WRATH OF THE GODS

MICHAEL G. THOMAS

First published in the United Kingdom in 2014
by Swordworks Books.

ISBN 978-1-911092-41-4

Typeset by Swordworks Books
Printed and bound in the UK & US
A catalogue record of this book is available
from the British Library

Cover design by Swordworks Books
www.swordworks.co.uk

WRATH OF THE GODS

MICHAEL G. THOMAS

CHAPTER ONE

The Alliance spread its influence from one side of the galaxy to the other, but with the construction of the first long-range Rift came a desire to explore further. If one could travel over three thousand light years in one direction, then why not travel to other just as remote locations? Information recovered from the Biomech ruins of Hyperion and Hades showed that a vast potential network of Spacebridges between multiple Nexus could allow travel to every star within the vast Orion–Cygnus Arm. This area of space encompassed over a thousand parsecs across and three thousand parsecs in length and included the world of the Alliance, as well as Betelgeuse, Rigel, the stars of Orion's Belt, and the Orion Nebula itself.

The Races of the Known Universe

ANS Dreadnought, Mars Orbit, 361 CC

Spartan ducked low and punched directly at her face. It was a fast, powerful blow, but even he wasn't quick enough to strike Teresa. She avoided the attack by the narrowest of margins and yanked at his good arm. She pulled him off balance, and he stumbled forward, only to trip over her leg and spin over onto his back.

"Come on, old man, you can do better than that!" she laughed.

Spartan flipped himself back to his feet and just made it. He could feel his back creaking a little as he moved, and he groaned, much to his annoyance.

"Spartan, get to it!" said Khan further back in the training hall.

It was a modest area to practice, but more than enough for their purposes. Weights and benches filled a third of the space, but it was on the mats that Spartan had returned to time after time over the last month. His wounds continued to heal, but the damage done to his bones and memory was long-term. Even so, he'd used the time to build up strength and stamina to levels not far from before he'd been taken prisoner. He looked to Khan and shook his head.

"You want some as well?"

A dull impact cracked against his temple, and he found himself staggering to one side until he could right his balance.

"Concentrate, this way," said Teresa.

Khan chuckled and looked to his right where Olik watched. There were another dozen marines, all watching with a mixture of awe and amusement. Teresa was their Colonel and commander of the entire battalion, yet on this ship she was sparring like any enlisted marine, and doing very well. Her speed and power was easily a match for the best of any of them even half her age. She moved around Spartan, her light form and perfect balance in stark contrast to Spartan's brutish movement.

"It's good to see them together," said Khan.

Olik nodded slowly.

"I saw what Teresa did on Prometheus. She is an insane commander. She takes risks and comes out on top every time."

Khan wasn't quite sure if that was the complement Olik intended. He was a seasoned warrior just as much as Khan was, but he'd had far less experience of these two people than he'd had.

"Spartan is much worse. You saw what happened down there when they worked together. Combined, they have the ability to rally anybody to their side and conquer entire worlds. They're probably more effective than even the Biomechs in that way."

Captain Rivers was standing in the corner of the gymnasium and watching silently. He could hear what the two were saying, and with every word found himself becoming more and more uncomfortable. Colonel Morato was a proven asset, but this sparring with a civilian on board their flagship. It just wasn't what he'd expected.

"Oh, I see you," said Spartan with a roar.

Spartan planted his feet firmly and locked his eyes on his wife's body. Like him, Teresa wore nothing but the physical training clothing used by all other marines. It was simple attire, a pair of long compression pants that fitted close to the skin and a short, close cut sleeved top. They were barefooted, and the tightness of the compression clothing emphasized every bump and curve in their bodies. Spartan and Teresa couldn't have been more different. Where Spartan was broad and muscular, Teresa was short, toned, and light skinned. Neither looked a day older than their late thirties, due to a mixture of diet, fitness, and the best medical regime the Alliance could offer. Teresa caught him looking at her, smiled, and then ran at him.

"Bit mistake," he said laughing.

She reached within a meter and then jumped out to the right. Spartan moved to block her, but she darted around to find the back of his elbow crashing into her chest and the back of his forearm against her cheek. The impact was hard and heavy, and it stopped her in her tracks. Spartan turned to face her, their faces just centimeters apart.

"I told you it was a mistake."

A trickle of blood ran from the corner of her mouth, but she spat out a little more and shook her head. Unlike Spartan, she began to move about, her feet light and fast on the mats. Spartan lowered his center of gravity and lifted his arms, preparing for the next attack.

"I don't think so, Spartan. If I want you on your back… you'll be on your back!"

A few marines near Khan let out a few catcalls, but a quick stare from the monstrous warrior quickly quieted them down. As he looked back, the two were wrestling before Spartan finally slipped and crashed to his back once more. Teresa leaned in to lock his neck.

"You see," she hissed.

Spartan didn't give up though and locked his legs around her thigh, pinning her between his legs. She was strong but nothing of the level that Spartan was. Every marine was exceedingly fit, but Spartan had always been just that little bit bigger and stronger than the average. Try as she might, there was simply no way to power her way out of the situation.

"And I said it was a mistake."

The two lay there, clamped together like some infernal machine with neither refusing to back down. Teresa pushed as hard as she could and instead fell down over him. As she lost her balance, she reached out and pinned both of his arms to the ground.

"Officer on deck!" barked one of the Marine sergeants.

Major Terson, the second-in-command for the entire 39th Battalion walked in. He spotted them grappling on the ground and waited for them to finish. Teresa threw a quick look at him and then bent down and kissed Spartan quickly on the nose.

"That's it...for now."

He released her, and the two rolled apart. Spartan lifted himself up slowly on one knee while Teresa jumped up as though she'd only just started her exercise regime. She nodded to one of her marines who tossed her a towel. Teresa caught it with her left hand and wiped her brow.

"Go on."

Khan and Olik moved to Spartan, who was finding it much harder to bounce back up.

"What's wrong, old man, you feeling your age today?"

Spartan straightened his back and quickly wished he hadn't. He tensed his facial muscles and powered through the pain. The doctors had done some great work with him, but nothing could alter the fast that the Biomechs had caused permanent problems with his limbs. He could even feel a numbing pain from his missing forearm. He looked at the artificial limb and found himself laughing. Khan watched him with amusement.

"You're going slightly mad, Spartan."

Spartan looked to him and angled his head while nodding.

"You might be right. Hell, after what we've been through, you'd need to be. Right?"

Major Terson moved closer to Teresa who was still wiping her brow from the exertions. A small pattern of blood on the towel marked where her lip was still bleeding.

"Colonel, an urgent flashcom from High Command.

The General is coming to Sol. He will be here in three days."

He noticed the blood and looked a little concerned. Teresa either didn't see his expression or simply chose to ignore it.

"Very good. Pass the word to the Captain. We'll need to regroup at the Mars Rift shortly. The fleet will need to make preparations."

He nodded and then left as quietly as he'd arrived. Spartan and Khan both watched him leave the gymnasium, and three more marines took their place on the mats.

"Three days," Spartan said in a questioning tone, "Is that going to be enough time to finish?"

Teresa shrugged.

"We'd better go and find Z'Kanthu and see how he's doing."

* * *

Z'Kanthu waited in the darkness deep inside the bowels of the ship. Try as they might, neither Teresa nor Spartan could ignore the increased security as they moved closer to the powerful machine. By the time they reached his temporary quarters aboard the ship, there were pairs of marines at every access point. He knew it was them before they entered the open door and into the large storage area. It was square in shape and outfitted with artificial windows on one side that gave the impression the quarters were located on the outside of the ship. It was a simple and yet effective way of creating the illusion of glass windows. A pair of Decurion machines waited like motionless sentinels on each side of him, their limbs hung down low and lifeless.

"Spartan, Colonel. I heard Khan making his way here as well. Where is he?"

Spartan approached and reached up to make contact with the machine's arm. It was an odd custom, but in the last few weeks, the two had become much closer than any had expected. It wasn't like the friendship between him and Khan, but closer than anything he shared with those in the Marine Corps.

"He's checking on his brothers. Their quarters are not much better than yours."

The Biomech flexed his limbs as if they were aching.

"There is nothing wrong with what I have been given. Space is a luxury we do not have, especially with the work we've been doing. Time is much more of a problem if we are to be ready for what we are going to be forced to do. I suspect that is why you're here?"

Spartan looked to Teresa.

"You know about the General?" Teresa asked Z'Kanthu.

The machine said nothing, and Teresa knew almost immediately that she'd simply answered her own question by telling him. Z'Kanthu nodded but said nothing more.

"Very well. Yes, we need to pull out of this area. The reports from the front are not good. Spascia is still holding, but Helios…"

She found it hard to continue describing what was happening. Spartan placed a hand on her shoulder.

"Z'Kanthu. You know how the Biomechs operate. They are launching ground invasions of all Helion worlds, but Helios Prime is something different. By the time they've finished, the world will be a sterile rock."

"Yes," he replied.

Teresa looked up at him and shook her head angrily.

"Yes? Is that all you have?"

The machine paused, perhaps contemplating her question and then answered.

"Yes."

Teresa looked down hopelessly and rested her head in her hand.

"We've been given this time on the promise we would be able to bring assets to the war. The assumption being we were enlisting Earthsec forces, but you've seen how successful that has been."

"I don't think the volunteer unit is going to change the war," Spartan said ruefully.

The day before he was aboard one of the many requisitioned civilian liners being hastily converted for war. The reality was this just meant clearing out the unnecessary junk, fitting stowage equipment, and marking them up as

Alliance vessels. Only a lucky few had been fully painted up, and even fewer retrofitted with point-defense turrets. Those they had recruited were a mixture of security staff, retired soldiers, and more than a few unsavory characters Spartan suspected would be as likely to steal and run rather than fight.

"Maybe, but we do have over a thousand of them so far."

Spartan lifted the corner of his mouth in a crooked smile.

"Oh, a thousand? Well, in that case."

Teresa shook her head in mock annoyance and looked back to the machine.

"How many are left?"

The aged warlord extended his hand and opened the fingers. A colorful hologram appeared showing a line of machines, each of them like him but different in minor ways. Some were larger, and at least one was multi-armed. All were massive though, and nothing like anything created by man.

"Following our defeat, the last of our kind fled out here. This is the last one I have any information on, the rest scattered out into the blackness. They may have lived, but for how long and without assistance," he shrugged; at least it was his best impersonation of the human gesture he was capable of displaying.

"The last of my kind should be buried deep inside this

object you call Makemake."

The image of the other machine changed to the minor planet. It showed a cool, lifeless rock. The object had first been discovered back at the start of the twenty-first century and had never seen any interest from humanity's colonists.

"Yes, we've already landed mining machines on the dwarf planet. Based on the information you've given us, we should have results within six to thirty hours. That's the problem; we have to move and soon."

Z'Kanthu looked at them both and then turned and looked out through the vast artificial windows. Like them, he would have known only too well that the windows were completely artificial. Yet even these fake windows gave him a view of something he hadn't been able to look upon for so many centuries. He looked back at Teresa and extended his hand to show the imagery of his comrades.

"Each of my brothers is worth an army to the cause. As you have seen, they were all buried along with their armies. Give me twelve more hours. There are things we can do to speed this up."

He looked out at the blackness of space, filled with the myriad of stars and objects.

"Tell me about the soldiers. Do you have enough ships for them all?"

Teresa looked to Spartan and back to the machine.

"It wasn't easy. Luckily for us, the casualties caused

by the attack on Mars freed up an awful lot of civilian vessels. We've commandeered enough transports for all the containers you've helped us locate so far."

Spartan rubbed his chin while she spoke. Finally Teresa finished, and he stepped a little closer.

"Tell me, old friend. Don't you think it's time we had a look inside one?"

The machine looked away from the windows and toward Spartan. If he'd been human, Spartan might have expected some form of insult. Instead, he stood there motionless, like a statue.

"Yes, we should examine one to be certain its contents have not spoilt. There are no guarantees that our procedures were infallible. Maintaining machines over such a period is difficult. Living matter is something even more…complex."

Spartan struck his arm.

"If there's anything your people are good at Z'Kanthu, it's managing hybrid living machines. Let's go and take a look."

Spartan was out of the door before he looked back and found the machine was still exactly where he'd left him.

"What?"

Again there was a pause, but finally the Biomech spoke.

"The control system. I am…uncomfortable with the programming you have supplied me."

Teresa looked to Spartan, and he could instantly see the

nerves coming to the surface. Spartan put his hands on his hips and looked at Z'Kanthu.

"What exactly aren't you happy with?"

Z'Kanthu moved away from where he had been waiting and took two short steps in the direction of Spartan. It looked like he might simply walk through the man, but he quickly slowed in front of him.

"The current system relies upon orders from a command figure that can be overridden by a Core transmission. It is a simple chain of command that has multiple levels of redundancy. What you propose…well…it is…"

Spartan looked increasingly impatient.

"What?"

The machine lowered half a meter and then stopped. A gentle hiss and whine from his motors now being the only sound anywhere near them.

"Dangerous."

Spartan nodded in agreement and then smiled.

"You can bet your ass it's dangerous. I want this Core concept removed once and for all. The only way these soldiers can fight for us is if their loyalty is without question. If they can be reprogrammed at will, then the Biomechs will always have a way to take them back."

"But this solution, it will give the Thegns complete autonomy. They could turn against your own armies, or even against your commanders."

Spartan now understood the machine's concerns.

"No, that's not it, is it?"

He stepped close to the Biomech so that his face almost touched his scarred metal armor. At this distance, the machine could have killed him by simply crushing him against the wall. He said nothing though. Teresa looked to Spartan as confused as she'd been a minute earlier.

"What do you mean, Spartan?"

He looked to her and then nodded to the doorway.

"He's worried that if we give them the ability to choose their own fate, they will use it to turn on their enemy. The one enemy that has spent their entire existence killing, mutilating, and torturing them."

"Biomechs," Teresa said under her breath.

Spartan looked back to Z'Kanthu.

"Somehow, I don't think they'll care too much about this rebellion of yours. They'll want revenge against you, Dersna, and any other Biomech they can find."

The machine made a few odd noises before speaking

"That is one of my concerns."

Spartan smacked his artificial left hand down onto the metal plating.

"Then we'd better make sure they understand what's at stake."

He then moved through the door with both of them following him. Spartan was sure he could sense one last question. He looked over his shoulder to see the machine walking just a few meters behind.

"What?"

"How can you be sure of their intentions?"

Spartan moved on and indicated toward the pair of red armor clad Jötnar waiting on each side of the wide passageway.

"Almost every one of the Jötnar was constructed by the enemy for one purpose. After capture, we removed the programming of every single one of them. Any born since have been clear of the command system of your people. Do you know what we've found?"

Z'Kanthu shook his metal torso from side to side.

"They are the most loyal, trustworthy, and brave soldiers in the Alliance. But even more than that, they have a hatred that is bone deep for anybody that would attempt to enslave or control them again. It's why they are such formidable fighters."

"Why are you telling me this?"

Teresa laughed.

"Because these Thegns have the potential to be more than just cannon fodder for your wars. They could be an asset to all of us, just like the Jötnar proved to be."

The two humans walked ahead, and Z'Kanthu trailed behind, trying to imagine what kind of universe it would be if the Thegns had free will. No matter how many different ways he looked at the problem, every single one ended up with him and his kin dead.

* * *

The storage hold on the port side of the ship was large, easily big enough to house four Maulers and all their assorted paraphernalia. Instead, this section of the ship was being used to store a number of the special containers collected from the other dig sites throughout the Kuiper Belt. Each was the size of a Cobra, one of the small Marine shuttles. They were rectangular and surrounded by a lattice of armored ribs that protected whatever lay inside. Two-dozen marines waited at their posts along the two entrances, as well as around the containers themselves. Z'Kanthu moved closer to the unit and placed both his hands on top.

"Wait there, do you know what is inside?" Teresa asked.

The machine looked back at her.

"This one carries the markings of On'Sarax. She is one of the youngest of the rebels. We fought together at the Battle of Fire where seventy of our brothers held the line. It was a major victory for us, but not for long."

"On'Sarax, a female?" Spartan asked.

Z'Kanthu looked at him, his machine eyes glowing bright red.

"Yes."

He pointed to the other containers.

"There are more of them bearing her mark and those of her bandon. They will contain the warriors, but it is this one that contains her."

He then looked back to the container and twisted two of the bars to reveal a hidden panel. He reached inside his chest and withdrew a pair of smooth cables and pushed them into the unit. Dots of color moved back and forth from the container to him. This went on for almost a minute before the colors flickered and died. Z'Kanthu rose to his full height and stepped back.

"Well, is that it?"

The machine remained completely still.

"Watch."

They waited, and for what seemed like an eternity nothing happened. Then a gentle hiss and clunking sound spread from one end to another. One of the ribbing bars turned and dropped to the floor. The others followed until all of those on one side had broken away. More noise came from the container, and then the entire panel on the side tipped over and crashed to the ground with an almighty crunch. Two of the marines moved from where they were watching, both with their weapons raised to their shoulders. Teresa lifted her hand and sent them back.

"Soon," said Z'Kanthu.

Dust now surrounded the unit as more panels and sealed layers of thin metallic film ripped away, and a dark shape moved. Spartan wanted to move ahead, but the sounds coming from inside did little to encourage help. Finally, an object appeared, a machine-like leg little different to

Z'Kanthu. The metal object touched the floor and tapped it. Another quickly followed, and then with a crunching sound the machine pulled itself out from the container and lifted itself up to a height not far short of Z'Kanthu.

"Wow, we have a second one," said Teresa.

Z'Kanthu approached and stopped two meters away. Both machines faced off like a pair of metal demons. This new one was shorter and much broader in shape. Its legs were of the same design, but instead of two arms, it carried two on each side, both hanging down low to the knees. There was no obvious head, but a single blue lamp flickered as it began to speak roughly where a face would have been. The two spoke for nearly thirty seconds, and then they turned to face Teresa and Spartan.

"This is On'Sarax. She is my old master at arms and my teacher in the ways of war."

* * *

Spartan, Teresa, and Major Terson walked quickly along the starboard access corridor. The ship was busy now as marines moved about carrying equipment for the new arrivals. There was a palpable sense of both urgency and danger every minute they stayed out here in Sol. The passageway was wide enough for four marines to pass along and lit by a series of floor and ceiling strip lights at regular intervals. On one side were short, full-width windows that showed a clear view of the empty space further away from Mars. Like all the windows on the ship, they were artificial, yet they served the purpose.

"Look," Teresa said.

She stopped for a moment and pointed out of the window. Spartan saw the shifting patterns of darkness, as the stars seemed to dance. All three of them knew what was coming, but a young private further down the corridor stopped and watched in surprise.

"What the hell is that?"

Another marine coughed to get his friend's attention. The man looked at the three senior officers and straightened up before continuing toward them. Spartan smiled at the man's surprise and looked back at the shifting colors.

"He's early, isn't he?"

Major Terson checked his secpad.

"Yes, by a few minutes at least."

The color shifted one last time before a kaleidoscope of color announced the activation of the Rift. In a single flash of light, a Spacebridge of just over four light years was created between Mars and Terra Nova. It was the miracle of science that had given the Alliance the ability to spread far and wide with minimal effort or resources. Instead of what they were expecting, a twenty-one ship civilian convoy entered the system. Teresa looked almost disappointed at their arrival. These were a mixture of freighters and passenger liners that traveled together for mutual protection. All were privately owned and decked out with a bizarre assortment of livery and insignia marking out their owners and interests. The only ships to stray from this were the two Liberty destroyers moving with them as escort. It was a timely reminder of the situation transport vessels now found themselves in throughout Alliance territory.

"Well, I guess this means things are starting to get back to normal," said Spartan.

Major Terson tensed his brow and frowned.

"This is different though. Until now, it's been rare for Alliance ships to make this trip. Earthsec are pretty militant about looking after their own territory."

"You don't say," muttered Spartan.

Major Terson looked at him, tensed a little, and then looked to Teresa.

"Sending Alliance ships in as escort is a clear message from Terra Nova. In the past, we've had to clear a flight plan well in advance with Earthsec. Why do I think High Command just sent these through without clearance?"

"Great," said Teresa, "so Terra Nova is flexing its muscles."

Spartan watched the shapes of the ships with a mixture of annoyance and curious fascination. He could already identify some of the markings from Euryale and Kerberos.

"Those ships have been around the block a bit."

He then looked back to Teresa and the Major.

"I don't really get it. Earthsec is something that had significance maybe before the Rifts. Now we are linked together by a matter of days, or hours in most cases. Sol is part of the Alliance, so why the hell do we let something like this even exist?"

Teresa looked almost as surprised as the Major.

"Well, the Alliance has an agreement with Earthsec. They operate semi-independently but under the protection of the Alliance."

Spartan shook his head and continued on forwards. He looked at the ships as they activated their thrusters and moved into high orbit around Mars. With the planet now secure, there were hundreds of other vessels dropping off people and supplies to the Red Planet. Even more ships were making preparations to travel to the other worlds and moons throughout Sol to ply their wares once more. Trade and industry was taking a chance in this system, but even as they tried to return Sol to some semblance of normality, it was clear that times had changed. None of the crews could have missed the new shapes of the huge cruisers and destroyers that had taken up positions around Mars and further away toward the Rift entrance itself.

* * *

Spartan watched the mainscreen inside the CIC of the massive warship with fascination. It had been some time

WRATH OF THE GODS

since he'd been on board such a vessel, let alone inside the CIC. Teresa looked at him and shrugged. Many types of military ships were now posted there, but it was the flagship ANS Dreadnought that caught most attention. It sat there, squat and foreboding, unlike anything owned or operated by Earthsec.

"There's nothing like a few warships to get things moving, don't you think?"

Major Terson looked to Spartan and finally nodded in agreement.

"This is a failed backwater; Mars was barely functional before the Biomechs attacked. Now, well, it's a ruin. There's little of value out here anymore."

Spartan couldn't really argue with that, though he had just remembered that Captain Cobb, the leader of the mission to Mars had just entered the CIC and was looking right at him.

Great, I wonder how much of that he heard?

The two had come to something of an understanding during the original operation on Mars. Now that it was over, he'd being doing his best to avoid the man. The officer was one of the sternest Spartan had met. Even on a ship of which he had no jurisdiction, he still strutted about as though he had some degree of influence on board. He moved past them and directly toward Captain Vetlaya who watched his arrival warily. He stopped and saluted.

"Captain, I bring greetings from Earthsec as the senior Earthsec officer in this territory."

She smiled and threw a quick glance to her executive officer.

"It is good to finally meet you, Captain. I understand some of your operatives are still being cared for on board one of our medical frigates. Is there anything your people need?"

Spartan didn't know the Captain, but he could see there was much more to her than the façade offered by her pleasantries. Though not particularly young, she was still young for the command of a vessel as significant as this one. Spartan looked to Teresa in her smart dress uniform and immediately felt a slight pang of nostalgia. He might be wearing clothing taken from Alliance stocks, but he was no longer involved in the Corps.

"Governor Trelleck thanks our armed forces for their assistance in this unfortunate incident. I have been tasked with facilitating the handover to our own security units on the surface."

Captain Vetlaya opened her mouth to speak, but Teresa interrupted her.

"Captain, perhaps this would be better left to the new delegation from Terra Nova?"

That put a smile on the Captain's face.

"That is an excellent point, Colonel."

She then looked back to Captain Cobb.

"Colonial matters are a little out of my jurisdiction, Captain. My forces are here by the order of Alliance High Command."

"But Earthsec has…"

She raised her hand to silence him.

"I've already answered. Now, let us discuss other…"

Spartan looked away to Teresa, but she had moved away and in her place was Khan. He still wore his armor, but at least it had been repaired, patched, and cleaned. Even so, he still looked as though he'd just arrived fresh from a warzone.

Well, I suppose he has.

"What are you doing up here? I thought you were busy swapping war stories with your friends?"

Khan's visor was open and showed his large, expressive face clearly. He lifted an eyebrow in mock pain.

"Me? Why are you here, Spartan? We're not in the Alliance military anymore."

He found it hard to stay serious though, and his face broke to a smile.

"They do have some good stories though. Did you hear about Teresa's command on Prometheus? They say she and Osk commanded the ground battle in some serious combat."

"Of that my friend, I have no doubt."

Khan took that as an opportunity to regale him of the details of the operation, with suitable embellishments from his kin. As their discussion continued, ANS Dreadnought moved silently in orbit above the surface of Mars. Spartan could see the colors and markings of one of the oldest and most famous planets in the human Alliance, while at the same time hearing of dismemberment and combat. Finally, he shook his head.

"Khan, the General will be here soon. Are you sure we've gone over everything?"

Khan lifted both of his shoulders in mock confusion.

"Probably. How could he refuse?"

Spartan raised his left eyebrow and sighed.

"Because right now we're in the middle of a bloodbath. You know how much trust there is from the average person toward your kin. Can you imagine how they will feel about this new plan?"

Khan considered his words.

"True, this will change things."

He then lifted the corner of his lip and chuckled. One of the junior science officers heard him and muttered something. Khan spun about and pointed at the man.

"What did you say, little man?"

The officer raised both of his hands in mock surrender and looked back to his station. Khan laughed quietly to himself.

"Yeah, that's what I thought."

CHAPTER TWO

Experience on the battlefield of the Helios System would finally introduce the concept of autonomous machines. The Khreenk and Byotai military both made extensive use of machines for war, though nothing to the extent of the machines of the Biomechs. The discoveries made by Colonel Teresa Morato and her taskforce in the old worlds of Sol were like nothing even imagined before. If Alliance High Command had even an inkling as to what she and Spartan were doing, they would have shut down the entire operation. Chance and timing would prove as important as the discoveries themselves.

Computer Science 101, 7th Edition

ANS Dreadnought, Mars Orbit, Sol

Sol was a shadow of what it had once been. Mars and Earth had seen millennia of colonization, along with the outlying moons and asteroids. With its peak coming just before the Great Expedition, it is now inconceivable that a place so rich on life, resources, and intelligence could be brought so low. Mars was now one of the few productive colonies in the Old World, a place where refineries and factories were the dominant features of the planet. In the past, the planet had been home to some of the largest colonies of Sol, but generations of neglect and failure had reduced the entire star system to something of a backwater. Local colonial administrations had been merged together, usually peacefully, but on occasion under force of arms. The Lunar rebellions of the twenty-second century cemented a firm belief in a strong Earth-based administration. Wars, famines, and plagues had done their own foul work, but it was the discovery of new riches in Proxima Centauri that did the greatest damage. Those that could leave did so, and those remaining fought over and destroyed what was left. Only the construction of the Proxima Centauri-Sol Spacebridge in the last generation had given the old planets of humanity a fighting chance at recovery.

The massive Alliance warship wasn't the only military vessel in orbit over the Red Planet. The capital ship was flanked by dozens of the new Liberty class destroyers fresh from the Promethean shipyards, as well as several veteran Crusader class heavy cruisers. This contingent of powerful Alliance ships had all recently arrived from

Prometheus where they had taken part in Admiral Anderson's complicated and ultimately successful plan to eliminate the Biomech presence in Alliance space. Their battleship gray paint appeared dull and uninspiring compared to the more colorful civilian vessels that had now returned to the shipping lanes.

A single Earthsec ship, ESS Dauntless moved with them, as well as its protective bodyguard of four Hammerhead fighters. Though technically Alliance territory, the old moons and planets of Sol still operated with relative autonomy under the guide of Earthsec and this ship bore is distinctive marking. It was a small price to pay for peace and security in the disparate worlds of the fledgling Alliance. Though nothing compared to the fleets currently battling in the Helios System, it was still a sizable fleet to orbit a planet so recently brought under control.

"Here they are," said the XO.

All attention turned to the mainscreen as another mighty flash filled with colorful light announced the arrival of yet more ships as four more craft entered Earthsec controlled space. This group was different though, as three of the ships were escorts for one of the Alliance's most secretive projects. Even ANS Dreadnought, a powerful Battlecruiser in her own right, was dwarfed by the great monolith of ANS Warlord. The super-battleship was the only ship of her type in existence, and based upon the large number of fighters deploying around her was considered a great prize. From some angles the great ship looked similar to the Conqueror and Crusader class that she'd evolved from. There was no mistaking the massive board hull though, or the huge number of weapon systems fitted on almost every surface. Those that knew of her had heard she was as powerful as an entire squadron of Crusader class ships. Whether it was true or not, few could doubt her power upon seeing her vast shape.

* * *

ANS Warlord, Sol-Alpha Centauri Rift, Terra Nova

General Rivers watched the colors flash and shudder as his view of Alliance space transformed between his eyes. As his eyes closed, he was only a short distance from Terra Nova, the capital world of the Alliance, and in the next he was over four light years away and moving toward the second oldest colonized planet ever walked on by humans.

Here we are, Mars.

His personal transport Mauler dropped out from one of the multiple hangar bays on the super-battleship and settled into a courier path with ANS Dreadnought, the flagship of the ongoing operation in Sol. Inside the heavily armored craft sat a small group of Alliance marines and him. The aged officer was the most senior military figure in the Alliance, and the Chairman of the Joint Chiefs. He was a man with as much experience fighting the Biomechs and their allies as the pinup man for the entire Marine Corps, Spartan. Many had opposed him even leaving Terra Nova, especially with the most advanced warship in service. But General Rivers was a man used to getting what he wanted, and the information he'd received in the last forty-eight hours made the journey a necessary risk as far as he was concerned. He wasn't even supposed to be in this sector, but all he could think about was what he had seen. He looked out through one of the armored portholes at the surface of the planet and gazed upon its unusual features.

Mars, what a place to hide under all this time.

The lines and colors of the world were certainly interesting, though after Prometheus something like Mars paled to insignificance. Centuries earlier the world may have been of importance, now it was just another failed planet with a ruined economy and a fractured social infrastructure. General Rivers had much bigger things to concern his time with than the history of a failed world. They continued on their journey between ships, and he looked back at the video stream on the screen in front of him.

Can it be true? Have they really found one?

The imagery showed several combat sequences where the Biomech rebel had apparently assisted the marines. In one particular section, the machine was overwhelmed by Thegn foot soldiers before being thrown to the ground.

Red armor-clad Jötnar smashed into them; a terrible melee ensuring those on both sides were torn about in bloody combat. A group of marines rushed in and helped to clear the Thegns before the battle was joined once more. The report, as well as the audio and video, confirmed in multiple mediums the stories were true. Even so, he still found it hard to believe a Biomech; one of the warlords of the enemy had decided to join them. Even more incredible was this tale of a rebellion that had brought them out to their own worlds in the distant past. He was far from convinced.

If this is true, can we really trust him?

The Biomech machine was a true wonder; an alien creature encased in the body of a machine that was centuries, perhaps millennia old. Its knowledge of the past must be immense, just as its technical and scientific skills would outmatch anything they currently had access to. That reminded him of exactly why he'd been granted permission to lead the small force to this rendezvous. He thought back to the last meeting over Terra Nova days before, and it filled him with anger.

They've got no idea what we're dealing with here.

It was a slow journey, made much worse by the new reports flooding in to him from the frontlines. Out here in orbit over Mars was perhaps the furthest he could possibly be from the war. Unlike the President, however, General Rivers understood Spartan and the opportunity this Biomech offered them. He'd seen the plan, the so-called Operation Citadel, and although it was sound in its short-term scope, he had little faith in its ability to win the war. Unlike many in the civilian administration, he was more than familiar with the Biomechs principle of playing the long-term game.

They're not attacking out of spite on some suicidal death or glory mission. These attacks on the Helios System are just the beginning.

The more he thought about it, the more sure he became. As he read the reports, the small vessel continued toward the waiting ship. For anybody that happened to be watching, it would have been almost impossible to spot alongside the flotilla of mighty warships as it made its way to the cavernous hangar of ANS Dreadnought. A pair of fighters, a single Hammerhead and one Lightning, flanked the Mauler. Both were veterans of the fighting at Prometheus and bore the scars of that battle with pride. General Rivers moved the imagery to one that showed the Black Rift and the mixture of ships already waiting there. He counted only Helion and T'Kari vessels, with no sign of any Khreenk or Alliance ships. The groups of ships moved about in a permanent series of orbits around the control station and its orbital defense platforms. All were waiting for trouble from either side of the Rift, and he could quite imagine the fear all of them must have been facing.

The enemy has a fleet, just days from the Rift. They can attack whenever it suits. So why wait? Are they waiting for something on the other side, or for the fighting in the Helios System to be decided?

He knew the most likely answer, but it wasn't one he wanted to consider. If they were waiting, then it had to be for something to happen, an event that had yet to take place before they could act. If true, that meant it could only be something that would turn the situation even worse for the allied races.

That's just what we need, more problems.

That was when he looked back at the feed of Z'Kanthu, the rebel leader. Every bone in his body told him to be wary of the machine. It had helped on Mars; yes, that was true, but how significant was that really in the scheme of things? He tried to imagine how else he could have escaped from the planet unless acting as a friend and ally to his own people.

What if the plan is for him to do something? Perhaps attempt to activate the Rift while working alongside our own ships?

General Rivers shifted uncomfortably in his seat. There would be little he could do until he could see the machine for himself. It was something he had to do because right now the war was not going well for the Helions, and that meant it was not going well for the Alliance. He'd already crunched the numbers with his opposite numbers amongst the other Allies, and they had all come up with the same result. It might take days, weeks, or months, but unless something drastic happened, the Helios System would fall to the Biomechs and their forces. This machine on Mars could be the catalyst that hastened their defeat, yet Spartan and Teresa's instincts were strong, and that was the only reason he'd even contemplated coming here, let alone allowing the machine to live freely.

What if Teresa's assessment is accurate? This could be a small army with inside knowledge of the Biomechs. It's a war-winning asset, if it's true.

He rubbed his forehead and lowered the secpad, turning his attention to the ship they had now reached. The squat shape of the Mauler moved inside, and vast sliding panels dropped into place behind it. After the first layer, it then moved through the airlock shields, another set of vast doors that also resealed to allow it into the pressurized section of the ship. It settled down on its landing feet with a crunching sound and then settled.

* * *

ANS Dreadnought, Mars Orbit, Sol

Teresa watched the dust cloud so carefully, one might have expected a horde of Thegns to rush out, each with their weapons raised and looking to kill and maim all that waited. Her hands were at her sides, but it was obvious she was nervous, or at the very least, extremely concerned at this arrival. A light mist of dust and vapor filled the air around the craft and partially disguised the side doors.

One by one they slid open, and metal ramps dropped to the floor with a clunk. Apart from the sounds coming from the Mauler, the entire deck was silent. With its tall ceilings, it could easily accommodate the larger craft, and the Mauler looked modest compared to the space around it. The figures that emerged on the ramp were anything but. First to make contact with the metallic floor was General Rivers. Dressed in his full regalia, he looked every part the war hero. A small party waited just in front of the ramp. All but one saluted him. He stopped and looked at them, four marines and a single Jötnar warrior.

"Spartan, I see you've forgotten your manners."

The Jötnar in the battered JAS armor laughed.

"As always. He is Spartan, after all."

The General extended his hand and found it quickly grasped by Spartan, who by now had returned to civilian clothing. He wore a set of off-duty marine fatigues, but at least he'd shaved, smartened up his beard, and washed his hair. Even his artificial arm looked more civilized with most of it hidden under the clothing.

"Always good to meet you, General. I see we're on the losing side of another war again. Are you here to get us back on track?"

He looked at Spartan and found himself wondering if the veteran warrior was being sarcastic or ironic. He hadn't seen the man for some time, yet whenever they did meet, it always seemed to be on unfamiliar territory, outnumbered, and in trouble. He smiled but instead of speaking, turned to look at Teresa and his son, Captain Rivers.

"This wasn't quite what I was expecting when I gave authorization for your little soirée into Earthsec territory. You understand we have a war on in the Helios star system? The initial reason for your extended operation was to finish the clear up of Biomech entrenchment in Sol. The last thing we need with the war is a new threat at home."

Teresa sensed he was just making small talk because they were more than familiar with the situation in Helios. The General couldn't keep his eyes away from the real prize though, no matter how hard he tried. The man sidestepped the welcome party and moved into the middle of the hall. On both sides was an entire company of Alliance marines and behind them the alien forces he'd heard so much about. He walked briskly past the first few ranks, watching the marines carefully as he went. Each wore the black and gray PDS Alpha armor and their personal weapons up to their shoulders. The group walked with him as he moved.

"I see you've increased access to more variable weaponry."

Teresa nodded.

"Yes, General. Every fireteam has access to at least one specialist weapon, usually the L48."

The old man raised an eyebrow at that.

"Interesting, I thought the standard procedure was to

phase them out, apart from the sharpshooter units?"

Captain Rivers sensed irritation in his father's voice.

"Experience has shown us that the L52 isn't always enough to get the job done. The L48 offers options in combat."

General Rivers tried to hide a smile and failed.

"Very true, the L48 certainly does offer battlefield options."

They were now past the last rank of marines and moved across a short open space until reaching the next unit. It was enough room to place another large unit, but instead the open ground simply increased the distinction between the sides.

"Here they are, General," said Teresa.

It was unnecessary, but she felt she needed to say something. This time they faced more than two hundred Biomech Thegns. He had first heard of them during the fighting on Eos, but this was the closest he'd ever been. Each waited shoulder-to-shoulder, little different to three companies of marines awaiting orders. They were motionless, waiting for their orders and nothing more. He looked at their skin, and finally curiosity got the better of him. General Rivers stopped in front of a random Thegn and touched its shoulder. The surface was a little warmer than he'd expected, yet it was hard and slightly rough to the touch.

"It's like elephant skin, but harder and more resilient,"

said Spartan.

Teresa pointed to the arm of the nearest Thegn.

"We did tests on some of the dead. It is definitely their outer hide, a hybrid skin and body armour. The tech teams think it's related to Graphene. I'm not so sure."

"Interesting."

They moved on and finally stopped at the great figure of Z'Kanthu, the Biomech warlord and commander of the new Thegn rebels. Like his foot soldiers, the great Biomech remained completely motionless. General Rivers approached and then walked around his legs. His son pointed out where the machine had sustained damage in the fighting on Mars. There were many marks and scratches, as well as clear puncture wounds from powerful weapons. The more he looked at the machine, the more he was surprised the thing was still able to move.

"And it is still alive inside?"

Captain Rivers nodded.

"Yes, General. Z'Kanthu sustained heavy damage in the battle, but he has been able to make use of the freed machines to repair and improve his armor."

Spartan placed his hand on the machine's thigh.

"The speed they got to work was impressive. Hell, I wish they could have patched me up in the time they repaired this armor."

The General didn't seem particularly interested, and after two full circuits around the rebel leader, stopped at its feet. Spartan could feel the eyes of the assembled marines watching them. Most of them had fought on Mars, and those that hadn't had already heard of the machine's skills and battle prowess from the others. Even so, he was still a Biomech, and General Rivers was the senior Alliance commander. This would be the perfect opportunity for one of them to strike, and every single person in that landing bay was thinking the same.

"So, Z'Kanthu, that is your name, is it not?"

The machine groaned ever so faintly as the motors and lumps of metal moved to bring his body closer to the man. The upper body lowered down half a meter and then stopped. Even while stationary, there were still almost silent hisses and whines from his armor.

"Yes, and what is yours? From your uniform you are a senior military commander. That is not a Naval uniform. You must be a Marine officer."

Spartan smirked a little at the deduction, an expression the machine quickly took on board. He was already becoming used to the machine's ability to identify, absorb, and digest even the most modest pieces of information.

"You are a General, perhaps one of the Joint Chiefs. You can only be General Cornwallis, head of the Marine Corps, or General Rivers, the Chairman of the Joint Chiefs."

General Rivers looked to Spartan and Teresa.

"How does he know all of this? Have you briefed him?"

He didn't look pleased, yet it was his son that answered.

"No, General, when the Biomechs arrived, they tried to get to him. While escaping, he tapped into Earthsec communications and databases systems. He's had access to all their data, plus pretty much anything else on the public databases. The names and details of all our key staff are on public record."

He raised his eyebrows in surprise at this and then turned back to Z'Kanthu.

"I see. Well, let's assume everything I have heard is the truth. What exactly are you offering us, and what do you want in return?"

The machine faced Spartan, its eyes softening slightly in intensity before it moved its focus back on the new arrival.

"I have merged my control architecture with the captured Core. This will give me full control of the already located and recovered soldiers. We have four complete bandon of soldiers that remained on your worlds. That gives us twelve partially operational Eques walkers, thirty-three Decurion assault machines, and three hundred Thegns. All are experienced and combat effective. Every hour we spend here increases the chances of finding more."

General Rivers listened as the machine rattled off the list of assets he now controlled. None of this was news to him, of course, but it was still of interest to him how the machine behaved. Teresa leaned in closer to him and spoke quietly into his ear.

"We've found them space in the storage areas of the ships. They don't need much room."

Even as she spoke, he found it hard not to notice the dozen red-armored Jötnar that flanked him on either side. All were veterans of the Battle for Prometheus, and now Mars. There were probably few other Jötnar that could claim to have seen so much action in a matter of weeks. Their PDS Alpha armor looked as similar as it was different to the model used by the regular marines. That was when the odd realization hit him.

We have more machines, aliens, and synthetics here than humans.

He wasn't sure how he felt, but it was certainly a strange feeling to have.

"I see. That is what you are bringing, but tell me. What else do you propose? A single Biomech rebel and three hundred or so machines is not an army."

The machine turned a few degrees to face Spartan. His body had been long stripped of its paint, and his pair of plasma weapons was currently hidden behind their mountings on his arms. Although much larger than the Jötnar, he still seemed to fit in with the theme of war machines and heavy equipment that filled the landing bay. He said nothing for a moment, finally answering the General.

"I will find my brothers, and together we can end the destruction brought by my kin's treachery. We have already found..."

Spartan lifted his hand, and the machine stopped. It looked to Spartan and then continued speaking.

"There are few of us left, and all are committed to the end of the genocide carried out in the past. If the... Biomechs are not stopped, they will lay waste to every world that has helped Helios."

General Rivers glanced to Spartan.

"Brothers? There was nothing in the report about there being more."

Spartan nodded.

"Yes, General. He says that he and his people fought alongside the Twelve until they were defeated and forced to retreat. There are few of them left now."

General Rivers looked at the monstrous machine and tilted his head a little to the right. He'd read the report multiple times, but only now was it becoming apparent the clearing operation in Sol was more than had been sanctioned by High Command.

"Where are the rest of your friends?"

The machine hissed and clunked before he pointed to the side of the ship.

"We scattered ourselves to the cold and darkness of the debris fields inside this star system. Any that still live will be buried deep inside the rock and metal we found here."

He then placed one of him hands across his chest.

"A handful of us scattered to other worlds to leave

information for others to follow. Most of those died in their efforts."

Spartan rubbed his chin as he listened to the machine.

"General, we couldn't share this through the Rift. You saw what happened when they found he was here. We faced a massive assault by all remaining Biomech forces in this sector."

"I saw the video feeds. Are you tell me there was no…"

Spartan shook his head.

"Oh, there's been ongoing combat throughout Mars, even after we took the Core. One squad of Decurions managed to destroy their communication systems before we could contain them. It's taken weeks to hunt them down, and in that time we've been busy."

He gave the nod to the young Captain ever present at Teresa's side. Captain Rivers was already checking on his secpad before lifting the unit.

"Here, General. We started here, between the orbits of Mars and Jupiter."

The imagery showed the Sol System, with its eight planets and massive asteroid belt that split them into inner and outer planets. He looked at it briefly, but although he'd never visited Sol before, he was very familiar with the stories of the old worlds dating back to the days of the early colonists.

"I am quite familiar with the asteroid belt. This was the first major area of mining and exploration, following the early colonies on Earth's moon and Titan. I fail to see how machines could have hidden out there for so long."

He then looked to Z'Kanthu.

"You're saying your people hid in our asteroid belt all this time?"

Z'Kanthu shook his head.

"No, just one. Most hid in the larger field out beyond your planets."

"The Kuiper Belt," said a familiar voice.

They all turned their attention to the man in a smart Alliance uniform and hobbling on a crutch. A metal frame ran down the side of his leg where it was pinned directly to the bone.

"Marcus Keller. Director Johnson told me to expect you here."

"Yes, General."

The man looked to Spartan and exchanged a cool but courteous look.

"May I?"

Spartan moved his hands out in front of him in a conciliatory position. The lines of Thegn soldiers waited in silence and could easily have been mistaken for a group of metallic statues, each one waiting as some form of foul sentinel.

"We've been following this trail for years now. With the damaged transport sites at the Anomaly, Hyperion, Terra Nova, Hades in T'Karan, and now finally on Mars, the puzzle has started to come together. Even the factories on Prometheus and Prime were built well before the worlds were settled."

Z'Kanthu moved his shoulder plates as though stretching.

"Yes. Before we went into hiding, we had tried to rebuild. The factories would create workers, warriors, and infrastructure. The Rifts would connect our new worlds that you now call home. The enemy tried to use what we had built, so we destroyed what was left, including our only remaining way home, the last gateway on your green world."

"Hyperion," said Khan with obvious reverence.

Z'Kanthu looked at the synthetic warrior as a child might look as a pet.

"Correct. Hyperion was our most complex construction, a way to reach an area of space near Helios, but not too close. Then they came, and most of what we had built was lost. My brothers that still lived joined me in this system, one that we knew was occupied by your young, primitive species."

He then looked to Marcus.

"Your assessment of our hiding places was most accurate. Any that remained were hidden deep inside the rock of this vast belt. It was our intention to wait until your species was advanced enough to discover us and awaken the remaining rebels. Only then would we have the tools required to end this war."

General Rivers took a step back and scanned from left to right. He examined the large numbers of marines, machines, and alien warriors before moving his attention back to the small group.

"Tools?" he asked, his face contorted in a suspicious frown.

"Yes, your people. The Biomech numbers were too great for us to match, not in the time we had remaining. Now that your own people have spread to many worlds, built ships, and powerful weapons, together we will be more powerful than we could ever be alone."

General Rivers looked at the emotionless machine.

"So you just assumed our local forces would authorize a full-scale search of the Kuiper Belt for your comrades, just so we could then let you lead us in some holy war?"

He then looked to Teresa.

"I left you in charge here specifically to secure this rear area prior to joining our buildup for Citadel. Now you're telling me you've actually been running errands for this machine?"

Z'Kanthu stayed silent as the General spoke. He listened and absorbed every word he heard until finally looking back at the assembled Thegns.

"We didn't just hide our kin in your system. What is left of our army is still here, buried out there on the distant rock fifty-two astronomical units from this star. By helping me uncover them, I have brought them all to you, to help in your war. I offer them to you to destroy the enemy."

General Rivers looked at the machine for several second before nodding. He walked away and indicated for his son, Teresa, Marcus, Spartan, and Khan to follow. They went past the lines of Thegns and finally reached the other side of the landing bay. Still he did not stop but moved toward where a pair of Maulers sat, each being worked on by a team of skilled engineers. Closer to the bulkheads waited small numbers of marines, all watching the General's movements. They were discreet, but Spartan had spotted their movement before the General had even made it halfway to the Thegns just after arriving. He finally stopped and checked their new arrivals were well out of earshot.

"I have just one question for you, and it's a damned important one."

He reached out his secpad and lifted it to show them a message. All it asked was could they trust Z'Kanthu? Both of them looked at it carefully, but Spartan replied first.

"General, there is no way for us to know. So either we help them, and use them."

Teresa pushed in.

"Or we leave this asset in the middle of our sector and hope nothing happens."

Z'Kanthu walked away from them and then stopped; General Rivers watched and called out after the machine.

"What stops you giving the order to these Thegns to turn on us?"

The machine twisted toward Spartan and back to the General. It said nothing, and General Rivers repeated his question before looking back to Spartan.

"Well? Is somebody going to answer me?"

"General, there is something else, something that only we know."

Teresa beckoned to a group of four marines who brought over a metal crate that was partially open. They moved it closer and lowered it directly in front of the officers. Teresa pulled open the lid fully so they could all look inside. Each peered in to look at the odd fusion of biological material and mechanics. It was still, silent, and smelt slightly off.

"I...I don't understand. This is the Core, isn't it? The one you captured and reprogrammed on Mars?"

Spartan nodded.

"Yes, and it's also the one that we destroyed forty-eight hours ago."

The General took a step back, almost stumbling as he listened.

"What? You've handed over control to one individual, this machine?"

He pointed at Z'Kanthu as he hissed his words. Spartan tried to explain, but the man just continued to back off, so Spartan marched off to the corner of the group of

Thegns. He tapped the first and spoke in short, simple English.

"Follow me."

The Thegn turned its head, looked at him, and then moved in behind him. The two walked back before halting directly in front of the General. Spartan looked to the warrior who was currently completely unarmed.

"What is your name?

"Forty-Seven."

General Rivers had never heard one speak. He didn't even know they could. The creature's voice was odd, a combination of artificial machine-like sounds and a strange foreign dialect mixed with a guttural tone.

"What are your orders?"

"Obey chain of command."

The reply was instant, and it remained next to Spartan like a dog waiting to be given permission to move somewhere. General Rivers was speechless and simply stared at the thing for almost a full ten seconds.

"I think somebody had better explain to me what just happened."

Teresa nodded quickly.

"We will, Sir. There is one more thing though."

She looked to Z'Kanthu and nodded slowly, as though there was a preselected signal. He extended both of his arms out and turned his metal fists around to present his palms upwards. His eyes pulsed, and then a detailed hologram appeared showing seven machines, each of them as different as they were similar. General Rivers looked at the imagery intently until spotting one that he recognized.

"That is Z'Kanthu," said Spartan.

The General continued to look at the other six, examining the limb arrangements, overall sizes, and mass. Finally, he turned to look at Spartan and Teresa.

"Is this what I think it is? Are these the rebels?"

Spartan relaxed his face just a little.

"Yes, General. More importantly though, they are here."

He indicated to his right just to the side of the spare Maulers. A massive hatch opened up that was easily big enough to push a Mauler inside of. It was one of the multiple loading lifts used inside the spacecraft. From the dark interior emerged a robotic shape, and then another until six more machines, each of similar build to Z'Kanthu. They moved closer and then stopped in a line of mechanical monsters with no intent on causing damage. One by one they lowered their torsos in homage.

"These are my kin, the last of the rebels left alive in this sector."

There was no emotion in his voice, yet Teresa was convinced she sensed something at the mention of the word alive. They had expected more, but these six were all they had been able to recover intact.

"General, we found four more that died in the last two hundred years. Automated mining machines digging on Makemake found the last one, but it died from exposure and decay years ago."

She then beckoned to the machines.

"These are the last of the rebel warlords, and each of them has pledged their allegiance to us in this war."

"Under whose command?" asked General Rivers suspiciously.

He glanced over to Z'Kanthu, but it was to Spartan that the machine looked.

"As the price for finding the rest of my kin, we agreed to the conditions of your officers, as well as a system of command."

General Rivers didn't seem impressed at this.

"What conditions?"

Spartan glanced at Teresa, swallowed, and then answered.

"The Core is the strength and the weakness of all life created by the Biomechs. Even the Decurion machines had minor organic components and basic levels of intelligence. We can control the Core directly or via Z'Kanthu, but does that give us any kind of guarantee?"

The General said nothing; he merely stared at Spartan impassively.

"So I took a chance. While we were well away from the planets, out in the Kuiper Belt, we tested a theory."

Teresa placed her hand on Spartan; now feeling it was time to take responsibility for the events that had unfolded.

"General. I authorized Z'Kanthu to send the signal to the first unit of Thegns. It was a failsafe procedure that deactivates and destroys the Core communication node. Only with authorization from a loyal Steersman or Core can this be done."

She tried to continue, but General Rivers stopped her.

"Wait, you're telling me you removed the control system for these soldiers?"

"Just as we did back on Prometheus, Sir," Spartan reminded him.

"You see these Thegns are intelligent, as smart as a basic trooper, but with conditioning and strength we cannot easily match. The Core system keeps them all under the thrall of the machines, yet I suspected that underneath they would have the same resentments Gun and the others had."

"Slavery," said the General quietly.

"Exactly. We freed one at first and the result were, well. Violent. It tried to kill us, but Z'Kanthu restrained it. It took a few hours, but eventually he explained that it could go wherever it chose, but if it chose violence, then he would be force to fight it. Do you know what it wanted to do?"

The General smiled that dark, grim smile Spartan had seen before.

"Tell me."

"It wanted to know where the masters were."

The General raised a questioning eyebrow.

"Why?"

Spartan looked at the Thegn.

"Forty-Seven. Orders?"

The warrior spoke in its own tongue, and Z'Kanthu was forced to translate.

"Its orders are simple. It will observe the chain of command as I have explained. Our Thegns and war machines have each vowed to observe the laws and commands based upon your chain of command in the coming fight. Not one of them has shown any interest in causing trouble. They will have their freedom."

"Yes, but what does it want? Can it even understand freedom?"

"Z'Kanthu spoke again, and the Thegn stepped away from the officers and approached him. He even seemed to recoil just a little as it spoke. Finally, the sounds finished and he looked to General Rivers.

"Forty-Seven wants to find the slave masters that forced him and his kin to fight and die. He has seen seventy-three of his comrades die in battle on both sides of our wars. He will not fight for any Biomech again."

"Uh, isn't that a problem?"

Spartan cleared his throat.

"Got something to say, Spartan?"

"Well, General, this Thegn and every one we have freed so far, wants just one thing; their freedom, but not our kind of freedom. They don't want or expect a normal life. They want the freedom to find, fight, and destroy the Biomechs once and for all."

"I don't understand, why? Are you telling me they have memories and feelings? Surely you do not believe they have a system of morality?"

Spartan didn't seem impressed.

"General, they are intelligent creatures that were built as expendable slaves. They had no free will but could see, feel, and understand what was happening around them. When freed of the Core, they operate under the basic laws of free will. But deep down there is something that has been simmering for centuries, just the same as with Gun and Khan. All they want is the chance for vengeance. Was Gun much different when we found him?"

"And who is supposed to lead them if they hold all Biomechs in such contempt. Will they fight under the command of our own officers?"

He looked up to Z'Kanthu as he spoke. The machine looked at him, his eyes flickering and then becoming brighter.

"They will fight for somebody our rebels can trust, one with a history and reputation as a hunter and killer of Biomechs. The Thegns are suspicious of your Alliance, and their knowledge of the Helions is limited. There is one they will follow though, the first of your people they ever met."

He then pointed at Spartan.

"He has been chosen as our war leader by the Thegns. Where Spartan goes, our bandon will follow. We are not interested in empire building or conquest. The last of The Twelve and all of our warriors pledge their lives to Spartan and to the end of all Biomechs."

General Rivers was stunned. He'd arrived with the intention of uncovering quite what was going and had instead been handed a fait accompli. He looked about the vast hall, at the marines, machines, and warriors waiting there for their chance for battle. Everything he had seen made him uncomfortable, and it was only the involvement of Spartan and Teresa that stopped him from shutting down the entire operation.

"So, you've created your own little army out here, then. What am I to do with you?"

Spartan stepped closer and pointed to the Thegns.

"We have seven Biomech warriors and three bandon of warriors. Let's use them as a spear point against the heart of the enemy. Just choose a target and see what happens. You won't be disappointed."

General Rivers heard the words, but all he could think of was that right now he had a big problem. There was a fleet of ships and an alien army right behind his own lines, and they recognized a civilian as their leader rather than his own generals.

"You will bring them to the rendezvous at the Admiral Jarvis Naval Station. Operation Citadel is almost ready, and there's no place safer than to have you alongside the rest of our forces."

To anybody else this might have sounded as a reaffirmation of his trust in Spartan, but he knew otherwise. The rebel forces might be powerful, but the assembled forces of the Alliance could easily destroy them.

"Very well, we will make preparations to link with the fleet."

"Yes, you will. In the meantime, you will return to my ship. We have other matters to discuss."

CHAPTER THREE

ANS Endurance was never supposed to enter an active combat zone. Only the critical situation, brought about by the change of course by Comet C34, moved her from a series of long-term projects and into the frontline. Helios would undoubtedly have fallen if the remnants of the comet fragment codenamed Thunar had reached the homeworld. Little is known about the fateful day when the combined forces of the Alliance, T'Kari, Helions, and Khreenk engaged Thunar and its fleet of ships. All that is known was that by the end of the fight, the enemy forces had been scattered and most of the Allies remained intact. Of ANS Endurance, nothing remained.

Ships of the Interstellar Navy

Orbital Platform Knossos, 70,000km above Helios
Three Crusader warships and a pair of Liberty class

destroyers activated their main engines and accelerated away from the destroyed defense platform. Dozens of Biomech ships pounded what little remained of the base while smaller craft hunted down lifeboats and escape pods to kill or capture those trying to escape. The rescue effort had been successful, and the five ships had achieved their objective of evacuating the station. Deep inside their armored hulls was the treasured cargo of escaped Helion soldiers and crew. The fight had been violent, but their escape was too slow.

Even as they moved away from the station, a Cephalon command ship spotted them. It was so close it easily disabled one before it could get away. As the engines built up to full power, a dozen lancing shots tore the engines from their mounts, leaving ANS Titania dead in space. The ship was an old warhorse, one of the first generation of Crusader class of ships and a veteran of the seven separate engagements.

This rescue mission would be her last. The other four ships put as much firepower onto the Biomech ship as they could, but in less than a minute they were long gone, and their sister ship was stuck in high orbit over the besieged world of Helios Prime.

With ANS Titania unable to move, the enemy warships took their time moving into safe firing positions. One by one, they began a systematic bombardment of her flanks. Shot after shot tore through her armor and rent open her bulkheads into space. Although unable to escape, she continued to fight with every weapon system at her disposal. Even her remaining fighter rammed the nearest Biomanta and set off a series of internal explosions that sent the vessel lifelessly into space.

In another fifteen minutes the ship was a wreck, a lifeless corpse, and to all intents and purposes dead in space and unable to fight back. Fires burned in a hundred places, yet there were many survivors aboard, and some took their chances with the lifeboats. That was when the boarding shuttles launched from the Cephalon.

One by one, they streaked across space and smashed into the ruins of the ship while fighters destroyed or towed the lifeboats back to their own ships. The boarding craft slid inside the wreckage like needles pushed into rotting fruit. Once stationary, entire squads of Decurion war machines clambered out and moved into the ship. Final volleys of gunfire from the four retreating Alliance ships caused minor damage to two of the Biomantas, but they had little effect on the boarding action.

The rescue for the orbital platform was over. Now the battle for ANS Titania would begin. Not a soul aboard her thought for a second it was a fight they could win. They were right.

* * *

ANS Conqueror, near Helios Prime

Helios Prime looked little different to the early days of the siege, yet every single person aboard ANS Conqueror knew the battle was going badly. Contingents from Helios and the Byotai had boosted the size of the fleet. But even when combined with the small trickle of reinforcements from T'Karan, it still only increased the fleet to just over a hundred and fifty ships. In any other circumstances it might have been an invincible fleet, but up against the Leviathan Ark and its escorts, there was simply no comparison. With every attack being repulsed, they were forced to withdrawal to the secondary deployment point at the entrance to the T'Karan Rift. It was the only way back to Alliance territory, and therefore the single most important piece of space to High Command. With no Rift, there would be no reinforcements, no counter-offensive, and also no way to evacuate Alliance personnel.

Admiral Lewis paced about inside the CIC, to the irritation of his officers. He'd been moving back and forth for nearly four whole minutes while they waited for the latest reports from the fleet, as the ships limped back to their holding position almost a day from Helios Prime. The officers spoke quietly, but there was clearly a mood of despondency on the ship, one brought about by weeks of death, loss, and failure.

"It was a good effort. We nearly succeeded, dammit!"

His voice was quiet, and few could make out what he

was saying even though the volume in the CIC was already almost silent. The tactical display behind him showed the last phases of his third attempt in the last month to relieve Helios Prime. The operation had begun four days earlier as a long-planned and rehearsed operation. The battle had been a three-pronged assault, using the Byotai ships under General Makos, as well as contingents from the T'Kari and Helios to engage the ships from two directions. Once busy, he had sent in thirty Alliance ships directly at the Ark Leviathan, the official codename for the largest and most powerful of the vessels unleashed by the Biomechs. He'd also sent in three waves of ships to the remaining Helion defense platforms that had been disabled weeks before, all under the cover of the general assault.

It should have worked.

He tried to get the images of the lost ships out of his mind, yet the thought of those that had been trapped would not leave him. At least four ships had been heavily damaged trying to evacuate orbital stations. It was the image of ANS Titania that hurt him the most. The loss of a ship was bad enough, but the boarding actions of the Biomechs were different this time. The last messages had been hours ago, and they had been filled with screams and horrors. The Biomechs had boarded them and were taking prisoners for their infernal war machine. The enemy was broadcasting life video feeds of the event on open channels so that anybody could watch. In the end, he had been forced to block the signal, knowing full well how the horror of the surgical assault would cripple morale in his defeated fleet.

There's a saying that they don't take prisoners, and in a way they're right. It would be better if everybody on board Titania put a bullet in their heads, because if they don't, in a few weeks or months we'll have to do it ourselves.

He shook his head and sighed.

It's no way for our people to die. The bastards!

Admiral Lewis could see the video feeds of the cruisers surrounding the Ark in his mind as clearly as when he'd seen them coming in live. At the time his flagship had been commanding the four divisions of ships providing long-range bombardment gunfire to the attack, as well as controlling the squadrons of fighters. It was the video of the ground assault as the Maulers and Hammerheads unleashed platoon after platoon of marines and Jötnar assault troops into the Ark. Leviathan was well named, and most commanders were still unsure whether to class it as a starship or space station. It made little different to him; it was a massive military vessel filled with troops and capable of terrible power. In the confusion of battle, they had even made it aboard for a full twenty-three minutes before they'd been beaten back.

So many gone, and still they control Prime.

He shook his head, recalling the elite Red Watch Jötnar outnumbered ten to one in passageways against Decurions.

Marines would have been wiped out in minutes, but the Red Watch had held the corridors to give the rest time to escape. Over ninety Jötnar had been lost fighting the rearguard. Each fought with such passion and skill that it wrenched his stomach just to think about it. All had died in the bloodbath, yet their kin continued to volunteer for yet more assaults.

"Admiral, are you all right?" asked his XO.

Admiral Lewis wiped his brow and nodded quickly.

"Yes, go ahead, continue with your assessment."

The Captain moved back to the computer display he'd been using and continued checking the new reports. Admiral Lewis watched him for a few more seconds before the imagery returned to his eyes, even though they were both wide open. The fight, for want of a better word, had been a slaughter. He had no idea as to the casualties caused against the enemy; they seemed able to simply shrug off losses like he might toss away an unwanted coat. He, on the other hand, had seventeen ships, nineteen hundred crew, and nearly three thousand dead or wounded marines.

We can't afford another battle like that.

The display above him showed the arrival times and location of each of the surviving units, and it was the percentage indicators that make his stomach shudder and ache. Some just showed a drop of a few percentage points, but one group was only at thirty percent strength, and he knew too well it had been a ten Liberty ship destroyer unit.

Seven ships lost, all from a single unit. Insanity.

It was his job to maintain the warfront though, and his orders were simple. With the largest force outside of Micaya and T'Karan, he would have to attack and harass the Leviathan whenever he was able. Every attack would reduce their ability to hit the planet, and that would ultimately save lives, as well hold off the possibility of an orbital assault on the planet. He stopped pacing and looked at his executive officer, Captain Marcus.

"Well, can it be done?"

The officer looked to Lt Vitelli, the ship's tactical officer before looking back and shaking his head.

"There's just no chance, Admiral. Even from orbit, they cannot breach the underground weapon system."

"Yes, but what is left down there to stop them?"

The XO shrugged.

"Contact has been lost with all their forces since our last attack. If we want to speak with them, we'll need to get a ship into low orbit. It's risky."

The raised eyebrows of the Admiral reminded that the man he was all too aware of the predicament they now faced. After weeks of combat, there really was little point in reminding him of such trivia.

"Admiral, what about the counterattack? I thought Citadel was supposed to resolve this?"

He closed his eyes and did his best to visualize the arrival of the fleet. In his mind, they would be like the cavalry in some ancient army story. But this was no story, and even another hundred ships would make little difference to what was happening out here.

"The Rift will be opened when, and only when Anderson is ready. We have only one chance with the counterattack. Our job in the meantime is to protect this Rift position against all comers. You saw the orders from Anderson. We will sacrifice every single ship if necessary to keep this point open. If they are able to turn their attention from Helios Prime, you can guarantee they will come in this direction. We have to keep them busy."

They both looked at the columns of ships still making their way back from the bloody engagement. The casualty reports continually updated, and both tried to avoid looking at the increasing numbers of dead and wounded.

"Our forces can't even reach half of their number, but we have nothing, and I mean nothing that can deal with the Ark. Every time we've tried to get close to it, they've hit us back hard. It seems they're happy for us to go anywhere else, providing their Ark is safe.

"Indeed. That is why we need to work out a way to remove that threat. As well as being a vessel capable of destroying any ship in our fleet, it's also the platform being used to conduct the continuous bombardment of Helios Prime. We have to find a way to stop it before Helios is lost."

Captain Marcus moved closer and wiped his brow.

"Admiral, is there much of Helios left to save?"

They looked at each other, and it was only then Admiral Lewis truly understood how far he had failed. He'd retained most of his fleet and those ships under the command of alien generals like Makos. Even the ships under Captain Perry were still available to him, yet his one job of protecting Helios had been a complete failure. The destruction of Thunar should have been his crowning achievement, when in reality it had simply bought the planet a few more days. His job had been to keep Helios Prime safe. Yet every ship he'd lost made not the slightest bit of difference to the outcome on the planet.

"You truly believe the planet is lost?"

Captain Marcus sighed.

"Admiral, I think we lost Helios the day the bombardment started. All that's left to know is how many we can save."

They both knew he was right, but that didn't make it any less painful for them. The Admiral looked back at the tactical display and then brought up the mapping information for the planet. It showed the underground Doomsday weapon system, as well as the positions for all ground units that were still waiting for the inevitable assault.

"So General Daniels is down there, waiting for them to attack. Can he hold when that happens?"

Captain Marcus lifted his upper lip a fraction and shook

his head.

"You've seen the reports from Spascia. They are fighting a smaller Ark and no mass-driver bombardment. They have managed to hold back dozens of assaults, and still they are holding the ground in the heart of the city. The ground attacks are of a level that far surpasses High Command's estimates."

He pointed at the imagery of Helios Prime.

"Based upon the size of Leviathan, I think we can assume that when they decide to strike, it will be short, deadly, and will overwhelm General Daniels in a matter of hours. Unlike Spascia, this Ark appears to be of a completely different level to the smaller ones."

"Just perfect. Still, just the mass of the thing is exponentially bigger than the Arks Belial, Astaroth, or Beelzebub targeted on the other worlds. Leviathan is like no enemy we've ever faced before."

He then pointed to the schematic showing the Doomsday weapon system and the remaining underground defenses.

"I suspect the other Arks are merely launching assaults to pin down our resources, ones that may or may not be successful. Why are they not hitting Spascia in the same way? Surely even the smaller Arks are capable of a massive bombardment from space."

"A diversion?" asked his XO in surprise.

"Quite possibly. Don't forget, these machines have only one short-term goal here. They need the Black Rift cleared so they can open a Spacebridge long enough to get help from their homeworld. If any of our ships remain at the Rift, or any of these Doomsday systems are operational, their entire effort would be wasted. The planetary weapons can do more than simply shut down the Black Rift for a period of time; they can shut down any Rift."

That stopped both of them in their tracks for a moment.

A grim-looking figure entered the CIC as the four marine guards ushered him inside. The man wore his PDS Alpha armor as if he expected an attack at any moment.

"Lieutenant Colonel Koerner, I wasn't expecting to see you for another six hours at least."

The man's helmet was off, his only concession to the interior of the ship. Both of the Naval officers noticed the lines running down from his forehead to his chin. The scars had been sealed up, but the damage to the rest of his body was well hidden by the armor.

"My boys are out there dying every day; I couldn't stay in medlab a minute longer. Meds will keep me going, and if I'm not mistaken, we have some serious work left to do. Am I right?"

"You could say that," grumbled Captain Marcus.

The Marine officer walked closer to the two with a pronounced limp and stopped next to the tactical screen. With a few quick gestures, he brought up the three-dimensional model of the primary weapon system on Helios Prime.

"I checked some of this data back down in medlab."

He pointed to a number of positions all around the surface.

"Notice anything strange about this picture?"

Both officers looked at it for some time, but neither could identify whatever it was the marine had found. An alert from one of the junior weapons officers distracted the XO for a moment. It was a pair of Liberty destroyers, and both were being pursued by a large formation of Biomech fighters. Admiral Lewis nodded to the XO.

"Problem?"

"No, Admiral, we can handle it."

While he assisted in providing covering fire for the approaching capital ships, Admiral Lewis looked back to the Colonel.

"I don't see the problem. What is it?"

The man pointed to the layout once more.

"They've had almost a month to disable this weapon system, yet after all this time, and hundreds of thousands of attacks, why have they managed to miss?"

Admiral Lewis could see the problem before the Colonel had even finished speaking.

"They aren't trying to destroy the weapon. They want to control it."

It was something he'd only just given much thought to, and the more he considered the possibilities, the clearer and more likely it became.

"So, they capture the weapon system and then can use it to control access to our own Rifts."

The Marine Corps officer lifted his lip a little.

"Why do they want control of the guns?"

Admiral Lewis considered his question and rubbed at his chin.

"There can only be one option. By controlling a single weapon, they will be able to cut off our forces from joining us here. Even worse, they will leave us trapped in this system, a sitting duck, if and when they are able to get the Rift itself open."

Both men came to the same conclusion at the same time, but it was the Colonel who spoke first.

"They are smart. If they capture just one of the guns, they can take their time finishing us off, and when they win, they head for the Black Rift. If they destroy the guns, well, that would be faster, and they could then still access the Rift."

"And whichever result occurs, they will have our ships pinned down well away from the Black Rift, making their arrival safer and more significant. Maybe we should have kept the fleet at the Black Rift instead?"

Admiral Lewis looked at him and considered the idea for a while.

"True. Without the Rift, their resources are finite."

The thought had occurred to him before, but it was only now that war had fully engulfed the entire system, he could see more clearly. His own resources were limited but were holding their own.

"The harder they push us here, the better the chance they have at the Black Rift."

He looked back at the ground positions for Helios Prime. The last dispositions were spread out, but even though General Daniels still retained sizable forces, it was perfectly clear to him what would happen next.

"When they make landfall, I would be surprised if the General will even be able to hold for twenty-four hours."

He looked back at the imagery.

"All I need to know is when will they begin the attack. Once they start, all of this will be over. We need an alternate plan."

He looked to his communications officer.

"Get me a secure channel with High Command on Terra Nova."

Captain Marcus heard his order and looked back to the Admiral.

"Problem?"

He shook his head.

"No more than usual. We need a new plan, and the Helions are not going to like this one, not one little bit. We need to move up the timetable. If the Biomechs take Helios Prime, they'll knock out our Rift home, and with it any chance of reinforcements."

He swallowed at the sudden realization.

"Hell, with the Rift gone, there will be no Operation Citadel."

* * *

City Docklands, Helios Prime

General Daniels looked up at the next wave of objects and shook his head angrily. This was the third day of the attack on this one section of the city, and little now remained of the taller buildings around him. The weeks of attacks on the rest of their planet had done their work, and the smoke and dust spread in all directions around them. This most recent attack had destroyed one of the few remaining identifiable parts of the city. Even as the orbital assault continued, the few remaining fighters reached up to claw at the falling objects. Sometimes they were successful, but with each hour the defenses became weaker. The thriving urban capital of the Helions was now a barren wilderness, its sounds now replaced by the shouts and screams of the dead and dying. The factional differences came to the surface daily as groups of Animosh, Zathee, and the others fought each other for food, clothing, and supplies. All the while, the ground forces of the NHA and the Alliance did what they could to help. Even so, this sector that General Daniels had selected was now different to the rest of Helios.

Just one big pile of rubble, not even the landing platforms and docks are operational anymore.

He had specifically selected the site of the massive battle during the early Helion Revolt as his base of operations, due to its proximity to the docks and storage facilities. He wanted access to arms, equipment, and fresh troops more than defensive terrain. Now he wondered if any of it had been of use. Those that had survived the first twenty-four hours now lived underground, in the many parts of the city left over from the horrific last war with the machines.

"General, reports in from the last weapon batteries. The surface-to-air missile batteries are down to their last crates of ammunition. The gun trucks ran out an hour ago," said Captain Hammond.

He nodded quickly and stepped back into the still intact bunker that had so far managed to hold against orbital attacks from the Biomech Ark still orbiting Helios Prime. Inside, moved a dozen officers as they assisted in the command of what remained of the scattered defenders on the Helion homeworld.

"The Doomsday Weapon, is it secure?"

His only remaining senior officer shook his head.

"No way to tell, Sir. We lost contact with them seven hours ago. Last reports said the comet fragments had destroyed the surface defenses. That means the Biomechs are clear to land troops right on top of them. The last transmission said the NHA would be sealing themselves in for a siege in the next six hours."

General Daniels shook his head.

"Brave, but it will not work. The Helions are not like us. They are vulnerable to a ground assault, and they lack the weapons or armor to win. What was their last recorded strength?"

"A little over two hundred warriors, plus an attached platoon of our recon detachment."

"That's not going to be enough to hold an underground fortress. They'd need double that."

He tried to remain calm, but it wasn't easy when the planet you were trying to defend was being smashed into oblivion from space. It was a cowardly way to fight, but there was nothing he could do from down here, nothing at all. His job was to protect the city and to keep the docks open for reinforcements.

"What's our own status?" he asked, dreading to know.

"Well, General, we're down to half effective strength; the rest are MIA of wounded. Air cover is gone, but we do still have plenty of ground vehicles left. We have enough units left to fill our regiment, Sir, no more."

That felt like a swift punch to his stomach. Most Marine regiments were based around four battalions, with one usually staying back to retain, resupply, and eventually to takes its place in the line. Numbers had been increasing, but it was generally assumed a battalion would be around twelve hundred men, and a regiment therefore nearly five thousand. That was half of the number he'd been allocated with for the defense of Helios Prime. So far, all he'd been able to do was to help with relief efforts and to assist in defensive fire against the objects hurled at them from space.

"I see. I recommend we shift two more companies to assist the Helions."

"Sir, look."

The man pointed at one of the larger displays that showed an external feed of their command bunker. It was angled slightly upwards so that the twisted wreckage of the city ruins filled just a quarter of the frame.

"What is it?"

"No way to tell. Our scanners can't cope with the orbital debris as it is. There are dozens, no, hundreds of them, and they're coming down near the weapon site."

General Daniels spotted the first of them as the dark shapes emerged from the fires of an orbital entry. As he'd seen on the footage from Spascia, this looked just like the arrival of the Biorays.

"This could be it. The attack we've been waiting for."

He nodded to the Captain.

"Send up the flares. It's time."

"General."

The man moved away and called out orders to the small number of officers that remained. What had been a matter of dull repetition, suddenly transformed into movement; marines appeared from hiding as if by magic, moving out from their underground lairs and into positions prepared weeks earlier. Even the vaunted SAAR robots drove out of their protective enclosures and into spaces with cleared fields of fire.

"Incoming!" cried an unknown marine from outside.

He ran in through the bunker's main door and slid inside, just as a long volley of gunfire shredded the masonry outside. The attack was followed by a bewildering array of explosions, and then the screaming sound of Biomech fighters overhead. General Daniels looked to the tactical screen that had started to flicker. From one side of table were scores of red shapes moving in fast from the south.

"General, reports of machines behind our lines. They're coming in directly from orbit."

He shook his head angrily. This was something he'd not heard of, yet it didn't surprise him. The Biomech war machines contained only a modicum of biological components and were easily able to survive a retro assisted landing on the surface. He grabbed the intercom and nodded to the communications officer to boost the power.

"This is General Daniels. The day we've been waiting for is here. Stay at your posts, and watch your comrades. We can survive this."

Part of the outer wall tore open, and in walked one of the dreaded Decurion war machines. The eight-legged thing made it halfway through before the marines inside cut it down. At close range the L52 carbines tore large holes in the metal. A marine bent down to look at the hole in the wall.

"No, get back!" barked a sergeant.

It was too late; a projectile struck the marine in the face and sent his body flying to the ground. General Daniels lifted his own weapon from its clamp on his body and flicked off the safety. At the same time, he mentally accessed the control to his armor and brought down the visor to protect his face.

"Get on the line. Hold them back!"

All non-essential personnel moved to the slits in the outer walls and through the blast doors that led into a dozen trenches and defense works around them. Even so, the explosions and gunfire seemed much less than he would have expected. As the fight continued, he walked back to the tactical display and looked at the first of the red shapes dropping in around the city. There was no obvious pattern that he could see. Then he remembered the weapons. Using his hands, he dragged the map to the side and noticed the lack of enemy forces anywhere near it.

The bastards are pinning us here, right where they want us so they can hit the weapon.

He spotted shapes outside, and a number of rounds clattered against the bunker. The return fire from the marines was impressive, and no further casualties were suffered. The attack seemed to end as quickly as it had started, without a single machine getting closer than the first.

"General, something is coming in on the emergency channel. It's coming from orbit."

"A signal?"

The officer nodded.

Admiral Lewis, it has to be.

"Then put it on the mainscreen before we lose whatever power we have left."

The man moved quickly and gave orders to the more junior in the bunker. Down here it felt cooler and slightly damp, but the dust still managed to seep inside and cover screens and equipment. The screen flickered and then showed a decayed image of Admiral Lewis.

"General, are you receiving me? I repeat; can you hear me?"

"The Admiral," said General Daniels excitedly, "Boost the power. Use whatever we have left."

"Yes, Sir."

The officers boosted the power from the last three storage banks, and for a short while the quality of the video improved.

"Yes, Admiral, we're here, but only just."

The image crackled and faded again.

"What is your status?"

General Daniels closed his eyes for a second and did

his best to hide his anguish.

"Admiral, we've lost over fifty percent of our forces here. The Helions' defenses are gone. We have no air cover, and the civilian casualties continue to climb. I'm down to less than five thousand marines over the six landing sites throughout the capital buildings."

"And the weapon?"

He shrugged in response.

"We've lost contact. Admiral, by the time they land the bulk of their ground troops, there'll be nothing left to defend."

"Understood. We have a small window of three hours before the Biomech fleet is back into position to launch."

"Uh, Admiral, we've got ships coming through already. We're preparing for the final attack."

It was hard to see, but he was sure he saw something approaching a grin on the Admiral's face.

"General. They are coming for you. That much is certain. We have already counted in excess of two hundred Biorays moving into position around the Leviathan Ark. They have twice that number of warships for force protection. When they land, it will be over."

The signal decayed a fraction, and General Daniels was forced to shout to his officers to get more power from the reserves to boost it.

"…the current ground forces are a forward party. You have two, perhaps three hours before the invasion starts. My estimates put a total assault force of around ten thousand shock troops, with an almost limitless of reserves following them up."

General Daniels found himself at a loss for words.

"Then this is it, Admiral."

"No," came back the start reply, "Not by a long shot. I can help, but only for the next hour, perhaps two. After that, then you are right. It will be over."

"They're Biomech ships!" shouted out a corporal.

General Daniels moved from the banks of screens and the dust covered tactical display and toward the doorway. Half a dozen exhausted looking marines joined him and looked up at the sky. Streaks of flames marked the continuing orbital bombardment, but it was the ships that all of them were stunned to see. First came one assault ship and then another until seven of the large warships screamed overhead. Their banks of gun turrets bombarded the surface, sending explosions and flashes rippling across the horizon.

"General. Helios Prime isn't the prize. They are not coming for you or the civilians. It's the weapon they want, and they intend on taking it."

The imagery of the Admiral shifted automatically to the helmet overlay rather than the screens inside the bunker.

"You need to send out a blanket evacuation order to the entire planet. Everybody not underground needs to hide, and fast. It will take weeks, perhaps months, but I do not believe the enemy has any interest in seizing Helios Prime immediately. Once they control the weapon and their forces dominate the Rift Network, then they will try and take control of this world. That does leave us a problem though, the weapon."

"What do you want me to do?" General Daniels asked.

He checked his carbine as he waited even though he already knew what the Admiral was going to ask.

"Deny it to the enemy. They will be there in three hours. I need you to render it useless in half of that."

"But the Black Rift Admiral."

"General, once they land their troops around the weapon, you'll be less than an hour from its capture. I promise you; after the first attack is over, they will be in control of the facility."

"Admiral, we have to try. Let me put..."

"No," came back the curt response.

"Soon as they begin the primary attack, I will be unable to land anywhere near the weapon installation. Get your troops to safety, or wait at the Doomsday Weapon. Either way, in ninety minutes, I will begin an emergency drop. Remember, in three hours they will hit, perhaps earlier. After that window, you're on your own. That weapon system must be destroyed by then. Under no circumstances can it fall into their hands. Do you understand?"

The image crackled, and he nodded to his

communications officer to put the reserve back into the bunker's defenses.

"Well, General, what are your orders?" asked Captain Hammond.

General Daniels looked back at the young officer and did his best to look calm.

"Son, we are gonna secure that weapon system, no matter what."

"And if we fail?"

He smiled at the question.

"Then we blow the place to high hell."

The General looked at the other officers who had heard the last part of the conversation.

"We're leaving this place. Send word out to all company commanders. It's time for all of you to go deep and do what they can to protect the civilians. We have security details helping with the defenses already. Join them and improve them as best you can."

He looked back to the Captain.

"I want a single picked company of marines. You know them as well as any of my officers. Get me three platoons of volunteers, and meet me in the vehicle pool in fifteen minutes."

He made to move off but stopped and looked back, an odd look in his eye.

"Oh, and make sure you bring some engineers along as well."

"The Doomsday Weapons, Sir?"
General Daniels laughed.
"Yeah, it's time we paid the place a little visit.

CHAPTER FOUR

Ships have always followed periods of modification, enhancement, and reevaluation. Even looking back to the wars of humankind on Earth nearly three millennia ago can tell us much. The Ancient Greeks utilized a wide variety of wooden ships, most intended for ramming attacks. Moving ahead came the development of guns and the great arguments of powerful guns versus quantity, an issue that would be decided in the Second World War. The balance of armor, speed, and power determined the makeup of a ship and its function in war. Today, the modular ship designs of the venerable Crusader, Conqueror, and now the Liberty class provide limitless configurations for the frontline.

Naval Cadet's Handbook

Old Spascia City, Spascia

Jack pulled open his visor and lifted the stabilized binoculars to his eyes. His internal optics had sustained multiple failures, yet the old piece of technology taken from stores were working as well as they ever had. The view to the east was little different to how it had been a month earlier. The substantial rocky mountains provided an impassible surface to land ships and shuttles on, and the turrets built directly into the rock made them all but impassable. At the base of the mountains was the gorge, a vast crag much like a river that split the city and ran in a crooked line directly to the mountain overlooking the ruined city. It housed the infamous planetary defense installation, one of only four in existence.

Doomsday Weapon, he said to himself with much amusement.

The name was nonsense, one presumably created by an Alliance officer with far too much time on his hands. It was generally know as the Planetary Defense Net to most of the Helions, yet the Doomsday Weapon was surprisingly fitting, given the circumstances. He glanced back at the horizon and the only part of Spascia not currently belching thick smoke into the sky. Even so, clouds of the stuff still managed to waft in the direction of the craggy cover.

"Any change?" Private Jana Jenkell asked.

Jack shook his head and concentrated on the view. He'd become much closer to the squad's medic since the catastrophic losses in the first assault on Spascia. Callahan was gone and so was Riku. Even the passing memory of her made him want to retch. Only Corporal Frewyn and

Private Jenkell remained from their original little group, and even the Corporal was a fraction of what he had been. His damaged arm had been patched and repaired prior to the siege, but since then he'd been forced to accept a brace on the arm to stop it moving too much. It was a simple articulated bracket, but it reduced his ability to fight, and he never stopped letting them hear how frustrated he was.

"Marines," said Corporal Frewyn as he dropped in alongside them.

"Have you heard the news?"

Jack and Jana shook their heads, along with the handful of others nearby.

"The Biomechs hit four cities further south an hour ago. This time they didn't bother with a ground assault. They just used nukes from orbit."

"What?" Jana snapped.

"Nukes?" Jack asked, but his words came out more as a confused statement rather than a question.

"Yeah, there's no information officially, but rumor has it the Biomechs are abandoning the sieges of five more cities and concentrating everything left on us."

Jack looked at him and then began shaking his head.

"No, that can't be. There are eleven cities and industrial sites under siege right now. You're saying they are giving them up to attack us?"

The Corporal nodded slowly.

"That's exactly what I'm saying."

He gave them a moment to let that sink in. Little information had come in over the last few days about the rest of the world, but the general opinion with the marines was that the sieges of the other locations were minor affairs, more designed to pin down Helion forces than to actually be decisive.

"We've got our own problems, anyway. Time will tell if they decide to raise their heads. Look, I've just been speaking with Jae Jaan and Tessuk. They say the machines tried an assault on the northern approaches of the mountain."

He pointed off into the distance and behind the planetary weapon system.

"Looks like they are working their way around the city and trying to get through the mountains while they mobilize their forces in the city ruins for the next big push."

Jack looked back to him.

"What happened?"

"The Khreenk is what happened."

The Corporal almost appeared amused at what he'd heard.

"Looks like nearly two hundred of those Thegns and a few war machines made it past the proximity minefield and right into a rear bunker complex on the lower slope. The Khreenk smashed them, and I mean smashed them. They had the high ground, good cover and best of all, supporting fire from the mountain guns. Looks like we had numbers and firepower on our side for a change."

Jack even seemed impressed.

"Yeah, the northern and western approaches are impossible to bypass with heavy machines and equipment. So all they can use is infantry, and that's slow, time-consuming, and vulnerable to air cover."

He looked up to the sky.

"You remember the second assault. That wasn't pretty."

The other two nodded, but Jack found it almost impossible to shake the imagery of that hellish assault. He'd played no part in the actual fighting, but he'd seen firsthand how the attack had unfolded, and how badly it had failed.

"Night assault from orbit and directly onto our prepared defenses was a big mistake," Corporal Frewyn agreed.

"I just wish they'd try it again. The ground spikes and defenses could easily finish off another few thousand."

Jana looked back to the Corporal and sighed slowly.

"I don't think they'll make the same mistake twice. Maybe they'll try and mine the place again," suggested Jana.

Jack gave her a look that told her no response was even necessary.

Corporal Frewyn indicated toward the mountains.

"The rock is hard as armor plate. Not even the Biomechs can mine through that while under fire. You saw what happened with the mining machine they brought in two weeks ago."

Both of them nodded in agreement. The underground battle between the Marine Corps and the Biomechs had gone on for three days straight and had already become something of a legend. Jack shook his head as he recalled what he'd heard.

"Yeah, I don't think they'll try that again. Marines and Khreenk underground can hold a lot of ground. It did keep them away from the artillery though."

As if emphasizing the fact, a barrage of heavy ordnance rumbled on the mountainside. The shells were launched from short-barreled guns hidden behind movable plates fitted at varying positions. Most had been installed in the first days of their arrival on Spascia. Far more had been installed over time, with each one turning the mountain into a veritable fortress. The shells were lobbed at a relative low velocity and arced overhead before falling down into the position only so recently occupied by the marines. Each one hit with a cataclysmic bang, sending dirt filled shockwaves through the streets. Even this far back the ground vibrated and lifted small amounts of dirt and dust from the floor. Before they hit the ground, a volley of counter-battery fire launched from the city ruins. The return fire was faster and directly targeted the mountain guns.

"Look!" Jana said.

Her outreached arm picked out a pair of the massive six-legged walkers known as Eques war machines. A shell had just exploded alongside them, and both had been hurtled out into the open of one of the ruined streets. Though hidden from view, a dozen marksmen armed with high-velocity anti-materiel weapons fired. Each shot punched a hole the size of a man's head into the machines' innards, and in seconds both were burning from scores of holes.

"Yes!" she said excitedly.

Then the return fire scored hits around the mountain. Almost half were slightly off-target, but enough struck home to damage gun mounts or kill and maim the crews. It was another of the vicious, morale destroying techniques used by the enemy, and day-by-day it whittled down the number of defenders.

All of the earpieces in their helmets activated at the same time. It was Lieutenant Elvidge.

"Theta squad, you've got hostiles half a klick away. They are tagged, but they went to ground the minute we spotted them. They're impossible to reach from here; you'll have to take them the old-fashioned way. Get there fast. I'll need you back here on the east side of the chasm by the end of today. Looks like they're mobilizing underground for another assault."

Jack felt a sickness in his stomach at this attempt of bravado. He knew exactly what the Lieutenant meant by the old-fashioned way, and it was far from pretty. Try as the man might, he was finding it harder everyday to manage with the close range gunfights and the brutal hand-to-hand combat. Just the idea pushed up his pulse, and he was forced to look away, open up his visor, and take another stim. They were small tablets, each no bigger than a pea, yet the effect was instantaneous. He felt his heart rate slow, and his thinking became clearer.

Just a few more, and after this is over, that's it.

He'd promised himself the same thing over and over for ten days now, but with the continuous barrage of attacks, his reliance upon the locally produced narcotic was becoming worse and worse. Jack wasn't the only one. He'd only learned of the drug when he'd spotted a pair of Territorial marines trading foodstuffs with one of the Khreenk. After a few of the tablets, he'd found them the only way to keep cool and levelheaded in the stressed environment of combat.

"Jack, you ready?" Jana asked.

He glanced back with a slight glazed look to his eyes. She angled her head a little as she looked, so he activated the visor. It snapped down with a clunk and blurred his features.

"Yeah, I'm ready. I think I'd rather stay on this side though than heading back over there."

His voice was low, almost monosyllabic, and he indicated across the chasm and to the city that could be seen off into the distance. It was the only viable route to reach the mountain with large numbers and heavy equipment.

But that doesn't stop them from trying to sneak in, does it?

The transmission from their commander continued in their helmets.

"The enemy is using a crevice to work their way along to the base of the mountain. Meet up with Sergeant Stone and force them back. We cannot allow a single soldier to make it inside."

Each acknowledged the orders and then moved down from their current position. The tagged location of the enemy was already within gunshot range, so they needed to keep their heads down low. In half a minute, they were back amongst the rocks and rubble that provided near perfect camouflage, as well as cover from artillery. Sergeant Stone waited with the rest of the squad plus a pair of Khreenk warriors. Jack glanced at them but didn't recognize the equipment configuration. They must have been a pair he hadn't seen before. He did recognize the stim pouch on the belt of the tallest soldier though.

"Move it, marines. We've got work to do."

As usual, the Sergeant led the ragtag band of warriors from the front. Gone was the rigid structure, and instead they found themselves moving as an ad hoc unit, a sergeant, two Khreenk, and ten marines drawn up into two teams. Jack and his comrades were placed in the gun team that included the Khreenk with their unusual mix of medium-range firearms. They moved a little further until reaching a clearing scattered with rocks and mixed cover.

"The only way for them to get past is to move through this area. It's big enough for an entire company to break through."

His eyes moved amongst the fighters until he spotted three of the Territorials, far less experienced marines and looking overwhelmed at what was happening.

"Don't think. Just remember your basic training."

The three looked to each other and then back at him. Sergeant Stone was already looking past them and to Jack, who did his best to avoid eye contact.

"Standard contact drill. I'll take the gun team to the right flank and prepare the ambush along the one side. Corporal Frewyn, you'll handle the rifle team down here."

Jack swallowed hard at hearing that. The gun and rifle team was something much more than equipment or training. The rifle team was the bait, and positioned to do just that.

"Corporal, you'll fan out and position scouts closer to their entry point. Give ground, and keep up fire until they're back into the killing ground."

He then looked to the team he would be taking.

"That's when we will hit them. Once they're scattered, they'll either fall to our guns, or we'll pursue them back to their entry point. Based on previous experience, they will do exactly what we would do in an ambush situation."

Corporal Frewyn nodded.

"Return fire and attack the ambushers?"

"Exactly."

Sergeant Stone turned his attention to the Khreenk.

"Do not block off their line of retreat. They need to make mistakes. If we surround them, they will fight like animals. Give them options, and we can control the ground."

The two soldiers looked to each other and began speaking. Nobody could understand a word they said, but that didn't interest Sergeant Stone. He just looked at the two of them and roared.

"Shut your mouths!"

Both looked at him, but neither even contemplated continuing with their discussion.

"Now, get into position."

He paused a moment while checking the most recent data from long-range scanners and drones.

"We've got less than six minutes. Jump to it."

With that, he was gone. The line of marines and Khreenk moved up to the one side and then slowly disappeared, continuing on to their chosen spot. The position on the one flank would give them a clear view of the Biomechs from just one side, but only if they emerged from the safety of the crevice. If they retreated early, there would be little chance of hurting them. Just five marines remained under the command of Corporal Frewyn. Jack looked at them and noticed they'd been lumped with the three Territorials. Though equipped in just the same fashion as the other marines, he knew they were far from the best the unit had to offer.

"You heard the man. Spread and follow me," said Corporal Frewyn.

He moved off with an odd gait, in part due to the injury that still hadn't fully healed. They moved a few more meters into the clearing and then fanned out on the hand signals of Corporal Frewyn. Jack and Jana moved to the front, and the others stayed back, each taking a position behind a suitably large piece of hard rock. Jack kept his eyes focused and moved another twenty meters to the front and then dropped down behind a long, lower ridge. Jana moved in three meters to his left and pulled her head down to safety.

"Good. I need eyes on the access point ahead. Let them in, but tag them as soon as they're spotted," said Corporal Frewyn.

Jack and Jana both acknowledged the command and moved the bare minimum to look ahead. The ridges and rocks provided vast amounts of cover in the shallow basin, but it was still just about possible to make out the end of the v-shaped ridge between two levels of rock. The enemy had been spotted entering the craggy gap, and if the estimates were right, they should be less than thirty meters from the exit point into the open space.

"I have eyes on the location," said Jack.

His optics were non-functioning, but the visor overlay was still working perfectly. As well as reminding him of his vital statistics, the technology was able to show him the position of his comrades, all of their ammunition status, and even the proximity of support.

"Good work, be patient. Get some mines out there."

Jack looked back and spotted an object sailing through the air toward him. He reached out in the nick of time and caught the proximity grenade. It was just the same as the four currently attached to his thigh rig.

"Jana, pass me your grenades."

The young marine reached down and rolled two of the objects over to him. She deliberately kept two back for her own use. Jack lifted the first and twisted the activate band to command trigger mode. With that, he hurled it off to the right and in the shadow of the largest rock. Twenty seconds later, he'd fanned them out in front of them, each of them set to the same setting.

"All done, Corporal."

"Good, now we play the waiting game."

He glanced to his left and checked that Jana was there. As was becoming routine for operations he was involved with, he half expected to see her dead or mutilated. It wasn't that he'd become morbid over time. It was simply a combination of experience and fear. He'd seen people he knew butchered in each of these operations, even the small ones, and this was far from small. They were outnumbered ten to one, and he knew only too well that those kinds of odds didn't suit them.

"Rifle team, I've got movement," said the Sergeant over the secure channel.

Jack lifted his weapon to the right of the rocky cover so that the barrel pointed at the narrow chokepoint. He instantly spotted the movement of a pair of Thegns. Both were armed with forearm firearms and kept their heads low.

They're learning…the bastards.

He was so tempted to pull the trigger, but self-control, mixed with experience and training, reminded him to stand his ground. He might kill them both, but the others would simply melt back into the mountainside. Few made it this far, but there was always the chance a handful could reach the planetary weapon system and damage or disable it. General Gun had reminded them more than a dozen times that if the weapon was disabled, it would give the Biomech a window, no matter how small a window to conduct their plans. Few doubted that the plan would involve a system-wide invasion.

"Jack, you ready?"

He nodded at Jana and looked back at the Thegns. More than a dozen had now moved out from the crevice cover and began to spread out in the clearing. All of this advance party was armed with firearms, and all were being very cautious.

Why? It's not like they are lacking reinforcements, Jack wondered.

He'd never been close enough to examine them like this before. Every single time he'd been in contact with them, they had either been shooting or stabbing at him. Like most marines, he'd assumed they were nothing more than pre-programmed or trained animals. More of them continued to stream out, and then came the shape that made his entire body shiver. It was one of the Decurion war machines. The fearsome eight-legged thing scuttled out from cover and moved along the flank of the unit. Jack looked back toward Corporal Frewyn and the rookies who would provide the covering fire for their withdrawal. He couldn't see them, but both were tagged on his visual overlay. He looked back and continued to tag targets to share with the other marines.

There are only two of us out here. What if we can't get back?

It was the fear of any blocking force to be trapped, and this was a scenario Jack had been through before. It was one thing to engage the enemy at range with firearms, quite another to hold back a concerted Biomech assault. He felt his pulse begin to quicken again before spotting a new icon on his overlay. He concentrated on it and used his retina to select the information for the object.

Combat drone. About damned time!

According to his information, the unit was waiting out

of sight just two hundred meters away. It was sending information to the marines on the enemy positions, but even more importantly, it carried a payload of laser-guided micro-missiles.

"Stay frosty, people. Let them in," said Sergeant Stone.

Half the Biomech unit was now out of the crevice and moving through the central part of the clearing. If they made it much further, they would have a chance to break out and move into the dozens of small tracks and gullies along the base of the mountain. Then there was a noise, a grinding metallic sound, followed by another of the machines appearing from the blackness. It was flanked by a small group of Thegns, as well as a larger, more substantial looking Thegn. This one was almost as big as Gun and carried a large gun in two hands. It pointed toward the mountain and muttered something in an alien tongue. Jack watched them, noticing how those at the periphery had dropped down low as if expecting something.

Something's wrong. They're spooked.

"Sergeant, what's happening?"

A short crackle muffled the first few words from the grizzled Sergeant.

"...do not engage. Wait for my signal."

The enemy was clearly attempting to jam the marines' communications. Like the weapons and armor they now used, it was all based upon lessons learned in their combat against the machines. Radio frequencies had been supplemented with direct-sight laser communications via drones and satellites. Although never one hundred percent effective, it did mean they could usually reach somebody, unlike the terrible disasters that occurred in previous engagements.

"Thirty more seconds. Two-thirds of them are out."

A howling screech came from the larger Thegn, and it ducked to the side and behind a series of large rocks.

"They've made us!" said Jack, "Do it, now!"

Jana took aim with her L52, and Jack did the same. As one, they opened fire at the Thegns in front and to the left of their position. Three were cut down in seconds, and many more were hit with stray rounds. Jack almost raised himself up to shoot as he noted the bloody impacts of the high-velocity slugs. Each one hit with a satisfying thump.

"Keep firing," said Corporal Frewyn.

Jack's magazine ran dry, and he reached down to grab another. It slipped into position, and he activated the high-power mode. A fusillade of small arms fire came back from the Thegns and hammered into the rock, each shot sending tiny pieces of sharp rock in all directions. Jack threw himself down, but more of the shots ripped into his position.

"Jack, we have to get back!" Jana shouted.

He looked up at her. She took aim, but two rounds glanced off her shoulder, leaving scorch marks and flashes of hot metal behind her. Jack indicated to those behind him.

"We need help here!"

There was nothing, and Jack leaned around the rock and fired three wild shots in the direction of the enemy. He had no idea if he'd hit anything, but the tactical overview presented a full image of the battle to him. He could see dozens of the enemy, and as expected, they had fanned out and were inching closer to him. He spotted a trio making a rush toward him.

No you don't!

He was scared but equally angry at their attempt to attack or kill him. Jack looked at the icons showing the grenades lying in wait amongst the enemy. All it took was a double acknowledgment from his eyes, and the further two exploded with a bright flash. Five icons representing Thegns flickered and then disappeared, and Jack found himself counting the confirmed kills.

Seven, come on, plenty more to kill.

Now he leaned around the corner and took careful aim. The group of Thegns was much closer now, and even more had surged in from the crevice. Two quick shots decapitated a pair of them, and then a round rushed back and removed the top of his cover.

"Screw this!" he muttered, more to himself than Jana.

Jack broke cover and scrambled back, zigzagging as he ran.

"Jana, fall back, now!"

He made it eight meters and then slid behind another series of rocks. These were only a short distance ahead of the Corporal and his group of rookies. As he slid down, a group of black tipped muzzles extended out and then answered with a bewildering roar. All blasted away in fully automatic mode, putting down a curtain of fire sufficient to allow Jana to also escape.

We can't hold them off, not like this.

Jack moved into a kneeling position and again raised his weapon. The Thegns had now filled two-thirds of the open space, and the Decurion machines were nowhere to be seen. He didn't hesitate and activated the final two grenades. Both exploded, yet the damage caused seemed insignificant compared to the numbers of warriors. A streak of fire rushed overhead and struck one of the rookies, who slumped down over the natural barrier and fell to the ground. Jack spotted dark blood running from his smashed head and did his best to ignore the damage.

"Jack, thirty seconds," said Corporal Frewyn.

It was impossible to see the marine from where he was sheltered, but the visual overlay on the visor marked his position. Jack sensed the nerves in his friend, but also the cool, dispassionate way that he spoke to them.

He's changed. He doesn't feel anymore.

"One last volley, give them everything we've got!"

Jack and Jana were already loaded and lifted their

weapons over the low cover. The roar of the gunfire was barely noticeable over the din of the return fire from the Thegns. Jack moved his eyes just a fraction and watched as scores of the things moved closer and closer.

"We're going to be overrun!"

"Calm down, Private," said Sergeant Stone over the intercom, "Now!"

The L52 carbine fire came down like an avalanche from one side. With no immediate cover, the Thegns were cut down like animals. Yet it was the unusual collection of alien weaponry carried by the Khreenk that did some of the most horrific damage. Unlike the marines, the Khreenk were a combat unit of individuals. Their armor and equipment reflected their history, and while some carried simple kinetic weapons, there were others with weapons of unknown origin. Streaks of green and blue energy crashed into the Thegns and burned through them, turning their bodies to ashen dust. Jack shook his head in horror and amazement.

"Private Morato, keep firing," said Corporal Frewyn.

Jack was already on it. The training was the only thing that could possibly work in such an environment. His weapon came to his shoulder and in went each clip, one after the other. He took aim, fired, and then moved onto the next. The battle became nothing more than a series of disjointed images to him now. Some of the Thegns managed to clamber out of the killing ground and rushed

Sergeant Stone's own squad. At least two marines fell before the Thegns were cut down. Jack was hit again, and miraculously his armor managed to deflect a bullet. Even the Decurions were smashed to pieces by broken metal from the variety of guns until finally the order came.

"Cease fire!"

It was Sergeant Stone's voice. And Jack was convinced he could almost sense a degree of sadness in the man's tone. One by one, the surviving marines rose to their feet. Jack almost laughed upon seeing the familiar face of Jana, still alive, yet white with shock. Corporal Frewyn remained, as did Sergeant Stone and the Khreenk. The flanking force moved down from their position and joined the rest in checking the bodies for survivors. A handful of the Thegns were still moving, but mercy killings by the marines soon stopped that. Jack moved out into the open and looked back toward the tear in the rock where the enemy had emerged. Bodies littered the place from the failed assault, and even he felt a little guilt at the way they'd performed such efficient butchery.

"What is it, son?" Sergeant Stone asked on seeing his face.

"This fight, it was barely a fight, was it?"

The Sergeant's face hardly altered as he looked at the young marine.

"Son, no fight ever is. They ain't here for an honorable war with flags and uniforms. This is genocide, plain and simple. Either we stop them cold, or their numbers and technology will wipe out every single one of us."

"Sergeant, you need to see this," called out one of the marines.

A handful of them moved to the crevice and to the man pointing at the body of the last Thegn. He bent down and pulled the figure up from the ground.

"What the hell?" Jana muttered.

"My father told me about these," said Jack.

Sergeant Stone's cheek twisted a moment before he spoke.

"Yeah, I know these. They aren't Thegns. These are closer to the things we saw in the Uprising back home."

Two marines lifted the body so that the others could see it. At first glance it was another bipedal warrior, one of the many types of foot soldiers used by the enemy. But this one was not a fully synthetic creature. It was much closer in size and build to a Helion or T'Kari. Its armor had been fixed directly into the flesh, leaving brutal marks and damage. The face was partially mutilated, and plating had been buried inside to connect to its bone structure.

"Yeah, they built these from the bodies of prisoners. If you ask me, they must have built these during their trip from Eos."

Jack looked at the creature and felt his throat burning, as if he was about to retch. It wasn't the creature that made him feel ill. It was that the enemy had managed to capture people on that world, a place where he had been fighting. The battle had been brutal, but the removal of people was something he'd never considered or even heard about. Sergeant Stone threw the body to the ground and looked into the dark crevice.

"If you ask me, I'd say they took these to replace the losses from fighting us in the assault on Eos."

"I thought we called that a victory, Sarge?" asked one marine.

"Watch your mouth, marine," Corporal Frewyn snapped back.

Sergeant Stone pushed his carbine into the darkness and was instantly rewarded by the shape of two more of the creatures. Both lurched out from cover and stabbed at him with blades built into their arms. He grabbed the first and yanked it out from cover, and then jumped into the gap to drive the bayonet on his carbine directly into its chest. The first scrambled about, but with plenty of marines there, it was shot to pieces while pinned to the ground.

"Secure this area. Jack, Jana, you're with me!"

Jack swallowed quickly, checked his magazine, and then moved in right behind the Sergeant. The crevice was just wide enough for an armored marine, but not much bigger. He moved forward, ever watchful of signs of the enemy while simultaneously trying not to step in the bloody remains of the creatures Sergeant Stone had killed.

"I've got movement. Keep your eyes…"

He went down as a Thegn dragged him to the floor. Immediately behind him was the metallic shape of the large Thegn. Jack didn't have time to think. He just aimed center mass and pulled the trigger. The carbine vibrated as it sent a high-speed stream of projectiles that clattered and smashed into its form.

"Jana!" he yelled.

She couldn't get past him and so placed her carbine on his shoulder and added her own fire. Deep inside the rocky crevice, the sound boomed just the same as when shooting inside a building. The Thegn absorbed most of the damage, and a line of holes ran from its thigh up to its collar. But instead of moving back, it grabbed the fallen Sergeant who was still stabbing at the Thegn that had ambushed him. The speed and strength of the injured Thegn commander was impressive, and in the blink of an eye, it had the Sergeant in a headlock right in front of its body. Jack lowered his carbine and put a single round into the creature still on the floor. It shuddered and then twitched in its death throes.

"Do it, Private. Take the shot!" Sergeant Stone ordered.

Both Jack and Jana took careful aim at the larger Thegn commander, but neither pulled the trigger. It continued moving from side to side, and the reduced space made it impossible to get around.

"Let him go!" cried out Jana, her voice a mixture of

rage and fear.

"This is Private Morato. We've got the enemy Thegn commander. He's taken Sergeant Stone hostage."

The veteran marine struggled, but the strength of this enemy warrior was too much for him. The more he struggled, the harder the thing squeezed him. Instead of fighting it, he looked back to Jack.

"Don't let it take me, son. Do it!"

Jack nodded and activated the high-power mode on his carbine. Jana saw what he was doing and glanced over to him.

"Jack, you can't."

He shook his head.

"No, there's nothing I can't do."

He took aim to the left of his Sergeant's head and squeezed the trigger. At this range, the blast was deafening and their vision partially obscured from the shattered dust and debris. Chunks of rock hit both the Thegn and the Sergeant, but it was enough to buy Jack the time he needed. He released his carbine, and it dropped down to hang on its sling. In one fluid motion, he snapped out his bayonet from its sheath and dived at the two. The Thegn still held the marine, but he'd fallen to the side and was struggling with the man. Jack grabbed at its left arm and then stabbed in a plunging action toward its neck. Even though it held Sergeant Stone with its right arm, the warrior was quick enough to deflect the strike to avoid the killing blow. Instead, the blade slid down and struck in its upper arm.

"Help me!" he cried.

Jana was already with him and tugging on the Sergeant. She pulled as hard as she could, but the grip from the Thegn was more like a machine than anything living. She pulled back her leg and kicked at it before finally being rewarded. The battered Sergeant slid forward and fell down on top of her, leaving Jack alone against the bleeding and badly wounded creature. He stepped back and adopted a fighting stand. He feet were spaced apart, and his left hand kept close to protect his face. In his right, he held the blade in a pick-grip, the blade pointing down to the ground. Then the thing began to cackle. There were no words, but it shared more in common with a laugh than any other sound.

"What the hell do you think is so funny?"

The creature dropped its wounded arm down and pulled out a serrated weapon as long as Jack's arm. The metal was dull, but the edge looked razor sharp. Again it made that sickening sound, and Jack realized this might finally be it, the end he'd expected for months now.

"Jack, stay down," said a familiar voice.

He had no chance to do anything and was yanked backwards and past Jana. In his place moved one of the Khreenk. It filled the crevice with its armored form and took aim with a squat, wide-barreled firearm. It made a single thud sound, and the entire center of the Thegn vaporized, leaving the remainder of its body to slump to the ground. The Khreenk turned its head around, and its visor changed from black to semi-transparent.

"Tessuk?"

The alien warrior turned about completely to look at Jack and lifted the corner of his mouth up. The translator caused a slight pause in his voice, but it wasn't enough to spoil the flow or intent.

"Correct."

He then nodded back toward where they had all started.

"General Gun has given orders for us to move off the mountain and back to the edge of the city. NHA regiments are holding a line two hundred meters wide in front of the Three Sisters. You will join us?"

Jack thought he heard a question, but the one thing the translator circuits had a problem with was intonation. Even so, Jack was just a private, and all he could do was to go where he was told. Sergeant Stone was now back on his feet and moved to the fallen Thegn. He looked back to Jack.

"We've heard about these ones already. According to the last reports, these are a low level command unit, one to give a degree of autonomy to the local ground troops."

Jack was surprised to hear this.

"I've not heard this, Sergeant."

The man smiled at his response.

"Well, now you have."

Tessuk pointed at the bodies.

"Our own information matches this. We know their forces are only partially autonomous. They rely upon Biomechs to command their armies, with command nodes providing a link in the chain of command."

"We call them Cores."

Tessuk looked back to Sergeant Stone.

"With this commander dead, their attacking force will fall back on their basic programming. That is until they receive new orders."

"So why are the last few heading back?"

A screaming sound of a low-velocity howitzer round whizzed overhead and vanished off far into the city ruins. Dozens more followed, as the myriad of gun systems fitted around the mountain put down heavy gunfire onto the lower ground around it.

"Because they're regrouping for another attack," said Jack.

Tessuk nodded feverishly in agreement.

"Yes, General Gun said an attack was imminent. Follow me, we have a pre-prepared position at the Three Sisters with more of my brothers."

There was no further discussion, and the small group of marines and aliens abandoned the position they'd fought so hard to defend and moved back around the slope. As they filed away, a large platoon of fresh Helion conscripts took their place. Jack looked at them as they went past and only then realized they carried just one thermal weapon between two. He grabbed one and stopped him, a short, scrawny looking man. His clothing was covered in a torn robe, and he wore a homespun covering on his head. His face was covered in a civilian respirator designed for workers in the deep core mining installations.

"What are you doing here? Where's the NHA?"

The Helion moved his right arm in an odd circular gesture and moved on.

"Private, they are the Ghosts," said Tessuk.

Jack watched another two move closely by before paying any more attention to the Khreenk commander. Both of these carried a box of ammunition, but it was the group following that truly stunned him. They were juveniles, teenagers to his eyes, and they wore nothing military other than poor quality quilted jackets and hats. On their shoulders they carried sticks with a cylindrical device attached.

"And those?"

Tessuk lifted his arms up as if not understanding Jack's words.

"Those with experience and training are using guns provided by the Animosh. The juveniles, well, they lack the training or the equipment to fight with our weapons. The lances are something we helped them construct."

Jack raised an eyebrow and his cheek twitched.

"You did what?"

Jana put her hand on Jack's shoulder but looked equally outraged.

"You've helped build weapons, for children?"

Tessuk looked to her and nodded.

"Of course. The Helion population of this ruined city is small, and we're using their resources to the best of our ability. The juveniles are quick in a fight and knowledgeable of the terrain."

He called to one of the young women who looked a teenager. After exchanging a few words, she handed her weapon to Tessuk. It was roughly two meters long and consisted of a simple hollow shaft to which a small device was affixed. Tessuk pointed to the tip.

"This lance is designed to be a single use device. The user simple stabs at their foe, and this charge will send a shaped warhead directly ahead."

Jack shook his head in horror, yet Tessuk continued his explanation.

"The materials are easily available from the mining supplies and allow even an untrained child to help in this fight. In the last assault, a team of civilians brought down an Eques walker on their own."

Jack lifted his hand to his face and wiped his brow.

"And how many made it back?"

Tessuk did his best to smile, but the translator was unable to hide its synthetic, inhuman voice from him.

"My friend, the Biomechs will kill every one of us. They do not recognize male or female, soldier or civilian. Children die the same as the rest of us. They are an asset, an expendable asset, and one we have to use if we want to live."

He tried to smile, but the alien expression came out more like a grimace.

"When this is over, they can always make more!"

CHAPTER FIVE

The origins of Spartan were always a mystery, with little to differentiate him from the myriad of other troubled men and women that joined the Marine Corps. Over time there were rumors that his parents had been killed, and the orphaned boy had grown up a variety of children's homes. Some information obtained in the War from the criminals on Prometheus collaborated this part of the story. Only those deep inside Alliance Intelligence had any real idea where had had come from, and even then, only in fragments. What little evidence of his past was destroyed long before the Uprising even began. It took the war with the Biomechs to bring the truth to the surface, a truth that even Spartan had never known.

The Rise of Spartan

The West Bank, Old Spascia City, Spascia

The images displaying on every marine's visor overlays was a shocking scene. In previous wars this kind of information would have been kept quiet for days, perhaps even years. The imagery from the drones showed the damage caused by the initial atomic strikes on four cities. They were small and lightly populated with much lower structures than on the Helion capital world.

Not any more though.

Fires burned in a hundred places, and long columns of refugees moved away from the ruins. There were other cities still controlled by the New Helion Army, but Jack doubted any of these survivors would be heading to Old Spascia City. The ruins were barely habitable before the siege. After a month of continuous combat, the place was nothing more than a shell.

Why do they even want this place now?

Jack trudged on, his feet lifting and dragging in time with the other marines as they trudged over the rocks and down to where the four landing pads remained.

"I can't believe they did it," said Jana, for what must have been the tenth time.

Jack looked in her direction but found it hard to speak. The shock of what he'd just seen had simply stunned him. Corporal Frewyn walked in front of them and heard Jana speak.

"It was gonna happen. Just be glad it hasn't happened here."

Jack shook his head miserably.

"We could be next."

They moved past a group of civilians who were arguing with a squad of NHA soldiers. After what almost sounded like the early stages of a fight, the group of civilians split up, the oldest taking a young child in the direction of the mountain. The others were directed back to the bridges.

Innocent or guilty, we're all in hell now, he thought.

All were protected by a pair of large tracked vehicles that had been modified with metallic rods extending upwards like giant spikes. Even as they moved alongside them, the two on the nearest platform started their engines and drove to one side. Seconds later an Alliance Cobra shuttle rushed in and landed. As soon as it touched down, the doors lifted up, and a squad of marines jumped in. The craft wasted no time in getting airborne, and the tracked mobile barrier vehicles moved back into position.

"Nothing will land there without permission," Jana said, doing her best to sound confident.

Jack wasn't the only one that could see the cables running around the flanks of the platform, or the burned shapes at key points in the foundations. He suspected they were connected to hidden charges designed to tear the platforms apart in an emergency. Sergeant Stone spotted him looking and pointed to the nearest cable.

"You noticed, huh? They're the last resort. If it looks like this place is under a full-scale assault, and they might secure the pad, well, then we set off the charges."

He stopped and looked back at the rest of the squad

marching in single file. He then leaned in to Jack, as though sharing some great secret.

"The trouble is if we blow them, we consign our resupply to parachute drops. Our ships can hide up there, but if they can't land," he shrugged, "No landing pads, no reinforcements, no heavy weapons, and no chance of evacuation."

They moved on past the pad and to the edge of the chasm. Even since they'd crossed the last time it had changed. The drop to the bottom was much too far down to see. It reminded him of images of Martian canyons, yet here the rocks were razor sharp and deadly to man and machine alike. The bridge was wide, easily big enough to drive a pair of Marine Corps Bulldogs along the entire length. Engineers had erected barriers every fifty meters to create a chicane effect to reduce access and drop speeds of anything making its way across. A female marine laughed from further ahead where she supervised a quadruple barreled flak gun.

"Look, Helion air cover. That's not something you see every day, is it?"

Jack looked up and watched the crescent-shaped aircraft scream overhead. It was fast and from this far away appeared more streamlined and advanced, but it didn't make it far before a pair of missiles had launched from inside the city and raced up to reach it. A series of dull thuds rumbled from the mountain that loomed ever present.

"Wild Weasel runs," Sergeant Stone said to anybody that was listening.

Jana looked to Jack for an explanation, one he would quite happily have kept to himself. She watched persistently though until he relented.

"It's a special type of mission performed by fighters to force them to use their ground-to-air weapon systems. Now our artillery will hit their launch sites and take out the missiles systems."

"Isn't that dangerous for the pilots?"

Jack raised his eyebrows in mock surprise.

"Uh, yeah."

Another pair of Helion fighters moved in, but this time they arced downwards and opened fire with wing-mounted rockets. These were not the precision munition usually associated with the Helions. Instead they were simple fin stabilized rockets that made a screaming sound as they loosed off to strike the ground. One explosion after another rocket the site that had already been pounded by artillery.

"Oh, man, they do not want to be down there!" said one of the marines.

On they moved, making slow progress over the bridge. It seemed to take an age, but it did give Jack the opportunity to turn his mind to something else. The chasm.

"Why did they build the city right here?" Jana asked.

Jack contemplated just shaking his head, but for some reason it was a question to which he actually had an answer for. During their retreat from Eos, he'd spent some considerable time studying the planets of Helios. Partially out of interest, but primarily to keep his mind occupied and away from the horrors of what he'd seen. These alien worlds contained so much he had never even heard of before, yet so much felt familiar. The roads, the vehicles, even the basic infrastructure had something that made him feel at home.

"Before the last war, this chasm was all water, right up to the edge of the city. Look, right there."

He pointed off to the east, in the direction they were currently heading, and picked out the cliff edge.

"Look at the top fifty meters. Notice the discoloration?"

Jana nodded. She opened her mouth to speak, but Sergeant Stone lifted his hand.

"Make way marines!"

A trio of Bulldog Mobile Gun vehicles approached, and the marines moved to the side of the bridge to let them pass. They were identical to the standard issue marine vehicle, apart from the large turret-mounted weapon. They were effectively wheeled tanks, each one a potent addition to the Marine Corps arsenal. As soon as they were past, the marines went back into the open space and continued their march.

"The colors show where the level of the water used to

be. The dams were destroyed in the last war, and the water rerouted to starve out the city."

"Why didn't they repair the dams?"

Jack looked to her and then to the city where shells continued to fall directly in front of them. It was strange for him as they advanced from the safety of their mountain stronghold and back across the river. The horizon was like something from a horror story. Thick columns of smoke rose up high, and fires burned in a hundred places. It was possible even at this distance to make out the tracer trails from a thousand different weapons.

"Jack?"

He looked back to her.

"What?"

"The dams, Jack, remember?"

Jana looked exasperated, but it had little effect on him. Every step they took over the bridge took them a step closer to the Spascia Meatgrinder, as it was becoming known.

"You know, for every ten marines we send back over these bridges, only half come back."

Jana sighed and shook her head in annoyance.

"I do know, Jack. I've been here as long as you. Now, those dams."

"Okay, okay. The dams are massive affairs. Why would the Helion authorities pay to rebuild them just to provide water to a dead city?"

He took another few steps before muttering so low only she could hear it.

"Nobody really cares about this city, not even the Helions."

They continued over the bridge in silence, but some of the other marines spoke to their comrades. There was a clear distinction between those that had recently joined the unit, and the most seasoned marines that had already seen weeks of combat. The newest spoke the loudest. They finally made it to the other side and on into the ruins of the city. The unit had increased to two under strength marine platoons with just a single squad from Jack's original unit. He counted them twice, confirming to himself that there were in fact just sixty-nine marines.

"Food?" asked somebody nearby.

Jack looked to his right, then his left where he saw a child of perhaps five or six years old. It was a Helion, with the facial markings of one of the Zathee families. It was a girl, her arm in a sling and cuts to her face. She extended her hand out and spoke again.

"Food."

The accent was thick, and it was clear to him she'd been schooled in the one word. He moved on past, not knowing what to say. He had no food on him at present and just a small quantity of water stored within the spaced armor of his PDS equipment. He looked over to Jana who just shook her head.

"Logistics will be through later with trucks. They'll get what they need then. We need what we have left for the fight. You know that, Jack."

He took another dozen steps and looked back to see the girl saying the same thing to the other marines; all with no offers of help or food."

"Marines, there they are!" Sergeant Stone shouted.

Jack could sense something close to pride in his voice, and he pointed at the dark black shapes ahead of them. It wasn't easy to make them out due to the mixture of dust and black smoke that seemed to be everywhere now. Only when the flashes from ground burst occurred could their shapes be seen.

"Ladies and Gentlemen, this is your new home for the next week. The Hotel Three Sisters!"

It was a joke, and a poor one at that. They moved the last few hundred meters to what had become the single most significant part of the defenses in the old city. Even while the battle continued on in almost all directions, the Alliance engineers had been busy expanding and improving the defenses. Jack looked back from his position outside the walls and to the mountain. The bridges were now fully obscured by the dust and smoke, but he could just make out the shape of an Alliance Mauler dropping down to land.

"This way," said the Sergeant.

Jack looked back and watched the double-layered

metallic door lift up on a pair of thick metal chains with a clanking sound. The entrance was big enough for a pair of Bulldogs to park next to each other. Even as it moved up, he could see four Alliance RAMs, each surrounded by sandbags and scanning the new arrivals for signs of the enemy. The gun mounts tracked from left to right, flashing green to signify they had passed the test.

"This place is completely different."

Jana nodded in agreement.

"You can say that again. I thought it was just an air defense installation. Three towers to cover the main approaches?"

Jack looked up at the nearest of the towers and then to the right where the next was almost four hundred meters away.

"I'd say this has changed."

Sergeant Stone heard them, waited to the side, and flagged them on.

"This is now the Spascia Fortress, the last bastion protecting the bridges. If this place falls, we'll be forced to blow the bridges and fall back to the mountain."

Inside was a hive of activity, and they passed scores of people busily preparing for the inevitable massive assault. It took considerable time to get through the layered defenses and past the triple layer of walls, barbed wire, and bunkers to yet another series of barricades. Jack tried to look confident, but Jana noticed the change in his mood.

"Jack, are you all right?"

His mind was now so fragmented he didn't even notice her talking. They passed the lines of troops and machines and into a secondary position inside the armored walls of the fortress. Unlike the previous positions, this one had been built over many weeks, and it wasn't just the layered walls. They could make out trench works and tunnels that were still being worked on. Jack brought up the overlay on his visor to examine the layout of the base.

"I thought so," he started, as though they'd already been discussing the design.

"The towers are positioned in a wide triangle, with a triple layer of walls and turrets joining them together. The entire site covers almost three city blocks and runs parallel with the chasm. We could put every marine we have left in this place and still have space."

They had not yet reached their destination and instead moved closer to the wall on the other side that would face the enemy lines. Jack instantly thought back to their position much deeper inside the city. He'd seen blood and casualties like never before at that point.

The passageway was cut directly out of the rock and concrete that months earlier had been the shattered remains of old Spascia City. This current route led to a series of bunker positions with commanding views into the city. The fire ports were small, just big enough to move a rifle low enough to hit targets. The engineers had learned from the weak defenses weeks before, reduced the gaps, and thickened the walls.

"Look," said Jana quietly.

She indicated toward a trio of Helions dressed in long, thick greatcoats and carrying more of those improvised weapons. Jack grabbed one as they were passing. She muttered something and shook him away.

"I don't get it, what are they doing?"

The unit moved into a wide position of four half bunkers, protected on all sides but the rear. Small doorways, just big enough for a marine to walk through, joined them together at the sides. The rear was completely open and allowed access to larger troops like the Vanguards.

"Okay, marines, you know what the mission is," said Sergeant Stone.

They each turned and faced the Sergeant but said nothing. They were formed up two deep and across two of the bunkers.

"The enemy is mobilized and ready. We just don't know when. It could be in five minutes or in five weeks. For now, we keep hitting them with the big guns."

He looked from left to right, watching the marines carefully.

"Many of them have gone to ground and are using the collapsed sewer and mass-transit system to get around. This fortified zone is built on the same solid rock as the mountain behind us. If they want to get to the chasm and beyond, they will have to come through us."

He pointed to each of the corporals in turn before coming to Jack's own squad.

"Each of your squads has an allocated zone. You will have a bunker to defend, as well as an allocated volunteer unit. Heavy units are in reserve."

A half-dozen Helions appeared around him; the long, thick greatcoats making them look even more depressing than the half-starved soldiers they'd seen back on the mountainside. Sergeant Stone opened his mouth to speak again but stopped upon hearing a marine shout out to his left. He glanced in the direction of the man and spotted something that completely altered his stance.

"General Gun!"

That was the first thing to get Jack's attention. He looked to the right and spotted Gun and his entourage of Black armored Vanguards and Jötnar with their Hyperion iconography. He stopped alongside a pair of flags. One was an Alliance standard, the other from Helios, and both were filled with dozens of bullet holes. Jack looked at him and wondered how many engagements the warrior had been in since arriving on Spascia. His armor was dented in a hundred places, and the paint had peeled or burned away on every flat panel. Even so, with his visor open, Jack could see the glint in his eye.

The crazy fool! He's loving this.

Jack shook his head, partially in exasperation, and

partially in amazement.

"We've received word from High Command. Our reinforcements are almost ready to hit back. We have a massive fleet, divisions of marines, and thousands of my own kin. The cleansing of this system will begin soon, and it will be glorious!"

There were few that could not get excited at the rousing sound of the warrior built for war. He towered over them all, encased in armor and marked from a dozen encounters.

"If we're to counterattack, and finally remove these things from Helios, well, that can mean only one thing. These Biomech scum will have one last chance to get rid of us before General Rivers brings fire down on them. If they delay, they will be caught between our guns and ships."

The marines shouted and cheered excitedly at the mention of the Alliance's most famous general. Even among the new and young recruits, the man was something of a legend. The Helions remained silent, and Jack could only assume it was because they couldn't understand him.

"This will not be easy though. In the last hour, the outer defenses have fallen. The 1st and 2nd Helion Militia are down to less than a quarter strength and falling back. That means we've finally lost control of the city."

He turned and pointed to the mountain.

"I have returned three-quarters of our forces to the mountain to reinforce it in depth. All that remains out here is us and this fortress."

Now the marines fell silent, the whooping and excitement quickly reduced to a more somber mood.

"Every city on this world is under siege, but none has taken such a beating as us. You've all heard the news of the atomic strikes on some of the other cities. The rumors are true. The machines have started a new genocide, and the only reason we're alive is because they want this site under their control."

Jack looked down to the ground as Gun continued to speak. He'd heard everything Gun had said before over the last few days, but it was the mention of the Doomsday Weapon that stood out to him.

Why not destroy it? If they want to capture it, then they must have a use for it.

He looked back to Gun, but the seasoned commander was far too wrapped up in his own speech to even notice the one marine.

"We've done what we can, but as of yesterday, there were over forty thousand more enemy soldiers redeploying from the south. They will be in the city in days, perhaps hours."

He lifted his armored fist and pointed to the sky.

"Ark Belial is well named. A worthless demon we will destroy, just like we've done with everything else they've thrown at us. A strong fleet of warships protects the Ark, and the blockade remains. We must hold this ground until relieved."

He looked to the marines, and Jack could see the worry on his friend's face.

What is it?

"Today I am issuing one final order; this is my no step back order. Any man, woman, or child of fighting age that attempts to retreat over the bridges will be sent back. Spascia will stay under our control, or we will be buried inside it."

* * *

ANS Dreadnought, over Terra Nova

The observation bubble was aptly named, a large dome that extended out from the hull of the ship. This kind of location would normally be off-limits, but in a safe sector of space, the outer shielding had been fully retracted and the anti-aircraft guns withdrawn into their housings. It was big enough for an entire platoon of marines, and far larger than needed for this small group. Several seats were fitted around the sides, but it was the fact the dome provided unrestricted views in all but one direction that made the place so successful.

"Nice view isn't it?" Khan asked.

Spartan nearly coughed at the odd question. He looked to his friend and could see he was being made fun of.

"Very funny, Khan. Where did you learn that kind of

humor?"

He feigned insult.

"Not from you, clearly."

Spartan looked back and watched the shape of Terra Nova. It was a strange place to be, even stranger to be here as a civilian, yet on board a military vessel. He felt just as out of place as he always seemed to be in this part of space. A number of figures strolled past and headed toward the officers' mess, not far from one of the public bars and recreation areas on the ship. He spotted Teresa approaching and waved for her to join them. While they waited, he looked down at the planet.

He'd been on Terra Nova on several occasions, none of them ones that he was particularly fond of. Worse than that was that the citizens of Terra Nova always treated him with a degree of contempt. It was as though it was his fault the machines' lackeys, under the auspices of the Echidna Union, had led a coup and established a Biomech core deep in the government buildings. They in the end controlled the Uprising and were responsible for so many deaths. But as usual, it was those that had brought destruction to the world that received the bulk of the blame. He shook his head, and Teresa put her hand on his shoulder.

"I know," she said quietly, moving alongside him.

It hadn't just been Spartan on that world in the final epic battle. Teresa had been there, a prisoner of the war criminals and their Biomechanical warriors. That last hour of combat was perhaps the bloodiest single moment in humanity's history in space, yet it had marked the end of the Union, as well as the Confederacy.

"All of that fighting, and still they blame us."

She sighed, but found it hard to disagree with his sentiments.

"We built something better after all of that," she said, trying as much to persuade him as her herself. Spartan shook his head slowly in disagreement.

"I don't know. Yeah, it's true we stopped the slavery and the war, but the same idiots are still down there, and the Biomechs are up to their old tricks."

He nodded to the watery orb below the fleet.

"And they're making the same mistakes all over again. There's no continuity, no real leadership. Presidents last a few months to a few years, and policy changes even quicker."

"At least the General is keeping them in line, where he can," suggested Khan.

Spartan tried to smile, but it simply wasn't going to happen. So he turned his attention back to the planet and thought back to the times where he hadn't been involved in full-scale combat. That was when he recalled the massive statue he'd seen amongst the lavish surroundings. It was something to do with an ancient event back on Earth; something during one of the many wars fought over thousands of years. The sculpture had been incredibly detailed, but even though it wasn't that long ago, he realized he had no idea what it looked like anymore. He shook his head and laughed to himself.

"What is it?" Teresa asked.

Spartan shook his head slowly.

"It's okay. I was just thinking of something I saw down there."

Teresa and Khan waited alongside him, and both were equally uninspired by the blue orb of the Alliance's capital. There were a great many ships outside, with General Rivers' flagship being the largest of the military ships. Even so, there were even more civilian ships moving about as though there was nothing even remotely resembling a war on. As at Mars, it was the shape of the new flagship that garnered most attention, especially by the local civilian ships, each of which was carefully moved on to a safe distance.

"Reminds me of Operation Perdition," said Khan wistfully, "I think I'd rather go through that again than all this rubbish with them down there."

Spartan's bones almost groaned at the memory of that event. It was something he tried to avoid where possible, even if it had been one of the few great successes of the War. It had also been one where a vast number of soldiers, marines, and civilians had died. Not least the brutal combat that the Jötnar had participated in so successfully.

"They really have no idea, do they?" Spartan asked quietly.

"About what exactly?" asked a new voice.

Spartan turned about and looked at Major Terson, Teresa's second-in-command. Teresa spoke highly of the man, but as far as Spartan was concerned he was just another Alliance officer. He'd not seen the man in combat, and until that happened, he was just another face to him in a uniform.

"The President has ordered a security unit to the ship to assist in the removal of our…"

He looked a little uncomfortable.

"…alien contingents."

Spartan narrowed his eyes a little and looked at the man carefully.

"Has this guy even seen what's going on out here? We've just smashed the Biomech threat in our backyard, and we have an entire legion of Biomech warriors on our side. We should point them at a target, not try and imprison them."

Major Terson looked to Teresa, but she looked equally stern.

"I'm not in disagreement. General Rivers said he would find a way, but the order still stands, and we are in Terra Novan space. High Command has maximum pull here."

Spartan nodded in agreement.

"Yes, putting autonomous Biomechs ground troops on Terra Nova is not a good idea. Not by a…"

"I quite agree," said a man with a clipped, familiar accent.

All turned to look at a man dressed in PDS Alpha Armor. There was no mistaking him for one of the marines on board ANS Dreadnought, however. He wore a dark red cloak pinned to the shoulders of his armor, and his visor was flipped open to reveal a smiling face. At his flanks were two similarly dressed soldiers, but both of them had their visors locked down to hide their faces. Normally, the marines made use of a dark gray and black tiger stripe pattern for their armor. These two wore bare metal so that it looked almost silver and completely unblemished. Major Terson looked at the man, and Spartan quickly deduced he knew him. Even so, all the Alliance officers quickly saluted, all but Spartan and Khan.

"Major," said Major Terson.

The man nodded politely but concentrated his attention on Spartan.

"This is Major Grant, commander of the Presidential Detail of the Terra Nova Colonial Guard."

Spartan looked squarely at the man's eyes.

"Yes, I recall the Guard. Weren't they disbanded after the Uprising? Rumors of collusion with the enemy?"

The man didn't even flinch at the insult.

"We're not the old Royal Guard. Their days are long gone, and that suits me just fine. The Colonial Guard is the honorary title for the 31st Regiment, raised just last year on Terra Nova. The Regiment is the largest in the Alliance, over eight thousand men and women."

Spartan shook his head in irritation.

"Yes, and every single one of them guaranteed to never have to leave their homeworld. I can't imagine they get to see much action."

The man moved his eyes a little toward to Teresa.

"Colonel Morato, your reputation precedes you. I have been…"

He stopped and lifted his hand while listening to something in his helmet. Halfway through he looked up to Spartan and scowled. His face tightened until finally he stopped and looked back at them.

"It would appear plans have changed. I have new orders from General Rivers to assist in your transit to the Prometheus Rift and on to your destination in T'Karan."

"I see," replied Spartan, "and how do you intend on doing that?"

The man took a step closer to Spartan. At the same time, Khan leaned forward ever so slightly, not enough to threaten but more than enough to remind the man that he was there. He'd been silent until now, but his patience was wearing thin. The Major stopped and looked to Khan with barely concealed contempt. Khan simply smiled back, but Spartan and Teresa could see the anger that remained.

"I see you retain the friendly attitude that I so admire about our capital."

The Major turned about quickly, unimpressed at what Spartan was saying.

"They might have a measure of equality now, but they will never be like us. They are Biomechs and always will be."

His lip almost trembled as he looked at Khan, the epitome of everything he'd obviously learned to hate over the years. Spartan's smile faded as the words from the officer bit deep into his psyche.

"And you haven't changed either. A world filled with collaborators and cowards. Let me guess, you lost people in the final battle for this planet? Were they on the side of the people, or the Union?"

The Major's cheeks moved just a little.

"Your invasion, Spartan, it cost tens of thousands of lives. When your ships arrived, the machines turned on the population and butchered indiscriminately. Warriors like him wiped out entire families in the time it took for these monsters to plant another flag on our capital. We already had things under control."

Spartan spat on the floor, narrowly missing the man's foot.

"You couldn't even control your bowels. Collaboration cost millions of lives. Remember that the next time you try and blame the very soldiers that came here and saved your worthless lives."

The man became even tenser, but something inside

seemed to click, almost as though a switch had been pushed. He breathed slowly, adjusted his uniform, and then stepped away from the situation.

"Your journey to the Admiral Jarvis Naval Station should take just a few days via the Interstellar Network. I will leave you to prepare."

Spartan made to follow him, but Teresa put her arm in his path.

"No, not this time," she said quietly.

Teresa then looked to Major Grant.

"We will be on our way. Just make sure you get the defenses down there ready."

He was already heading for the door when she fired a parting shot.

"You'll have to take care of any issues while we're gone, but don't worry, we'll be back to help clean up when this little war is over."

He looked to the wide grin on Khan's oversized head and then stormed off muttering.

"Looks like we've made some new friends," said Khan.

"That wasn't wise," Major Terson suggested.

Teresa shrugged.

"Perhaps, but he's not the one heading to the frontlines with a war fleet, is he?"

Spartan noticed her expression change when her secpad buzzed. She lifted it up and read the message before looking up to the small group.

"What's happened?" Major Terson asked.

"It's the General. He's issued orders for an emergency advance to the AJ Naval Station. Helios is under full-scale invasion, and Operation Citadel is being moved up."

"Yes!" Khan growled, much to the annoyance of Major Terson.

Only Spartan seemed unfazed by the news.

"Spartan, you know what this means?"

His jaw twitched a fraction.

"This was going to happen anyway, but we've got more important things to worry about for now."

"What could be more important than this?"

Spartan looked into the man's eyes, trying ever so carefully to ascertain exactly what kind of a man he was dealing with. Realizing he had neither the time nor the inclination to waste any more time, he looked back to Khan and Teresa.

"We need to sort out a backup plan, and fast."

Major Terson looked confused.

"I don't understand. Operation Citadel is designed to put a major surge of Alliance personnel into the Helios System. We will flood Helios Prime and its moons in the first day, and then move out to retake all territory currently being contested."

Spartan reached out and Teresa looked down to her secpad. Spartan nodded, and she quickly handed it to him. With a few deft taps, he twisted the unit about so the Major could see it. His expression transformed in an instant.

"No, this cannot be true!"

Spartan raised an eyebrow.

"Really? The Biomechs aren't stupid. In our Uprising they just provided the tools for a war, to weaken our people ready to be taken control of by them, if and when they won."

Khan listened but hadn't been privy to the information on the device.

"What's happened?"

Teresa took it back and examined the screen.

"It's all over the public networks. Helion terrorists have attacked the planetary defense installations on Libuscha and Micaya."

"And?"

She shook her head bitterly.

"Libuscha is offline. A team breached the Helion security perimeter and vaporized the power station. It will be out of action for a month, maybe longer."

She moved her eyes to look at Spartan. He looked equally concerned.

"Micaya is much worse though, look."

Spartan ran the back of his hand along his chin as if in deep thought. The imagery showed ruins and columns of smoke rising high up into the sky.

"They hit Micaya with a civilian liner. It looks like the ship dropped out of orbit and went nuclear just as it impacted. The planetary system didn't even have fighter cover. That means the only functional weapon systems left are on Helios Prime and Spascia."

Spartan looked at each of them in turn.

"Operation Citadel is our only shot at protecting the worlds of Helios, and I promise you, it is going to fail."

Khan and Teresa said nothing, but Major Terson looked stunned.

"What? The combined ground and space forces will smash aside the Biomechs. How is that a failure?"

Spartan pointed out to space.

"Because while we're busy wasting time fighting, the real event will be taking at the Black Rift. As soon as they have control, or can destroy the remaining planetary systems, they can launch their final attack on the Black Rift. What will stop them then? We've got only a handful of T'Kari and Helion ships with the tech to shut down a Rift. Do you think the Biomechs will let them get a line of sight on the Rift?"

Again he turned his attention back to Teresa.

"We need to see Z'Kanthu. There has to be a way to end this, once and for all. We cannot let this cycle continue indefinitely. Even if we manage to stop them, they will be waiting, and I can promise you this; no matter who wins on Helios, the enemy will have agents and machines hidden somewhere. Long after we're dead, they will try this again and again till they win."

Khan punched his hands together in agreement.

"Spartan's right. We need a plan, a real plan, a war winning plan."

CHAPTER SIX

The modern Marine Corps experienced the same punishing siege warfare as its cotemporaries in the Uprising. This new professional military was very different to the divisions of warriors that fought on worlds such as Euryale, Proxima Prime, and Hyperion. The Vanguards were now a common sight on the battlefield, as were entire companies of Jötnar in their own armor variants. The newly created 24th Regiment, raised on Prometheus and recruited from the ranks of Jötnar throughout the Alliance, was something else entirely. This regiment was completely synthetic and armed with close fitting body armor based on the Alpha armour used by the Corps.

Great Battles of the Confederate Marine Corps

ANS New Carlos, upper atmosphere of Spascia

Commodore Hampel rose from his bunk and rubbed his eyes. The alert buzzed gently, yet even its reduced volume pounded through his skull with the impact of a hammer. He shook his head and reached for his secpad. A countdown flickered on its screen, and when he brushed it aside, it revealed a continuously updating schematic of the enemy dispositions over Spascia. It was then he noticed it wasn't his alarm that had woken him; it was an alert from the CIC. He tapped the video communicator on his desk.

"What is it?"

"Commodore, we're detecting changes in the enemy fleet," said Lieutenant Morgan, the ship's XO.

"Such as?"

He was already looking at the secpad and the arrangement of capital ships around the Ark. He needed no more information to understand that the fleet was relatively invulnerable while positioned in that way. There were no Alliance ships anywhere near the enemy fleet; all his own ships were either on the ground at safe locations, or still in the air around Spascia. It had been the only way to preserve his fleet, by bringing the ships down to the planet itself. Those unable to assist had been sent back toward Helios Prime to regroup with Admiral Lewis.

"They are moving Sawfish and Bioray warships into the upper atmosphere."

"Well, we've been waiting for them. I'm surprised it's taken so long. Have you contacted Admiral Lewis or High Command?"

"Yes, Sir, flash traffic has been sent to both."

He pulled on his tunic and threw back a single glass of cool water from the dispenser at the side of his desk. It tickled his throat as it ran down but did its job of quenching his thirst for now. Commodore Hampel pulled on his hat and marched straight out of his quarters and into the passageway. A pair of Marine guards saluted as he left him room, but he was in such a rush he only managed a barely discernible nod.

"Are they coming for us?"

"I don't think so. Their course will bring them in toward the Biomech positions to the east of the ruins. So far there's no obvious sign they are heading for our ships. With our dispersed positions, it would be easy."

He walked as quickly and calmly as he could, but the seriousness of the news sent adrenalin surging through his body. The fighting over the last weeks had been unlike anything he could have expected. Instead of acting as a fleet, the dozen remaining capital ships had operated as carriers and ground batteries, supplying firepower and air cover wherever they could. Though not ideal for the task, the Crusader and Liberty class of warships were capable of atmospheric flight, but the prolonged operations had consumed vast fuel and ammunition resources, as well as nullifying all their direct-energy weapons.

"Send the alert to the other ships; I need everything we have in the air and over the old city ASAP. This is it. This is the attack we've been waiting for. We cannot let Old

Spascia fall!"

He took another four steps before the ship began to shudder and groan. ANS New Carlos had stayed airborne since entering the atmosphere weeks ago, yet even at a height of twenty kilometers from the surface, the effect of gravity and the density of the atmosphere made the ship slow, plodding, and difficult to maneuver. Even so, as the ship fired its engines, he was pleased to detect the motion of the vessel as it moved in the direction of the city.

How far away are we?

He looked at the secpad and made a mental note of the location of his own ship as well as a Crusader and three more Liberty destroyers nearby.

Yes, you might land more troops, but you're gonna pay one hell of a price to land them at this city.

He rounded the corner and toward a pair of double doors leading into the small CIC. He walked through and directly into the path of his XO.

"Get me through to General Gun. He needs to know what's happening."

Lieutenant Morgan pointed at the nearby video projection running on one part of the large holographic display unit. He couldn't argue about the sophistication of the technology, or even the degree to which it allowed a smaller crew to operate such an advanced vessel. Still, he'd seen what happened to ships under stress, and he was beginning to wonder how they would manage if this single unit was damaged or failed in combat.

I guess we'll find out, won't we?

"Commodore, we're ready," said a familiar voice.

He moved closer and spotted the face of the General and his entourage of grubby-looking warriors. Jötnar in the overly bulky JAS armor waited nearby with a mixture of heavy and close combat weapons. As the image stabilized, he could see the damage to their armor, and it wasn't just the odd individual; this damage showed on every single one of them. They were near a bunker complex with multiple towers and a deep trench off to the General's flank. Even though it was incredibly dark, the flares flashed every few seconds around him and bathed the position in vivid white and yellow light.

"What's your status, General?"

Gun nodded and looked to his left where an officer was asking him something. It didn't take long, and then he was back. Another streak of light filled the background, and a pair of bodies was thrown high in the air from a blast. More and more of them came down, and even Gun seemed to shake from the impact.

"As ready as we'll ever be."

"General, you've got the reports on their movements?"

The Jötnar nodded.

"Yeah, they're sending in the next wave. This is the biggest one yet. If you ask me, this is it. They mean business."

"That is my understanding," explained Commodore Hampel.

He touched his moustache as he watched the scene.

"I am bringing everything I have left to bear on this one. You won't be on your own in this battle. Everything the Alliance has that can fly is making for Spascia City, as we speak. When those Biomech bastards arrive, they'll pay one hell of a price."

A series of explosions rippled about Gun, and he looked to the side and lifted his arm to point. As he moved the pintle gun mount on his shoulder, it tracked and then flashed and rumbled a dozen times. Gun glanced back to the screen.

"That time is now. Let them come, I say. It's time we decided this, once and for all!"

* * *

Three Sisters Fortress, Old Spascia City

Two nights had now passed at the Three Sisters, and still the Biomechs had refused to attack in force. They'd had just as much time as the defenders to prepare, and their underground trench works were no less sophisticated than those of the marines. With each passing day, both sides became further and further entrenched, making all out assault even more fruitless than the day before.

The fighting hadn't ended though, not by a long shot. It wasn't that they hadn't stopped the artillery strikes and sniping, but the grand assault everybody had expected simply hadn't arrived. Small groups tried to penetrate defenses at key points, but on every occasion they were beaten back. After days of this kind of fighting, a good many marines had decided the Biomechs were not interested in taking the mountain by force. Instead, they intended on waiting them out and simply wearing them down through fatigue, and lack of food and ammunition. It was a cool and calculated plan, but as each day ended, it became clearer the defenders were living on borrowed time.

A triple volley of heavy guns sent high-explosive rounds directly into the heart of the defenses. Two exploded out in the abandoned streets, and a third hit one of the abandoned structures half a kilometer west of the Three Sisters. The round shattered and sent burning fragments in all directions. The structure was solid and easily brushed off the weapon. Flashes of light from the explosion lit up the entire city block, and anything not already burned to a crisp quickly caught fire.

"Incoming!" called out an unseen marine.

Another four rounds came in and hit around the city, yet even this level of attack didn't wake up the marines still sleeping. After weeks of combat, they had become adept at resting when they could, even during sporadic attacks like this. It was the third fireteam's turn to take watched, and Jack and Jana had joined a pair of rookies to get some rest. All four lay curled up in their armor, each with their weapons close to hand. A single SAAR robot sat patiently like a large dog as it watched over them. The single weapon system on its back tracked from left to right, continually checking for signs of danger.

The bunker had been untested in battle so far, but the thick roof and stowage compartments at least allowed the marines some degree of security. The vision slits provide a good view of the eastern approach, sited to allow those inside to shoot over the lower outer walls. The position of the bunker was part of the line joining two of the towers while the third lay directly behind them toward the river. Fog lights were carefully position to light the killing ground cleared around the fortification. The lights on inside the defenses were low-level red lights that could only be seen from inside, and only barely.

"Helion patrol coming in, Sir," said one of the corporals.

"Open the gate," said Lieutenant Elvidge, that night's officer of the watch.

A pair of marines pulled on the metal pulleys to lift the thick metal gateway. It was a low-tech solution, but one not easily bypassed with advanced technology and robotics. As it reached the halfway mark, the metal screeched. There were some dents and imperfections in the steel runners, and it made a sound like nails being dragged across metal.

"What the hell?" Jack said.

He jumped up and promptly rolled from where he'd been lying down and dropped to the dusty ground. His legs were frozen stiff, and no matter how quickly he tried to move, he still hit the ground with a thud. As he lay there groaning, Jana opened her eyes but remained on her side. She looked down at him and smiled, but he couldn't make out her face in the pitch-dark condition. Only when a flare burst above the base, did he see her looking down at him.

"What's it like out there, Sergeant?" Lieutenant Elvidge asked.

His voice was slightly interrupted by the sound of the chains, but Jack could still make it out. He sat up still on the floor and shook his head. This low down he couldn't see what was happening, so with a groan he stood up, stretched his tired legs, and hobbled to the main viewing slit overlooking the doorway. There he spotted the Lieutenant and a pair of Khreenk warriors. A small NHA patrol, each dressed in the dull uniforms that were now more like brown than the original flamboyant yellow. With only red lighting, their clothing looked closer to the grays and blacks of the marines. They carried thermal rifles on their shoulders and wore lightweight packs filled with provisions and spare ammunition. Their heads had been covered with colorful tall helms, but now were replaced by a simple combat helmet taken from the marine stores.

"Sir, they're coming this way, and fast," said Sergeant

Stone.

It was only a few words, but they were enough to make Jack's pulse quicken. He looked back to Jana and the two rookies. All three were watching him expectantly. Light from the pylon-mounted searchlights scanned back and forth and cast long, deep shadows in the ground. Corporal Frewyn ran into the bunker before any of them could speak.

"We're up!" he said excitedly.

The two rookies were on their feet in a flash and fumbling about for their magazines. Corporal Frewyn, ever the stout character, waited calmly as the others got themselves ready.

"How's the arm?" Jack asked.

The Corporal grimaced, tilting his head in the direction of the wounded limb.

"Not great. Still, after you've been on this rock for a while, you stop noticing things like that."

The crump of distant artillery brought all of them back to the harsh realities of the grinding attritional campaign that Spascia had now become.

"We've got bigger things to worry about, right now."

Sergeant Stone moved toward the rear of the bunker, with Lieutenant Elvidge close behind. Two-dozen marines assembled in a loose line at the rear of the bunkers and stood smartly to attention. The officer's visor was up, and the flashes of artillery and flares lit up his face, casting hard-edged shadows across his cheeks.

"Marines, this is it. We've just had word from Commodore Hampel. All units have been activated. You can…"

He was cut off by a great shrieking sound. He looked back, and the bright reds and yellows of hundreds of rounds of artillery and rockets arced overhead, reached their apex and then came down like rain all along the defensive zone. Not one block was spared as the mixture of ordnance came down one after the other. A screaming sound came from further away, and Sergeant Stone pushed the officer to one side as a multiple warhead split and rained fire down on the bunkers. A few unfortunate marines and Helions were caught out in the open and tore apart in the blink of an eye. Explosions ripped through the complex, but the damage was minor. Lieutenant Elvidge picked himself up and nodded toward Sergeant Stone.

"They'll have to use something a little more impressive than that kind of artillery if they want to breach the Sisters."

"Sir!" Corporal Frewyn said.

He lifted his arm and pointed at a dozen blue trails high up into the sky. Each could be followed back to positions deep inside the enemy lines through the city.

"Why aren't the counter-battery guns firing?" Jack asked.

Sergeant Stone cleared his throat.

"Because it's time, son, because it's time."

He pointed in the direction of the mountain, not that it could be seen from their current position. Additional lines of bunkers and gun positions blocked their view, and even if they could see out and beyond the eastern walls, all they would see were the smoke covered bridges and the mountain beyond.

"They are saving themselves for the assault."

Then he looked back to Jack.

"Trust me, when this one starts, you'll thank them. They can put down a lot of fire in a short amount of time."

A high-pitched whistle came from the left, quickly followed by a formation of seven Animosh riders.

"What are they doing here?" Jana asked.

The seven small craft vanished off into the blackness of the night, with nothing but the odd explosion highlighting them against the sky.

"Animosh, I thought we'd heard the last of them," muttered Jack.

The little craft were more like motorcycles than anything else they'd seen. Jack's first experience of them was back on Helios Prime during the first stages of the revolution. The Animosh were the Helion paramilitaries and had used the flying bikes to hunt down rebels. With small, flat-ducted fan engines at each end they were noisy but incredibly maneuverable.

"This time they're fighting with us," said Lieutenant

Elvidge.

Sergeant Stone looked to the officer and shook his head.

"Until how long, Sir?"

"Until we win, or they die. Either way, we've got bigger problems today."

A triple volley of flares soared up into the sky, and at the same time the klaxon changed to the emergency alert. This one was different, and the change in the postures of the marines was instant.

"The breach alert!"

The sound could mean only one thing; the defenses had been penetrated already. Lieutenant Elvidge put one foot onto an ammunition locker and pointed his sidearm to the bunkers and trenches. Jack looked at him and noted with a modicum of amusement how the man had changed. His first impression had been of an insignificant officer, one with little experience and a lot to prove. Now the man looked as hardened and experienced as any he'd seen. His armor was dented, and there was a bullet impact mark on his shoulder that should have taken his arm off.

He's changed.

"Marines, to your posts. Remember Gun, not one step back!"

Jack and Jana moved to their post, and Corporal Frewyn joined them. Another four marines moved in alongside them and lifted their L52 carbines onto the cool stonework. Jack and Jana lifted their own weapons. Frewyn did the same.

Here we go again.

Jack looked to his left and right, checking the others were there. Seven of them in this one pillbox arrangement made a tight fit, but at least the walls were thick and angled correctly this time. The slots for the guns were small, but with the visor overlay he could also see the shapes of machines in the distance.

"How many are there, Corporal?"

The veteran marine tilted his head just a fraction to look to Jack.

"Who knows, Jack? Probably all of them."

He then looked to Jana.

"Something tells me we're gonna need your services."

Jana pointed to the stack of boxes to her side.

"Don't worry; we're all stocked up here."

"It doesn't matter. The machines don't take prisoners. Not anymore."

He wasn't speaking to anybody in particular; it was just a general gripe. The words had little effect on veterans like Jana and Corporal Frewyn, but to the four other inexperienced marines it was electric. The fear was palpable, made significantly worse as their imaginations took over. Corporal Frewyn moved from his position and struck Jack on the shoulder.

"Private, control yourself."

Jack looked into the visor, and even through the darkened material the Corporal could see his eyes flickering.

"What the hell are you doing?"

He struck Jack's emergency seal, and the visor slid up to reveal the young man's face. A thin sheen of perspiration ran over his forehead, but it was the eyes that got his attention. The low-level internal lighting inside the helmet showed him almost enough, but the occasional flare burst lit them up so that he could see the patterns in his retina.

"You're high, you idiot!"

More shells dropped down over the defenses, and then a number of whistles blasted. They were unusual, unlike anything used by the marines. Right after the sound came dozens of Helion militia, a mixture of male and female volunteers with their improvised weapons. Some moved quickly, eager for the fight, but the majority had to be encouraged to move on by uniformed NHA soldiers.

"Corporal!" called out one of the new recruits.

Both Jack and Corporal Frewyn turned their attention back to the vision slit and the lower defenses in front of them. The gate was down and locked into position. Dozens more marines protected the lower walls and trenches running on either side of the entrance. Jana spotted the first of the Eques, those mighty six-legged war machines they had now fought so many times. One clambered out from a smashed wall and was immediately hit by three of the L56 machine guns. The continuous streams of gunfire tore chunks of armor off before it dropped to one of the lead knees.

"Yes!" howled a marine from the front trench.

The machine tipped over and almost crashed onto its stomach before one of the middle legs interceded and righted the thing. As it leveled, a flank-mounted sponson swiveled and opened fire. The rounds chewed fist-sized holes out of the masonry defenses, but they held up to the attack. Everything darkened to the west, with just the occasional artillery fire flickering and putting the ruined city into silhouette.

It's coming, Jack thought.

He watched patiently, but deep down he knew the attack had not yet begun. A single Eques walker was nothing compared to the horrors they'd faced over weeks of siege warfare. His helmet's scanning modes were having a hard time locking down on heat signatures, due to the vast amount of ordnances moving about and the wrecked buildings blotting out the distant view. More flares arced up and flashed, lighting up their position and the few hundred meters of cleared ground around their position.

"Gods!"

The very ground ripped and shuddered. Dozens of shapes, each the size of a Bulldog vehicle, pushed up like spear tips. What was beneath was anybody's guess, but from the shaking of the ground, there was most definitely something down there.

"I thought you said they couldn't mine!"

Corporal Frewyn watched the shapes slow down and then come to a stop. He looked confused and turned back to Jack.

"I don't know. Intel said the rock this close to the chasm was too thick."

Jack pointed at the shapes.

"Maybe that's why they're coming out just in front of us, then."

Gunfire glanced off their thick armored flanks, and still they push on upwards. Then the first one stopped, and a pulsing light ran about its structure. Sergeant Stone appeared as if from nowhere and roared.

"Get down!"

Jack didn't hesitate and reached out, grabbed Jana, and pulled her down. A bright white pulse blasted out in all directions as the nearest of the objects detonated. More and more followed, each detonating just below the surface. Clouds of dust bellowed out from the craters, and Jack was forced to switch to his mixed thermal and infrared targeting mode. He almost stumbled back at the sight.

"Jana, look at this."

She moved to join him, but he was far too engrossed in the scene before him. Hundreds of shapes erupted from the ground in front of the defenses. They were like thickly spreading lava. Corporal Frewyn looked on in surprise, and it took Sergeant Stone's presence to force them back into action. He appeared behind them and barked orders at two marines.

"Get your squad to the left wall. You, I need ammunition and more flares at the CP. Now move it!"

Both men rushed off to complete their chores, and he turned to put his attention on the secondary run of defenses. A shape appeared at the top of a low wall off into the distance. He flipped out his sidearm and put two rounds into its head at a distance of at least thirty meters. As the thing slid back amongst its comrades in the dark abyss outside the defenses, he looked at the marines.

"I've seen all of this before. It's the same bastardized tech we saw in the Uprising."

With one arm extended, he point to the distant creatures.

"A generation ago we mistakenly called those things Biomechs."

He opened his visor and spat on the floor. The bitterness and hatred was starker than even Jack would have thought. A flash from the flares lit up the saliva to give it an almost silvery look to it.

"Those things aren't Biomechs, no more than General Gun is a Biomech. Those things, well, they are the lowest form of foot soldier; a thing created for combat no matter the cost. Each is made from the butchered remains of prisoners. I can promise you now that some of those are Helion and human prisoners from Eos."

Jana looked to Jack with surprise.

"I don't understand. We've never..."

Sergeant Stone lifted his left hand just a little and pointed to the wall.

"I can tell you from experience they can tear apart ten men. From their harvested organs, bones, and tissue they are able to produce warriors, each fused with other hardware and wiped minds. It gives them expendable warriors that will fight until every last one is dead. And they can do all of this in a matter of months, perhaps even weeks."

Three of the new recruits began shooting as targets appeared from the dust and mist. They fired long bursts, and Corporal Frewyn turned away from the Sergeant and snapped at them for their lack of discipline.

"Short bursts, and pick your targets."

The sound was already deafening but right behind them, far up into the mountains, came the heavy artillery. It started with just a few dozen thumps, followed by the entire mountain lighting up. Hundreds of high explosive, thermite, and armor piercing rounds surged down from the position. The accuracy and rate of fire was astounding, yet the effect on the defenders was electric. Each time a shell smashed down into the ruined city, a yell would erupt from them. Khreenk, marine, and Helion alike shouted out after each blast.

"This is incredible," said one of the marines at the vision slit.

Jack shook his head as he watched the bloodbath.

"It won't last. They are expecting this. You just watch…"

On cue, the hidden weapons of the Biomechs began their own counter-battery fire. It wasn't as impressive as the bombardment coming from the mountain, but it wasn't far off. Worse were the sight of more than forty Biomech fighters, and even a handful of Bioray transports moving over the city to provide aerial fire support. The guns reduced in number until only sporadic shells came down to the east. The marine looked to Jack with an expression of horror about him.

"That's it?"

Jack nodded and tried to smile.

"For now."

Almost as though it was a premade scenario, a pair of the creatures leapt over the outer wall. They must have used the bodies of the myriad of fallen comrades to reach the position and landed directly in front of the marines. Corporal Frewyn lifted his carbine to his shoulder and pushed its muzzle into the firing slit. Two short bursts were all that it took to cut down the things.

"Now watch that wall. If anything else comes over the top, you'll know what to do. Right?"

All of them nodded and turned their attention to the fearsome horde moving closer and closer. More of the things dropped over the wall, but the weight of defensive fire easily cut them down. Corporal Frewyn looked back to Sergeant Stone and shook his head bitterly.

"Those poor bastards."

He then lifted his carbine and selected the high-power mode.

"It's our job not to just win this battle; now we have to put all of them out of their misery. We kill them all, every damned last one of them."

Jana opened her visor, retched, and then vomited. Stone ignored her and nodded at the vision slits.

"Put some fire down!"

The view from the slits gave then a look out over the outer lower walls and to the ruined city. Dark shapes of metal machines filled the skyline, and thick black smoke mixed with the night to reduce the visibility to only a few hundred meters. Out of that darkness came ten, then hundreds, and finally thousands of the enemy. Jack took aim and opened fire. The targeting mode on his visor tagged the first thirty of the enemy, and then he lost count.

Keep shooting.

One magazine went and then another. Then he realized he'd used five. A quick look to his side showed the others were still blazing away. Their own gunfire seemed insignificant next to the entrenched heavier weapons. Even so, the swarms of foot soldiers continued to try and breach the outer walls.

How many are there?

He activated the overhead view that took in data from

the scouts as well as the aerial drones. It showed a massive ocean of red completely engulfing the last remaining outpost this side of the chasm. Jack almost choked as he looked at their situation.

"Corporal, have you seen this?"

"Not now!" he snapped back.

The ground rumbled and shook, and then three Eques walkers appeared outside the walls. All of the defenders continued to shoot at any available target, and one Eques was brought down. The second soon followed, but not before collapsing down onto the wall. The mass of the thing, combined with the barrage of mortars, rockets, and gunfire tore open a section ten meters wide. Scores of creatures poured through, along with almost as many of the terrifying Decurion war machines.

"Aalkab!" shouted the NHA officer.

He ran out from where he'd been waiting just to the side of the bunkers, directly toward the breach. More and more of the machines moved in, and explosions ripped along the wall. The marines and robotic defenses tore them apart, but still they came. Two managed to reach a SAAR robot and tore it apart before a pair of Khreenk warriors moved into the open and blasted them apart. They too were then killed by overwhelming numbers of the terrifying Biomech creatures.

"We can't hold them," Jack said quietly.

A marine runner dropped a metallic box next to him

and tapped him twice on the shoulder. He looked down and saw the twelve magazines fitted into the box.

More ammo, great!

With a quick movement, he grabbed at the box, pulled out the nearest magazine, and slid it into the L52 with a clunking sound. He then took aim through the slot and found an unlimited number of targets. It was like some hellish breach that limitless monsters streamed through. Jack pulled the trigger and emptied the magazine in one long, noisy burst. He could see the Eques walker as it climbed over its fallen comrade. Around its legs lay scores of dead creatures, crunching and tearing under the weight of the machine's metallic limbs.

"Look!" said Jana in terror.

Jack moved a little to his left and continued to fire. A group of seven Helion civilians were out in the open and running toward the Eques machine. Their long, thick coats broke up their outlines, but their Marine Corps helmets marked them out as soldiers, of a kind at least. They carried no firearms. In their hands they carried their spears, each fitted out with a powerful shaped charge. They moved with speed but little skill, as they clambered over the bodies to reach the enemy.

"Give them covering fire," Corporal Frewyn shouted.

Jack, Jana, and the rookies took aim at the eastern wall. There were hundreds of targets, but it was the small screen of Thegns and the biological monstrosities moving on all four legs that were the current problem. Jack emptied round after round into the Thegns that had now moved in behind the wall of dead from both sides. A flicker of white light marked return fire, but Jack ignored it and kept on shooting.

They can't get us inside here.

He knew it wasn't true, but by trying to convince himself, he hoped it might bolster his already failing confidence. The enemy was not holding back and surged ahead. They hacked with their blades and shot at any one they could find in the killing ground between the breached outer wall and the next line of defense. Three Helions were cut down in the opening volley in the first few seconds. The remaining four managed to reach the metal monster and stabbed at it with their long spears. As each one connected, the tip exploded in a blinding white light. Two of the Helions were vaporized in the blasts, but the others survived long enough for the ruined machine to fall down onto them.

"Poor fools," Jack muttered under his breath.

He could see another group of the Helion volunteers charging out and stabbing their weapons into Decurion machines and even a team of Thegns. Each time the result was the same, as bright blasts would destroy the enemy and also sometimes the user. The outer wall was untenable now and dozens of marines, Helions, and Khreenk abandoned their positions and ran back under the cover of bunkers, robots, and turret fire.

"Incoming!" Corporal Frewyn cried.

A flaming object streaked down from the sky and crashed into a pillbox just behind their position. The structure was torn apart, and a dozen Decurion assault machines leapt from the vehicle. The Corporal turned about and faced them, his carbine held low to his hip. He managed to squeeze off just three rounds when the first one reached him. It lifted two arms to stab at him, and then Jack was there. He put a single high-power round into its center mass and continued to empty a magazine on the normal setting. The machine staggered back and dropped to the ground.

"Thanks, Private. Your left!"

Two more of the machines were heading for the side of the bunker and managed to catch one of the marines. In one swift stroke, the young man was decapitated, and the second man took a swipe that left a gash from his stomach to his collar. Jana screamed as she fired her own weapon at the machines and then turned back to help the badly wounded man.

"What do we do, Corporal?" Jack asked.

He slid in yet another magazine while watching the shapes moving all along the eastern wall. It was now breached in a dozen places, yet less than half of the enemy troops were able to make it through. He took aim and fired again, and again.

"We keep fighting!" said the Corporal through clenched teeth.

CHAPTER SEVEN

The Zealots of the Uprising were an odd mixture of religious organizations and individuals. One thing they all had in common was a religious zeal, built and encouraged by the influence of the Biomechs. Even after the Fall of Terra Nova, it was never entirely clear how the machines had been able to influence so many different peoples. In time, the last dark days of the ancient Great War would give up pieces of information, one of which was the pact, signed in blood between the vanquished leaders of Carthago and the mysterious group now known simply as the Sons of the League.

Origins of Echidna and the Zealots

ANS Titania, near Helios Prime

The ship had been dead in space for an hour now, and still the fighting raged on inside. This was no conventional boarding action though, as there were no valuable systems still functioning inside the warship. The battle was over the very bodies of the crew, and they were making the enemy pay for every soul they took.

The port gunnery deck was a mass of twisted metal, yet the crew of six had managed to construct a primitive barrier in just minutes. The lack of gravity meant they had been forced to jam equipment and containers amongst the wreckage to deny access through the three breaches into the rest of the ship. Just as before, the machines attacked, but this time the Decurions took their time. Three of them approached and began carefully pulling and cutting at the barriers.

"What now?" asked ensign Harris.

The young officer almost choked as he asked the question. Lieutenants Matius and Ingo Morato looked at each other and then to the young man. Ingo spoke first.

"Use any weapon you can. We'll get to the weapons locker."

He turned and pushed away back into the darker section of the deck. Two of the lockers had already been raided but right at the back where a gun-loading mount had been shattered, lay another. Ingo pulled on a grab handle and drifted silently through the ship to the unit. He crashed into the metal frame without a sound and yanked on the handle. It pulled open to reveal two magazines and a single thermal pistol.

"That's it?" Matius asked, landing alongside him.

Ingo pulled out the pistol, checked its slide operation, and pushed in the thermal clip. He tucked the second into his utility belt and then looked back. Both of them were dressed in their Navy Personal Defense Suit, a much lighter variant of the gear used by the Marines Corps and now used by a small number of frontline crew. It was designed to function as a basic protective layer against fire, flash burns, and the vacuum of space for short amounts of time. Unfortunately for the crew, it was completely unsuited to the rigors of combat with Decurions, as was made evident by the countless mutilated corpses floating about the ship.

"Lieutenant!" screamed one the crew defending the barricade.

Ingo was already heading back when he saw the machine punch through the metal and stab one of its arms into the ensign's torso. Metal extended out of his back, and then with a vicious yank, the thing pulled his still living form through the broken metal barricade. Another machine approached and grabbed the body. There was no attack or mutilation; it simply turned and moved away as if taking some wondrous prize from the ship.

"Lieutenant!" cried out the man once more.

Ingo felt his throat go dry, but he knew what he had to do. Locking his left arm onto the nearest grab handle, he lifted the weapon and took aim. It was a short-ranged pistol, but the howling man was not far away. Lights flickered along the grip, and he squeezed the trigger. A blast of super-heated metal rushed out and struck the man in the arm before embedding in the metal limb of the Decurion. The crewman barely noticed the impact, and Ingo fired three more times before hitting his comrade in the back of the head. Heated blood, brain, and tissue splattered against the bulkhead. Then the machine was gone, still pulling the shaking body with it.

"Animal!" shouted Ingo, even though the sound went no further than his helmet.

Another Decurion appeared and a pair of Thegns. Their special hide was either resistant to a vacuum, or it was resilient enough to allow the warriors to fight for a time in the shattered remnants of the vessel. One lifted its arms, and they flashed white. Two crewmen were killed by the burst. The next Thegn took aim and Ingo again lifted his pistol. He pulled the trigger until the magazine was dry and one of the Thegns spun about dead. The remaining warrior looked at him and then threw himself at the remains of the barricade.

Matius grabbed Ingo and pulled on his shoulder.

"Brother, we have to go. One pistol won't stop them!"

* * *

ANS Conqueror, near Helios Prime

Admiral Lewis watched the video feed being transmitted

from the robotic squadron. The mood in the CIC was as silent and somber, as it had been since the failure of the mission. The four X57 drones were spaced apart in a wide formation and still accelerating toward the scene of the vicious battle. Their optical scanners were able to provide a grainy, yet surprisingly detailed view of the remains of the Knossos Orbital Platform as well as the shattered hulk of ANS Titania. Dozens of Biomech ships waited like predators around a carcass. The view sickened him to his stomach.

"How much longer?" he asked.

"Three minutes, Sir," answered his tactical officer.

It wasn't long, and the thought of the poor few still trapped inside the ship made him want to retch. He forced his body to cope and watched the video. Instead, it came to the XO to change the subject.

"Sir, we have forces ready to move in on Helios."

He looked to Captain Marcus and nodded.

"Very well. Give the order. We'll do what we can for the General. This assault of theirs is taking up most of their ships. The plan's simple, and that's why it should work."

"Yes, Sir," said Captain Marcus, "We'll move in low and fast and provide ground support for the General."

"Exactly. One sweep, though, that's all we can risk. We are outnumbered, and they know it. One run, and then we come down low and take as many off the surface as we can. We get only one shot at this."

His XO saluted and moved to the tactical display to help with last minute arrangements for the strike. Admiral Lewis looked back at the footage of the four drones. They seemed to be moving at a snail's pace, yet the numbers on the screen showed otherwise. Soon they would reach their target, and he could only hope it would help the crew of Titania.

Gods save them.

* * *

Lieutenants Matius and Ingo Morato pulled themselves past the three dead crewmen and toward the port gunnery escape hatch. It led directly out of where they'd been hiding and further into the shattered interior of the warship. The final remaining crewman pushed past them, ignoring their cries and vanished through the gap. Matius looked toward Ingo and spotted the shapes of the remaining Thegn and the other two Decurions. Both were now almost through the barricade of broken cases, ammunition boxes, and equipment.

"Follow him!" Ingo said nervously.

Matius went through first and activated his helmet-mounted lamp. The dull yellow device bathed the dust-filled interior with a wide beam. Though it enabled them to navigate through the ship, the light also exaggerated the shadows and silhouettes to create an even more terrifying environment than the blackness had been. Ingo moved to the hatch, turned back, and took aim. He pulled the trigger and nothing happened.

Last clip, you fool.

He reached down, found the final magazine, and snapped it into the pistol. He took aim once more, firing shot after shot. The first hit one of the Decurions, and four slammed into the Thegn, opening up a deep wound. With its outer skin breached, it seemed to lose consciousness as quickly as any other creature in an airless environment.

Just that machine to go.

The last rounds bounced off the hardened metal of the machine, with just two managing to burn through into its torso. Although it continued to move, something else caught its attention. In a few seconds it had scuttled away, using its eight limbs to pull and drag its weightless form into yet another section of the ship. The last bullet from the pistol embedded in the bulkhead just half a meter from the machine as it disappeared.

"Dammit!" he snapped.

He spun about, lost his grip, and found himself spinning out of control. Then he was grabbed and pulled him into the blackness. He kicked out and struck something hard.

"Hey, watch your feet, Ingo!"

He stopped spinning and found himself face-to-face with his brother. Both of their Navy PDS suits were covered in a mix of dust and splatters of blood. Ingo noticed a globule of something foul on the side of his brother's visor and could only hope it was from the Thegn.

"Which way now?" Matius said nervously.

They were inside one of the long passageways that served multiple sections of the ship. It was wider than many of the other sections and had clearly been a primary escape route during the battle. Bodies were drifting about, along with spheres of blood moving in a myriad of directions, many of which left their mark on walls. Even worse were the sights of crew members torn apart by the hundreds of kinetic shells that had ripped through the vessel.

"This way!" Ingo answered.

He pointed further inside the ship through the blackened corridor and toward a pile of wreckage. Part of it moved away, and from within it a single Decurion moved. One crewman opened a hatch and looked at Ingo before seeing the machine. He tried to get back though the hatch, but somebody else behind pushed him and into range of the machine. It reached out with a pair of razor sharp limbs and stabbed at the unfortunate soul. Two puncture wounds appeared, followed by a third, but by then the man was already dead. The hatch clamped partially shut, but the machine was on it in a flash. With a quick tug, it pulled open the piece of metal and gave chase.

Matius tried to move, but Ingo pulled him back.

"No, it's too late for them. It's too late for all of us."

They looked at each other for what seemed like an age. The ship was slowly being torn apart from within, and one crewmember after another ripped apart literally limb from limb; or even worse, they were being dragged off to the Biomech ships. Then Ingo's face lit up.

"The port launch bay. There's a pair of unarmed drones still there."

"So?"

Ingo smiled and struck his brother on the shoulder.

"We can program it to travel back to the fleet. There's more than enough stowage space to hide inside. We have enough air to make the journey."

"Are you sure?"

Ingo shrugged.

"Do you want to stay on this ship and wait for those things to find you?"

Matius should his head, and the expression on his face told his brother everything he needed to know. They'd been in scrapes all their lives, but never something as terrifying as this.

"Good, let's do this, then."

Matius nodded quickly, almost too quickly.

"I know my way around the ship, and I know a few shortcuts that might help. We want to keep away from the main access shafts as much as possible. Remember the boarding training we did that week after meeting Jack?"

The mention of his half-brother appeared to make

Ingo look even more miserable and depressed than he had been during the machines' attack.

"I remember the fight we got into. We would have made him pay if it hadn't been for that moron of a sergeant."

Matius frowned at the mention of the fight. It seemed like so long ago, but none of his memories of his brother were good. They'd been forced to live with him for some time as children, and although he was the youngest of the three, there had never been any kind of love between them. The Morato brothers were inseparable, and Jack Morato; well, he was seen as nothing more than an imposter. A child from that monster of a man called Spartan, a man unlike their father who they had never met.

"What was Mother thinking?" Ingo grumbled.

Matius smiled at his brother.

"Are you armed? Tell me you've got something."

Ingo pulled out a knife from the utility belt on his armor and held it up in front of him. He tried to strike his twin brother playfully with it, but it was neither the time nor place for such frivolity.

"What's wrong with you, Ingo? We have to get out of here!"

His brother looked back over his shoulder as if expecting another of those dreaded machines to appear. The dark interior was barely lit now, with nothing but sporadic light from the damaged red lighting still functioning. Their suits were still equipped with external lamps on the helmets, but even with them on full power, much of the ship was hard to make out. The loudspeakers still working attempted to operate, but only those in the parts of the ship that hadn't been opened to the coldness of space would have heard them. The sound crackled inside the brothers' helmets.

"This the XO. All sections are breached. The Captain is dead, along with most of our officers. Do not attempt to evacuate the ship. We are surrounded, and enemy ships are taking the lifeboats. Do not let them take you! We have a team heading for…"

The sound of the officer's voice vanished and was replaced by screams from inside the ruined warship. A dozen gunshots blasted out, and the clatter of metal on metal. Finally came the sound of heavy breathing, and the man was back.

"The CIC is losing air. Fight them, kill them, but do not surrender."

Once more the sound of gunshots overwhelmed the microphone, and then a high-pitched squeal of the compartment depressurizing. The Morato brothers could only hope the XO was wearing his PDS suit, or else he would be dead in seconds.

"Well, what now?" Matius asked.

Ingo had no idea and just looked down at his blade as if it might offer him some kind of valuable insight. As he might have expected, it did nothing other than reflect the light from his brother's lamp. Finally, he looked up, his eyes bloodshot and his expression stern.

"We do what the XO said. We find whoever is left alive and fight back."

"With what? How?"

Matius noticed the odd look on his brother's face. It was the expression that usually meant they were about to get into trouble.

"We get everybody still alive, all the weapons we can find, and then we get the hell out of here."

Matius still looked confused.

"Uh, you do realize the ship is gone?"

"Oh, yeah, but I know where we can find more."

Matius pulled back a few centimeters in surprise. For a second, he thought his brother was referring to a lifeboat or Captain's yacht. It was only the expression on his face that gave away his intention.

"You crazy fool, brother. You want to take one of theirs?"

Into lifted his blade between both of their helmets.

"They are working through this ship, a methodical harvesting of what we have left. I doubt they even have guards posted on the nearest ships. We'll board one and take it as a prize, just like we read about in the Academy."

Matius didn't seem convinced, but it was a plan, and anything was better than waiting to die.

"What about the drone? I thought you wanted to escape to the fleet?"

"You heard the XO. They are attacking craft leaving the area. If we do that, they'll probably destroy us as we leave. No, we'll leave this ship the way they are boarding us."

He thumbed toward where he thought the exterior of the ship was.

"We'll leave through the breaches using EVA belts and take the nearest ship. Are you with me, brother?"

For the first time in hours the two nodded in grim unison. Ingo looked to his left and then to his right, making sure there was no sign of the enemy. Then he activated a wide-band transmission on the open channel.

"This is 1st Lieutenant Ingo Morato, acting gunnery officer. Are there any surviving officers? I repeat, are there any officers still alive?"

They waited but not a sound came back.

"Maybe they're hiding?"

"Maybe, Matius."

Ingo looked at his brother and contemplated what might happen if they were the only ones left. He tried to remain calm, but it was almost impossible with the situation they were in.

"This is Seaman Apprentice Bevan; I have two more survivors with me."

Ingo closed his eyes with relief.

"Get any survivors you can find near the port side passageway, and grab what weapons you can find. Meet us at the port drone launch bay. You have four minutes.

Don't be late!"

* * *

Ingo and Matius arrived in the drone launch bay to find the craft smashed in a dozen places and wedged into one of the smaller hatches. A broken body lay between the metal, and blood covered both sections in dark gore. Holes in the outer skin had ripped open the vessel to the elements and anybody that might have survived the bombardment. Even so, there were another five crewmen and a single Marine corporal. All six wore their sealed suits, and two carried thermal shotguns. Only the marine carried an assault weapon in the form of an L52 carbine.

"Who's in charge here?" asked the marine.

Ingo looked about the group and quickly determined they were all non-commissioned ranks.

"Where's Bevan?"

The marine looked on impatiently as one of the crew lifted his hand.

"That's me, Sir."

The marine looked back at the two new arrivals and shook his head slowly.

"In this situation we need combat leadership. I suggest that..."

Ingo shook his head.

"No, not today marine."

Matius nodded toward his brother.

"We're the senior officers on this ship. We have a plan, and each of you will have a part to play," he answered while pointing to his brother and himself.

Three impacts shook the vessel, and a number of metal containers broke free and drifted about them. Then the sliding door to a smaller passageway pulled open, and a Thegn pulled itself inside. The marine opened fire first, and then the two Navy crewmembers blasted it with their shotguns. The head of the thing was torn apart, and the ruined body drifted down into the section.

"Hell, yeah!" laughed the marine.

His voice was nervous but tinged with a level of bravado none of the others felt.

"Any more coming?" Ingo asked.

The marine shook his head.

"No chance. Every section this side of the ship took the brunt of the bombardment."

"Starboard side?" Matius asked.

Two of the crew shook their heads in unison.

"No, the machines have been clearing through there. If anybody is left, then they're trapped. We were the last out of the medical bay when they attacked. They...they..."

Ingo reached out and touched the young crewman on the arm.

"I know."

He glanced at his brother who was already opening the

front of the pair of massive lockers at the side of the room. The door spun away, its hinges already shattered by one of the many assaults on the ship. Inside were dozens of EVA utility belts, many of which had sustained damage. Luckily, there was more than enough for the tiny group of survivors. He handed them out one at a time, and they pulled them on and tightened the straps.

"Anybody not used them before?"

All of the crew lifted their hands, with just the marine smirking.

Matius lifted his belt in front of him, and the ends began to lift up with the momentum.

"Okay, this is the standard issue S21 EVA Belt. You should have been trained on these back in the Academy."

He noticed Ingo handing out the last belt and pushed it toward him. The unit spun gently, and he reached out to catch the device. It was a thick item and constructed much like a utility belt but with small nozzles fitted into evenly spaced hexagonal shapes along the outside. He pulled it around his body and clipped it on.

"Make sure you activate suit pairing with your gear. If you don't, then you'll have to go on full manual control."

Matius laughed at the suggestion.

"And trust me, you do not want to use these on manual."

Even in such a terrible environment, he still couldn't shake the memory of the time the two of them had participated in a joint training mission. It had been with a unit of marines from one of the Kerberon ships and hadn't gone well. His suit had lost contact with the belt, and he ended up spinning out of the arena and out into the kill-zone. Two of the referees had to bring him back, to the amusement of the marines.

The suit instantly detected the nearby presence of the device and automatically paired, simply waiting for command authorization. He tapped the button, and the two synced together. The suit's internal computer ran through a series of diagnostics that took only a few seconds, and then checked the fuel counters for each of the small reservoirs on board.

"Mine's only half full," said one of the crewmen.

Ingo glanced at his brother and back to the man.

"That's okay. Half is more than enough to clear this distance. A full tank should be able to last up to an hour… or so."

All of them looked to the brothers, and they were ready. Each wore a fully functioning EVA belt synced to their gear, and between them they carried a modest array of weapons.

"Okay then, what's the plan, Sir?" asked the marine.

There was bitterness in his voice but also a mild sense of nerves. Ingo could hardly blame the man. Their situation was dire.

"What's your name, Corporal?" asked Ingo.

The man looked at him carefully, as though not even

entirely sure whether he intended on answering his question. He was a middle-aged man, probably one of those that had joined later in life with thoughts of missed opportunities. His jet-black eyebrows and short cut black hair were in stark contrast to taut, pale skin.

"Corporal Vlad Makarov, Sir."

"Okay, Makarov. It's pretty simple. Our ship is dead in space, and if we stay here, so are we."

One of the crewmen started to speak, but Ingo spoke over him.

"The engines are gone, so is power and our weapons. There is no chance of rescue and even less chance of this ship surviving the hour. The only reason we're still alive is because they're taking their time."

He pointed to the broken armored walls.

"Outside there are dozens of Biomech ships, but the nearest is a Bioray, one of the smaller assault transports. They must have used it to bring the Decurions here to our ship."

"Yeah, so?" said the marine, his tone even more irritable.

"Well, the two of us have been fully debriefed on the capabilities of these craft. We know their layout as well as their access points."

"How the hell would you know that?"

Ingo pulled himself toward the marine with surprising skill. Although he and his brother were both junior ranks, they had spent some time on the optional zero gravity training in readiness for advancement. Ingo, in particular, had his eye on an engineering post, and the course was a requirement. He twisted and then moved alongside the marine.

"Corporal Makarov. Are you going to fight me all the way on this one?"

The marine was as surprised at Ingo's speed and dexterity, as much as he was at his attitude. He said nothing so Ingo continued.

"We're going to leave the ship and board theirs."

The group was completely stunned, and not one of them knew what to say. Matius moved alongside his brother and adjusted one setting on his belt.

"There's an access hatch directly across from here. Two hundred meters through the debris field and we're inside. Thegn weapon racks are near all the main doors. We get inside, arm ourselves, and then fight back."

Again there was nothing but silence from them all. Matius instead looked to Ingo.

"Brother, are you ready for this?"

Ingo smiled, trying to reassure both himself and his brother.

"Of course. It's time. Let's go."

* * *

The small group of Alliance personnel reached the

halfway point in just over eleven minutes. They moved at a slow speed with the thrusters making micro-adjustments to keep them on track. The distance between the hulk of ANS Titania and the Biomech Bioray was short, yet most of it was taken up with pieces of debris, broken fighters, and scores of frozen bodies. Ingo and Matius led the group of eight away from the ship with nothing but a faint stream of gas marking their movement. They'd stopped and pulled themselves to the side of a large piece of shattered decking.

"Another three minutes and we'll be there," said Ingo as they waited.

"No more cover from here though. We could use all the fuel we have left and get there faster."

Corporal Makarov nodded quickly.

"I agree. We've got enough fuel to get back with some to spare, or we can use it to halve the time to the hatch. Two minutes and we're inside. You're sure they have the guns inside?"

Ingo nodded slowly.

"Yeah, we've seen the interior imagery of one we captured. The information is good."

"Captured?"

Matius pointed in the direction of the enemy vessel and then tapped his own visor.

"Maybe we can have this conversation another time? My air is running low, and we're out in the void here."

The Corporal grinned in a sinister, almost lopsided way. He then looked down to check his carbine was still attached to his thigh mount. Ingo checked the entire group was there and then nodded at the ship.

"Right. We enter the open door and go for the weapons. Once we're armed, follow us. We'll go for the command center and take control of the ship. Ready?"

Each of them nodded, but none seemed especially eager.

"Okay, follow me!"

Ingo pushed away from the wreckage and drifted to the side before activating his thrusters. The small puffs from the belt decreased as his course stabilized and then he was off at speed. Matius and the marine were close behind, and the other crew moved in a loose clump. They drifted toward the vessel with surprising speed until finally Ingo struck the hull of the craft. He hit it hard, much harder than intended and rolled off to the side.

"Hold on!" Matius called out.

His brother decelerated and struck just a meter from the hatch. With one hand grasping one of the many outer ribs, he reached out and grabbed Ingo's hand before he slipped away.

"Slow down next time, you fool!"

He tried to sound cheery, but it was hard to do so when moving in on the outer hatch of an enemy ship. The three with weapons checked them for the last time and then Ingo gave the nod. The marine pulled himself in first, and Ingo followed. It was black inside, perhaps even darker than the space outside. At least when they had been drifting the short distance from ANS Titania, they benefitted from the reflected light coming off the planet Helios Prime. There were no windows in the Biomech ship, so one by one they had to activate their lights.

"Get ready!" Ingo said.

The lights came on within a second of each other and bathed the interior with a dull yellow. Dust and filth gave their lamps a wide beam effect. It wasn't the light that shocked them, however, it was the damage. From the outside the ship looked fine, but the interior was little different to that of their ship.

"Looks like we did a bit of our own damage here," said Corporal Makarov.

A green light flickered, and two lifeless Thegn corpses drifted from view to reveal a Decurion. It was missing three of its limbs, yet moved as efficiently and as terrifying as when it had all eight.

"Shoot it!" cried one of the crew.

Corporal Makarov was on it and emptied a dozen rounds into the machine before its light cut out, and the body drifted out as lifeless as the Thegns.

"Look," said Matius.

He pointed to the left where the wide shaft led further inside the ship. A gentle light at the end altered as dark shapes moved about.

"There are more of them coming."

The two brothers looked about in a panic and then spotted the gun racks on the walls. Nearly half were empty, but there were still more than enough to go around.

"Grab a weapon and get ready."

All of them, even the marine grabbed one of the alien rifles and then pushed themselves into the dark corners of this part of the ship. There was ample cover to go around, and the outer hatch was ever present, a constant reminder of how they could escape, but only into space.

"Now!"

Ingo took aim and pulled the trigger. Flashes erupted from the muzzle, and he spun backwards to strike the wall, completely forgetting about the most basic of Newtonian physics. Even so, the rounds smashed into the first Decurion. More and more appeared until the passageway contained more than twenty, and still more arrived. He opened his mouth to shoot, but all of them were now shooting. The noiseless battle was surreal, and yet almost melancholy to watch. A machine would be wrecked, yet continued to move in the same direction while more pulled and pushed to get past.

"Keep shooting!" he cried.

It was much too late though. The first three machines tore into the crew, quickly dispatching the first two in seconds. Corporal Makarov howled over the intercom and then pushed his way forward at the machines. He held down the trigger on his gun in one hand while firing the carbine in the other.

"Look!" Matius said excitedly.

Ingo looked to his left and spotted the shape of two Alliance drones rushing past the ship. It was a surreal moment. He was on the alien ship, and a friendly robotic fighter was just outside. He was so distracted that he didn't even see the blade from the machine as it punched through his chest.

"Ingo!" screamed out his brother.

He wanted to help, but there was nothing he could do. Instead, he pushed away from the bulkhead and back to the hatch. One of the other crew tried to do the same, and they crashed into each other, blocking either from getting out in time. A Decurion moved in and stabbed at him, but Matius managed to beat aside the attack with the side of his arm, but it still managed to open up the armor with a gash that cut deeply into his flesh. He cried out in pain, and at the same time the suit pumped in a special sealant to plug the gap, as well as a burst of painkillers. That was when he saw the fighters.

"What the hell are they doing?" asked the crewman.

Matius heard the man but could only watch from his peripheral vision as a machine tore his right arm off. His attention was drawn inexplicably toward the first of the fighters as it vanished in an explosion. It looked like a small blast, but the flash continued to expand until it engulfed ANS Titania and then moved closer to him.

Nukes, he thought miserably. *We never had a chance.*

The speed of the explosion was impossibly fast, just as he'd learned about atomic weapons in space. There was no shock wave as such, just an incredible expenditure in heat and radiation before it dissipated. Matius didn't even have time to blink as he was struck. The Biomechs, the machines, and the ships vanished from his mind as the entire area superheated to incredible temperatures. The fight for the Bioray and ANS Titania was over.

CHAPTER EIGHT

Some Alliance politicians argued for a rapid expansion out of local systems and directly into the Orion Nebula. Most, however, advocated concentrating on the newly discovered and partially terraformed sites at Epsilon Eridani. An even smaller group began to gain prominence at Terra Nova with a simple, yet extremely divisive idea. Rather than heading out to the star with dreams of conquest and expansion, they instead looked inward and back to the old world. The Old Earthers focused their attention on Earth, Mars, Lunar, and the old satellites that still housed small populations. This radical organization advocated nothing less than a massive expansion and exploitation program of these old colonies.

The New Colonies

11km above Helios Prime

Admiral Lewis watched the screens and tried to stay calm and collected. It was necessary not just for the crew, but also for himself. He'd seen the reports coming from T'Karan, but there was no time to wait. The fleet might be on the verge of arrival, but with the enemy already on top of the planetary defense system, there was now a time factor involved. He looked at the timers and shook his head in amazement.

If they make it inside and activate the system, they could stop Citadel before it begins!

If he'd had just ten more hours, he could have delayed and used the massive number of ships and troops for a real offensive. Instead, he was now using all that remained of his forces in a single knockout blow on Helios Prime. Even as the ships moved into position, he imagined the horrors of the fleet not arriving from T'Karan. With the Rift closed, the Alliance would be stuck with what remained of their forces in the Helios System.

If the Rift is brought down, we'll lose this war.

It was nothing more than simple mathematics. The Biomechs had more warriors and more ships in the system. Even if the Helion, Khreenk, and Alliance forces won every battle, they would still lose the war. And once the Black Rift opened, it would be the endgame for every soul.

It cannot happen.

He did his best to banish the thoughts from his mind and concentrate on what was around him. He couldn't change what the Biomechs were planning on doing, but he could command his own assault, and that might be enough to turn the tide in their favor. The disposition of the rest of the Alliance force was exactly as he'd planned, and those ships allocated to this operation were moving directly behind him. He could see the Crusader and Liberty class ships, as well as more than thirty Maulers. It was an impressive force but a fragile one. The smaller craft had been designated the rescue portion of the mission, with only a third carrying troops on board. The rest were being kept deliberately empty in expectation of a major evacuation. Even so, all were equipped as gunships, and he had little doubt their guns would be needed.

"Four minutes," said Captain Marcus, as much for himself as for Admiral Lewis.

The heat from re-entry into Helios Prime's atmosphere was incredible, and no matter how they faced the ship into the descent, it was clear they were taking quite a beating. Panels and antenna burned and melted, but it was no more than the ships had been constructed for. He looked to Captain Marcus, who like him, was doing his best to remain calm.

"She'll hold together. This is what the outer skin was constructed for."

He was right, of course. All of the new generation of ships had been designed to be as flexible as possible. One of the many requirements had been the ability to operate different modules, dependent on the mission. The first

Crusader class was the first, though the changes to different configurations were complex and time consuming. The newer designs, such as the Liberty class and the latest tier Crusaders were built specifically with the facility of modification in a matter of hours. The real improvement, and the one that he was taking full advantage of right now, was the ability to enter a planet's atmosphere. This was more than just a change to the structural design and integrity of the ship. It required changes to aerodynamics, as well as power and propulsion.

"What was that?" Captain Marcus asked as three alarms activated simultaneously.

"Dorsal stabilizers," said the Chief Engineer.

The man was one of the oldest, if not actually the oldest officer on the ship. He was short and bald, yet his voice pierced through the CIC like an angry sergeant major.

"It's gonna get a little rough."

He was right. No sooner had the alarms started, and the ship began to shudder. It started as a minor rumble but quickly became a constant vibration that ran from every direction. The view from the mainscreen was black and red with a mixture of flame and smoke, and then it cleared. Admiral Lewis almost staggered back at the view.

"Just look at that."

They had already seen images of the surface of the world, but experiencing the hell that was Helios Prime truly was a sight to behold. The planet was known to be one massive city that spread across every landmass with clear warm skies. Now the planet looked like it was made from jagged rocks. Where once there had been mighty city blocks and towers that reached up into the clouds, there were just heaps of rubble. Skyscrapers vied for position amongst the destroyed overpasses and collapsed landing platforms.

"The General was right; this world has been burned to a crisp. How could anybody live down there?"

Captain Marcus nodded in agreement.

"The reports in the last weeks confirmed the orbital bombardment had destroyed all of the remaining infrastructure. Daniels and the rest have been in hiding or underground since the attack began."

He looked away and might have spat on the floor if he'd been outdoors and on his own.

"This isn't war. This is simple extermination."

They both looked on at the vast pillars of smoke rising from every direction. The surface of the planet was almost impossible to make out in places. Both men had been on the surface before and had seen the jewel of the Helion League. Their planets and star systems were developed to a certain extent, but only the Helios System contained anything more than a single useable planet. Though they liked to boast of their five star systems, the reality was that they controlled a total of seven worlds, with three of them outside of Helios and barely functioning as colonies. It was true there were also small research and industrial sites on some of the moons like Eos, but in reality, only Helios Prime was fully functioning.

And now look at it.

Admiral Lewis looked on at the surface of the world and shook his head slowly. It was an image he knew he would never be able to remove from his mind.

"It really is a hell world down there."

Captain Marcus pointed to one of thousands of fires that continued to burn. The color was much lighter at the base than he would have expected, and that could only mean that it was burning even hotter.

"I thought the fires would have stopped weeks ago. Our drone assessments showed the primary damage wasn't caused by the Biomech bombardments; it's the fires that have ruined Helios Prime."

Admiral Lewis sighed, but he knew his executive officer was right. While the attack continued, it was almost impossible to go outside and attempt to fight, let alone stop fires, administer first aid, or provide any other assistance. It was a bitter, cruel way to fight a war.

"It's true. What's happening down there is little different to the Great Earthquake of San Francisco in 1906. The quake did considerable damage, but it was the damage to the water system that stopped their ability to put out the fires."

He raised an eyebrow, recalling the article he'd read

many years before.

"They lost something like eighty percent of the city in that fire. It went on for days, and thousands of people were killed. If they'd been able to fight the fires, a much larger amount could have been saved."

Captain Marcus nodded in the direction of the mainscreen.

"Well, they didn't have Biomech bombardments and aerial attacks to contend with. Frankly, I'm amazed this world hasn't already been sterilized after all of this. Even if we secure the installation, this world is still a total loss."

It was the tactical officer that spotted the first flight of Biomech craft racing across the ruined city at low-level. Mixed in among them were a much smaller number of Helion interceptors. Missiles and gunfire flickered between them as both sides took casualties. A single fighter broke in two, and the larger section fell to the ground in another column of smoke. The explosion added to the fires still burning and then vanished from view, obscured by the myriad of other disasters to befall the planet.

"How can anybody still be alive down there?"

He wasn't really talking to any of the other officers. It was more a rhetorical question. He continued running ground and aerial scans to check for signs of trouble. With so much smoke, fire, and dust in the air, the sensors were having a hard time sifting through the data. The thick mixture of smoke and dust heavily obscured even the optics.

"What the hell was that?" demanded the XO.

The ship shuddered one more time and then began to settle as the inertial stabilizers began to take effect. At the same time another jolt shook the ship. He looked to the tactical officer who was feverishly checking systems. He stopped and looked to the mainscreen.

"There."

One of the cameras showed an external view of a large metal plating section that had ripped off. Scorch marks ran nearby, but it was hard to tell if it was the heat from re-entry or combat damage that was the cause. The ship's continuing decrease in forward velocity also assisted in the reduction of buffeting. More sensors blared, and this time it was the tactical officer's turn to sound worried. He moved the imagery away and brought up a pair of images from two different sets of optics.

"I knew they'd be here. We have a Biomech warship on an intercept vector. Twenty degrees off the starboard bow. She's a big one."

Both senior officers looked at him with a mixture of surprise and amusement showing on their faces. The use of such archaic navigational terms was rare these days, especially in the modern Alliance Navy. Yet being on another world, with enemy ships at close range, it seemed bizarrely the right thing to do. On any other day, Admiral Lewis might have taken pleasure in knowing he was in a combat situation not unlike one from Earth's nineteenth century. Back then, entire fleets of wooden and metal ships had met in epic battles, each side squaring off to engage with solid shot. Not today though, he had more serious issues to concern himself with.

"What is she?"

Schematics and a live feed moved directly to the mainscreen. At first, a dark shape obscured the view, but then it pulled back and the focus altered. The shape distorted and then became clearer, even though it was still surrounded by smoke and haze. The ship was big, easily the size of a Crusader class, perhaps almost double the size. Helion fighters raced about it while the monstrous ship simply ignored them; like a dog ignoring a few insignificant fleas.

"It's a Ravager variant, must be. The hull's the same configuration, multiple gun turrets and quite a few hangars. Wait. She's opening…"

"Brace, brace, brace!" shouted the XO over the intercom.

The officers in the CIC grabbed emergency handles or their buckles as they waited for the inevitable. Even the marines waiting near the main doorway grabbed the nearest handles that also doubled up as the way to move through the ship when in a zero gravity environment. Admiral Lewis watched the screen, and flashes of light appeared along the hull like hailstones.

"Here is comes."

The first volley struck along the flank of the ship. Dozens and dozens of hardened projectiles slammed through the outer skin and into the layered armor. One by one they smashed, with only a small number actually missing the large Alliance warship.

"Sir, shall we intercept?"

Admiral Lewis shook his head.

"Hell, no. Pass the word; all ships will continue on their present course."

"And the Biomech ship?"

He looked to his XO with a surprisingly angry expression on his face.

"Damn them all to hell, Captain. Give them a passing broadside and concentrate on the task at hand. That ship is a distraction, nothing more. We will get to Daniels and give him the help he needs."

The XO was already issuing orders to the tactical and communications officers. More junior officers quickly moved back and forth on the deck to get back to a safe location before the next shot hit. Admiral Lewis paused and then gave the XO a quick nod.

"It wouldn't hurt to get birds in the air, though. It's time for our fighter jocks to earn their pay, and I've got just the thing. I want a path cleared from here to the General. If anything comes within range, blast it. Once there, they can establish a security perimeter up to thirty kilometers in radius of our landing zone."

The wedge formation of Alliance ships kept on course and opened fire with kinetic weapons. This far down into a planet's atmosphere their direct-energy weapons were less than useless. It was common knowledge that particle beam weapons would dissipate at even short ranges. Instead, the power was used to boost the inertial stabilizers and good old-fashioned guns activated. Rapid-fire kinetic railguns joined with even older auto cannons to fill the sky with super-heated metal.

"Beautiful," said the XO in a quiet, slightly somber tone.

The wedge formation of ships and their escort Maulers put down such a weight of fire that the entire flank and nose of the Biomech ship was wreathed in flame. By the time they had reached just a kilometer away, the Ravager was already losing height and heading for the city. A pack of six Maulers followed it down, blasting at the ship's engines with merciless aggression. They barely made it away from the explosion as the capital ship crashed down into the city ruins.

"There it is," said Admiral Lewis.

The mainscreen showed the close-up view of their objective, a distant and well-protected part of the city. Ground based weapon systems blasted up high into the sky, but from this far away it was almost impossible to tell if it was friendly or hostile weaponry. There were very few missiles being used this far into the orbital siege. The battle had come down to flak guns and gun turrets, all old but reliable technology. Indicators on each side of the mainscreen showed their current height and speed, both of which were still falling at a high rate.

"Sir, we're on course for the weapon's location. General Daniels' forces have activated the tracking beacon. They are at the installation," said Lieutenant Vitelli.

"Good, we might have a chance yet."

He looked to the communications officer. He could quite easily send the signal electronically, a simple activation command, but this was no ordinary mission. He was about to order the bulk of his functioning vessels into what could quite easily be a suicide mission.

"Comms, put me on with our strike force. It's time to get this operation into action."

It took less than three seconds.

"You're on, Sir."

He wiped his brow while grabbing his seat harness. Even with the stabilizers at full power, the rocking had started to return, and stray rounds from the ever-increasing number of Biomech ships and fighters would only make it worse.

"This is Admiral Lewis. Operation Barndoor is a go. All of you have the target coordinates. Stick to the schedule. I don't want any heroes today. If you go down, get underground fast and dig in for the long haul. This is a sweep and rescue operation, plain and simple. Good hunting to you all. See you on the top side."

It was short and simple, no more than was necessary for such a careful, preplanned operation. He tried to keep it lighter than his last message, knowing full well how fear and nerves could spread and cripple an operation. They might have only the most slender of chances, but there was no reason why he needed to share that with anybody more than his immediate entourage. He deactivated the intercom and looked to Captain Marcus, who gave him the nod.

"This is it, then. Daniels destroys the weapon, and we pickup whoever is left."

Admiral Lewis tried to smile, but it was hard when he could see the look on his tactical officer's face. His stomach lurched upon seeing that look, one that only ever happened when they were about to be punished.

"What is it?"

His tone was dulled, as though he'd just seen his own fleet blown apart. The man moved three smaller images onto the mainscreen. All of them showed an area of space near the enemy Ark.

"They must have detected what we're doing, Sir. They already have ships on their way down from orbit."

"What? How soon?"

Lieutenant Vitelli shook his head.

"At the current speed, they'll pretty much be there the

same time as us."

He tightened his jaw and then pointed at their target.

"Accelerate. There's no way in hell I'm leaving the General in the lurch. We end this, today!"

* * *

Underground highway, Helios Prime

The Bulldog left the ground for a brief moment as they hit a rough piece of rubble. When they came back down, the armored personnel carrier lurched to one side before the driver was able to recover their position and put down more power. The underground tunnel system was extremely wide, yet the constant bombardment over weeks had forced many vehicles underground, all of which had been subsequently abandoned. The Bulldog smashed a civilian transporter aside that had blocked the route and then pushed on. In the pitch darkness, only the large front-mounted lamps provided any kind of illumination.

"How long do we have?" General Daniels asked.

Captain Hammond checked the drone scans for what must have been the tenth time.

"They are coming in right now. Drones show their craft will be landing directly above the planetary defense installation."

Daniels smacked his armored fist against the side of the vehicle.

"And they will be able to gain access before we even pop our heads out from under the ground."

He was frustrated but not because the enemy was coming. His real annoyance was from the fact he'd been hiding on this planet for so long now, with almost nothing to do but wait and repair their defenses; all the while the enemy just sat in space and fired down on them. Now, when the time came for him to act, he was going to be late.

"If they take control of the complex, they'll be able to block of this entire planet, perhaps the entire system."

He then looked directly at the Captain.

"You know what that means, right?"

"Yes, Sir. They can shut down the Rifts to all other systems, including T'Karan. We'll be trapped out here with only the ships we have left, and the enemy poised to enter through the Black Rift."

He thought about his words as though unsure whether to speak.

"I don't understand why we can't just open the Black Rift ourselves, and then immediately collapse it."

General Daniels laughed at the suggestion.

"That's actually not a terrible idea, but neither the T'Kari or the Helions will go for it. After the last war, they have something of a genetic memory and fear of what might happen if it opens."

They hit another bump, and if it hadn't been for the

mag-restraints, both would have struck their heads on the metalwork of the vehicle. The engine howled loudly as the driver put every ounce of horsepower into the drivetrain and pushed them onwards. Right behind them came enough vehicles to transport the entire combat company. Inside the armored vehicles waited just over a hundred volunteers, all experienced and all eager to finally get to grips with the enemy.

"General, we're coming to the surface...now!"

The internal viewscreen showed the view from the top hatch as they moved out from the dark tunnel and back to the surface. The inferno all around the facility took even General Daniels by surprise. At the same time, an internal speaker burst into life.

"It's Admiral Lewis," said the Captain quietly.

"Alliance landing craft will be with you in six minutes. I repeat; all Alliance forces are to withdraw underground or to the landing grounds around the weapon platform."

One by one the Bulldogs raced out and moved in on the monstrous structure. The highway was half-filled with debris, but it was clear enough for them to wind their way through. Up ahead was the clamshell-shaped roof that covered the entire site. Around it were ten-meter tall walls that had been breached in a hundred places.

"Look at that," said Captain Hammond.

His voice was dull, tinged with bitterness. General Daniels could hardly disagree though. The site was one of the most secretive on the entire planet and had been constructed well away from any urban centers. There were the remains of hundreds of industrial buildings, towers, and at least two military air bases. The lower level highway ran alongside one of the outer walls and was sunken nearly three meters below the ground level of the fortified walls. Overhead were smoke and vapor trails from a hundred aircraft. Biomech fighters tangled with Alliance Hammerheads and the ultra sleek Helion scout fighters. All of this paled with the dark shapes of a dozen or more Bioray landers that were only a short distance from the compound.

"Any word from the Helion garrison commander? His name is Kossl, I think."

The Captain shook his head.

"There's massive signal distortion around the site."

"We're going in, General," said the driver.

The lead Bulldog swerved left and up the bank to crash through one of the large breaches in the wall. Another nine followed behind and did the same, each grinding the broken masonry to dust as they powered over the debris. The low clamshell roofing structure made the entire site look relatively modest in size. One of the four ramps leading down to great metal plated blast doors betrayed its more sinister purpose. That was where they spotted the first of the enemy.

"Gods, we're too late."

The Bulldog skidded to a halt just sixty meters from the massive blast doors. Bodies and rubble littered the place, and a single Bioray burned off to the side where it had crash, presumably during its attempt to land.

"Everybody out and secure that damned facility!" shouted out the General.

The doors slid open, and one by one the Bulldogs deployed their fireteams of marines onto Helion soil. General Daniels was out with the first wave and found his visor was forced to darken automatically as a series of blinding grenades exploded not far away. He looked back and located five more Biorays moving in low, their gun turrets already picking out the Bulldogs that lay out in the open.

We might have enough time, if we hurry.

He glanced over to Captain Hammond.

"Keep one squad back and watch the entrance. Let Lewis know what we're doing. We have to take this place."

The man saluted and then barked orders to the small unit. At the same time, the General ran down the wide ramp to the blast door that was wide open. A pair of his marines had already reached it and was checking the bodies on the ground.

"Four Thegns and two NHA soldiers," said the first.

The Corporal on the right checked another soldier and looked back.

"General, this one is a Helion officer. Looks like the

machines gained access somehow. They must be inside."

He looked at the bodies and noted the thermal scoring and holes in their bodies.

"Those are not blades, son. They are heat weapons."

He looked to the left and then to the right, checking on the rest of his unit. There were two full platoons of marines, with more coming down the ramp. All were kitted out in their battered PDS Alpha armor and carrying a motley mixture of L52 carbine, L48 rifles, and even the odd looted Helion shotguns. A single SAAR robot squealed and creaked as it rumbled down the ramp behind them.

"This facility is all that stands between freedom and the destruction of this entire star system."

He'd been breathing fast and tried to slow down just for a moment, trying to calm down, to relax before the real fight began. As he checked around him, he could see more vapor trails from even more Biomech ships.

Where the hell are you, Lewis?

"We go in fast. If it's not Helion, you put it on the ground. I want this entire site cleared and under our control in less than fifteen minutes. Understood?"

The first squad had already moved behind the rubble to hide themselves from view. Others were positioning mobile barricade units and activating the hardware to create a series of taller structures to fight behind. One placed his L48 onto a v-shaped rock and extended the bipod. In just a few more seconds, the entire squad was in position and waiting to hit any enemy forces moving in on the ramp.

"Good. Follow me."

General Daniels was first through the blast doors. He stepped into the darkness to find all the lights off, yet he counted dozens of small fires throughout the first few sections of the wide passageway. It was big enough to stand an entire squad shoulder to shoulder and ran more than two hundred meters off into the distance.

"Move it!"

The General increased speed, first to a fast walk, then a jog. Finally, the entire unit accelerated to almost a full run. Then one of the marines spotted movement, and the battle for the defense installation began in earnest.

* * *

ANS Dreadnought, T'Karan

Spartan walked around the small group of Biomech war machines for what must have been the fifth time. It was a walk tinged with impatience and more than a little annoyance. ANS Dreadnought had been transformed in the last twenty-four hours into something he thought he would never have seen. Most of the marines had been moved off to other ships in the flotilla, leaving just a single company on the ship, under the command of Captain

Rivers. He'd been around their kind many times before, but this was a first for him, the chance to look at and study them without being tortured or interrogated. Each of them was as similar as they were different. Some were tall and lithe; others short and squat like a tank. Yet every one of them shared the worn and battered look of Z'Kanthu. He felt a slight shiver as he spotted a wide machine, its legs thick, and the low hanging arms came equipped with horrific-looking pincers. One of the arms moved a little as he watched and then went still.

They are old and tired. A bit like me, I suppose.

He found it a little amusing and glanced to Khan who walked alongside him. The two had much in common with the machines they now walked amongst. All had suffered at the hands of the enemy, and all of them had seen vast bloodshed. The one common ground, however, was the desire for vengeance. It was now no longer about ending the war. It was time for a total victory.

"Maybe we should have stayed longer. For our efforts, we've been given seven Alliance ships. That's it. One for each of our seven guests we found. Maybe we could have found more than the eleven bandon. Will that be enough for this fight?"

Khan shrugged.

"Maybe, maybe not. It doesn't matter, anyway. You've seen the video feeds. Gun and Jack are fighting on Spascia, and it doesn't look good. We have to act, and fast."

Spartan nodded in quick agreement. Even though they'd moved as fast as they could, there was no more time to search. They would have to manage with the forces they'd found, all of which were now part of this fleet. All remaining stowage space had been allocated to their news guests on this vessel, as well as space about six Liberty class destroyers recently configured for transport and now designated the Black Ships. Gone were their three mission bays, replaced by three large habitation blocks, each suitable for housing a large number of marines. Between them they could carry all the machines and their horde of warriors.

"Helios Prime is in an even worse state. I don't think they can hold down there. You've seen the reports on the public nets. They're bad enough as it is. When you look at the Alliance military reports, you can see how bad it really is."

To Spartan's surprise he realized Khan appeared to agree with him.

"Really, you, too?"

Khan shrugged.

"The bombardment has smashed the planet. Every time Admiral Lewis has tried to help, his ships have been crippled. The only chance the world has is the operation. And if we throw everything at Helios Prime, what will happen to Spascia?"

Spartan nodded and looked back at his friend.

"True. I don't think it will make much of a difference either way. The machines don't want Helios anymore than we really do. All they want is control of the Nexus and the Black Rift."

He indicated toward the group of Biomech war machines.

"That's why I think the only way we can help our friends is to do this. We will have to accept their sacrifice on Prime and Spascia. It's up to us to do what the others cannot."

Even Khan appeared to find this thought unsettling.

"Millions will die if we don't use our full strength on Spascia and Prime. This plan will divert the bulk of our strength from where it is needed the most."

He paused before pushing it any further, but not even he could keep from saying the obvious.

"When we go through the T'Karan-Helios Rift, we will be taking a single engineering station with us. It is the only way we can build a stable Spacebridge, but they'll hit us hard. It's the only way we can save Spascia."

He swallowed.

"Jack and Gun will die if we don't get to Spascia soon."

Spartan listened but couldn't find the words to answer his friend. He already knew the implications of Operation Citadel. It was a powerful fleet, one that even now had been reinforced by his forces. Even so, few believed it would be enough to beat back the machines and clear the system for good. And then there was always the Black

Rift, that terrible part of space where all feared to visit.

"Will it work? Should I go through with it?"

Khan considered his words for a few seconds.

"Maybe, but Gun and Jack will pay the price. When the General finds out though, hell, he is not going to be pleased. Have you told Teresa?"

Spartan lowered his head and rubbed his brow.

"No. She's only just heard about ANS Titania. They were involved in the last attack around Helios Prime. The mission report says we fired atomics at any ships about to be captured. Their ship is missing. I wasn't sure if…"

Khan stopped and placed his paw on his friend's shoulder.

"If there was a chance they could survive, then they will have. Teresa is strong, and even though you don't get along, I can promise you her children are just as tough."

He looked at the machines and wondered how many were listening. It was a stupid question, of course, because he knew that the machines were ever conscious and able to watch and record without even moving.

"Spartan, Teresa needs to know about this mission. If we go ahead without her knowing, well, you know her rage. She'll never let you forget."

Spartan knew he was right, but that didn't help him at all with the decision.

"Khan. None of us will forget this. Whether it works or not, we will still be the ones to be punished."

Z'Kanthu listened to them both and waited until there was silence.

"You were both prisoners of the enemy, were you not?"

Spartan nodded, but Khan just looked at the machine suspiciously.

"Something like that. They had us for months, torturing and interrogating us. Why?"

Z'Kanthu moved closer, looking at Spartan carefully, as though scrutinizing every square centimeter. One of his arms extended out and moved closer. Khan instinctively brought his hands up, ready to fight.

"What is it Z'Kanthu?"

"The machines, they have ways of manipulating people. In the past, my people used living computers to transfer information and memory?"

Spartan looked to Khan and raised an eyebrow.

"So?"

Z'Kanthu pressed his hand against the side of Spartan's head and shuddered. He then took a step back and beckoned for Khan to approach. He moved forward cautiously but when close enough the machine touched him as well.

"Okay, what the hell is going on?"

"The machines, they have been inside your minds. Both of you have been infected with their indoctrination."

Spartan was convinced he could sense disgust in the machine's voice. Even so, the very mention of the word infection sent a shudder through his body.

"Infection?"

"Yes. You both have the programming to be living Cores, to command and be commanded by machines."

Spartan shook his head.

"No way, nobody controls me."

Spartan straightened up and then turned about completely before stopping to face the machine.

"Really?" it asked.

Spartan's felt his body shudder, and for the first time he began to understand what the machine was trying to tell him.

"You just did that?"

Z'Kanthu nodded slowly.

"Can you fix it?"

Again the machine nodded.

"I can do better than that…I have an idea. How much spare storage do you think your brain has, Spartan?"

He reached for Spartan and touched his head once more. This time he did not let go, and Spartan found he lost control of his legs and finally dropped to the floor, limp as a dead fish. Khan stepped close and blocked Spartan's fallen body with his own.

"What have you done, machine?"

Z'Kanthu lowered his arms and presented them in a humble gesture.

"I have given him and myself a shield, a defense against

the machines. I can do the same for you?"

Khan refused to move and simply shook his head.

"Hell, no. You remove that stuff and then you tell me what you've done to him."

CHAPTER NINE

The Decurion war machine was first encountered toward the end of the Uprising. Some say there had been sightings on other worlds, but it was the violent battle on Hyperion where they were found in large numbers. In the past, the Biomechs had simply provided the technical knowhow and basic leadership for the war effort. At Hyperion, they attempted a direct intervention through the ground-based Rift, and the Decurions fought against marines in bloody and violent combat.

Robots in Space

Alliance Taskforce, Helios Prime

The formation of Alliance ships bore down on the ruined city like a horde of angry birds of prey. Smoke trailed from ANS Harbinger, one of the older Crusader ships, yet she continued at the same speed as the others. A large fire had spread through a hangar on the starboard side, following three suicide attacks by Biomech fighters. They had already cut their way through the Biomech fighter screen and were now just a kilometer from the Defense Installation. At this range, they could now make out the six Biorays that had just landed, and even the columns of troops charging out from them and toward two separate ramps. A clump of Bulldog wheeled armored personnel carriers lay burning near one of them.

"Magnify," said Admiral Lewis.

The ship shuddered just as it had done since the real fighting had begun. The gentle hum of point-defense turrets served as a constant reminder they were moving through a growing cloud of Biomech craft, most of which were the tiny fighters.

"Yea, that's the place."

Dozens of Eques walkers moved about in the open, and hundreds more Decurions swarmed over the multiple entry points into the underground structure. Tracer fire from the nose and dorsal guns tore into the ground around them, but they continued to pour out and toward the ramps. The Alliance capital ships were now close enough to make use of their guns, but they were limited in choice of targets as they screamed overhead. At the same time, the groups of Maulers swept down on the target with their own small gun turrets blasting away at Biomech foot soldiers.

The number of landed and burning Biorays told Admiral Lewis this was exactly where he needed to be. He just wished he could make his ships hover over the objective where they could do the most good. Coordinating ground assault operations using capital ships was a subject rarely covered in the Academy. An image in one of the old paperback manuals did come back to him, and the thought immediately put a smile on his face.

Yes, that is perfect.

He watched as an Eques walker lost a leg to a missile launched from a Hammerhead. It stumbled, dropped to one knee, and then took another missile in the upper body that triggered a series of multiple explosions. Decurions scrambled over the wreckage and kept moving into the installation. There was a good chance many were already inside. Another three Biorays moved in to try and land, and even though they took considerable fire, all of them managed to find a space and skidded down amongst the others.

"How the hell did they get through?"

Admiral Lewis was all too familiar with how many troops they carried, and he knew that General Daniels had just a single company at his disposal for this operation.

I need to give him more time.

He looked to Captain Marcus and pointed at the mainscreen.

"I want the destroyers to follow a pylon turn on this

location."

He pointed at the center of the large open area next to the clamshell roof.

Captain Marcus nodded and turned away to coordinate the attack. The Crusader ships were slower and much harder to maneuver in this atmosphere, so he concentrated their use as barriers to block off the Biomech reinforcements. It took less than two minutes for the first two Liberty destroyers to fall into a close radius circle around the selected point.

"Admiral, they're in position."

"Good. Let the bombardment begin."

The idea of the pylon turn was something dating back to the early twentieth century air racing. It referred to the way an aircraft or multiple aircraft could move around a fixed point on the ground so that an imaginary line could be drawn from the side of the craft to the point.

"Admiral!"

Both senior officers looked to the mainscreen. A pair of Biomanta warships and five Biorays had broken through the Alliance fighter screen. They were heading for the underground facility. There was no need to issue orders though; the ships' captains were all aware of what needed to be done. Dozens of Alliance ships opened fire with a monstrous bombardment of railguns that tore the stern from one Bioray and cut a Biomanta clean in half.

"Beautiful," said Captain Marcus.

The broken Biomanta spun out of control and crashed into two of the Biorays. The whole mass of smashed metal and flesh tumbled from the sky, leaving just a single Biomanta and two Biorays. The surviving ships tried to avoid the gunfire, but even as they moved away were pursued by eleven Hammerhead and Avenger drone fighters. Admiral Lewis moved to the tactical display with its multicolored view of the battlefield. More importantly, he began to smile as the pylon turn started to have an effect.

"Just look at that," he said happily.

Captain Marcus nodded in agreement.

"Reminds me of the video streams of the NATO air sorties in the Afghanistan conflict."

The Admiral looked to his XO with a surprised look on his face.

"I never took you as a history buff, Captain."

"It's about aircraft, shooting the hell out of the enemy, Sir. What is there not to like?"

He couldn't argue with that. Even at the mention of that ancient conflict, he could recall some of the video streams. Though fast jets and helicopters had been used in that war, it was the large four-engine planes with the flank-mounted heavy weapons that had given him the idea for the pylon turn in the first place. That war had much in common with the Uprising back in the Confederacy, a time where insurgents and suicide bombers fought against advanced mechanized forces.

Things don't change as much as people would have you believe.

He looked back to the live feeds and the seven destroyers moving around the target at a distance of just under three kilometers. For ships of that size, and inside a planet's atmosphere, this was effectively point-blank range. If it hadn't been for the permanent threat of a death, he might have actually enjoyed watching the ships at work. Gunfire bounced off them as hundreds of small arms reached up and stabbed at the massive gray vessels. Only the most powerful weapons could have even the slightest chance of doing any kind of significant damage. He spotted a single Eques walker stop. It then pivoted and raised its gun system to engage one of the destroyers.

Let them burn.

They were all the air defense destroyers, each one armed with eight quad 20mm coilgun turrets that were perfectly built to shred missiles, fighters, and light armor. The first opened fire, and then one by one the others joined in to bring down a fiery rain upon the Biomech ground forces. Two Biorays were set alight, and more than half a dozen Eques walkers were cut in half by the weight of fire. Captain Marcus nodded with pleasure at the carnage.

"Admiral, this sure is a beautiful sight."

More of the machines spread out from the landers, but now the Alliance ships had their range. In this environment they proved devastating against the Decurions, Thegns, and even the heavily armored Eques machines. Every time a squad tried to reach the facility, it was smashed to pieces by gunfire.

"Good...damn good. That should take some of the pressure off the General."

"Sir!" Lieutenant Vitelli called out, "Enemy warships coming from the south."

Admiral Lewis felt his stomach lurch.

"Numbers?"

He looked to his tactical officer and found the answer in his face. All he needed to do was to put a number on the threat.

"Uh...I've not seen anything like this before, Sir. We have fifty plus Biomantas and the same number of landers. There's more though, Sir."

"What do you mean?"

Lieutenant Vitelli indicated toward the mainscreen when he changed the view of the defense facility to one of the smoke-filled sky. The imagery was shaky and filled with digital noise and artifacts.

"What am I looking at?" Admiral Lewis asked.

"It's Ark Leviathan. It's coming down through the atmosphere."

He almost choked at the news.

"Coming down? Has it been forced down here? That means the end of the bombardment."

The young officer shook his head and looked back at

the dark shape beginning to fill the sky. It shared much in common with the arrival of the other warships from orbit, with one massive exception. Size.

"It's slowing down, Sir, and it's coming down ten kilometers from here. There are more ships coming down with it."

So, this is how Helios dies. They smash the planet within an inch of its life, wait until the warriors are dead, starving or dying. Then, with almost no defenses left, they unleash their hordes.

"Animals!"

He signaled to Captain Marcus.

"We not going to be here for long now. Make sure the ship is ready for a quick escape. As soon as the General is done, we're out of here."

The ship shook violently, and this time suffering far worse against the increasing number of enemy vessels. The gun turrets of the Alliance vessel loaded, fired, and reloaded until their barrels began to overheat.

"We're running out of time."

The rest of the Alliance ships showed up on the tactical display and presented a layered cylindrical defense over the installation. Smaller shapes indicated the fighter and drone squadrons busily running circles around the larger vessels. No matter where Admiral Lewis looked, he could see the bright red tendrils of the Biomechs moving in. He wasn't simply outnumbered. He was trapped.

"How long until we're stuck here?"

Captain Marcus was already speaking with three other officers. He twisted about to look to the Admiral.

"Seven minutes, eight at a push. After that, they'll be able to hit us all the way off this world."

"Very well."

He selected all of the Maulers in the vicinity of the facility.

"This is Admiral Lewis. Phase II is a go. Get our people out of there."

* * *

ANS Warlord, Admiral Jarvis Naval Station, T'Karan
General Rivers marched along the wide passageway running below the spine of the warship. Just behind him moved a pair of marines, each carrying their carbines low and at the ready. The passageway was flanked on both sides by a long ribbon of artificial windows that showed the perfect view of space. Unlike the rest of the journey, this one showed just two things. On one side was the vast Admiral Jarvis Naval Station, the largest and most advanced military installation in the Orion Nebula. To the left waited scores upon scores of ships, everything from Liberty class destroyers up through the many Crusader class vessels. There were even a large number of modified civilian transports bearing the markings of Hyperion. He shook his head, partially in amusement and also in

annoyance.

Damn Jötnar and their refusal to follow orders.

Their ships did at least carry the red stripes that marked the bows of most Alliance warships. It was clear they were there because they wanted to join in, and not because they had been told to come. He had nothing but respect for Gun's people, but he could easily understand why so many people had a deep down fear and mistrust of them. They were simply more independently minded than any other citizens.

One day, that problem is going to come home to roost.

He lifted his hand to his face and rubbed his forehead gently.

But that's for another day.

His expression was far from happy, and any officer that turned to salute quickly moved away to avoid his gaze. He moved in silence, the guards mute sentinels, each looking for signs of trouble. They reached the end of the passageway and a hexagonal open space with a pair of high-speed elevators waiting on each side. Another pair of marines watched each entrance and saluted as he stepped inside. Only when the doors hissed shut did he pull out his secpad and look at the data again.

"The fools, I told them we needed to act, and fast."

He scratched at his nose and placed the device back in its sheath on his thigh. Yet even with the object hidden away, he could not hide the imagery he'd seen of the attacks on the two Helion worlds. It was bad enough that Helios Prime and Spascia were under full-scale siege, but the news from Micaya and Libuscha was staggering.

Now we're on the back foot and they'll press their advantage.

In less than forty-eight hours, they'd gone from having a taskforce at the Black Rift and four planetary defense bases to just two. He had serious doubts of the ability for the Helions to defend the Black Rift, let alone be able to hold it for particularly long.

If they can negate our ability to close the Rift, we can expect a full-scale assault into the system in seconds.

It was a terrifying and incredibly sobering thought. One made far worse at the realization that the forces in Helios were just the remnants of the war long ago. He dreaded to think what might lay in wait thousands of light years away at the planets of the Biomechs.

The doors hissed open and revealed the spacious landing bay of the largest Alliance warship ever built. Even he had been impressed by the vastness of the vessel. It was excess in every possible way and amused him after the speeches and arguments directly after the Uprising.

What did they say? We need fewer ships, ones that would be cheaper to build and more flexible. Now what do we have? Hundreds of Crusader and Liberty vessels, and now this behemoth.

He wasn't wrong either. This wasn't just the largest military vessel ever constructed. It was also the most expensive, complicated, and heavily armed known to exist outside of the Biomech inventory. He turned his attention to the landing bay and the complete lack of personnel. He'd ordered the place cleared prior to his arrival, with no more than his personal guards staying back and watching the entrance. There were many Hammerhead fighters and Maulers lined up, but one in particular sat in the center. The craft carried a pair of red stripes, and a squad of marines waited outside for protection. Waiting in front of them were Khan, Spartan, Teresa, Major Terson, Marcus Keller, and his son. It was a veritable ensemble of the lost and damned of the Alliance.

"You should see what you look like."

He walked right up to them and stopped. Even as the marines started to salute, he shook his head, irritated at the ceremony.

"We go through the Rift in three hours. All that's left are the marine transports coming from Kerberos, what is it?"

Spartan took one step forward and met the General, almost as though he was trying to head off the old man. Both warriors faced off, years of experience allowing them to size up the other without even speaking. Spartan finally broke the silence.

"General, we've spoken with Z'Kanthu and his comrades about your proposal."

The General knew them all well enough; especially Spartan from his years of experience in the field to know something was up.

"What is it, Spartan?"

"Together we have come up with a plan. A way we can end this one once and for all. It's not the officially sanctioned Alliance plan, though."

General Rivers looked at him, and then to Teresa, and finally to his son.

"A plan? We already have a plan. It's called Citadel, and it's guaranteed to smash the enemy hard."

None of them said a word, and he looked at each of them, noticing the subtle changes in their faces that had occurred over the years he'd known each of them.

"Come on, then, what's so special about this plan of yours?"

Captain Nathaniel Rivers looked quickly to Teresa and then back at his father. He was clearly uncomfortable in his presence, something he'd never really discussed with the others.

"Citadel will hit them hard, for sure. But the Biomechs aren't stupid, Sir. We can guarantee they will open up the Black Rift no matter what we do, and when that happens, this war is over."

The General didn't seem very impressed.

"You're here are my request because Spartan said something about a critical problem with the operation? What was that, just a ruse?"

A scraping sound came from the Mauler waiting behind

the small entourage. The shape of Z'Kanthu moved out through the double hatches that were big enough for three Vanguards to exit from. Immediately behind him stepped On'Sarax, the shorter and broader of the two Biomechs. It began speaking in a dull, monotone computerized voice that was almost feminine in tone. Spartan noticed the change and wondered if they'd make adjustments to their vocal units specifically for this meeting.

"We have formulated a plan, a very risky plan, that could end this war in one battle."

General Rivers looked at the two machines and then waved off the marine guards waiting at the Mauler. Both had arrived with the craft, yet neither were people the General had seen before. Once they had moved back inside the craft, he looked back at the machines.

"Well?"

On'Sarax spoke, but not a single component of her metal figure moved. The Biomech might easily have been a metal statue than a leader of hundreds or even thousands of years of age.

"We have detailed knowledge of the Black Rift, as well as the enemy's domain. It is after all, our own world as well. Get us to their homeworld, and we will end this conflict."

General Rivers almost choked at this.

"Nonsense. You fought a war and you lost. What has changed? Don't tell me you think you can force them to not fight, because if you could have done that before, why didn't you?"

On'Sarax twisted to her right and looked to Z'Kanthu. They said nothing, but there clearly a conversation going on. After a few seconds, both turned their attention to the General.

"We plan on doing something the enemy would never expect."

"Really? And what would that be?"

His tone was becoming more and more frustrated as the seconds ticked by. So far, he'd heard them speak; yet they had told him nothing of substance. He was aware of planets, ships, fleets, and sieges. But this plan lacked anything more than a few vain dreams. He needed more, and they knew it.

Z'Kanthu decided to speak.

"We want the Rift opened. We must take advantage of the enemy's greatest weakness."

There was silence, but each knew what the question was. Z'Kanthu broke the silence with just a single word.

"Hubris."

General Rivers turned away from the machine and sighed. He began to move away and then looked back, his body still only half turned. The machine took this as a signal to continue speaking.

"If we attempt to fight them with force of arms, I can guarantee we will lose. In our own war, we lost millions of soldiers and thousands of ships. Even combined, you and your allies do not have the strength to bring about a total victory against the machines."

Teresa had been silent until now, but finally she spoke.

"No matter how powerful they might appear right now, the forces waiting in the worlds of The Twelve will be innumerable. Our own low estimates put their number of Arks at more than the strength of your entire fleet."

General Rivers tightened his brow at this new information.

"I've not heard this before."

It was more a question than a statement, but the machine chose to continue with its own line of inquiry.

"General, if we are bold, we can use the enemy's moment of victory to our advantage. When they are strongest, they will also be at their weakest. This is the perfect moment for us to strike."

Spartan and Khan both nodded in agreement at this last part. It was Teresa that finished off the proposal, however.

"General, in the end of times, this is the last thing they would expect. Even as their ships sweep in, we will move in behind them and launch a strike that will make Terra Nova look like a..."

She then looked to Spartan.

"What was your word…a picnic?"

Spartan couldn't help but smile at that, but the General remained completely impassive. There was a short pause as he considered all of their words. He had great respect for all of them, especially Teresa. Even so, he found the idea barely believable.

"What?" he snapped back, more viciously than he'd intended, "You want us to open up the only thing stopping them from total annihilation? To what end? If they have the kind of numbers you're talking about, you will be utterly destroyed. We don't even know a thing about their worlds, just the scattered relics of the Helions."

"No," said Z'Kanthu, "You have us. As the last of The Twelve, we know our old worlds, the navigation routes, and also the capital. We have all been there, the heart of the old Empire and of the galaxy."

Spartan shook his head as the General spoke.

"General. We plan on taking the fight to them. Let me lead whatever you can spare. I will take any forces you can give me. I'll use them in a single massive strike. We'll hit them hard, and we'll hit them again and again. I don't care what we have available. I'll use atomics, viral warfare. Hell, I'll use my teeth, hands, and feet, but by God, I'll make sure we end them. I'll leave nothing on their worlds but the dust of their vaporized souls."

General Rivers looked at him and found himself speechless. The bitter vitriol coming from Spartan was unlike anything he'd heard him say before. He was well aware of the man's treatment by the Biomechs, but this was something else. Only then did he notice the swollen features around Teresa's eyes. The light was low, but as she moved a little, the glow from the lamps fitted under the Mauler showed where she had rubbed away the tears.

Something's happened, something terrible.

It fell to Khan, who as always seemed to keep quiet until the last possible minute.

"This is the way it was always going to be, General. Do we want to whither away one soldier at a time, or do we want to fight them the way my kin were born to fight? A single battle, a bloodbath to tear the Biomechs from their world and see them burn like they would see us burn?"

He looked at Spartan, Teresa, and now Khan. He opened his mouth to speak, but his secpad beeped instead. With a single quick motion, he pulled out the unit and lifted it to his face. His expression transformed as he read it, and then moved his eyes back to them.

"They've hit Helios Prime. Big time. Admiral Lewis thinks they're going for the weapon. They already have troops on the ground and are fighting all around the place. The Ark that was over Prime, it has dropped through the atmosphere and is moving into position over General Daniels' position."

He swallowed as though trying to hide some terrible truth.

"If the Biomechs take just one of the facilities, they'll control the Rifts."

He glanced over his shoulder and back into the dark

recesses of the landing bay.

"We're going through now. The rest of the reinforcements will have to come through when they're ready. Admiral Lewis and General Daniels have put out a general distress call to all forces. Either we go through now, or we might end up stuck here."

He began to move away, but Teresa stepped toward him.

"What about our plan?"

He shook his head in partial annoyance.

"I understand your concerns, but this is war, and we have to make difficult decisions. My orders are to secure Helios Prime and to protect this Rift to our own system. The Black Rift is a luxury we cannot afford to interfere with. If Spascia and Helios Prime fall, so does everything else. We'll secure both…"

Spartan shook his head angrily.

"…and then see about your plan. I will not take risks with the limited resources at our disposal."

Even as he spoke, he could see the look on Spartan, Teresa, and Khan's faces.

They don't want to save Helios Prime; they want vengeance, nothing more and nothing less.

He liked the idea of a glorious last battle, but unlike the rest of them, he was aware of what state the Alliance was in. Without Helios, there was nothing to hold back the Biomechs.

This is a war of attrition, and Helios Prime and Spascia are the rocks that we'll use to grind their bones to ash.

* * *

Planetary 'Doomsday Weapon' Defense Installation, Helios Prime

Dust filled the passageway as more and more shells smashed around the compound. The attack from the Alliance ships was much more focused than anything they'd faced by the Biomech ships in orbit. The very foundations seemed to shudder from the near continuous smashing of shells and rockets in an area the size of a stadium. Even General Daniels found it hard to disguise his smile.

"Admiral Lewis wasn't kidding about the air support."

They had moved through the long corridor and were trying to make their way through a wider section. Doorways on the flanks led to smaller rooms running in parallel and gave the marines through points to try and breach.

"General, the primary passageway is secure," said Captain Hammond.

He looked at the young officer and to the direction they'd arrived from. Even at this distance, he could see the flashes from the handful of defenders still holding the position from outside.

"They can't hold them for much longer out there," Captain Hammond added.

A flurry of gunshots from the right turn further into the compound sent them all to the walls, trying to find anything to hide behind. The return fire from the marines was intense and silenced the defenders, if only for a few more seconds.

"General Daniels, this is Admiral Lewis. What is your status?"

Three more shots rang out, and one of the marines fell down, a hole in his shoulder armor. Another shot hit nearby, but his comrade pulled the wounded man out of the line of fire. General Daniels lifted his own carbine and fired a burst in the direction of the Thegns that had secured the point just ahead of them.

"Keep moving, we cannot let them take control!"

He took two steps and grabbed Captain Hammond by his left shoulder.

"Captain. Get them inside and seal the door. We cannot let anymore of those things in here."

"What about the ships?"

"Don't worry about them. I'll deal with it."

The officer turned and took a single fireteam of four marines with him to the main door. The doorway they were trying to get through was nearly four meters wide, and the thick metal door had jammed as it dropped down halfway. In the gap below the frame were five Thegns, all with firearms and firing almost continually. The General looked to the two-dozen marines in this section and signaled them.

"On my mark, put down every ounce of fire you have. Then follow me."

He didn't ask for suggestions or clarification. There was no time for that kind of thinking. The facility was already overrun, and according to the data given to him by the Helions, the primary control center was on the other side of the door. He reached for a flash grenade, twisted the timer, and tossed it to the door. Two other marines watched him do it and threw their own devices in after his.

"Ready…Now!"

He jumped from the modest amount of cover near the door and ran. He made it three meters, and then the marines opened fired. They held down their triggers as they moved. Each blasted at the doorway with a mixture of automatic and high-power rounds. The flash alert sounded on his helmet, and he instinctively closed his eyes. It was unnecessary; the visor was synced to the grenades and automatically blacked out as the first detonated. The system was simple and worked much like that used on welding equipment and helmets.

General Daniels reached the doorframe and found his path blocked by three of the horrific soldiers. He took aim, but the first took a dozen hits and stumbled backwards. He didn't even worry about where the fire had come from and crashed through, his own carbine rumbling as he went. Then he was through, and more marines poured in behind him.

"Keep moving forward!"

Two Thegns tried to grapple with them, but General Daniels kept going, firing only at those directly blocking his path. He relied upon his comrades to deal with any they missed. They swept inside and followed the path to the control center. All that separated him and his marines from their objective was the metal-framed glass door. He ran at it and threw his entire weight into the door. The glass cracked and shattered in five places. Two more marines arrived alongside him, kicking at the door until two sections ripped off. One of them stepped inside, and General Daniels followed behind him.

"Secure the facility, fast!"

He looked to his marines and gave them quick, short hand signals. More of them poured in through the breached doorway and into the control center. It was a big place and on three levels made of semi-transparent metal. Banks of computers were laid out in rows on the top two while the lower level was filled mainly with large liquid cooled cases. Scores of Helions civilians hid and cowered behind the equipment, while a tiny band of NHA soldiers ran in from the top level. They stopped when they ran straight into a squad of Thegns. One of the biomechanical soldiers looked down and raised a weapon.

"General, look out!" cried out a marine.

The man lurched out to the front, and a burst of thermal

energy struck him in the stomach. The man spun about and dropped to the ground writhing in agony. He wanted to help the man, but the mission pushed to the front of his mind. He directed his marines to put down fire on the enemy's position. The Thegns were already gone though, as were the NHA soldiers.

"Useless, every single dammed one of them!" he snarled.

The NHA had proved less than reliable in the last week, and now he had to secure a site they had promised was near impregnable. More shapes moved to the right, and ten carbines raised as four NHA soldiers moved from the shadows. An Animosh officer led them toward the marines and stopped in front of the General. Just like his men, he wore a dark orange, almost scarlet breastplate and tunic that was covered in a black cloak.

"What's your status?" he asked the alien, "Is the defense installation operational?"

The Helion leader's face was covered, and his long robes ran down to his feet, easily hiding his features from view. His face was covered in a half mask, something closely resembling a gasmask rather than a fully enclosed helm like the marines, though the top was finished off with an elaborate crest. General Daniels lowered his carbine just as the last few shots rang out inside the structure. Captain Hammond moved to stand alongside his commanding officer.

"Sir, there's something wrong with the outer door."

He was barely listening. His attention had moved to the bodies on the ground near one of the vertical computer displays. There were multiple Helion dead, and all were wearing the civilian clothing of the computer support staff. Every one of them had been killed, but it was the thermal wounds that almost slowed his heart to a stop. He looked to the Captain and nodded down to the bodies.

"They weren't killed by the machines."

His voice was quiet, yet all the nearby marines could sense the ill feeling in his tone. Dozens more marines were now inside, and all of them kept their weapons raised, each expecting trouble. Most of the marines moved off to search the levels, but a core group stayed near the doorway around their commander and lifted their weapons, scanning for potential signs of the enemy. General Daniels kept his eye on the Animosh commander and spoke quietly over the internal audio network.

"Captain Hammond, the outer door?"

The officer nodded.

"Sir. There is a computer override in progress. I've position the SAAR robot to guard the entrance. We have an entrenched squad waiting for them."

Both of them looked to the Animosh and noted more of them seemed to be coming out from the darkness. First there were less than a few dozen, and then there were six groups, each numbering between five and ten Animosh warriors. They carried an odd variety of weapons that included short thermal rifles, shotguns, shields, and maces. The later weapons were closer in style to the weapons used in Earth's Middle Ages.

"General, we have Maulers on the ground. You have three minutes to blow the site, then get your asses out of there."

He opened his mouth to speak and then noticed the expression on the Helion's face. At first he was confused, but it was clearly a smile, and far from a friendly one.

"Human," it started, with an extended emphasis on the first syllable.

A pair of marines ran to the base of one of the computer systems and opened a case on the ground. The front slid to one side, revealing a complex timed thermite charge. The second one took out a control unit, but one of the Animosh soldiers stepped toward them and pointed its weapon at them. General Daniels spotted the problem and stepped toward the Animosh leader. One of its retainers said something in their alien tongue, but he did recognize one word.

Lyssk!

His brain was already powering ahead, but deep down he knew exactly what was happening. He stopped and felt for the catch on his carbine. None of the other marines appeared to have worked out what was going on, but he was sure of it. A quick scan from left to right of each level logged and tagged the Helions on his targeting computer. The numbers were about equal, at least based on those he could see.

"Marines, it's Justitium Lyssk!"

He dropped to one knee and lifted his carbine. The Animosh must have been expecting trouble because they still managed to open fire first. Captain Hammond was first to die. The unfortunate man was hit four times, twice on the chest and twice in the face. Before his body even hit the ground, the entire command center exploded in a violent firefight.

"Admiral Lewis, it's a trap! We've been betrayed. Justitium Lyssk is here…"

He ducked to one side, blasting one of the Animosh with a short burst. The enemy leader had moved back, his path protected by many of his followers. He tried to go forward, but the return fire from their rifles and shotguns proved too intense. The armor of the marines was proof against many small arms, but in tests, the short-ranged heat weapons of the Helions proved easily capable of melting even the thick plating of Vanguard armor.

"He has control of the facility! I repeat. The Planetary Defense Installation is under enemy control!"

CHAPTER TEN

The Battlecruiser was the ship design made famous in the bloody days of the Uprising. Fast, powerful, and filled with the latest in railgun technology. After that costly war, there was a great push for more flexible vessels that could function as capital ships, escorts, and even transports. The subsequent expansion into the Orion Nebula showed that this class, though extremely capable, would need modification. The design was stretched and extended until it produced the powerful Battlecruiser known as the Conqueror class. This ship could be outfitted as an assault ship, carrier, command ship, or even a simple ship of the line. As the war with the Biomechs continued, so the importance of these powerful ships increased.

Origins of the Battlecruiser

Admiral Jarvis Naval Station, T'Karan

The Naval Station was more than an Alliance staging

post. It was the most substantial military installation ever built outside of the core planets. What was even more impressive was that its key components had been shipped and assembled in less than a year. Month by month, the automated mining and engineering machines of the Alliance continued to extend and enhance its capabilities as they burrowed deep into the original piece of drifting flotsam. The station was now close to the equal of the old Titan Naval Station in orbit over Proxima Prime, and coming close to the capabilities of the Prometheus Station.

The station's cavernous shipyards, research facilities, and troop barracks made it the equal of an entire star fleet. It wasn't just its size that gave it its power; it was the substantial defenses that would only ever be built on a facility constructed on the frontline. Raised towers, turrets, and fast launch bays had been removed from scrapped warships and fitted to cover every approach. Fighter squadrons crewed by Alliance and T'Kari pilots ran patrols throughout the T'Karan System, and escort class vessels protected convoys between planets, moons, stations, and the Rifts. In many ways, T'Karan was the most militarized and also the least populated part of the Alliance, an odd, but necessary arrangement in such turbulent times.

Admiral Anderson walked back and forth while the senior officers continued to discuss the latest news. In the center of the room was a massive holographic model of the Helios System, with lines connecting it to the worlds of the other alien domains, as well as the Rift gateways leading to T'Karan and the Black Rift. It was a strategic map, and the amount of red as opposed to blue and green showed just one thing.

We're losing, he thought.

It didn't surprise him; the situation was hardly unexpected based upon the forces at their disposition. He looked at the imagery and then to those senior officers and officials; many presented by virtual presence projectors inside the Naval station's Command Center. This was the central strategic post in the entire Alliance, and where Admiral Anderson had conducted combat operations, logistics, and intelligence missions. Even so, there was the ever-present oversight from Terra Nova, and right now, the very people that put him there were holding him back. The station's communications officer caught his attention.

Finally, it's here.

"Priority message from Intelligence Director Johnson has arrived, Sir."

The video stream and associated material transferred to his personal screen. At first, it was nothing other than a series of hexagonal shapes he had to manipulate to match his personal security mark. After a few more seconds, the imagery dropped to the bottom and was replaced by a short summary from Johnson himself. He read the few sentences and began shaking his head in a mixture of surprise and shear annoyance.

That idiot. That complete and utter idiot!

The report lacked video, and he could see why. Without reading it again, the material began to break apart as the time-delayed decay routine scrubbed every letter from his system.

So, the President has called on the Senate to give him full military control. He wants to go past me and the other commanders. Why?

"Admiral, the President is ready," said the same officer.

"Good, put him on."

The shapes of the President and a number of his senior advisors appeared. The imagery was almost perfect, with only the smallest degree of digital noise and corruption. All wore sharp black suits and were immaculate, from their shiny shoes to their dark ties. The very look of so many reminded the Admiral of the images of the Kerberon underground, with its criminal gangs and black marketers. The very thought of their plotting and scheming sent a shiver down his spine.

Calm down, you fool. They've not said a word yet.

That part was true, but the alert from Johnson had given him just seconds of advance notice. It wasn't much, but it did allow him to do one thing. With his fingers moving quickly, he keyed out a short message and hit send.

He'll have to get here fast.

"Admiral. I've some major news for our forces and outposts in the Orion Nebula. We've seen the reports from Helios, and quite frankly, we are stunned at the successes of the enemy."

The station's chief communications officer caught his attention with an emergency alert summons. It was a rare event, and standard protocol required the officer to interrupt him, even when in the middle of something as serious as a meeting with the President of the Alliance.

"Sir, Admiral Lewis has sent a flash alert. The enemy is trying to assemble a blockade over Helios Prime. He is sending his last ships down to assist with the evacuation of the planet."

Admiral Anderson knew what that meant for him, though. By making that decision, Admiral Lewis was committing his Naval forces to the battle and would be unable to leave. Operation Citadel would have to be launched to both assist the Admiral in his operation, but also to give him even the smallest chance of escaping the hell that was now that world. Even as he looked at the reports, he could hear the annoying drone of the President from his left ear.

"…but new information from the Anicinàbe is greatly disturbing and has caused a major crisis here on Terra Nova. I have received petitions from Euryale, Kerberos, and Prime about our heavy losses on the frontline. The public wants to know why our troops are dying."

Admiral Anderson looked at the man and wondered why this news was arriving literally the moment he was about to give the order for the largest operation in Alliance history. The idea of a crisis so far from the frontline was almost amusing. The only worlds hit by any kind of enemy attack in recent times was on Mars and at Prometheus. Even the ambush near Terra Nova had been in pursuit of a battlegroup heading for Prometheus. He wasn't aware that Terra Nova had faced a single direct threat in years. The time delay caught up, and it was now time for him to respond.

"President Harrison. I am on the cusp of sending our entire expeditionary force through the Rift. My ships are waiting just a kilometer from the Rift, and their troops and weapons are loaded and ready for battle. Admiral Lewis needs to be relieved and fast. Can this discussion not wait?"

The delay was short, but enough for him to be able to check on the arrival details of another three Alliance ships. They were all veteran Crusaders from the initial arrival in T'Kari space. There were also two small T'Kari escorts traveling with them, a reminder that the almost extinct race was still about, and keen to do their part. He might have been pleased at their arrival, but this contact from the President made him nervous. Instead of speaking with their captains, he now had to spend time with what he considered barely better than amateur bureaucrats.

"We've just received word from our counterparts inside the Anicinàbe territories. As you know, the entire region is something of a problem, with no central government and multiple tribes in a constant state of flux."

An image appeared alongside the President. It showed a number of alien ships of similar designs in a prolonged engagement. The configuration was vastly different to the kinds of vessels used by the Alliance, with their emphasis on speed and elegance. Both fired powerful weapons that inflicted substantial damage before one accelerated away, leaving a trail of broken debris behind it.

"The fighting between three of their factions has intensified, and there has been a series of violent raids between many of the factions themselves, especially this one known as the Red Scars."

Another man, one unfamiliar to Admiral Anderson now began to speak.

"Apparently, this group takes their name from the fact they were originally outlawed by the other tribes. They cut themselves as a reminder of the generations of slavery and torture they suffered at the hands of their own people."

Text appeared alongside his images and confirmed the man as Kocho Trajchevski, the Secretary of State for the Colonies. He hadn't even heard of the man before, let alone the title.

Another civilian department created in the middle of a damn war.

The man brought up images of the Byotai border that appeared alongside him.

"Our ambassador on the Byotai homeworld confirmed

they have redeployed their forces to protect their trade routes. The Anicinàbe are no great friends of theirs, but it is this group of raiders and pirates known roughly as the Red Scars to us that are causing most of the trouble. The Byotai pushed them back across their border, but that has created an even bigger problem."

He moved a set of stars maps and schematics to the tactical display. The imagery was also duplicated automatically onto the screens in the command center around Admiral Anderson. One in particular appeared over a mining world. The Admiral was forced to lift his hand to the side of his face for a moment, to hide the expression showing that he found impossible to mask. The sheer anger he felt right now was rising, and he knew that every minute spent talking probably meant another ten dead marines.

"...this is Karnak, one of the disputed Anicinàbe worlds. The Byotai chased the Red Scars here and assaulted their base of operations. The Byotai took it with heavy losses and are refusing to cede it to the Anicinàbe, not until they receive certain security guarantees."

Admiral Anderson listened carefully, but at the same time brought up details of this new department on a secondary display. He had been given de facto military and civilian jurisdiction out in the Orion Nebula, and this new department sent a chill up through his body. He operated through the military chain of command, and that meant he answered directly to the civilian government though the Secretary of Defense. General Rivers might be the highest-ranking man in the military, but it was his job to advise the President and the Secretary of Defense, and technically lacked any authority over combatant forces.

So, it is a new department created by the Alliance Senate to deal with Colonial Affairs outside of the core Alliance territories. And why I am not surprised that Hyperion and Hades come under this jurisdiction?

He began to shake his head in annoyance, and then lifted his hand to stop the man speaking. As expected, the sound continued for several seconds before the delay was accounted for, and the man stopped.

"I am unfamiliar with the Secretary of State for the Colonies, President. I have heard most of this information already, though. Intelligence Director Johnson has provided detailed and very thorough reports from all fronts over the last weeks."

Again there was the long and thoroughly annoying pause. This time it was the President's turn to speak.

"Admiral, I appreciate the confusion. My cabinet has been reshuffled in the last few days. A full briefing has already been scheduled for all civilian and military departments of the Alliance. It is clear that a cohesive civilian structure needs to exist both here in Alpha Centauri as well as in the colonies."

He seemed uncomfortable at the last part.

"That is why I have put forward the proposal under Clause 72 of the Alliance constitution. It has been voted on, and I have been given a three-month emergency term as the first Magister Populi. My brief is simple, specifically 'rei gerundae causa'."

Admiral Anderson sighed as he heard this.

It's nothing more than a three-month term dictator. It gives him legal immunity and the ability to issue any and all decrees, and military actions for that period.

The President was still speaking and now moving to the end of some grandiose part about the war effort.

"...We are reshaping the internal organization of the Alliance to better fit the challenges of the Biomechs and our alien partners. Until territories are self-sufficient, they will be managed by this new department, in partnership with the military, of course."

He paused, and Admiral Anderson knew that it was time for the real speech, the one that even the President, the elected leader of the entire Alliance, seemed nervous about broaching.

"Our military forces are scattered and vulnerable. Admiral, I cannot give you authorization to start Operation Citadel. I have consulted with General Rivers on our current situation as well as my own staff, and there is little agreement on a way forward."

Again there was that pause.

"That is why I have decided to take full control of this

situation. From today, all strategic decisions will be taken through High Command, here on Terra Nova. It is time for central control and leadership of this shambles of a campaign."

As he spoke, he seemed to increase in confidence, as though saying the words themselves made him feel stronger and more significant.

"It is my intention to use this opportunity to pull back to our borders, to entrench and prepare for the real battle. The forces for this operation would be much better served where they are, not on some fanciful suicide mission. With this hammer, I will force the issue with the enemy. There must be some common ground. A way to avoid an all out war between us."

Anderson shook his head in frustration as the words tumbled from the President's mouth. His entire command staff was there, each helping to manage and conduct the war effort, and now this man wanted him to do it with one hand tied behind his back.

When is the man going to grow some balls?

After what seemed an age, he finally hit the mute button and lifted his hand.

"President Harrison. Operation Citadel is poised to enter the Rift. Even as I speak, the fleet is ready. Hundreds of ships, tens of thousands of warriors, and even ANS Discovery; her paint is still not completely dry. They are ready to do what needs to be done. Spascia and Helios

Prime are a priority, as are the lives of our armed forces."

The icon representing the unarmed ship stood out more than any other around the Naval station, right on the edge of T'Kari space. Data alongside it confirmed its size of more than a kilometer long. She was the sister ship of ANS Beagle, the vessel that had constructed the reverse Rift in T'Karan to link back to Prometheus.

"We cannot simply cancel the operation, not because the situation has deteriorated more quickly than expected. If we do not act, we will lose thousands of men and women on Helios Prime, Spascia, and Eos. Half of our fleet is currently in the Helios System, Sir."

He lifted his eyes and watched as the small cadre of senior officers updated the details on the multiple frontlines. The look of the place was reminiscent of the planning rooms and control centers used back in the twentieth century to conduct battles and air interception. The vertical panels showed everything from the invasion of Helios Prime to the ongoing siege of Spascia. General Rivers walked into the room, and all of those military personnel actually physically present saluted. It was a quick, efficient mark of respect; one that he ignored. He walked past the more junior officers and stopped alongside Admiral Anderson.

"Admiral, what's the problem?"

He tone was curt, but not specifically directed toward the other officer. Admiral Anderson changed the General's center of attention simply by moving his eyes to the side and toward the holographic images of the civilians. He noticed the pale, scrawny shape of President Harrison, as well as his new Defense Secretary.

"President Harrison, Defense Secretary. We have a major situation here."

He glanced briefly at Anderson who gave him a barely discernible nod to continue. Though few words had been said, there was clearly something of a conflict of interests between the Defense Secretary and General Rivers. Admiral Anderson couldn't but fail to notice how the General had ignored the other senior members of the President's team.

Ever the statesman, he thought, a smile almost forming on his face.

"Gentlemen, we have a window of minutes, perhaps only seconds. Helios Prime is about to lose control of its weapon system, and with it will be our ability to send in help. Either we go through now, or we leave Helios and the other races to their fate."

He leaned in a little closer.

"We have a commitment to them and our people. One that will not be forgotten if we betray their trust."

There was the usual lag with the encoded Rift-to-Rift laser communication used between capital ships, stations, and planetary installations. As he waited, the General looked to his old friend.

"Admiral, we're in serious trouble here. The report

from Admiral Lewis is much worse than I expected. Even if we go through right now, I don't know if we'll be able to help Lewis and his forces."

Anderson nodded in agreement.

"I know. The fleet is ready, but now we have this…this fool of a dictator."

The image of the President flickered and instantly betrayed the visual presence device as something wholly artificial. It was strange how something so small could completely transform a person's attitude. Yet as Admiral Anderson watched the image of the President, he found the man's ability to command faded along with the quality of the transmission.

"I'm sorry, Gentlemen, but after receiving the news from Helios Prime and the Anicinàbe, it is clear the Helions and our allies are incapable of offering effective resistance. We must withdrawal and entrench."

He beckoned toward the Defense Secretary to continue.

"The Senate voted on this very issue and has made its decision. The results were unanimous. Each of our colonial senators has determined that the fleet, and our marines must be ready to defend our interests, not aliens' interests, and that we must ensure Prometheus and the key worlds back here are protected. T'Karan is to be the buffer zone. That's why we're sending additional reserves. The only way this can be done is with a clear, simple strategy. For too long the borders of our Alliance have been unruly, lacking focus."

General Rivers shook his head in irritation. He could see Admiral Anderson was no less impressed than himself. The Defense Secretary continued.

"We must do what we can to protect our own border. That is what the people want, and that is what they pay us for. The Helions are our friends, but this war is one they began millennia ago. It is not our business. Open the Helios Prime Rift, and bring our ships home. If necessary, we will shut down the Rift to Helios until this situation is resolved."

General Rivers ignored the message, as he continued to speak and instead looked at Admiral Anderson.

"What about our troops? It will take months to get them all back, if at all. Five hours ago this operation was a go. Now there is a discussion on Terra Nova and everything changes. We do not need a dictator. We already have a clear mission."

His emphasis on the word discussion couldn't have been any clearer.

"Admiral, it is not the decision that was the problem. It was the question. You know how these votes go. Have you even seen the proposal they put forward?"

He held up his secpad so that only the two of them could see the content. The Defense Secretary was still talking, and both men glanced at his image as though paying active attention to what he had to say. The report from the Senate was long and complex, but the summary was easy enough, and the effect of the General's face was near instantaneous.

"As I said, it was the question. The Defense Secretary simply put the idea across that alien interference was putting our forces in harm's way. While we fight on alien soil, it is our troops that are dying, and at the same time we're facing the enmity of the Biomechs. He put forward a measure stating clearly that our war effort is to be used to defend our interests, not those of others, and the best way to do this was with a single civilian figure to coordinate our strategy."

General Rivers shook his head slowly.

"It would make sense if the strategy was to win this war. This will cost us lives, allies, and territory. The Biomechs couldn't have planned a better strategy for us. Why now? What's changed?"

Anderson raised an eyebrow and indicated toward the Defense Secretary.

"There's something going on between those two. Maybe it's a power play, or some secret deal, but I do know that the Vice President and the Defense Secretary met before the Senate was called into session, right after news of the assault on Helios Prime arrived."

"A coup. So this is just a power grab, right in the middle of a war? Just because they think the end is coming. So is the President in charge here, or is it those two?"

He looked to the ground and muttered under his breath.

"The selfish, power grabbing bastards."

Neither said anything for almost four seconds. The delay might have gone on longer if Admiral Anderson hadn't noticed the Defense Secretary had finished his speech. He looked at both of the civilians, and for the first time the obvious tension in the President.

He knows something is up. He's being pushed into something he knows is wrong.

"President Harrison. I understand your concerns, but in times of war you have the authority to conduct operations for sixty days without senatorial approval. It is not the job of the body politic to dictate military strategy, especially in times of war. You do understand that the Biomechs are not looking to punish just the Helions? There is a reason they were behind our own civil war."

General Rivers had composed himself and joined in right after the Admiral finished.

"They have the technology and location information for this place. With or without this Rift, they will be coming for us. Either we defeat them on Helion soil, on their worlds and with their forces to help. Or we fight the war on our own worlds. Either way, winning this war is down to us. If you bring back half of our people now, you will be stabbing the dead in the back."

Once more Admiral Anderson tapped the end of transmission button so they would know he'd finished speaking for the time being. It was an odd procedure, reminiscent of ancient radio communications on Earth. As they waited for the reply from Terra Nova, he looked back the General. He started to speak and then spotted the changing red patterns showing on one of the vertical boards. It was the representation of air and ground forces beginning the last stage of the campaign against that world. The Secretary of Defense looked flushed at this rebuke of the strategy, and his face tightened slightly.

"The military operates under the control of the civilian government, and that means all tactical command, including yours in T'Karan and Admiral Lewis in Helios, answer directly to me."

He then pointed at the General.

"General Rivers, as Chairman of the Joint Chiefs you advise myself and the President. As you know, you are not granted with the authority to command combatants."

"Really?" the General spat back, even though the time sync would be completely off for any kind of conversation and response. He then looked to Admiral Anderson, his face positively dripping with venom.

"This man, he is a complete and utter moron. We need continuity in times of war, not a strategy that changes with every new face. Even in the Uprising, we at least had clear plans and goals. What the hell is going on here?"

The President looked at them both with bitterness on his face. He shook his head slowly as he spoke.

"I suspected you would refuse to accept my lawful authority, Admiral Anderson, even after I have been granted a lawful term of three months to end this crisis. My first task in this role will be the complete reorganization of the outer colonies. I have created the new Office for Colonial Affairs, under the control of Kocho Trajchevski. He will be dispatching governors to each of the new regions, all of them to be administered by the Office for Colonial Affairs, here on Terra Nova."

He motioned with his hands as they effectively encompassed the entire area of space around him, and then motioned for the man to speak. Kocho Trajchevski had an air of importance about him, as though he'd been in this position of authority for months or even years.

"My jurisdiction includes Epsilon Eridani, Gliese 876, Procyon, Sol, and, of course, T'Karan."

Admiral Lewis' face twitched at the mention of T'Karan. He looked at General Rivers who continued to listen, stoic and impassive to the end. Anderson spoke quietly and away from the sight of the civilian.

"This Kocho Trajchevski has just made himself commander of six entire star systems. Are you telling me the citizens of the Alliance granted the President the post of first Magister Populi so that he could create a personal fiefdom for this man?"

He looked back at the virtual presence and the continuing speech from Kocho Trajchevski.

"Naval and Marine Corps commands in these outer territories have been amalgamated in this new structure and will be commanded by civilian regional governors. Only Terra Nova, with its cadre of reliable, dutiful citizens can provide the leadership we need. The Governor of T'Karan is en route and will be coming through the Prometheus Rift within twenty-four hours. You will answer directly to him upon his installation on the Admiral Jarvis Naval Station."

Admiral Anderson looked at the tactical screens to his right and the urgent indicators coming from ships around the Helion homeworld. A series of news and urgent reports had just arrived from Admiral Lewis. It wasn't particularly different to the last one, but it did report that two Crusader ships had been lost in low-level combat. The ships had been crippled and then crashed into what remained of the city.

"Helios Prime is almost gone, and with it goes the rest of the system."

He spoke quietly, almost too quietly even for the General. Then he stopped and moved his eyes to look at the seasoned commander. There was more than concern showing now; there was a palpable look of resolve about him.

"We have to act, General. If others are unwilling, then we must act alone. As the senior military commanders out here, we have a duty, no, we have a responsibility to see that this is done."

He considered his next words carefully.

"If it comes to it, will they follow you, like before?"

General Rivers smiled in reply.

"Admiral. The entire Marine Corps exist to protect the Alliance. We have thousands of marines trapped out there. You'll be hard pressed to find a single man or woman that would refuse to help their comrades. In the Corps, we don't leave marines behind. What are you asking of me, Admiral?"

He knew what was being asked, but he needed to hear the words. The President and his staff looked on, with the Defense Secretary in particular arguing profusely with one of his colleagues. The return audio was still muted, but neither of the senior commanders let their faces be seen as they spoke.

"I want you to help me prosecute Operation Citadel. Once we're through the Rift, we will fight this until the war is over. We will need a cohesive strategy, out of their control."

He nodded in the direction of the virtual presence.

"This is treason, my friend, you do know that?"

Admiral Anderson nodded slowly in reply.

"General, the acts of this government are treasonous. They will see everything we've built destroyed and our people left out there to burn. These outer worlds are not playthings for the President's civilian buddies. This is war and we need to win."

His words were tantamount to treason as well, but he saw nothing but agreement in the eyes of his old comrade. He then turned back to the holographic representation of the President that was still effectively on hold as they waited for their reply. General Rivers had to do no more than give him the nod for him to proceed, which he did without hesitation. Both turned back to the virtual presence devices and activated the return audio mode.

"President Harrison, Defense Secretary. Under the Uniform Code of Military Justice, I am refusing your command. Your orders are unlawful under the Constitution of the Alliance. You are willingly allowing citizens to be slaughtered in the name of expediency; something that even an authorized term of dictatorship cannot allow. This attempt to usurp the chain of command in T'Karan and our other outer colonies betrays the constitution itself. You were granted a term to help prosecute a war, to ensure victory and minimal losses, not to exploit our people for your own personal gain."

He swallowed. The next part he knew would be his moment, the time he drew his line in the sand, a line that he could never retrace. He'd spent years in the military, had fought with honor both for the Confederacy and now the Alliance. Turning against the system he'd defended was far from easy. He spent a number of seconds composing himself, and that gave the President time to reply, something he'd intended on disallowing.

"Admiral Anderson. You are hereby relieved of your command. General Rivers, you will take over provisional control of the station until the Governor arrives. You will then return to Terra Nova for...debriefing."

General Rivers looked to Admiral Anderson with a single raised eyebrow. The Admiral's expression had already changed though, and it was one the General hadn't seen in a very long time.

"Until I receive lawful orders from an authority recognized by law, I will be launching Operation Citadel immediately. In less than an hour, we will have forces over Helios Prime, and we will succeed. We will assist our forces and arrangements with our allies, as agreed by the Senate."

He paused and then reached out to touch the slider on the side of the unit. The image of the President vanished in mid-sentence, even as the man had started to reply to the previous message sent by the two officers. The others officers in the room fell silent, waiting and wondering what was happening. Most continued their operation management, but at least three looked to Admiral Anderson for guidance. He looked at them and tried to smile.

"It is time for leadership and hard decisions. I am sending command clearance directly to Admiral Churchill at Prometheus. He is already waiting there for this order."

General Rivers was a little surprised at the forward

planning on display here. Admiral Anderson checked the General's face one last time and then turned to his command team.

"We have just received illegal orders to order our ships back and to abandon Helios and our people. There are over a hundred thousand Alliance men and women on the other side of that Rift. The planetary defense system is almost gone, and when that happens, our forces will be on their own."

He wiped his brow and found his forehead completely dry. Even so, his hand shook like never before.

"Until such time as Terra Nova regains our trust, we will be cutting off our ties with them."

He looked to his communication's officer and gave a quick nod.

"Even now, Admiral Churchill is fortifying Prometheus against any threat, foreign or domestic. Nobody can get through to T'Karan without bypassing Prometheus first, and his forces will not let that happen. The chain of command has been broken, and until such time as it is reestablished, General Rivers will be our Alliance representative."

There was a cool, hard feeling in the large command room. With little time for emotion, most of them had been busy carrying out their jobs. Now they were being told that for the foreseeable future they would be unable to return home. One man, a short science officer lifted his hand.

"Admiral. This is treason, isn't it?"

Anderson knew that by ignoring the President he was in serious trouble. The crime of treason was still a capital offense.

"No, son, it isn't. We are under no obligation to carry out an illegal order, and I suspect our own government has other reasons for this withdrawal. While we are out here fighting this war, they are playing politics with all of our lives. When were you asked to vote on President Harrison being made dictator?"

He looked to General Rivers who raised an eyebrow at his question. It was a good point though. The vote had been news to him, and he suspected none of the military personnel posted outside of the core planets had been given the opportunity to vote, a requirement for any kind of change in the constitution.

He's right. There are few orders more illegal than the ones coming from Terra Nova.

There was no respect for the post when it turned on its own people in the middle of a crisis, and even less for the Senate that had given the approval for such measures. Admiral Anderson spotted the look of resignation and agreement on his face and tried to imagine what the future would bring when the war was over, assuming it ever ended.

There is going to be one hell of a reckoning. That's for tomorrow, though.

He noticed General Rivers was smiling, an event that was quite unusual. It was the first genuine smile the man had experienced in days, perhaps even weeks. Admiral Anderson turned and headed for the door. General Rivers went with him.

"Is that what you came for?" he asked.

The General looked to his old friend.

"I expected nothing less. I take it you're coming on this operation?"

Admiral Anderson finished the authorization procedures and then sent his prearranged communiqué directly to Prometheus. General Rivers raised an eyebrow in amusement at the fact that it was already written and ready to go. As soon as it was marked as sent, the Admiral took a step away from the room. He then stopped and looked back at his staff. The base commander, a young female officer with dull red hair approached him.

"I have your orders, Admiral. We will maintain patrols and build up the reserves."

"Good work, Captain. Expect contact from Admiral Churchill within the hour."

He nodded to the General, and both men headed for the door.

"I'm looking forward to seeing my new ship," said Admiral Anderson as they walked through the doorway and out into the bright passageway.

"What's she like?"

It was an unnecessary question because he'd been actively involved in the design and construction phase. There wasn't a ship in the Alliance inventory that he wasn't intimately familiar with. Even so, unlike the General, he'd so far spent no time on the completed ship since she'd entered service, and like all great ships, they earned their reputation through their actions and experiences, not their designs.

"She's big, very big," was all General Rivers had to say on the subject.

Admiral Anderson smiled to himself at that. There were many words to describe the monstrous flagship of the Alliance, but big was perhaps the fairest. He nodded in agreement.

"I can't argue with that, General."

CHAPTER ELEVEN

The press of Proxima Prime and Kerberos made a great deal of noise during the first years of the Emergency as it was then known. Before the Uprising began there were many attacks on Confederate installations, facilities and convoys. It was then that the press came down hard on the machines and equipment being used to combat the terrorists. As this fighting changed into an insurgency, so did the tactics. Roadside bombs and improvised devices were used to smash through the hulls of vehicles and heavy cover and defensive positions for ambushes. Early models of the Bulldog armored fighting vehicle were designed and put into production as a direct counter to this problem. Even the L48 rifle came under scrutiny, but its powerful ammunition and ability to hit targets behind cover guaranteed its future for many years to come.

Reports of the Proxima Emergency

ANS New Carlos, Old Spascia City

The ship lurched hard to port as seven missiles exploded along her flank. Even as the stabilizers kicked in, a great volley of gunfire reach up from the ground and smashed into the belly of the warship. Holes ripped open the outer plating, wrenching the lower three decks apart and exposing them in more than a dozen separate places. The ship twisted about, and three more missiles screamed overhead and exploded impotently. Two Biorays swept down to rake the Old City, but another Liberty destroyer moved into their path and fired a full broadside into the nearest before they collided. The shattered remnants of both dropped out of the sky and down to the ruins below.

"Report!" Commodore Hampel called out.

Thick blood ran down his forehead while he held a bandage on the wound. The pain had faded and been replaced by a dull throbbing feeling that almost put him to sleep.

"Multiple breaches, two turrets offline. We can't leave this place, Sir. Not now."

The ship moved into a spiral and then leveled off above a Bioray that was busy racing to the ground to offload a large number of ground troops. Return fire from the ship clattered against the damaged plating of ANS New Carlos, but it wasn't enough to stop the pursuit.

"In range, fire!" said the XO.

In her dual role as both XO and tactical officer, she selected the confirmed weakness of the enemy ship and sent the command confirmation. All remaining gun turrets, both on the frontal section and in the weapon modules, tracked about and took aim. One by one, the quad cannons blasted small holes across the top of the ship before striking its cargo area. The ship still managed to limp down, but Lieutenant Morgan continued firing on the vessels, bringing a rain of superheated metal down upon the occupants of the craft. As its doors slip open, just a handful of warriors staggered out.

"Good work," said Commodore Hampel.

As he spoke, he felt the pain returning to his forehead. The ship shuddered again, and this time it sounded as if every single alert and warning went off at the same time.

"Cephalon command ship on our stern!" Lieutenant Morgan stated.

She didn't wait and issued orders directly to the helmsman, who plotted a bizarre series of twists and turns. This far down on Spascia the Liberty class destroyers had a major advantage in terms of speed and maneuverability, as the Cephalon command ships were almost impossible for a Liberty class ship to bring down.

"Our only chance with that thing is to get down low and fast."

The helmsman exhibited great skill in bringing the ship down to almost three hundred meters above the city ruins. At this height, only the most experienced, and slightly deranged officer could hope to pilot such a vast warship.

Streaks from the Cephalon's few kinetic turrets rushed past and crashed into the buildings below them. Each blast vaporized building after building, killing Alliance troops, NHA soldiers, and Biomech ground forces indiscriminately.

"Great flying, keep it up," said the Commodore.

The swerving about wasn't helping his head, but it did give him an opportunity to assess the battle. The holographic display showed the fleets from both sides engaging in a bloody battle, yet from what he could see the Three Sisters and the two bridges were still under Alliance control.

We've got a chance, not much, but a chance.

He'd sacrificed what was left of the fleet on the burned world of Spascia. The best they could hope for was to continue the siege. With no Alliance fleet left to break the blockade, he'd now forced the planet to succumb to a mind-numbing siege. He just hoped that in the long run they could win it.

"Watch out!" called out an unseen officer.

A powerful double blast from the Cephalon managed to strike just above the engines. The energy from the weapon was incredible and embedded its projectiles a third the way inside the superstructure before detonating one of anti-ship mission modules. The explosions started off small and then rippled through the lower section of the ship. The mood in the CIC transformed in a matter of seconds, as the ship itself turned from being damaged to being no more than a lump of inert material plummeting to the ground.

"We're losing power. Stabilizers are gone. Engines failing. Commodore, she's dead in the air."

Commodore Hampel looked to the hybrid main display and tactical projection unit, but it was already flickering and missing key data on the battle. He could see both sides were still taking a heavy punishment in the battle, but they were going down, and from what he could see, they were be coming down less than a kilometer from the Alliance frontline.

We did our part. We can do no more.

The display flickered again, and then two-thirds vanished from view. Half of the lights shut off, and only a handful of emergency lights returned.

He tried to stand, but the straps held him in place, something he'd already forgotten about. He grabbed for them but his arm went limp. His eyesight began to fade, but his hearing seemed fine. He could hear the shouting from officers and the booming sounds of gunfire raking the sturdy little ship.

"Commodore!" cried out the XO.

Even above the din of battle, he knew her voice. She remained calm yet assertive. She continued to issue orders to the men and women aboard the ship even as they continued on their unstoppable destiny with the ground.

"Brace, brace, brace!"

* * *

Jack pulled himself down as low as he could along the eastern tower. Every few seconds another heavy shell would drop down around their position, and each time it was followed by a cloud of dust and the screams of wounded soldiers. He could already hear the next one, the dull howl of a subsonic high-explosive shell falling down lazily into the defensive cordon that was now the only piece of land still held east of the chasm.

When is this going to end?

Every barrage that struck around them shook his bones. He was sure his internal organs shuddered each time the ground trembled. The walls had been smashed and battered in a hundred places, but even after all this gunfire the towers of the Three Sisters remained. The forty-meter tall, sixteen-sided monstrosities were completely out of place in a normal city, yet alone a place like Old Spascia. They were now the only buildings still intact. Every single structure around them stood no taller than two stories, and all heavily damaged or even partially collapsed. A howl from some unspeakable monster off to the east was quickly silenced by a salvo from the roof-mounted weapons. The four twin 128mm railguns shook the ground as they fired; bright arcs of burning dust marked the paths of the shells.

"Look," whispered Jana.

The shape of more than ten Eques walkers could be made out far off in the distance. They moved through the rubble, their gun turrets blasting away at anything they could find. They had already moved past the outer walls that had long been breached and made use of the broken walls and pillboxes as shields from the guns of the marines.

"Drones!" called out an unseen marine.

The gentle clatter of small arms fire hammered around the broken defenses. Jack looked up and considered returning fire, but he recalled what had happened three hours earlier when three of the machines landed near the northern wall. A squad of Helion volunteers had rushed out, only to be shot down by the drones' internal weaponry. He began to inch back as another marine from fifteen meters away did just that.

"Jack!" Jana cried out.

Jack ducked down behind a broken down SAAR robot, just as a burst of fire hit near him. Jana pulled at him and helped him get further back, but more rounds struck. One bounced off his left joint and embedded into the SAAR robot. Unable to hit him, the machine twisted about and opened fire on the other marine. It put a dozen rounds through the poor warrior's visor, killing him instantly.

"Animals," he muttered under his breath.

Jana looked down and slid open the lip of the weapons stowage bin. Inside was a pair of the Khreenk short-ranged surface-to-air missile systems. They were simple units, each one no bigger than an L48 rifle and fitted with a pair of short-range missiles. She lifted out the first and nodded to Jack.

"Bring it down."

Jack placed the unit on his shoulder and tapped the activation toggle. Normally, it would connect to a Khreenk warrior's armor, but he was forced to use it manually. The flip-up sight projected a small red circle over the drone and flashed to show a target lock. Other details also appeared, but none of them made any sense to him.

"Do it, Jack, come on!"

The machine must have spotted him because it opened fired once more. The small arms fire struck around the barricade. One of the SAAR robots rotated its turret and engaged the aerial vehicle with its own weapons. In seconds, the small machine was falling from the sky, trailing smoke. The robotic warrior was replaced by a cloud of dark shapes that materialized as hundreds of the butchered semi-human warriors leapt in. With the outer wall gone, it fell to the central defenses along the lower levels of the ground to provide the backbone. This was all that remained of the substantial earthworks and pillboxes constructed by the Alliance engineers. The defenders had dug more trench works and pushed debris and metalwork ahead to create a series of tall barricades that joined the towers into a triangular fortress.

"It's time!" said Corporal Frewyn.

He lifted himself to his feet and moved up to the barricade. There were small slits that they could see through without having to expose themselves to fire. Jack was next and groaned as his left leg refused to function properly. The joints on the PDS Alpha armor had been causing trouble for hours now, and without some maintenance it was only going to get worse. A series of low-velocity shells struck the barricades and blew holes into the frontal sections. A single breach was created twenty meters from where they waited.

"Here they come!" said the Corporal.

Jack and Jana were alongside him, along with the rookies, Privates Jon Yule, Simon Hardman and James Rozoff. A few days before they had been total strangers with an almost insignificant level of experience or ability to offer. Now they were veterans with more experience than most marines had in an entire career. Private Rozoff moved his Helion thermal rifle about and put two rounds at point blank distance into a pair of Thegns. The weapon punched deep holes through their bodies, and then he ducked back down.

"Yeah, that's how you do it," laughed Private Yule.

The enemy was everywhere, with most moving in small infiltration groups about the eastern side of the fortification. The largest group swarmed around the Eques walkers and made for the center of the defenses, a point equidistant between the three towers. Further along the barricade, another trio of Khreenk took up station and next to them a SAAR robot. To their left an entire marine squad, led by the newly promoted Lieutenant Cemgil Kurt ran toward the breach and spread out around the rubble. Corporal Frewyn pointed to an area in front, and the marines spread out to form a firing line.

"Kneel!"

It was barely necessary, as their training had already kicked in. Every marine knew that if they were still for more than a fraction of a second, they would drop to one knee. A little longer, and they would go lower, and longer still they would start scraping material for cover.

"Aim."

Each lifted their weapons to their shoulders and took careful aim. Jack watched a trio of Thegns scouting ahead of a Decurion. They moved behind a jagged piece of equipment and vanished from view for a moment. He continued tracking to the right, assuming correctly that the shapes would reappear. Three more Thegns scuttled ahead.

"Fire!"

Jack was the first to pull the trigger. The rest followed, and the entire barricade lit up with small arms. Most used the reliable L52, but a handful had now moved to weapons taken from fallen NHA and Khreenk warriors.

"They're coming over the top!" Jana yelled.

She swiveled about and aimed right above them. From the ragged top of the barricade came the first of the horrific butchered creations. For every one that made it over the top, another two were cut apart by the myriad of tower guns. Four of them fell down and landed next to Jana. Private Yule didn't hesitate and drove his bayoneted carbine into the chest of the first. The next one smashed Jana's weapon from her hands, and she was forced to pull out her sidearm. The motion was quick, and she put a round into the thing's face before it could reach her.

"Aim low and put them down!" said Corporal Frewyn.

Jana pulled Jack back and struck him on the helmet with the base of her pistol. There was nothing at first, so she struck him again, and this time he looked at her. His expression was confused and lost.

"Get yourself together. We're in trouble."

More Thegns appeared on the right this time. She put a hand on Jack's carbine and pushed him about to face them.

"Shoot them, now!"

Jack muttered something and then pulled the trigger. He didn't bother taking much aim and emptied the entire magazine. Luckily, his wild shooting coincided with dozens of the enemy surging through. The bullets struck four in quick succession.

"Drop the mag, reload," he said in a near robotic tone.

The magazine slid and dropped into the dirt. He didn't

need to look and easily pulled out another and slammed it into the base. Jana fired a burst and then glanced over to him, making sure he was okay. This time he fired in short, accurate bursts, and each one hit an enemy soldier as they rushed about inside the compound. Fear had vanished, as had any other semblance of emotion. He simply loaded, aimed, and fired; motion drilled into every marine over months of training. The flashes of the explosions barely registered to him, not even the three bullet wounds he sustained in the hip.

"The base is breached. Remember General Gun's orders. Not one step back!" Corporal Frewyn called out.

Yet another Eques walker pushed through a section of the defenses thirty meters away, and its turrets rotated to blast up to the towers. A series of small flashes marked where the gunfire struck. Jack aimed at the machine, but then he heard movement. He twisted about and took aim, expecting to see a Thegn with its weapons pointing right at him. But he was looking into the eyes of the haggard young female Helion. She led a group of five teenagers, each wearing a quilted jacket and carrying one of those assault lances tipped with explosive. Another pair followed, both of them buckling under the weight of a heavy metal tripod and a Marine Corps issue L56 Mark III support machine gun.

"Biomech!" said the Helion.

She turned and pointed to the machine. The pair of

civilians dropped their tripod and began connecting the two ammunition bins to its feed. A blast of blue energy vaporized the first, but the second readied the weapon and turned it on the massive machine.

"Get down, you idiots!" Jana shouted.

Jack turned back to the fighting and continued shooting at any targets that moved into his sight. The female Helion looked at him with a confused expression, stunned at his coolness under fire. At the same time, a blast from one of the massive Eques walkers crashed down amongst the group, instantly killing two and injuring another. As the teenager screamed out in pain, the others ran at it with their weapons.

"Stand your ground!" Jack said in a stoic, emotionless tone.

They ignored him, either deliberately or because they had no idea what he was saying. In all the violence and carnage, he often forgot that it wasn't just marines fighting here. With Helions, Khreenk, and humans there was a bewildering array of language and dialects. As Jack kept shooting, he felt warmth returning to his body. He took a step to his left to get a better view, but again his leg slowed him down. He assumed it was the armor, not for one minute realizing that his armor had been breached and his leg torn by the bullets. Even so, he began to see what was happening.

It's a wonder anybody knows what the hell is going on here. We're overrun.

More of the Helion civilians ran out from their hiding places and attacked the machines with a bloodthirsty ferocity. A handful carried thermal weapons, but most were stuck with the improvised mining weapons.

Brave, but bravery won't keep you alive, he thought.

The group mixed with those already there and then ran into the marines that were still fighting, and managing to knock one of them over. Another Helion jumped ahead and stabbed at the machine, only for the explosive to fail to detonate. A Thegn shot the Helion down and moved on to the next, the warrior operating with calm and efficiency in a similar fashion to Jack. The next Helion in line lowered the lance and charged. This time the device exploded on impact and took the Thegn and the Helion with it in a yellow flash. It even managed to partially damage the nearest Eques walker's leg. Jack swallowed, the feeling of lack of control beginning to return.

Keep in the fight. You can do this.

Again he reached down for a magazine and found nothing. He looked to Jana, but she was too far away and busily helping to patch up two fallen marines. He looked to his left and found nothing but bodies and fighting. The tripod-mounted L56 sat impotently, both of its Helion crew now dead. Another Helion vanished in a bright blast, and he stumbled. The horror of the exploding Helions should have stunned him, but for now he felt numbed to the horror.

"Jack? Jack?" Jana was calling.

She lifted herself up and moved to him. He turned to her, but his face was blank, perhaps stunned at what he'd seen. She grabbed his arm, but he pushed her away and hobbled over to the knocked over tripod. Behind him, the surviving Helions threw themselves into the swarm of enemy troops. It was a futile gesture, and for every enemy they killed, they lost two or three of their own. Explosions and flashes engulfed the area, and they were quickly shrouded in a mixture of dust and debris. More gunfire from the towers ripped into the moving shapes, the projectiles striking friend and foe alike until there were no more siege lines, just individuals fighting to the death.

Even as the Biomechs streamed through the breaches, the smaller guns of the nearest tower opened up with quad-mounted auto cannons. The combined firepower turned the ground into a bloodbath, yet still they came. Two Eques walkers were felled, but the following seven moved closer and closer. Gunfire flashed off their thick armor plating, and Thegn foot soldiers swarmed around their legs, taking careful aims at any defenders daring to raise their heads.

"The breach!" Lieutenant Cemgil Kurt cried.

The officer looked no different to the other marines, apart from the subtle stripe he'd added at some point in the last day. He pulled himself up, waved to his marines, and then rushed at the breach. He vanished into the maelstrom with his marines alongside, their bayonets fixed. Even as they vanished from view, a pair staggered back and then collapsed. More flashes of gunfire, and then two Eques walkers pushed through the gap and into the compound. Jack dropped to his knee and pulled the L56 machine gun from its mount. It was heavy, and he was barely able to move the thing. He turned about and lowered the unit onto a chunk of rubble. Five more Thegns rushed toward the marines. That was when he pulled the trigger. The five barrels poured round after round into the enemy, shredding the wall of flesh in seconds. Corporal Frewyn saw his chance as Jack continued to put down a heavy barrage of covering fire.

"Let's go!"

He stood up from his position at the barricade and moved in to flank the machine. Jana took aim at its torso and fired a high-power shot. The blast ripped a small hole into the plating but had no discernible effect on its operation. The others joined in, firing a mixture of shots, but nothing seemed to slow it down.

"Jack, Jana to the left, the rest of you with me," said Corporal Frewyn.

They clambered over the rubble and did their best to ignore the streak of gunfire all about them. A fireteam from another platoon fell back from their defensive position just as a massive explosive charge tore it to pieces. The wounded marines staggered about, each badly hurt from the blast. One screamed across the open communications channel as his armor burned from a molten stream of thermite. Jack aimed at the poor soul's helmet and pulled the trigger. It was a mercy killing, and right now he felt nothing but a burning inside of him that made him want to kill.

"Jack, there's more of them," cried Jana.

Jack turned to aim and spotted what must have been at least a hundred Thegns, with a similar number of monstrous creatures moving with them. Sergeant Stone appeared at the corner of the tower right at the base, and with a pair of marines flanking him. Both carried the L56 Mk III machine guns in improvised thigh mounts. He pointed at the horde and shouted something. Both marines poured a withering hail of ammunition at them. The Sergeant then look back and gave a hand signal.

"What's happening?" Private Hardman asked.

Private Rozoff shook his head as he kept shooting.

"No idea, man, no idea."

Jack could almost smell the fear coming from the two men, yet neither balked at their situation and continued shooting. Jana spotted the shapes first, and for a brief moment, Jack almost turned his gun on them. They were larger than marines, much larger and closer in build to the warriors of Gun's own people. One after the other the heavy robotic suits stomped passed them.

"Vanguards," said Jack, almost in awe at the sight of them.

There had been a time when the Vanguards were to become the standard trooper for the Corps, but the cutbacks after the Uprising meant they were never more than the heavy assault element, always vying for position with the Jötnar. Jack looked at them as the six heavily armed marines ran directly into the path of the horde. They stopped fifteen meters from them and then locked their legs. Each lowered its center of gravity and then aimed with both arms. Jack counted four L48 rifles fitted to them, each fed by motorized ammunition hoppers.

"Kill the bastards!" Private Hardman yelled.

The large caliber rounds exploded on impact, and in seconds the ground before them became a pool of shattered flesh and bone. Ten, twenty, and then at least thirty of the enemy were dead. But from the ruined bodies came more, and behind them the inevitable Decurion war machines, those fearsome metal monsters that moved with a speed and agility bordering on the impossible.

"Get down!" Sergeant Stone shouted.

Not one of them gave his words a moment's consideration and dropped to the ground as though they expected all hell to break loose. Jack pushed his body down low, expecting a lance of heat at any moment that would melt his armor. Only the Sergeant stayed on his feet, as the massive black monolith appeared overhead.

It could easily have been no more than a black cloud, but the hundreds of white dots flickering along its underside betrayed its true purpose.

"It's the fleet, finally!" Corporal Frewyn said happily.

The first barrage landed short of the machines but still managed to strike two Eques walkers from above. Then more fire came down, this time from two more ships, and then the entire fortification came under a rain of burning fire. Jack watched an entire squad of Thegns falling back, only to be cut into tiny pieces by hundreds of large caliber rounds. Explosive shells landed deep inside their formations while missiles arced down to strike the heavier pieces of equipment.

"Incredible," said Jana.

Jack smiled for the first time in days.

"You can say that again."

The enemy was not beaten, not by a long shot. Even as their formations were torn apart, they moved to find cover or closed with the marines. More Vanguards ran in from the right, along with a formation of three Bulldogs, each filled with marines. The reinforcements spread out amongst the defenders, and the battle began to turn minutes before the site had been overrun. Now the rear walls and barricades had stabilized, and the machines were being pushed back to the shattered eastern walls of the Three Sisters. Jack and the others moved to follow the pursuit, but Sergeant Stone waved them back.

"We aren't moving out of this compound. You stay here, and get ready for the next attack. This ain't over, nowhere near."

He threw a glance at the group, quickly assessing their status and capacity. He had the basic information to hand via his visor, but there was a great difference between cool hard numbers and the reality of the situation.

"Casualties?"

Corporal Frewyn shook his head.

"No, Sergeant, we're okay here."

Sergeant Stone made to move, but the Corporal caught his eye.

"Are we winning, Sergeant?"

The shell came down twenty meters away and directly on top of a broken down Bulldog. The force of the blast smashed a hole inside the vehicle before sending its wheels, small turret, and onboard stores flying away in every direction. The Sergeant flipped over the dark overlay on his visor, but the transparent part stayed exactly where it was. He was taking no chances.

"They hit the last two intact bridges with a Decurion assault. They managed to get a Bioray right over them before the Khreenk put the thing down. They've now put troops and combat robots at both ends. NHA and our marines hold the landing pads on the west bank."

"What about here, Sarge?" Jack asked.

"Son, we're still here. That's all that matters."

He pointed at the small group.

"Every hour we hold this line, is an hour that those bastards are stuck out there. We control access to the mountain, and that means we control the weapon. We need to buy time for General Rivers and the others."

Another pair of shells swept overhead, but this time the ground-based radar controlled interceptor guns were on target. Two missiles rushed up and exploded in the path of the shells. With a flash of light, they were gone, and small pieces of burning material dropped down over the base.

Lieutenant Cemgil Kurt staggered back from the fight with the Eques walkers. He moved to Sergeant Stone and dropped down to one knee. Sergeant Stone grabbed him to stop him from falling.

"Son, are you hurt?"

The officer tried to speak, but no sound came from his equipment. Sergeant Stone activated the visor, and it flipped open to show the man's white face. Every time he tried to speak, a gurgle of blood bubbled from the corner of his mouth. He nodded in the direction of the ground. The Sergeant looked about but could see nothing other than three discarded carbines.

"A weapon?" he asked.

The officer spluttered blood once again. Jana moved closer to check but stopped a meter away. None had noticed, but she had a clear view of the thick piece of metal from a Decurion's limb that must have been blown off. It was half embedded in the man's back and pushed deep into his upper body. Jack looked at her, and she shook her head gently, in a way that was barely discernible to the mortally wounded man.

"Son, take this."

Both turned about and watched Sergeant Stone hand over his personal carbine. It bore the marks of many engagements, as well as the painted pattern of his previous unit, one that not even Jack recognized. The officer took the weapon, pulled the feed handle, and turned back to the fray. He moved after a squad of Thegns that were falling back while shooting.

"Drive them back!" shouted the Sergeant.

The small group of marines moved ahead slowly one step at a time, putting down a weight of fire that made it impossible for a single Thegn to offer much in the way of resistance. Only a single Decurion stood its ground, a dark black model, dripping in blood and missing an arm. It dodged a number of rounds before charging back at them. Somehow the machine managed to reach close enough to strike at the wounded Lieutenant. It stabbed at him, but the man was almost as quick and evaded the strikes. A pair of Vanguards ran from behind a broken bunker and blasted at the thing, tearing off two limbs.

"Die!" yelled the Lieutenant

He threw himself onto its torso. At such a close range,

it found it difficult to strike him, and the two tumbled down into the dirt. His weapon gone, the man resorted to his bayonet and pistol, shooting and stabbing in equal measure until the two rolled to a stop. Jack stepped in and placed his boot on the machine's torso, but it was still, as was the Lieutenant. Blood dripped from a dozen more puncture wounds on his body. It was then that Jack realized the shattered spike in his back was the missing limb from the black armored machine. He reached down and tapped the visor release button. It hissed open to reveal the man's face. Blood covered half of Lieutenant Cemgil Kurt's face, yet his expression was calm, almost happy. Jack pressed the button again, and the visor slid shut. He straightened up and looked to the others.

"He died the way he wanted."

Sergeant Stone shook his head.

"No, Private, no marine dreams of dying with a spike in his back. Dream of victory, and staying alive."

He looked to the wave of marines surging out to the first line of defenses around the Three Sisters. They were already heavily engaged with the enemy troops, and the fighting was again bogging down.

"This battle ain't over. It's not even halfway there. They need our help down there. Follow me!"

CHAPTER TWELVE

Justitium Lyssk was one of the most infamous characters from the days of the Helion Uprising. After the initial revolution, it was he that was granted a full term as Justitium, a role he had been given to help stop the violence. Many believe this was simply the final stage in his rise to power and prominence amongst the Irkerk, Yuulen, and Sh'Dori people. Little concern was given to the Zathee, even though this one group outnumbered the other three combined. Justitium Lyssk's name has since been linked with violence, murder, and reprisals of a kind never seen before in the Helion League. His overthrow sent him and his forces into exile, along with a large band of Khreenk mercenaries.

One hundred famous names from the Centauri Alliance

Planetary 'Doomsday Weapon' Defense Installation, Helios Prime

Zeta Team consisted of just four female marines, the last

survivors of the regimental special weapons unit. They'd trained for technical operations, specifically computer control, hacking, and remote communication, but never had they trained for such a specific and critical mission. Sergeant Maria Harvey stopped and lifted her arm in the classic halt position. The other three immediately froze and dropped to one knee. Two of them carried carbines, but the third held a portable EM pulse unit. It was as big as a child and weighed nearly twenty kilograms.

"What is it, Sarge?" Private Cooper asked.

She placed the pulse unit on the floor for a moment, partially to allow her to reach for her sidearm, but also to give her just a few seconds respite from its weight. As they waited, a pair of Animosh appeared on the level above them.

"Nobody move a muscle," said Sergeant Harvey.

All four waited in silence while the Animosh moved about doing whatever it was they were there for. As each second ticked by, they could see the icons flickering and vanishing as yet more marines died throughout the complex. During the short pause, Sergeant Harvey checked her mapping information and estimated the time until they would reach their objective.

Two more levels to the targeting level. We can do this.

Then the Animosh moved away, and the place was clear, as though it had been abandoned for days.

"Go," she said quietly.

As before, the group moved ahead and onto the gantry moving around the shaft. Try as they might, it proved almost impossible to stay silent. One foot followed another, and after what seemed like an eternity, they were past the next level and continuing on upwards. Sergeant Harvey looked over the edge and down into the pit.

I could drop all our grenades down there. What would that do?

It was tempting, but her orders were simple. Every part of the assault force had a mission, and theirs was the option of last resort. While General Daniels would attempt to knock out the weapon itself, four other teams would attack key components to stop the weapon being used against Alliance forces. Their job was to hit the targeting array, the part of the complex monitoring the targeting matrix, computers, relays, and most important of all, the massive motors required to move the weapon's emitters. This part of the site had much in common with a ground-based observatory but on a grand scale. By damaging or disabling this area, it wouldn't give the Alliance control of the facility. It wouldn't even allow them to fully target anything else. Most importantly, it would mean that the only viable target would remain the Black Rift, the area that the system was specifically constructed for.

* * *

The battle for the heart of the underground facility was

not going well. What should have been a rapid assault had transformed into a violent battle of attrition. More importantly the Alliance forces were up against a terrible deadline. Every minute they delayed in completing their objective meant they were a minute closer to the Biomechs reaching the site. If they failed, the enemy would control the weapon and be able to shut down the T'Karan-Helios Rift. With no ability for reinforcement, there would be no Operation Citadel, and no way to save Helios Prime. General Daniels knew this. But each time he raised his head, an entire fusillade of shots would clatter down around him.

We have to make this work!

A burst of fire off to the right managed to attract the attention of his tormentors, at least long enough for him to take careful aim at the next level above him. Two rounds struck nearby, but he chose to ignore them and pulled the trigger of his carbine. A short burst rattled about those above, and one staggered and stumbled, falling to his death. Then he was back in cover and checking for more enemies. The next one was in his sight well before the body of the first had even stopped twitching.

One down. How many more to go?

The next target was an Animosh marksman that was taking his time to pick off marines. It was a difficult shot from this angle, but as the alien leaned forward, he slightly exposed his lead arm. Sensing he might get just the one shot, he changed to high-power mode and unleashed a triple blast, hitting the target like the discharge from an automatic cannon. The projectiles ripped up through the forearm, bone, and armor, and then directly into the jaw.

"Good shooting, Sir," said Private Uchenik.

The middle-aged marine was a single parent, one of many who'd lost her husband in the Great Uprising and found herself falling on hard times. Now she was a marine in her late forties and in the prime of her life. Good training, food, and medical support allowed her to participate in physical activity that would have been limited to those under thirty a few centuries earlier. Another two marines ran past her, and one was hit in the neck. The marine fell down, and Private Uchenik pulled him to safety while checking him for injury.

"You're fine, marine, just a flesh wound. Now get back at it."

With a push, she shoved the man back out whereby he turned around and poured more fire into the enemy positions. Another pair joined in with him, and they moved off to the right where a group of marines was hunkered down beside banks of computers. Finally, the marine's clip ran out. He dropped down alongside the other marines and reloaded.

It's not fair, thought General Daniels. *These are good people. They deserve better than this.*

He checked the timestamp and felt his stomach lurch.

When they arrived, the marines were pumped up with adrenalin, partially out of the tension created by such an important mission, but also due to the inactivity they had been plagued with for so long now. This was the one thing they could do down here, and now they were stuck. The icons representing the ships of Admiral Lewis showed they were circling the facility, and as far as he could tell, they were doing a fine job of keeping the enemy from entering. It couldn't last though.

We've been down here way too long. Either we take this place, or we leave.

He'd given the order for two attempts at a breakout, and both times they had been forced back. The Command Center proved to be defended by much more than just the contingent of Animosh soldiers. There were now a number of machines moving along the upper levels and using large-caliber guns to shred any marines daring to cross the killing ground that led into the facility. Only two small groups had made it out, and he'd sent them for two different targets. All he could hope was that by keeping the battle going, he could draw the fire of the enemy and give them the opportunity to do what had to be done.

"What now, Sir? We can't reach the control systems for the weapon," said Sergeant Jones.

The General didn't recognize the man's voice, but the details on his visor overlay showed him to be one of the volunteers from the engineer unit based at the docks.

The man was an expert in computer control systems and shielding, skills that could earn him good money in the private sector. For whatever reason, he was now a marine just like the rest of them, a man in a suit of modern combat armor and carrying nothing more than an L52 coilgun. He looked at his overlay and shook his head in frustration. The number of enemy units had double in the last minute.

They must have another way inside.

Then a truly awful thought occurred to him.

Or they were already here? But why wait this long before acting?

He looked back to the enemy positions, shook his head, and then took aim.

"Thin the herd, marines…we need options."

The exchange of fire continued in every corner of the control center, from their current level right up to the highest point. Marines and Animosh fought with firearms, as well as thermal glaives, pikes, and bayoneted carbines. As the casualties mounted, there was no change in the location. Justitium Lyssk still controlled the systems, and that meant he had the weapon.

He checked the mapping information and on the status of his other teams. One squad had managed to circumvent the control room and was heading for the gunnery level. Another had broken further underground but was being held back on the way to the reactor systems. Zeta Team was making the greatest progress from what he could see.

"Zeta Team, do whatever you have to. We're running out of time, but make sure the weapon cannot fire!"

Justitium Lyssk knew the facility well, and his forces made good use of the multiple floors, cover, and hidden access points to quickly surround and cut off large parts of the Marine force. The Helion soldiers wasted no time in annihilating the nearest marines with a devastating series of ranged attacks while they tried to fall back and regroup. General Daniels continued scanning the enemy positions and tagged those he found. The information was quickly shared between the surviving marines and allowed them to fire, even without looking at their opponents.

One group of marines, led by Sergeant Aderyn, picked themselves up and tried to push ahead, only to move straight into a mixture of anti-personnel grenades and hidden charges that had been placed along the floor. A series of explosions rippled along the lower level and shredded the unfortunate marines. Others tried to slip further inside to avoid the shooting but also found themselves surrounded in a matter of seconds. Each of them died, and died well; but in less than five minutes, the entire assault force had been halted and forced to ground. Now the remaining marines gave ground slowly, each moving from cover to cover as they fell back from the killing ground. Heat weapons exchanged fire with coilguns, but the numbers were on the side of the defenders, as was knowledge of the local terrain.

"Sir!" called out a marine.

General Daniels moved his glance and looked in the direction of the man's hand. He spotted the shape of Lyssk, who then quickly moved back into cover.

"Leave him. All units fall back to the rendezvous point."

The man's details flashed up on his visor. It was twenty-two year old Corporal Saleem. A rookie from Kerberos, this was his first combat posting, and already he'd tagged and killed three Animosh warriors. This time he either failed to hear the General, or simply chose to ignore him

"With me, let's bring the bastard down!" called out the man.

"No, damn you. Get back!"

The Corporal lifted himself up and moved out from behind the tall storage unit. Three rounds crashed down alongside him, but he stepped away just as they landed. An entire squad rose to their feet and chased after him out into the open. General Daniels lifted his carbine while cursing to himself. His orders had been clear, but inside this deathtrap, he was quickly losing control of his scattered and panicked forces. The weeks of siege and bombardment had done little to calm their nerves, but as each marine fell, so did their desire for revenge increase.

I need to get them back. We're too exposed out here. We can't withdrawal though. I have to keep up the pretense that we intend on taking this place. If they get a moment's respite, my people will be screwed.

"Give them covering fire!"

He was the first to take aim, but then others joined in. Each did their best to help the Corporal and his forlorn hope of marines. They made it to a ramp leading to the next level before a pair of thermal proximity grenades detonated and killed him instantly. Another marine fell to the ground and screamed out for help. The others tried to pull the wounded man back before being struck by round after round from the darkness.

Bastards!

General Daniels twisted to the right and narrowly avoided a direct impact to his face. The thermal round burned through the metalwork of the nearby workstation, showering the hidden marines with sparks.

Close.

The move wrenched his back, and he felt another surge of pain. He breathed in hard and tried to avoid the spasms running up through his leg. He'd taken a lancing strike above his knee from an unknown alien weapon, and it had left a wide scorch mark on the plating. The armor had stopped the weapon penetrating, but the kinetic impact had been substantial enough to fracture two bones. Emergency sealant had locked the leg, but that now meant he limped as he moved.

"Admiral Lewis, this is General Daniels, are you there?"

A sound like that of a voice came back, but it crackled and was heavily distorted. It could be down to enemy action, or merely by being so far underground and inside a shielded structure.

"Admiral!"

A rocket smashed into the ground ahead and sent a single marine staggering back, his helmet glowing from the heat bloom of a phosphorus charge. They were banned weapons in the Alliance, and the mere sight of the burning material filled the General with a barely concealed rage. He knew he needed to conserve what was left of his force. Continuing this action would do nothing other than get the rest of them all killed.

"I can't hold the landing zone for much longer. Biomech forces are coming down in large numbers. You have seven minutes to get out of there. After that, you're on your own."

"Admiral, we're in trouble down here. We have no way of taking control of this site, not yet. Our only chance is to knock off or temporarily disable the targeting."

There was a short pause, and then an Animosh solider appeared from a duct above the marines and dropped down amongst them. He fired two powerful shots at close range and then disappeared into a tiny shaft and back into the structure. A marine tried to chase him, but a proximity grenade set off a flash and filled the immediate area with a thick dust, blocking their vision for several seconds.

"What was that, Sarge?" cried out one of the marines.

Another hatch in the ceiling opened up and a barrel

pushed out. This time the marines were ready and hit it with a fusillade of shots. A mortally wounded Animosh fighter dropped down and hit the ground hard. He was quickly dispatched with a bayonet by the nearest private.

"Marines, fall back to the intersection!"

He pointed in the direction they had arrived from. The intersection marked the point of four corridors and was easily defended, while providing access to the entry access ramp and armored doorway. He also knew they had a squad further back, as well as the SAAR robot.

"Move it!"

He took the lead and lurched back while firing short bursts at any targets he could find. The Animosh knew the site well and proved adept at hiding their cloaked forms in the shadows. He reached the doorway and ducked inside as three blasts tore chunks from the wall. More marines staggered out to join them and moved passed the line of seven marines. These had already stopped and dropped to their knees while behind them another three moved up close, each with their guns lifted. They provided a wall of flesh and armor for the retreating marines to fall behind.

"Movement, quadrant six!"

It was an unknown private that called out the warning. No sooner had he finished speaking, and a pair of marines staggered and then collapsed to the ground in front of them. They were the last few stragglers, and both were riddled with the holes formed by the deadly heat weapons of the Animosh. Behind them came their attackers, the feared paramilitaries of the old Helion state. Five of them rushed the corner, directly into the sight of the line of marines. General Daniels spotted them and barked out his order with calmness.

"Fire!"

A single L52 was capable of causing heavy casualties through weight of fire, but when fired in such a coordinated way, the effect was devastating. The marines fired in the rapid mode, whereby each barrel fired alternately and then loaded in another magnetic charge. The first volley shredded the formation, but the second finished them off. The Helion warriors took at least five bullets each before smashing to the ground in a huddle of blood and gore.

"Cease fire!"

General Daniels looked in the direction of the enemy and waited for signs of their foe. Icons on his visor showed his remaining troops, and he noted only half had made it past him and to the intersection or beyond. The remainder were pinned down or moving throughout the structure to escape the threat of the Animosh.

I need more men!

* * *

Sergeant Harvey lifted her head and looked around the corner of the narrow doorway. Inside were two rows of large computer screens plus six Helion men wearing military fatigues but no armor. She started to move her leg and then spotted the four Animosh paramilitaries. As with the others, these fighters wore long robes that covered their garish armor. There was a mixture of thermal weapons in their hands. They kept moving about and looking back in the direction of one of the doorways further inside the room.

"Where does it go?" Sergeant Harvey asked.

Private Cooper glanced quickly and then also ducked back.

"I think that shaft leads back down into the main control room. Where the General is still fighting."

Sergeant Harvey smiled; at least it looked like a smile to her comrades. She looked at them one at a time, doing her best to look calm and collected. They were technical specialists, but like all marines, they were trained as riflemen.

"We have to take this place. We secure the room, and then get the device into position. We go in hard...and fast. Understood?"

Private Cooper lowered the device to the ground, but Sergeant Harvey shook her head. She then lowered her glance just a little to focus on the device itself. Her meaning was clear, but she felt it important enough to explain.

"We don't have time to come back. You stay behind us. Ready?"

They nodded in the affirmative. Sergeant Harvey moved up to the doorway and looked inside one last time. The operators were all still busy working away at the computers. Only then did she see the massive screen off to the right. It showed the shape of the planet, as well as several moons and a nearby Rift. Flashing red shapes around it showed objects appearing every few seconds. Her heart almost shuddered when she spotted the dotted line moving slowly from left to right.

They're pointing it at the Rift. We don't have long!

She didn't hesitate, not even to check on the current position of the Animosh guards. The proximity flash grenade was in her left hand, and it was already out and flying through the air.

"Now!"

All four marines burst through the doorway and made it three meters before the grenade activated. Their visors turned black and then cleared almost as quickly. The Helion technical staff did absolutely nothing. The shock of the attack, combined with the flash of the grenade had stunned the entire group. Time appeared to slow as the marines surged inside, all firing as they went. This was controlled violence at its most extreme. Over fifty rounds had been expended from their coilguns in seconds, and two of the Animosh were already dead. The bodies lay slumped on the ground, riddled with dozens of bullet holes. The others were well trained though, and instead of fighting back against the overwhelming force, they stepped back and made for the other doorway that would lead back to their comrades.

"Sarge!" Private Cooper called out.

Sergeant Harvey had already seen them and chased after them as fast as she could. A thermal round struck her left arm and partially embedded itself in the armor. The super-heated projectile hissed and burned away against the armor but caused no immediate damage.

"Secure this room, and set up the device!" she barked.

More shots hit near the marine, but the two Animosh were barely taking aim. They had now run out of the doorway and were blasting away in the vain hope of deterring their pursuer. Private Cooper watched her vanish with her coilgun raised and firing short bursts at the two Animosh, and then looked to the others.

"You heard her. Secure these civilians; I need three minutes to connect up the amplification nodes."

The two moved in amongst the Helion engineers and moved them away from the equipment. One reached out to a control panel, and Private Cooper thrust out with her carbine so that the still burning hot muzzle pressed against his cheek. The unfortunate soul winced in pain and muttered something, but the marine simply applied more pressure against his face.

"Yeah, that's right. You think about it...then get the hell back!"

An understanding of the English language was completely unnecessary, and he quickly stepped back. The other two marines moved the prisoners to the other side of the control room and covered them with their weapons.

"Okay, you're clear," said Private Alexandria.

"Good."

She bent down and opened up the unit. She removed from the side a wireless sensor package and then moved along the control units. The device was able to match the control signals from the motors and actuators directly to the major circuits in the room. It took more than thirty seconds, but she finally stopped at a long bank of curved machines.

"Here, this is where the motor drive actuators control circuits are based."

It was more for her than the others, but with the key control system identified; she went to work preparing the equipment. Most of its bulk was taken up by the power pack and capacitors. The unit had been activated for more than ten minutes and already showed as being charged for use. It was one of the assault kits being distributed throughout the Marine Corps for damaging or destroying Biomechanical machines and equipment, known as a pulse generator core, of more colloquially as a Pulsegen. Four sets of blue lights flickered in ever increasing patterns as the device increased in potency. There were also four pairs of thickly ribbed piping with magnetic clamps attached.

She pulled them out one by one and attached them to the key areas around the weapon's control circuits.

"Is that going to do the job?" Private Alexandria asked.

Private Cooper shrugged.

"There's enough energy to knock out every circuit within thirty meters. This tech will reduce it down to just three, but it will cause permanent damage by sending pulses throughout their entire system. This is the heart of the control system. If we're lucky, this will stop the weapon."

Private Alexandria gasped in surprise when she looked at the massive display on the wall. More and more objects were coming through the marked Rift, and the dotted line from Helios Prime was now just ten or so degrees away from anchoring on the new target. She looked back to Cooper and shook her head.

"We're running out of time. Whatever you're going to do, do it fast!"

* * *

Four more marines had been killed in the withdrawal to the intersection, but now they were in the main corridor and able to control the space with gunfire. Shots bounced back and forth between both sides as the Animosh attempted to move in through the flanking corridors, but for now they were safe. Each time a Helion appeared, a dozen or more rounds hit them. He moved back, trying his best to disguise his limp until he could see the dust shrouded entrance. He checked the indicator on his visor that showed just over thirty marines in this part of the structure.

No much, enough to do one thing, though.

The Helions had not been keen in giving out information on their facilities. With each day of the bombardment, however, he had been able to get more and more out of them. The basic layout of this facility was available to him, with just the power station segments off limits. It gave him enough to formulate a plan.

We need to hit them fast. What can we do to change this around?

He used his eyes to scan through the blueprints until he reached the reactor entry points. Flashing lights from behind them caught his attention, but then one of the horrific Decurion war machines appeared. He'd seen images of them. He'd even fought their kind before, but never had he seen one configured like this. It scuttled into the corridor and waited.

"General?" called out a sergeant.

"Wait!"

The machine stopped as if its operator had just pressed a button. Shadows behind it moved about, and then a number of Animosh warriors moved into the corridor with their hands raised in apparent surrender.

"We will discuss terms," it said in a machine-like voice.

The speaker inside the General's helmet crackled long enough for him to hear the voice of Admiral Lewis. The sound was still heavily damaged, but it was partially audible.

"...fire, one chance to land...get out...sector four is overrun...Operation Citadel is a go...I repeat...scouring of Helios Prime in T plus five hours."

The rest was garbage, but it was enough for him. If the Operation was going ahead then that could only mean one thing, the entire fleet was coming through the Rift, and they expected to find the Biomechs on the surface and in great numbers. Citadel was supposed to be a massive counterattack. The word scouring almost made him cringe. It could only mean they intended on a massive orbital strike before landing. That meant he needed to get off the world, or under it before the rockets came down.

We have to destroy this place. It's our only chance.

The lights around the frame were already flashing, but a loud warning siren drew his attention. He looked at the doorway from where they had entered. A single entrenched squad waited alongside an SAAR robot, its weapon system ready and alert.

"What's going on? Do not let it open!" he said to the nearest marine.

The man was already running toward the door when it started to lift up. It made it just a few inches before the man managed to hit the correct sequence and locked the mechanism.

"Outstanding work, Private, outstanding."

He then looked back to the Helion and shook his head while slowly lifting his weapon.

"Son…"

He pulled the trigger and sent a triple round directly into the Animosh trooper's face. It staggered out of sight, and the rest of the marines blazed away at the small group of Helions and the single machine. Two more were killed before the others gave ground, leaving just the machine to return fire. It was quickly silenced by the marines, but not before taking another one with it.

Yes, we will bring the entire place down on top of us.

His mind was resolute now, determined to finish the job they had started. It might have worked if it were not for the doorway and the bright light coming from the end of the tunnel.

"General, the door!"

He dropped down and took aim, his training and reactions instantly taking over. The door moved slowly and then hissed up with a great cloud of dust. A blast of dust and debris came from outside and ran along the length of the corridor.

"Watch your fire," he said quickly.

Two thirds of those inside trained their weapons on the doorway, while the rest kept a watchful eye on the other areas used by the Animosh. Even though he suspected he would be disappointed, General Daniels hoped against hope that this would be the help promised by Admiral Lewis.

Here it comes.

The area around the door flashed white, and then shapes moved on through, each silhouetted against the bright background. A few shells landed and exploded further out and on the ramps. The additional blasts sent even more dust into the underground facility. General Daniels tensed up, but all he could do was wait.

"General, Biomechs!" the man closest to the doorway cried out.

The first shape to emerge was a pair of Thegns. They rushed in and fired from their arm-fitted firearms. They were quickly cut down but not before wounding a marine. More came in after them, and then came the Decurions. Not one, but dozens of them. Five more marines were shot and then butchered where they stood. General Daniels watched the carnage from just twenty meters away. The Biomechs poured in like water into a pipe, crushing all that stood in its path.

"Marines, to me!" he yelled.

Those marines still able to move rushed to their commander. Gone were plans of escape or destruction of the base. The last marines formed up in a tight knot around their General like an ancient schiltron formation. Rounds clattered against their armor, but even a direct hit on one of their visors failed to deter the last of his command in their mission. One by one, they turned about and aimed their guns at the approaching Biomechs.

"Kill them all!" were the last words most of them heard from General Daniels.

Not one of the marines noticed Justitium Lyssk and his bodyguard of Animosh fighters at the opposite end of the long corridors. They stayed in the shadows in case they might be seen and watched in silence. It was like some form of sickening piece of entertainment, yet each watched blissfully at the final stand of the General, and the great onslaught of the Biomech reinforcements as they continued to surge through the outer doors and into the facility.

CHAPTER THIRTEEN

Why did the Alliance choose to travel to the Orion Nebula when there were already mysteries galore in Alpha Centauri? What so many failed to understand years after those tumultuous events was that the Alliance had only just come out of its own terrible crisis. With the Uprising still fresh in the minds of the adult population, there was a thirst for change. Alien worlds, cultures, and opportunities provided a distraction for a population tired and battered from years of conflict. The prophesied war with the Biomechs created a focal point that even the conservative haters of the Jötnar couldn't ignore. As has been shown so many times before, even a hint of a potential external threat can move attention from home.

The Economics of Exploration

ANS Warlord, T'Karan-Helios Prime Rift

T'Karan was once the domain of the T'Kari, an old and proud race that like many before it had been smashed by the might of the Biomechs. In the past, the T'Kari had lived on worlds throughout these star systems and many more. Each of these domains had been linked by the intricate series of short-ranged Rifts. Since the Biomech War, all that remained of this once advanced race were eight planets, an asteroid belt, and a myriad of moons. Most of these worlds were dead rocky objects or frozen ice worlds that offered little to the living. The remnants of their colonies were spread throughout the planet Luthien and the many moons such as Hades.

Today the T'Karan System had been transformed, but this wasn't a change in ecology, it was a change in its military and political status. With the star system now the single point in space connecting the Alliance to Helios, its fortunes had changed. The Admiral Jarvis Naval Station was the largest naval facility outside of Alpha Centauri, and the military buildup was larger than anything seen in humanity's history. Ships ranging from civilian transports through to apocalyptical battleships filled the shipping lanes. Some were just weeks old, but there were also a few old vessels dating back to the Uprising, and even several old war barges that had been towed into orbit around the station. These primitive craft were similar to those still used in Sol to protect planetary colonies and to guard shipping lanes. T'Karan was more than just a star system. It was now the frontline for the war against the machines, a place where ships and warriors from dozens of worlds were congregating for the vast Operation Citadel.

Admiral Anderson and General Rivers watched the Rift to the Helion warzone as it flickered and flashed. The mainscreen showed the view in perfect detail, with each ship showing up as the size of a man's head. Squadrons of ships were moving as quickly as they dared through the tear in time and space. The first to enter were the mixed formations of frigates and Liberty destroyers. Unusually, there were also large numbers of fighters moving throughout the formation.

"The Rift is still up. Has General Daniels secured the site?" asked the Admiral.

He didn't need to ask the question; the reports were already coming in via the ships already around Helios Prime. Even more obvious was the look on the General's face, a look he had seen many times in the past.

"Helios Prime is overrun. Satellites show over eighty thousand enemy ground troops, and more are coming down by the minute. The last order given was for all forces to move underground. The war for Helios Prime is over now. It is time for the resistance.

"Not if we can help them in the next twenty-four hours," said Admiral Anderson.

General Rivers shrugged at this suggestion. He'd seen the dispositions of his own forces and those of the enemy. He had no doubt the Alliance could lead a successful counterattack against the Biomechs. In fact, in some odd way, he actually relished the opportunity to engage them in open combat. His real concern was that Prime was just one battle of a much more serious conflict. As always, the Black Rift loomed dark and foreboding into the distance, and he had little doubt that it had its part to play.

"Admiral Lewis is running a last ditch attempt to evacuate our ground forces. He's already picked up several units, but the enemy is growing in strength. If he stays much longer, he could lose the fleet."

Admiral Anderson nodded impatiently and gave the nod to the helmsman.

"Take us through, now."

A low rumble shook through the massive vessel as its main engines powered up, and then they were moving. At first it was hard to tell if they were traveling particularly quickly, and this wasn't helped with little around them to give an impression of speed. Then they were heading toward the Rift at even greater speeds. It was only when a transport came back though and into T'Karan space that it became clear the ship was traveling at a considerable velocity. General Rivers nodded to a group of ships waiting off to one side.

"The Black Ships, they will be following right behind."

It was a statement, not a suggestion, and one he knew the Admiral was wary of. Few in the military would doubt Spartan or Colonel Morato's resolve in the face of the enemy. This was different now. They were carrying a deadly cargo, and one that could potentially turn and bite the very hand that fed it. Both watched the vessels warily as flames pumped out from the rear. It was a simple gesture, but it signaled their intent to follow, and they joined the column of ships heading for the Rift in surprising time. At the center of the Black Ships was a single Alliance heavy warship, ANS Dreadnought. It was the additional group of civilian transports that surprised the General.

"Uh, what are they doing here?"

Anderson threw a quick glance in their direction.

"Yes, the ships from Hyperion. Recognize the markings?"

General Rivers smiled.

"Jötnar, of course. How could they not be here?"

Admiral Anderson sent off a batch of order notifications to three of the capital ships before returning his gaze to the large screen. The shapes of the civilian transports and passenger liner were unusual to see, especially in pseudo-military markings.

"Yes. It looks like Gun's kin are anxious not to lose out on this one. They've hired or bought an entire squadron of heavy transports and mining ships for work on Hyperion, Prometheus, and now out here in T'Karan. They are licensed to haul freight and ore between nine locations right now, yet are they doing that today?"

The General smiled, and Admiral Anderson continued. He pointed to the nearest of them.

"Now those ships are filled to the brim with Jötnar. Many came from Prometheus, but the majority are from from Hyperion. Some of them are new generation, born using the equipment we helped install on Hyperion. A lot will never have seen combat before."

He didn't seem particularly worried about the last part, but he was definitely uncomfortable with the entire affair. He paused and looked to General Rivers whose expression was almost impossible to fathom.

"And do you know what?"

General Rivers raised an eyebrow in answer. Admiral Anderson's face changed color as the vessel entered the Rift. Bright colors and flashes altered his skin tone and even seemed to distort the man himself, and then they were through.

"I wouldn't have it any other way."

The General nodded in agreement.

"True, very true," he agreed, "There's no more reliable or violent soldier than a Jötnar. My last visit on Hyperion was just over a year ago. I witnessed the birthing of sixteen new Jötnar. The equipment takes nine to ten months to fully develop a fetus, but they come out the size and strength of a teenager."

They were through the Rift, and although General Rivers had done his best to ignore it, now that they were through his body seemed to relax. The other side looked little different, apart from the subtle shades of yellow and orange caused by gases and dust in the Helion System. Hundreds of ships lurked near the Rift, the majority being Alliance in design. The strangest was the long lines of liners and transports from a dozen worlds, each making for the Rift.

"What's going on?" asked the General.

Admiral Anderson sighed as he looked at the same imagery.

"That, my friend, is what happens when an enemy like the Biomechs arrives, and offers nothing but genocide to every soul it meets."

He nodded in the direction of the nearest vessel, a dull gray heavy transport that was badly damaged on a side of its hull. There were markings in an alien tongue running down one side of the nose section.

"Helion liner with Zathee designators. They are refugees with seven thousand civilians on board. The designation on the side shows their origin as the moon of Gaxos."

"The first Biomech attack. I thought NHA forces had retaken the moon?"

"We have, but this ship left months ago. Would you want to go back to a place that had been fought over and nuked from orbit?"

He looked back to the ship and spoke to himself.

"While those of us that can fight do so, there will always be others that are forced to flee."

More shapes flickered behind them as the rest of the

fleet came in. A tiny number of T'Kari ships. Some of the few vessels still remaining also moved alongside the heavily armored Alliance ships. A single squadron of six private security craft from Kerberos was also present, but they seemed to be hiding back behind the military vessels. Light from the hot star of the Helios System put orange and yellow hues on the flat panels of the ships, while the opposite sides vanished into cold blackness. It was an impressive sight.

"Right, let's see how we're doing," said Admiral Anderson.

He looked down at the horizontal tactical display with its multi-layered three-dimensional model. Each planet in the system was shown by a while orb, and colored details highlighted troop numbers and status. Other icons marked the multiple fleets of ships from all sides, the majority focused around Spascia and Helios Prime. He looked at each and then stopped at reaching the more distant planet of Gaxos, and its moon Eos.

"So that's the closest friendly territory to the Black Rift, and we have full control of the place. What assets are available, if needed?"

General Rivers nodded and checked his secpad while looking at the tactical display.

"Limited marine forces, but there are three full divisions of NHA soldiers. All are veterans of the cleaning up campaign. We do have small groups down there, including

Captain Carter and a company of recon marines."

Anderson wiped his brow. The fleet was now almost fully assembled, and the enormity of what needed to be done was clear. He commanded hundreds of ships and hundreds of thousands of men and women. He moved his hands as he selected each of the planets and checked the information. Now that they were in the Helios System, he was able to take advantage of the terabytes of data arriving every minute to his flagship. Individual regiments, starships, and space stations sent reports and requests for help.

"So, we still have two planets under enemy occupation or under siege, and both are surrounded by enemy fleets."

He selected the larger of the planets and pulled his hands apart to enlarge it.

"The Helios Prime Ark, codenamed Leviathan is in the atmosphere and leading the assault on the Helion homeworld. General Daniels has vanished, and Admiral Lewis is evacuating marines from the surface."

"Eighty-five percent transfer complete, Admiral," said the tactical officer.

Admiral Anderson nodded but said nothing in response. He had just minutes, perhaps seconds until the entire fleet was in position. Then, and only then, would he sanction the deployment to the enemy war zones. He glanced at the disposition of his forces and almost panicked while looking for the massive engineering vessel, ANS Explorer.

There she is.

The ship dwarfed even his flagship in both length and bulk. Even so, it took him several seconds to actually find the vessel amongst the myriad of craft coming in from Alliance space. A dozen Liberty fleet defense destroyers stayed close to its hull as well as thirty fighters.

"Eighty-eight percent."

General Rivers showed his secpad to Anderson.

"I'm getting some pretty serious contact from High Command on Terra Nova. They are trying to hold back the last few ships."

Admiral Anderson barely even looked at the data.

"Churchill will keep them in order. He's already locking down the border."

General Rivers rubbed at his cheek.

"You know they'll make us pay for this, assuming we actually make it back."

Admiral Anderson almost laughed at his suggestion.

"General, I think we have far greater concerns today than whether we'll be in trouble when we go home. Let's save our people and end this war. We'll deal with the consequences when the fate of the galaxy doesn't rest on our shoulders."

It was a tongue-in-cheek comment, but General Rivers couldn't but help feel the words were harsher than normal.

He doesn't think he's coming back.

They both looked back at the tactical display and the

other planets being held primarily by the NHA ground forces.

"So, so with Eos recaptured by the New Helion Army, we have a jump-off point to the Black Rift, if and when it becomes necessary. Captain Carter's forces have captured several pieces of Biomech equipment that might prove useful."

He then moved the vast distance to the hated Black Rift, the one area of space every race tried to avoid. Icons for Helion, Alliance, and T'Kari forces showed around the Rift station. Of real concern were the three red blocks representing Biomech forces nearing the Rift. Alongside their icons were numbers and statistics concerning the fleet disposition, velocity, and more importantly, their ETA.

"Two hours, that's all we have. Goddamn two hours!"

The news was hardly new, but the data had updated in the last minute, showing the enemy vessels had adopted an odd tactic. Even General Rivers appeared surprised at what he was seeing. He pointed to the segment in question that was far ahead of the other two-thirds of the fleet.

"A third of their fleet still hasn't reversed course. There is no way for them to be able to play a part in an assault on the station or the Black Rift defense force."

Even as he spoke, he could see what was going to happen.

"You're partially correct, General. The other two sections will hit in two hours. This other splinter group started their deceleration much later. They will arrive in forty minutes, perhaps a little more. Their increased velocity will take them to our forces and then beyond."

"You're kidding? A strafing run."

"Perhaps, or it could be a suicide run on the station."

While the two contemplated this, the sirens continued to blare through the warship. Crewmembers moved to their stations, readying for the start of the massive operation. A number of fighters had already detached from the port hull where they had been attached to increase the number of fighter craft for the operation. There were more than a dozen fighters and a similar number of drones waiting just behind ANS Warlord. Admiral Anderson creased his brow a little and then put the focus of the display on the two other planets important to the Helions.

"They have two more Arks heading for Micaya and Libuscha. When they land, we can expect at least…"

"Admiral, reports from the surface. There's a major energy bloom in progress. The planetary defense weapon is firing."

The color seemed to drain from the faces of the two senior officers.

"The Doomsday Weapon," Anderson said through clenched teeth.

He turned about and bellowed at the mixture of officers through the CIC.

"Get everything through the Rift, and fast!"

The mainscreen altered its angle to show the Rift back to T'Karan. As before, more and more ships came through with their engines blazing hot in the icy coldness of the void. Two transports narrowly avoided a fatal collision as they arrived simultaneously but on a converging course. Only the quick actions of their helmsmen narrowly averted disaster.

"Keep them coming!"

The sound inside the CIC almost doubled as the officers did their best to manage the array of transports and warships as the last few tried to rush the gauntlet before the inevitable.

"How many more?"

"Uh...seventeen, no, sixteen more ships to come through, Admiral," said the tactical officer.

General Rivers pointed at the shape of ANS Devastation, the only surviving ship of her force that had been lost en route from Prometheus. The Black Ships waited patiently alongside, with the bright shape of the Rift right behind them; a cruiser appeared and then another. That was when the weapon struck. The effect on the Rift was instantaneous as the invisible beam slammed into the phenomena and began breaking down the carefully managed Spacebridge. They all watched in horror as just three-quarters of the cruiser appeared. The entire aft section was missing, and the vessel belched gas and flames from its ruptured compartments.

"Battlestations!" the Admiral shouted.

The ship was already at a high state of alert, and the call to battlestations was almost unnecessary. More than anything it drew the attention of the officers to the two men and to the new predicament.

"Get lifeboats out there. Fighters in the air, we're going to war."

"Admiral, we have an emergency broadcast from the Black Rift defense force. They say something is happening out there."

He then looked to the General when the communications officer called out.

"An urgent message from ANS Dreadnought."

The two senior commanders looked at each other and spoke at the same time.

"Spartan."

"Admiral, he wishes to speak with both of you."

"Put him on."

Anderson angled his head just a little.

"What might the great Spartan want now?"

The imagery from the Black Rift appeared on the mainscreen. The defending ships looked tiny alongside the station, especially this far from the Helion star. What caught his eye was the ripple and flashing effects in the background.

"Is that what I think it is?" General Rivers asked.

Anderson shook his head in amazement.

"They are trying to open a Rift, the crazy bastards. They are going to open the Black Rift."

He rubbed his forehead in frustration and then looked intently at the General.

"ANS Explorer can create a short-range Rift, but only one."

"Yes, and the plan is for Spascia. We split the fleet and overrun the Biomech forces at Spascia and Helios Prime. Are they ready?"

* * *

ANS Dreadnought, T'Karan-Helios Prime Rift

The Conqueror class warship swiveled about along its axis to take up a lead position ahead of the Black Ships. Several more civilian transports also moved in with the Hyperion flagged vessels. It was a tiny number compared to the rest of the fleet, yet combined the force had the capacity to spearhead an assault, or even take over an entire space station or small moon. Small groups of Biomech fighters had been left silent and deactivated near the Rift, and they were already moving in to attack the smaller Alliance ships. Before Operation Citadel could begin a massive dogfight was already underway.

Spartan watched them go via the live external feed inside his Marine Corps helmet. He'd expected there to be resistance as they came through, but a cloud of fighters would do little to halt their progress. He looked to Teresa, noting her smart armor with its embellishments as befitted her rank. His equipment was right from Marine Corps stocks and no different to that worn by the rank and file. It felt strange to be in the uniform of the Corps, even more so as he was still technically a civilian. Even odder was the fact that he was now on hold with Admiral Anderson, the commander of the entire Naval operation.

"That's thirty-five ships leading the fleet already. The rest are moving into columns, just as planned," said Khan.

The nerves amongst the officers were already frayed as far as was possible. This deployment was the first and last attempt to recover Helios Prime and its colonies. There was no backup plan, nothing other than the shutting down of the T'Karan-Helios Rift and losing contact with everything they had discovered.

We don't have long, Spartan thought.

The cool fear, the stricken nerves, and the sense of what was to come had spread to every part of the ship. As more imagery arrived of the assault on Helios, it could only get worse. Each of them had seen the live streams from the surface, the burned and destroyed cities, the heaps of corpses, and the hundreds of ships that continued to drop off more and more soldiers. Helios Prime had already fallen, and all that remained were those that had made it underground.

The imagery of the destruction wrought on the last

few ships coming through the Rift was terrible to watch. Spartan nodded in agreement, but the faces of Admiral Anderson and General Rivers appeared in his helmet.

"We're ready to deploy. What do you need, Spartan?" Anderson asked.

"Admiral. What's the status of the Rift?"

There was a pause that seemed to last forever. Spartan, Teresa, and Khan were all that remained of the officers that had taken part in the fighting on Mars. Major Terson and the other Captains had been sent to their new posts aboard the six Liberty class vessels known as the Black Ships. Deep inside these vessels waited eight of the eleven bandon that had been discovered, as well as the six other Biomech commanders. Three more bandon waited patiently inside the landing bay and storage areas of the massive warship. Spartan stopped and looked at the imagery of the two officers.

"Admiral?"

Still there was no answer. The small group moved about the deck and examined their forces. This wasn't the first time they had run this inspection, but it was the first time since Spartan had authorized the removal of all core programming from every single one of them.

"Spartan, there is activity at the Black Rift. We have T'Kari ships on standby as well as two Helion cruisers. If they manage to open the Rift, we will have it shut in seconds."

Spartan shook his head in annoyance.

"Admiral, they won't open the Rift unless they can keep it open. What about their own taskforce?"

Again there was a pause.

"Spartan, make sure you're ready. I'll be in touch shortly."

With that brief answer, he was gone.

"Well?" Teresa asked, "To Spascia?"

Spartan could detect the hope in her voice, a tone that was tinged with a little fear. Jack was on Spascia, as well as Gun and an entire host of people they knew. He was also well aware of the effect the presumed death of her other two children was having on her. Teresa's face was pale and strained, something he found difficult to take in when he tried to plan for the coming campaign. They continued past the lines of warriors, even as squads of marines ran back and forth with equipment. Now each of the creatures and machines had been given full and complete control of its faculties. There were now subtle differences in the way they waited and watched, ways that only somebody familiar with them would have noticed.

"What are they doing?" Teresa asked.

Khan and Teresa flanked Spartan as they walked down the line between the groups of Thegns. They had adopted the same shape of dark gray worn by the Marine Corps but with colorful embellishments on their heads, chests, and shoulders. Every bandon had a unique color scheme, and every twenty bore colored markings on their heads or torsos. Spartan tilted his head slightly to look at her. It was Khan who spoke, his voice lower than normal and tinted with something bordering reverence.

"The Thegns chose their own leaders, and the first decision they then made was to create a military structure. They chose units of twenty and then colors and symbols to go with them."

Spartan started to speak, but the image of Captain Vetlaya appeared to each of them.

"We've got a problem, a big damned problem."

"What is it?" Teresa replied.

"The Helion ships at the Rift. They've turned their guns on the T'Kari. It's a massacre out there. Our own ships are trying to help, but what isn't destroyed is being hunted down."

"Helion? Why?" Khan asked.

Spartan seemed to be the only one not surprised at the news.

"That will be the Animosh and their allies. They'd rather operate as vassals of the machines than let the Zathee take control of their own worlds."

Teresa swallowed slowly, considering what was happening, but it was the Captain who continued to speak.

"We have no way of closing the Rift. My science teams estimate it could open any second."

Spartan looked to Teresa, the look of fear clearly written

across her forehead. She wasn't stupid, and Spartan knew that. With the Rift possibly opening, there was no way the fleet could move to the aid of Spascia, at least not in the short run.

"Colonel Morato. We have…"

The image of the Captain moved to the side to be replaced by a much larger one of Admiral Anderson.

"The enemy has begun the activation procedure to create a Spacebridge to the Black Rift. Operation Citadel will continue as planned, but a force under my command will move to the Black Rift and stop any further ships from arriving. All ship commanders will receive their orders shortly. Those that remain will continue under the authority of General Rivers to recover Helios Prime and then Spascia. Prepare to move out."

As he continued to outline the revised plan, Teresa turned and looked to Spartan.

"Continue to Spascia?"

She reached out and grabbed his arm.

"If Explorer doesn't create a bridge to Spascia, it will take weeks to get troops to the planet. Does Jack have that long?"

Spartan swallowed, but he couldn't lie. Teresa had been a marine longer than him now. She knew the odds, and she knew the situation they now found themselves in. He also understood the effect of losing her two children was having, even though she did her best to hide it.

"Teresa, if we ignore the Black Rift, they will come through, and this entire operation will be over. Helios will fall and so will our forces."

She shook her head.

"No. We could evacuate both planets, leave Helios and this damned Black Rift."

Khan pulled his head back in surprise at this suggestion.

"No, that's not going to happen. It will take weeks to evacuate our forces, and to where?"

Spartan nodded in firm agreement.

"Khan's right. With the Spacebridge to T'Karan gone, there's nowhere we can go. Helios is where our future will be decided."

Teresa tightened her grip on his arm and looked intently at him. Her eyes strained, and he could see the fear beginning to turn into something else.

"I've lost Matius and Ingo. I won't let Jack die on an alien rock, not alone, not this time. You never saw him on Helios, Spartan. He's not like us."

Spartan looked to Khan, but this time his old friend had little to offer. The three of them waited alone in the midst of an army of alien life. If they'd had the time to consider what was happening, they might have appreciated the irony. Instead, it came down to Z'Kanthu who marched toward them with a guard of Thegn warriors. Though armed and equipped as normal, the Thegns wore their new colors and unit markers with an odd look of pride.

He moved right up to them and then stopped.

"The data from the Rift, I know the signature."

As usual his voice was monotone and machinelike. All three looked at him and waited for him to continue, but the machine waited for them to speak.

"Well?" Spartan asked impatiently.

A light flashed on his chest, and then a holographic representation of the Helion System appeared. It moved and then stopped at the Allied fleet and station near the Black Rift. The imagery flickered about but proved stable and detailed enough for them to see individual ships.

"Yes, the Rift. We just received contact from Admiral Anderson. He thinks the Rift is about to open."

Z'Kanthu lifted himself up half a meter, and then shook his body as if to say no.

"This signature is similar to some of the technology being developed back during our own war with the enemy. If the T'Kari and the Helions had not forced them back when they did, this equipment might have been used."

Teresa stepped closer to the machine.

"What does it do?"

A motor whirred gently before he answered her.

"It is the next development of the Rift generating technology. A single station or massive ship could create a stabilizing field from within the Spacebridge as it travels through. Providing the station stays on both sides of the Rift, it can keep it open, even through spatial disturbances."

Spartan and Teresa failed to understand, looking to each other for clarification.

"Disturbances?" Khan asked, "Like the weapons used by the T'Kari?"

Z'Kanthu answered with a hissing sound.

"Yes."

Teresa understood the implications immediately.

"Z'Kanthu, you're saying the Biomechs could get this machine into position and hold the Rift open indefinitely, even if our allies use the Rift collapsing technology? Does it even work?"

Z'Kanthu lifted his metal shoulder in a mock shrugging action.

"I do not know. It was an experimental machine in the war and was never tested. They have had hundreds of years in exile to perfect it though. If they have made the system work, then they will definitely use it."

Spartan looked to Teresa.

"If he's right, this could be the end."

Her eyes widened, and she found it hard to speak.

"Spartan, you and Khan will have to stop them."

She started to move away. Spartan grabbed her shoulders and turned her back around.

"Where are you going?"

"To join General Rivers. We will take care of the planets. You take Khan and the rest and end this war. Understood?"

Khan's eyes narrowed as he listened. He knew how hard it had been for Spartan to be separated for so long. Now it looked like they would be splitting apart once more. He watched as the two spoke quietly, and then Teresa turned and walked away, never looking back. Spartan finally turned around to look at him and Z'Kanthu. His eyes were red and his face taut and hard.

He's ready, thought Khan.

CHAPTER FOURTEEN

The Hyperion flagged starships chartered by the Jötnar marked a first for their race. Private security vessels had, of course, been used in the past, but never had so many been hired and retasked before. When the fleet arrived in Alpha Centauri, it wasn't just the official military forces that arrived for the fight. The so-called 'Black Ships' bore the iconography of Hyperion as well as the distinctive markings of the Jötnar families. These ships would take private warbands of Alliance citizens into battle alongside the professional Marine Corps regiments. Most, if not all, probably thought they would be fighting to assist their kin on the battlefields of Helios Prime and Spascia. In reality, the bulk of these forces would follow Spartan and his comrades in a desperate rush to the Black Rift.

Origins of Private Space Travel

ANS Conqueror, over Helios Prime

Admiral Lewis held onto the straps as the ship took a broadside from a Biomech Ravager. The ship had managed to pull alongside in a gap created by three of the Alliance ships. The accuracy of either ship at this range was irrelevant. Instead, it came down to the loading speed and potency of the kinetic weaponry.

"Report!"

Lieutenant Vitelli and Captain Marcus feverishly checked the reports coming in. The XO spoke first.

"Hull is breached, minor damage. All systems are nominal."

He looked at the mainscreen that showed an enhanced, heavily stabilized view of the massive underground defense installation. The roof and nearby road system were heavily damaged, yet he had no doubt the majority of the system was intact, protected from attack by the deep tunnels and thick armor.

"What about Daniels?"

The XO looked at him and shook his head.

"We've lost contact with his forces inside the facility. The Biomechs have breached three entrances now and are establishing a perimeter."

A pair of hypersonic missiles detonated just short of the underside of the massive warship. They exploded prematurely, but the debris smashed into the armor plating with such force it could be felt this far inside the ship.

"We have to get out of here," said Captain Marcus.

Admiral Lewis looked at his XO and then to his tactical display. The icons showing the number of Biomech vessels now inside the planet's atmosphere had increased exponentially. Even more worrying was that the Leviathan Ark had now breached the lower atmosphere and was heading directly for them, along with hundreds more vessels.

"Just look at them. We're outnumbered five to one already, and their numbers are increasing."

The lower gun turrets continued firing, each targeting any ground forces or landers that were now working their way through the city ruins. Thegns, Decurions, and Eques walkers numbered in the tens of thousands and were working methodically street-by-street and block-by-block. The Admiral watched as a pair of quad guns shredded an Eques walker as it tried to pursue a Helion civilian vehicle down a rubble-filled street.

"And the weapon?"

"It's still firing, but it's off course by eighty-two kilometers, and the gap is widening," said Lieutenant Vitelli.

He turned around and looked at the Admiral. He looked as surprised as the rest of them.

"There was a massive, highly focused AMP pulse throughout the one section of the site. The accuracy failed after that, and now it is way off from the Spacebridge."

"Great, so we can reopen it, but only when the space

distortion stabilizes. How long?"

Nobody answered the rhetorical question. It was well known since their first encounter with the T'Kari that the technology used to collapse Rifts was unreliable at best. Sometimes the Spacebridge could be reopened in hours, but on other occasions it could take days, week, or even months. All Admiral Lewis needed to know was that the longer the distance, the greater effect the distortion would have.

"We're on our own for now. At least Anderson got through with most of the fleet."

A number of new alerts sounded, but what really caught his eye was the number of shapes approaching the upper atmosphere.

"Whose ships are those?"

Captain Marcus checked several of the IFF transmissions. All Alliance ships were required to have the equipment fitted, and each vessel transmitted a unique code. He double-checked what he had seen before looking back to the Admiral.

"You are really not going to believe this."

The view on the mainscreen split in the middle to show the view of the ground battle as well as the sky. Hundreds of white streaks leapt up into the sky from ground forces blasting away at the new arrivals. Black shapes sheathed in smoke and flame smashed down through the sky. As the largest and first of them came lower and began to slow, its shape became more obvious. Each of the races had a particular distinctive look, and the bow of this ship was known to every one of them.

"It's one of ours," said Lieutenant Vitelli.

They watched dozens more ships come through with long trails of smoke behind them. The craft came down in multiple waves, each batch heading for different parts of Helios Prime. The largest of them all made directly for Ark Leviathan that was beginning to settle over the surface near the Doomsday Weapon. The ship's communications officer began to wave feverishly and then called out.

"Admiral, we've got an urgent wideband transmission coming from that ship."

"Put it on the speakers."

The sound crackled but cleared up as its strength continued to increase. The sound that came out was unmistakable to most of the officers present, none more so than Admiral Lewis himself.

"General Rivers?" he gasped.

The name sent a calming wave throughout the CIC. The man might technically be out of the actual combat chain of command, but out here, and in such a warzone, there could be nobody better to have on your side. General Rivers was a warhorse, a man who lived and breathed war. He'd fought for decades, and news that he had arrived was exactly the kind of news Admiral Lewis needed.

"...Operation Citadel has begun. If you have weapons,

use them. Helios Prime is under the control of the Alliance. My plan is being sent out to all unit commanders. Mobilize all forces and prepare for battle."

Admiral Lewis looked about the CIC and could have wept at seeing such looks of happiness showing on their faces. Only a man like the General could have instilled such a feeling through the force, even for people too young to have ever served under the man.

"…we will not leave this world until every single Biomech warrior is dead or captured. Operation Citadel will cleanse Helios of every taint of the enemy. My name is General Rivers, and I am taking command of Alliance operations on this planet. Let the battle begin!"

A cheer of pure excitement rippled through the CIC. Admiral Lewis almost laughed in relief at what he saw on his ship and only imagined the same would be felt throughout the rest of the fleet. He grabbed the intercom and selected the wideband channel to all of his forces.

"This is Admiral Lewis. Our reinforcements have arrived. Operation Citadel is a go. I repeat; Operation Citadel is a go."

He checked back on the tactical display to make sure it was not just a handful of ships. His smile widened as ship after ship appeared as they came through the atmosphere. Ships of a dozen classes hurtled downwards with their cargos of warriors, fighters, and weapons.

"I am deferring all ground forces to the control of

General Rivers. We're not leaving. We're staying, and we're going to win this fight!"

He deactivated the intercom and beckoned toward his XO.

"I need to speak with General Rivers. We've a campaign to coordinate, and something tells me he's going to want to handle the ground operation."

* * *

General Rivers watched the unfolding battle from the CIC of ANS Ticonderoga. He could see the courses of the first forty or so ships from this position, but it was the state of the planet that stunned him.

"What is it?" asked the Captain of the ship.

General Rivers looked back at the woman, Captain Jeanie Wilson. She was one of the oldest ship captains in the fleet, and from what he'd read she had originally served as a marine. Damage to her legs had forced her out of frontline combat, but she'd fought hard and worked her way back up as the Captain of the massive vessel. She was taller than most of those in the CIC and lacked any discernible sense of humor.

"The planet, it's in a much worse state than I expected."

He looked back at the battered, sterile environment filled with shattered skyscrapers, fires, and smoke. Dozens of ships lay discarded and smashed, with fires raging deep inside their engine, ammunition, and reactor cores. Most were Biomech vessels, but he counted at least three Crusader ships lying broken and burned on the surface of Helios Prime.

"That's what weeks and weeks of bombardment will do to a planet, General. Don't forget the underground system, though. The Helions were not stupid. Our reports show that in the last war many of them were forced to shelter against the Biomech weapons. There is just as much under the surface as there was above it."

"You're not wrong, Captain; we're already getting reports from scattered marine squads and platoons across the planet."

He turned about and focused his attention on the scores of icons popping up across the planet. Many were of different sizes to show the estimated strength of those still alive and able to fight. Different colors showed Marine Corps and NHA forces separately, with many of the NHA units now broken up into smaller forces.

"We need to reach those we can help the fastest. We'll take the weapon, docklands, and this fortified region to the south first. We'll need secured landing grounds to control these areas, fast."

A dull groan vibrated through the hull as the retro engines burned and began the final deceleration prior to reaching a combat altitude. In less than a minute, the ship had halved its speed and still it continued downwards.

"Gunnery system is armed and ready, General."

He lifted his hand to his mouth and looked back to the tactical screen. The ships remaining in orbit were already engaging Biomech warships, but it was the large force under Anderson that concerned him. The icon representing ANS Explorer showed it had finished deploying, and scores of heavy warships were waiting nearby. He also noticed that Spartan's contingent was still there.

"General, I see you're in the thick of things, as usual."

He looked to his right and smiled as the form of Colonel Morato walked into the CIC.

"Teresa, I thought you had transferred before we began the descent. What about Spartan?"

She looked uncomfortable at his question.

"I assume he is with Khan? Those two are inseparable."

Teresa raised one eyebrow and then nodded in agreement.

"He's going with Anderson and the others to the Black Rift."

General Rivers appeared to find this intriguing.

"Yet you are here, why?"

He realized why before she could answer.

"Ah, Jack. I understand."

One of the Marine liaison officers approached, and he took a moment to explain exactly where he wanted his landing parties before turning back to Teresa.

"We must deal with Helios Prime first, but I have already

sent orders for a force to take the Rift control station to Spascia. If we're lucky, we might be able to reactivate the Spacebridge and send them help."

"And if we can't?" she asked calmly, even though her heart was pounding inside.

"If we can't, then we'll get there the old fashioned way."

"That could take weeks."

He nodded in agreement.

"Yes, you're right. So the quicker we secure Helios Prime, the better."

"I know this world well. Let me help you."

General Rivers knew that only too well, and they quickly went to work at the tactical display. Both quickly identified the strongpoints of both sides and diverted forces and air cover where they were needed. As they arranged for the landing of thousands of marines, he looked back to her.

"You understand that if Anderson and his forces fail at the Black Rift, this entire effort will be in vain? Your son can only be helped if Anderson succeeds."

"I know, General. That's why Spartan is there. I couldn't leave Jack alone, though. With Spartan at the Rift, and me doing what I can here, we'll be giving him the best possible chance."

General Rivers touched her arm, and his face almost seemed to soften in sympathy.

"Teresa, with the two of us plotting this battle, we have the best chance we could ever have."

He looked to the map and then back to her once more.

"Spartan is a great man and an even greater warrior. He's not the greatest strategist, though. Leave him to help in whatever bloodbath is coming to that Rift. I can promise you this; he will extract one hell of a toll in blood from them."

* * *

ANS New Carlos, Old Spascia City

Commodore Hampel tried to open his eyes and instantly felt the sting of pain in his right eyebrow. He forced them open and found warm air pushing through the broken visor on his helmet. He hadn't even noticed the thing on his head, but the broken material on the edges clearly showed where the transparent visor had once been.

When the hell did I even put this damned thing on?

He lifted his right hand and found the thinly armored glove was missing, and his hand lacerated in multiple parts. He moved it to his face and touched his cheek, half expecting to find blood and gore. The stinging pain was a relief, if nothing else.

I'm alive, that's a start.

The naval version of the PDS armor was similar to that used by the marines but lacked the protective qualities of that combat gear. This suit was designed to provide a sealed suit for EVA work and evacuation in emergency situations.

One additional benefit was that all naval clothing was heat and flash protected, a critical requirement to uniforms and clothing aboard warships. It was a lesson learned hard back in the Great War.

"Sir, can you move?" asked a familiar voice.

He looked up into the dust-covered helmet of another crewman. The visor lifted up and revealed the face of his executive officer.

"Lieutenant Morgan."

He coughed, and the pain sent red spasms of pain through his back.

"It's good to see you."

The younger officer looked up to the sky and pointed.

"The fleet is hammering them, Sir. Look."

He turned his attention upwards and watched as scores of large shapes dropped down like a meteor shower. Many more fighters swirled about in a deadly battle that saw one after the other tumbling down in flames. He looked back down and around him. The ground looked like a mall of some kind. Every floor had been shattered, yet a number of staircases partially remained, and crew in their PDS armor sheltered behind whatever cover they could find. Further away moved the massive shapes of Eques walkers. He'd seen imagery of them before, but never in these kinds of numbers. He spotted at least thirty in just this one area, and each of them poured fire down into the positions held by his crew. He tried to stand and felt a dizzying spasm through his body.

"No, Sir, you need to stay here," said Lieutenant Morgan.

She leaned in closer and pointed in the direction of the machines.

"We landed right in the middle of the city. There are three Marine units plus a single NHA company trying to defend thirty city blocks."

A rocket screamed overhead and vanished far into the distance. It was followed by a mechanical howl and scream, something he had never heard of before.

"What's that?"

His XO shook her head.

"New to me, Sir. It must be a rallying call or something for their troops."

"Lieutenant!" called out a crewman who was hiding next to the broken staircase.

She looked back and spotted him and three others taking aim at a squad of Thegns inching their way up the ruined street. Eques walkers had moved in behind them, and their turrets were moving back and forth as they searched for targets. Something moved off to the right, and three of the walkers blasted it with hundreds of rounds.

"Hold your fire, and keep your heads down!"

More noise came from behind them, and she spun about, her sidearm raised and pointing directly at the face of a battered-looking Alliance marine. Four more appeared, each in an even worse state than the rest.

"There's an assembly beacon at the transit complex., about three kilometers from the chasm. It's the bastion for this zone. This place has less than a minute before they overrun the place. You coming with us?"

She looked down at Commodore Hampel. With a great effort he lifted himself to his feet, even though the effort almost caused him to pass out.

"How many of you are at this bastion?"

The marine shrugged.

"No way to tell, Sir. I do know that General Gun is sending reinforcements to that exact spot though, fresh troops, machines, and supplies. It's got to be worth a shot."

The machines fired again, and this time the sound was considerably louder.

"You're right there, marine. Let's go."

With just a single word from his XO, the survivors of the Alliance warship abandoned their positions and followed the marines through the winding chasms and chambers of the broken city. Only Commodore Hampel bothered to look back once they reached a safe distance. He hadn't even noticed the remains of the ship while they had been so close. At this greater distance, he could make out the broken spine of the Liberty destroyer. There were twenty or more fires burning throughout the hull, and sections of the aft were scattered over a wide area. He spotted movement, and then a single Eques walker appeared in the middle of the wreckage. It kicked at the broken metal and then blasted away inside at unseen targets.

"Bastards!" he muttered.

Without thinking, he reached down for his sidearm. A hand stopped him and pulled his arm back.

"No, Sir, we can't help them now. We got out everybody we could; those left were trapped inside or too badly wounded to move. The machines are finishing off anybody they can find."

He shook his head and tried to grab for the gun again.

"What about prisoners? You know they take them to use in their machines."

Lieutenant Morgan shook her head in disagreement.

"No, Sir, that's not what's going to happen here. They aren't here to mobilize numbers for their war machine. This is a full-scale assault. Just look at them."

He did just that and almost had to avert his eyes when he saw the myriad of Decurions clambering all over the wreckage. Even at this distance, he could see them stripping the broken vessel to get inside. Lieutenant Morgan placed his arm over her shoulder and helped him continue their movement to the bastion.

"Sir, there's nothing we could do for them. All we can do is save what's left. This battle won't be over today. They've got entire armies on the surface already. The war for this place is only just starting."

They continued forward over the barren and desolate

surface of what had been the jewel of the Helion League. Just months before it had been a planet filled with towers, a beacon of success and civilization. Now it was another burned out husk, like so many planets that had fallen before the machines of the Biomechs. The battle for dominance continued with mainly fighters on both sides engaging in a perpetual dogfight. Every few minutes one of them would break free and rush down to strafe ground targets. It took nearly twenty minutes to cover the ground from the crash site to the outer defenses of what was now known as the bastion. The position was actually one of the many transport hubs that had suffered during the bombardment. Many wide highways and rail routes ran through or nearby, and all had been taken over by Alliance and NHA troops.

"Wow," said Lieutenant Morgan.

If it hadn't been for the raging sky battle, they might have stopped. Instead, they pushed on while soaking in what was happening around them. Dozens of fresh Bulldogs were moving out into new positions, while entire columns of Vanguards ran off in half a dozen directions. Even more regular marines moved weapons systems and equipment into positions. Through the smoke and off into the distance they could make out a Liberty class destroyer sat impotently on one of the landing pads. It was one of the transport-configured models, with its three mission bays given over to troops and equipment. Squad after squad ran down ramps and toward their deployment zones.

"This is much more like it," said Commodore Hampel.

His voice was much weaker, but the sight of so much Marine equipment and manpower seemed to calm him. Lieutenant Morgan checked the status indicators on the collar readout of his helmet and then looked ahead to the fresh marines. The Commodore dropped to one knee, groaned, and fell to the floor. Lieutenant Morgan tried to stop him, but his weight, combined with the surprise of him falling, left it too late.

"Medic! I need urgent medical attention, now!"

She dropped down alongside him, and a pair of cannon rounds whisked overhead, slamming into a fast moving Bulldog. The armored vehicle flipped over and crashed into a wall. Incredibly, the vehicle didn't explode or catch fire, and marines quickly arrived to drag the shocked and wounded men and women from the wreckage.

* * *

Low Orbit, Helios Prime

A small number of Biomech transports and two Ravagers were all that defended low-orbit at the point selected by General Rivers. Both of the two capital ships were torn apart by the concentrated gunfire of the first twenty-two Liberty destroyers as the fleet screamed down from orbit. Lines after lines of turret fire tore holes through the Biomech ships while the following Crusaders blasted them apart with their own guns. It was a savage and bloody opening to the Battle for Helios. The enemy was not slow in responding, however, and once ships had deposited their Biomech infantry, they quickly turned around and formed defensive squadrons to counter the new arrivals. Hundreds of Biomech fighters were forced to abandon their attack runs on the surface and turned their attention to the ships coming down from orbit.

A myriad of vessels cascaded down from space, their engines and weapons filling the skies with heat, light, and flame. More than fifteen separate groups arced downwards toward their preselected targets. These vessels had been waiting a long time for this battle, and now everything appeared to hinge on a tight timeframe. Some had reached the assembly point just hours before, but many had been there days or even weeks. A large contingent had also been present under the command of Admiral Anderson when it had assisted in the destruction of Biomech forces making for T'Karan. Now that core of seasoned and experienced vessels provided the heart of the force making for the surface.

Most of these groups of ships were aimed directly at the known hiding places for Marine Corps and NHA units. Some of these units were still in contact with High Command, but many had been forced to go into hiding since the Biomech invasion had begun. A few of these massive assault groups were also sent directly at the enemy's own landing grounds where they continued to disgorge troops into the fray. General Rivers and Colonel Morato, of course, led the single biggest formation. This included the bulk of the force's Vanguards plus the most experienced Marine Corps units assembled for Operation Citadel. They made directly for the site of the Planetary Defense Installation in a massed spearhead formation.

The majority of the Alliance infantry transports and assault ships continued in their falling orbit over Helios Prime. It took a number of minutes to move through the upper atmosphere, and the heat from the high-speed descent would easily burn off any obtrusions on ships' hulls. Once down and slowing down, the ships began deploying their descent hardware. For most, this involved the extending of low-level flaps and control surface while for others a number of heat-proofed veins would extend out to help reduce the speed and increase control in an atmosphere.

A single Liberty Destroyer lost an entire mission module and an engine, as minor damage to its hull allowed super-heated gases to rush inside and melt apart a series of bulkheads. The ship shuddered and twisted and then flipped about under the massive stresses. What remained of the shattered vessel spun about; flames rushing from every direction. It was a bloodthirsty and tragic start to the assault, but nothing was stopping the attack, not even the natural power of Helios Prime.

A smaller number of frigates and warships stayed in orbit and made for the remaining Biomech ships that had formed a defensive cordon. Both sides were roughly matched, but there was one major difference. The Alliance already had what remained of Admiral Lewis' fleet in combat, and this meant for the first time the Biomechs lacked air superiority.

The largest ship in the formation was the venerable ANS Ticonderoga, a Conqueror class Battlecruiser that had been outfitted for Naval command and assault operations. Her mission bays were optimized for Marine Corps usage, and General Rivers had moved his own command staff to conduct the Battle for Helios. A dozen Crusader class warships came down right behind as escorts, and more than double that number of Liberty class destroyers. Many more heavy transports and Liberty class troop carriers moved in right behind them. Once they had slowed down enough, the ships opened up access to their hangars and launch tubes. It was this final stage that marked the transition from transport to attack.

Drones launched first and then came the fighters. Lightning and Hammerheads screamed out from their mother ships, rushing off to engage the enemy. Maulers and even older landing craft then followed, each filled with marines and Vanguards, moving to the surface as fast as they dared while jinking to avoid gunfire and surface-to-air missiles. Many were hit during the descent, but the heavy armor on the Maulers took most of the fire. Only two were shot down, and both managed an emergency landing under extremely heavy fire. By the time the first Maulers were on the ground, there were also Hammerheads swooping overhead to provide close air support.

CHAPTER FIFTEEN

The war machines of the Biomechs were almost unchanged from their great struggle with the Helions and their allies. The forces that assaulted Helios Prime and Spascia were not the primary forces of the Biomechs, they were simply the survivors of that war so many generations before. Most of the Biomechs had been cast into the Black Rift, to be forever trapped in their own domain so many thousands of light years away. As the Alliance made its way closer and closer to seeing this Rift activated, some began to speculate on what might be found on the other side. Would the Biomechs be exactly the same as those encountered so far? Or would the Great Enemy that had been in exile for so long have evolved into something more horrific and terrifying?

Evolution of the Biomechs

ANS Dreadnought, T'Karan-Helios Prime Rift

Spartan marched through the ship with Khan standing

right beside him, as they had done on a hundred other occasions. This time there was a subtle difference, one that neither of them ever would have expected. On Spartan's other flank stood the implacable form of Forty-Seven, the Thegn soldier Spartan had spoken to first of all during General Rivers' visit. All three were armored from head to toe, though unlike the other two, the Thegn's armor was natural rather than added on. All of them also bore the star symbol of Hyperion. Spartan had given Khan the chance to choose something in the hours as they were waiting and had almost immediately regretted it. Khan simply chose the symbols often used by his own people. In theory, this should mean nothing more than putting the mark of Kerberos or a city of Proxima Prime on their armor. The reality was quite different, and each human they passed seemed to confirm that. The star of Hyperion looked more like a jewel, reminding all they met of the interest his people had in the mysteries of the world they had called home for two decades.

All three were unarmed, save for blades carried about their person, a concession even Spartan was unprepared to make. They moved through the corridors and passageways with speed, and everywhere they went they were met with odd looks. The Thegns were hardly surprising to see on the ship, but this far inside and so close to the command center of the vessel, it was most odd. Spartan looked to the alien foot soldier and raised one eyebrow in question.

"Forty-Seven, are your warriors ready?"

The alien continued walking forwards and said nothing. It did look at him with an odd, slightly confused look, rather like a small dog. Khan laughed at the failure in communication.

"Spartan, you remember what Z'Kanthu said. They are limited in their intelligence, and they cannot speak our language, not yet."

Spartan sighed and tried again.

"Forty-Seven, Bandon status."

The Thegn seemed to comprehend some, if not all of what he was asking this time.

"Forty-Seven, ready. Bandon ready."

Khan swung out and struck Spartan with his a right arm. The impact hit hard and forced Spartan to stumble before righting himself. He might have hit back, but a squad of marines was marching directly towards them. He might not be a marine any longer, but he was still in charge of thousands of soldiers, and his respect for the service had never dimmed.

"See, you just need the right words," laughed Khan.

They approached the entrance to the CIC, and a pair of marine guards blocked their way in. Spartan took a step closer, and both guards lowered their carbines.

"I'm here to see the Captain."

The two men said nothing, but one appeared to be speaking to someone over his communication system.

The second looked at Khan from head to toe, barely able to conceal his disgust at what he was looking at. Spartan glanced at his friend.

"Must be another Terra Novan. We've got fans everywhere."

The Thegn soldier waited in silence, not even moving when one of the guards made a disparaging remark to his comrade. The other chortled with amusement before finally straightening up and standing to the side. Both men saluted and ensured there was plenty of space for the three to move inside. The Thegn and Spartan went in, but Khan lingered and then stopped. Spartan spotted him but chose to carry on while shaking his head. He glanced back to see what would happen.

Khan looked at one and then to the other before sniffing them. The act was like that of an animal sniffing something new or unusual. The two marines looked at each other and chuckled. There were many in the Alliance that saw Khan and his kin as nothing more than animals, beasts of war that were suitable for nothing else. The taller one began to say something, and that was when Khan saw his chance. He lunged at him, and the man shook and took half a step backwards. His rushed action also made him fall over, his honor being saved only by the bulkhead nearby.

Khan roared with laughter and carried on right behind Spartan. The tall marine moved in behind Khan and made to strike him, but the other marine grabbed his arm. Khan tilted his head just a fraction so that he could see what was happening and began to laugh. Both marines then faced them, watching as the party went deep inside the CIC and away from their reach.

"Stupid children," he growled in mock annoyance.

There was a visible tension as the three entered, with each of them being watched carefully. Spartan noticed the looks, but it had little, if any effect on him. His was used to this kind of response, especially from those worlds with limited contact with other races.

I'm not in the Corps any longer. Neither is Khan or Forty-Seven. We've come across this rubbish a hundred times.

As he approached Captain Vetlaya, he wondered what exactly they would be classed as now. He was a retired Marine Corps Officer, and Khan was a synthetic being, created by the enemy's technology in the Uprising. Forty-Seven was a foot soldier of the enemy regime, a soldier whom only recently had been granted complete free will via the captured Core on Mars. Even Spartan wasn't completely comfortable having the warrior so close, but with the machines now firm allies; he had to do his part. By keeping the Thegn that was most honored of those recovered at Sol, he was making a statement to all of them. The Thegns were his allies, and he trusted them. At least that was what he needed them to feel. He just had to hope the modifications made by Z'Kanthu were both correct and permanent.

"Legatus Spartan, you've arrived at an...interesting time."

He looked at the Captain and then around the CIC. Dozens of faces looked back, and not one seemed particularly pleased to see him. It was not that different to how things had been before, but at least as a Marine officer he had been due some degree of respect. Now he felt like an outsider, somebody that perhaps shouldn't even be on the ship. It was only then he realized the title he had somehow been awarded.

"What's happening with Explorer?" Khan asked.

Spartan could barely contain his smile at the question from Khan, even though his friend had now interrupted his question regarding his position.

"Explorer is preparing to establish a Rift, Tribune."

Both Spartan and Khan looked at each other and then back to the Captain.

"What the hell is it with these names, Captain?"

The young officer looked a little taken aback at this. She turned, spoke to her XO, and then nodded toward a modest screen near her arm. Several images showed the two of them along with their service records and security details. More importantly, the screen also showed the other bandon, their attached Marine Corps liaison officers, and a codename for their taskforce. Spartan instantly noticed the name for Khan's title.

"Tribune?"

Now it was Captain Vetlaya's turn to smile.

"Yes, Legate. In the last thirty minutes, a number of new orders have come in from Alliance Command. General Rivers himself has reinstated both of you into the Alliance military, with honorific titles befitting your special status in this campaign."

"Legate?" he said again, but quieter this time.

Captain Vetlaya tapped the device, and the image of Spartan enlarged to show a rough chain of command for him and his assorted forces. At the same time, the imagery on the mainscreen changed to show a Rift being created before their very eyes. Spartan's eyes widened as he watched the ever-growing shape near ANS Explorer. The distortion flickered and rippled before settling down to create a temporary and instantaneous Spacebridge between Helios Prime and its destination. An image of Admiral Anderson appeared to the right, and all of the senior officers stopped and watched.

"Men and women of this fleet. Our hand has been called, and it is time for us to act. General Rivers is leading the fight here, and even as I speak, we have warships making for the surface. The campaign to reclaim this star system is well underway."

Spartan looked to Khan and back to the screen.

"We will follow a different and equally important path."

Khan nodded as the Admiral spoke.

"Animosh sympathizers and traitors in the Helion fleet have committed their last treacherous act. Just hours ago, they turned their guns on the T'Kari and small number of Alliance vessels guarding the Rift station complex. Latest reports show the area has stabilized, but the fight is ongoing."

The mood seemed to change in seconds in the CIC. There had been reports of the fighting there, but the main signal chatter indicated it was far less significant that it appeared.

"It is our mission to take the fight to the Black Rift, the gateway to the Biomechs' domain, and the thorn in the side of both the Helion League and the Alliance. Even now, the first enemy vessels are minutes away from reaching the defense force and adding their numbers to the traitor Helion ships."

Spartan leaned in to Khan.

"If they can open that thing, you know what's coming through."

Khan raised both of his eyebrows in surprise. There had been much speculation, but in reality there wasn't a soul in the Alliance that really knew.

"What do you mean?"

The loud voice of the Admiral drowned both of them out.

"It is our duty to keep it shut, no matter the cost. All ships, stations, and personnel are expendable for this mission. If anything comes through, you will do everything…and anything to stop them. Good hunting."

That was it, nothing particularly detailed, just a quick and direct call to arms for the fleet. Even now, the first ships in the massed formation were already altering their course and making for the Rift. The first to make it was ANS Warlord, a ship that at this range looked like a behemoth. A handful of Helion vessels move in nearby, but their sleek hulls and attractive lines were nothing like the brutality of the double-hulled Warlord. Where they had aesthetics, the Alliance ship had armor, and where they had weapons, ANS Warlord had banks of turrets. The flagship was a monster, a ship built in a rush by simply throwing together everything available in one shipyard.

Captain Vetlaya signaled to her XO.

"The enemy advance force is due in minutes, and the rest will be two hours behind them, so we can expect action from the minute we arrive. Get them ready. This one is going to be bloody."

The ship was already at maximum alert, but it would have been foolhardy to suggest anything less. As the XO sent orders to each of the vessels' stations, the Captain looked back to Spartan and Khan.

"You don't have long. I suggest you return to your troops. Anderson is leading the vanguard. We will be following in the third group, along with the rest of the Black Ships."

Khan pointed to the icons representing the unofficial vessels from Hyperion.

"And them?"

Captain Vetlaya looked back to Spartan as she answered.

"General Rivers' last order before heading for Helios Prime was to grant all of these ships a temporary commission in the Fleet."

Khan pulled his head back a little.

"Can he do that?"

Spartan interjected.

"Who cares? Official or semi-official, we're all going through."

He then turned his attention back to the Captain.

"Before we go, what the hell is this Legatus and Tribune business all about?"

Captain Vetlaya was clearly agitated with so much to be done. She considered sending them away, but it was clear the two needed something, no matter how brief.

"Look, a Legate, or more properly, a Legatus, is the title used long before the Confederacy. In that period, armed forces were raised and sent on operations under the command of important citizens for the length of the campaign. The Martian revolt in the twenty-third century A.D. required an emergency expedition that was led by a retired General who was granted Legate of the expedition."

She nodded as Spartan began to understand.

"It is an odd term, but one we are vaguely familiar with in the Navy. You are granted full autonomy within the constraints of this campaign in the Orion Nebula. Once back in Alliance territory, you and Tribune Khan will revert to being honored citizens of the Alliance and lose your position in the military."

"Great, so we're Alliance commanders, providing we never go home," said Spartan.

It was a bittersweet offer, and one he knew was almost certainly the best General Rivers could have done at short notice. It was a solution of sorts, but it also provided some problems later on. He turned to Khan who looked equally troubled.

"We've got nothing to worry about until this is all over. All we need to do is win and to survive this thing. What are the odds?"

The last few words came out a little louder than he'd intended, and he managed to attract the attention of a number of officers. Even Captain Vetlaya appeared unimpressed at his suggestion. Spartan nodded and then made for the door. He stopped and looked back, with Khan standing there along with the Thegn.

"Well, you coming? We've got a battle to plan!"

They chased after him, but before they reached the corridor Khan spoke out.

"What do you mean, we know what's coming through?"

Now Spartan looked confused.

"We saw the plans on the Biomech ship, don't you remember?"

Khan shook his head in confusion.

"No, Spartan, I never saw a thing to do with the Black Rift."

Spartan seemed unfazed by this and continued down the corridor with the Thegn right beside him. Khan dropped back a step and thought back to their time on the prison ship. He remembered the questioning, the torture, and the machines. But try as he might, he could not remember a dammed thing about the Rift. Even worse though, he had no memory of Spartan ever mentioning this before. He increased his pace to catch up.

"Spartan, can we handle what's on the other side?"

Spartan didn't stop, but he did twist about to look at his old friend. He didn't bother speaking. There was no need. The look was the same look Khan had seen in the eyes of the walking dead monsters sent in battle by the Biomechs. It was a look off insatiable, uncontrollable violence.

"Khan, there is nothing here that can keep them back. Nothing. This fleet, these ships, they are just delaying the inevitable."

Then his eyes narrowed, and the color almost came back.

"You and I, Khan, we know who they are."

He placed both of his hands onto Khan's forearms.

"Only we can stop them, my friend."

* * *

ANS Warlord, T'Karan-Helios Prime Rift

Admiral Anderson watched the mainscreen and did his best to keep his pulse under control. They inched closer and closer, and he knew that at any moment they would reach the Rift and then be propelled through to the other side of the star system. The journey time was two hundred and twenty-four light minutes away, yet the Rift allowed them to reach the target in an instant; there was no traveling time in the Rift. It operated merely as a doorway into another part of space.

"Six seconds, Sir," said the XO.

Anderson could see the clock and was counting down in his head. Every single ship in his fleet was ready for the battle. The plan was simple, one of the simplest he'd ever come up with.

"Two seconds."

The Rift filled the entire mainscreen. He swallowed and then blinked. At the moment his eyes opened, they were in a completely different part of space. Before them was a strange series of flashes and distortion. He ignored them and moved his attention to the rapidly updating tactical display. There he could see the small number of defending ships, as well as the traitorous Helion vessels.

"We're being targeted," said the XO.

"You all know the drill. Escorts will deal with the Helions. The rest will form up in a defensive formation at the designated coordinates.

"Aye, Sir."

Ship after ship appeared. They quickly moved off with sixteen escort vessels making for the Rift control station. They immediately engaged the five remaining Helion cruisers in a mid-ranged battle that saw gunfire and missiles exchanged at a high rate.

"Incoming communication from the T'Kari commander, Admiral."

"On screen."

The face of a T'Kari commander appeared to the right of the mainscreen. At times like this, it was imperative the view consisted primarily of the ongoing action, in this case the fight around the Rift station.

"T'Kron?" Anderson asked, surprised.

"Admiral, good to see you. We have a problem out here."

The imagery behind the alien showed emergency lighting and some considerable damage. The translator on his suit created a subtle degree of lag. It wasn't enough to impede conversation, but it was enough to make it look as though the alien had been dubbed into another language.

"The first wave of Biomech ships will be here in less than a minute."

"I know. My ships are deploying to form a defensive

laager around the proposed Rift site."

T'Kron shook his head in disagreement.

"No, Admiral. My exiles have only seen this signature twice before in our history. The approaching ships are doing something we've not encountered in this system."

"Well?"

"The signature matches a Biomech Rift opening sequence. We have records in our files of this being the precursor to the early stages of Rift creation."

Anderson shook his head in disbelief. He glanced over to his XO.

"Are the ships in position?"

Captain Decker nodded.

"Yes, Sir, ninety-one capital ships and escorts in a standard laager pattern formation."

It was far less ships than he had intended for any one mission. The rest of the fleet was busy fighting in orbit over Helios Prime or landing troops on the surface of that devastated world. The combined force would have given him more than three hundred ships of various classes and ages. He'd stripped out most of the frontline ships for this operation and left the transports and commercial vessels with the General for his own mission. He looked back to T'Kron.

"How many ships are coming this way?"

"Fifty-six ships, Admiral. They are advancing in a crescent formation around three Cruiser class ships."

"Any suggestions?" asked the Admiral.

T'Kron might be an alien, but his time with humans had allowed him to learn and partially adopt some mannerisms. This time he tried a laugh. It didn't entirely work and sounded more like he was choking. When he was finished, he pointed off to his left.

"We destroy them as quickly as we can."

* * *

ANS Ticonderoga, Helios Prime

General Rivers watched the battle from the safety of the armored hull of the ship. Small arms fire struck the metal plating every few seconds, but nothing short of heavy firepower would be able to damage, yet alone bring down such a massive vessel as ANS Ticonderoga. Captain Wilson gave specific orders to keep them high enough to command the battle, yet not too high that the Biomech ships in low orbit could track and attack them. General Rivers pointed to the tactical display, specifically the planetary defense installation.

"The Rift to T'Karan is down, and that facility might still be operational. It's the only one still able to shut down this system."

"What's the plan?" Teresa asked, "What is more important? Stopping them using it again, or capturing it for our own use?"

General Rivers didn't hesitate.

"The weapon could fail at any moment. I will not waste more lives trying to take control of the site. I want it taken out of the picture. It's a wildcard that can stab us in the back at any moment."

"Assault team?"

General Rivers looked at her and shook his head slowly. There was something about his expression that left her feeling more than a little numb. Instead of speaking, he accessed the ship's arsenal and displayed it next to the tactical screen.

"We use bombardment missiles."

"Atomics?" Teresa asked with horror.

"No, not on a friendly world. Not this time. We have a much more primitive weapon. It's time to go old school."

The three-dimensional model of the weapon showed a relatively simple object. At first glance, it looked like a guided free fall bomb with an aerodynamic shape and small wings to assist in targeting.

"Ten thousand kilograms of Composition H6, all delivered in a single blast."

"Air blast bombs," said Teresa, "How will that help though? The facility is deep underground."

Now the General seemed especially pleased with himself.

"The facility is irrelevant, Colonel. Just get the order out to our people. They have three minutes before the bombs start falling. When this is over, that weapon won't be firing at anything other than rock."

He then looked back at the tactical display.

"As for the rest of this place, it's time to introduce these machines to a purifying flame."

Teresa had never thought of the General as a particularly pious man. He'd never spoken like this before, but the ruined world and the massive numbers of enemy troops changed this battle into one like no other.

"Send in the destroyers."

Both of them watched two lines of Liberty destroyers spread out in waves over the ruins. All of them were equipped as transports, but their manifests showed no troops on board. Teresa tapped the icon of the first ship and almost staggered back at what she saw.

Bombs, all bombs. All of those ships are fitted out for bombardment. This was his plan all along.

* * *

Helios Prime

General Daniels opened his eyes to the sound of loud gunfire; he instinctively reached for a weapon, a weapon that was no longer attached to his body. He opened his eyes and began lifting himself up. His eyes focused, but very slowly to reveal the interior of a shattered building. A shape moved closer, and he lifted his arms to protect himself.

"Sir, we're buttoning down. Cover your face."

The unknown man waited in front, and others ran about before taking cover.

"What's going on?" he asked, his voice weak and pained.

"It's the General. He's started an aerial bombardment. It's time to let them all burn!"

Now he found the strength to lift up into a sitting position. It was only then he could see he was actually resting on the wreckage of a broken civilian vehicle. The building to the right was almost completely gone, and crates and chunks of rock had been positioned to form temporary walls and barricades. Squads of marines ran about to find cover while at least twenty Vanguards hunkered down along one side and continued firing off into the distance.

What is happening? Is this winning or losing? Where are my marines?

Even from this position, he could see the metallic forms of Eques walkers marching down streets and blasting away. The entire surface and its thousands of shattered buildings, streets, and skywalks seemed to be overrun with the machines and their hordes of minions. He looked up at the black sky and the continuing trails of smoke from drones and fighters.

This war will never end, he thought hopelessly.

A Liberty destroyer rushed overhead with a Biomanta

hot on its tail. Both fired away at each other. At the same time, a dozen or more fighters moved in close to attack both of them. Then he spotted two long lines of shapes high up in the sky. At first glance they could have been clouds, but the uniformity of the formation was what really caught his eye.

"Here it comes!" cried out a marine.

One of the Vanguards twisted about and lifted its massive metal arm.

"Stay down, all of you!"

It was an almost angry tone, and General Daniels could only assume it was a Marine Corps non-commissioned officer. Only they seemed to have such anger and authority in their voices, especially in such tense situations.

Light!

He could have been blinded, if it were not for the great clouds of dust and smoke already surrounding their position. Far off into the distance came the bright flash that expanded out with great speed.

Atomics?

More and more of them came down until the entire skyline was alight with flashes. They flickered like a wondrous firework display until finally all of them vanished behind the great cloud of dust.

"Shockwave!" shouted the Vanguard, again in his stern tone.

General Daniels tried to move, but his leg was numb

and his strength long gone. He rolled to the right and directly into the bloody ruins of a dead Thegn warrior. The blast wave hit like nothing he'd ever experienced. It howled through like a tornado, uprooting wreckage and shattering stonework as if they were paper. The internal speakers in his armor did nothing, and his communication and tactical updates were all offline. He moved his eyes to the left and then felt the storm of air pulling at him.

Now what?

He grabbed the wrecked vehicle and found a curved piece of metal jutting from the side. He wrapped his left arm around the section and then his right, just as another shockwave blasted past. A Vanguard appeared, staggered, and then tipped over backwards before vanishing off into the blackness.

CHAPTER SIXTEEN

Some regiments of the Confederate Marine Corps can trace their lineage back to the colonial militias on the colonies of Sol. These citizen units were trained each month to deal with raiders and threats to shipping and ports. There were even occasions where Legates were granted a short term of tenure to conduct specific operations. Every one of these operations included a core of colonial troops, as well as larger numbers of private security and volunteers. The mixed fortunes of these ad hoc units led to the creation of larger, permanent military forces that would provide a core of fighting men and women for both sides in both the Great War and the Uprising.

History of the Marine Corps

ANS Warlord, Black Rift

The massive warship took up its position to face the new arrival. Instead of facing bow forward, the ship had rotated fifteen degrees to port to allow the starboard batteries to also fire. The bow emitters could still target up to twenty degrees on either side and this, combined with the dorsal turrets, would give them the optimal firing pattern.

"All ships in position and ready to engage, Admiral," said the XO.

"Good. Let it begin."

The first weapons to fire were the missiles from the Liberty destroyers. As the slowest of the weapons, they would still be the last things to strike the enemy ships. Then came the massed guns of the ships of the line. The small, medium, and large caliber railguns sent shells of different types directly into the approaching formation of ships. Most of the rounds were nothing complicated, just chunks of shaped metal known as solid shot. A significant number of rounds included the infamous Sanlav rounds, a special type of ammunition invented in the Uprising for use aboard Confederate warships. Based on the ancient design from Earth, the shell would break apart at a fixed distance to shower the target with a small cloud of deadly projectiles.

"We've got good hits," said the tactical officer.

The mainscreen showed the small fleet of ships as they surged toward the Alliance defenders. Flickers of light marked where the projectiles had struck, and larger explosions indicated where substantial damage had been caused.

"Enemy fleet has sustained eleven percent casualties."

Admiral Anderson looked at him for a second and then again to the mainscreen.

"What the hell is going on? Why are they not firing?"

He stared intently at the screen.

"Magnify, I want to see the second line of ships. What are they protecting?"

The imagery altered instantly to a grainy video stream. In reality, the telescopes were at maximum zoom, and the camera shake made the footage almost impossible to view. Multiple layers of error checking and correction produced a low quality, but useable image. At first, he could see nothing more than a cloud of ships, and the majority at the front taking damage. Two had completely disintegrated while most of the others were still taking damage.

"That thing."

He pointed to a pair of wide hulled craft. Both were immediately behind four more ships that were positioned to take all of the fire.

"They will reach us in forty-five seconds, Admiral."

The fleet continued pounding the Biomech ships and caused even more damage. The closing speed was like nothing any of them had seen before. Even if the ships activated their engines at maximum burn, there would be no way they could slow down or stop before rushing right past the fleet and the Rift Station.

"Wait, I'm getting a reading from their ships. A power

reading, the levels are off the charts, Sir."

"Keep firing. I want those secondary ships brought down!"

The particle emitters on the larger ships fired their powerful beams right at the ships. Even at near the speed of light, they were unable to stop the entire force. By the time the first ship reached the Rift Station, half of the vessels were wrecked or smashed. One ripped through a Crusader, and the wreckage of both spun off into the void at incredible speeds. That was when the unexpected occurred. All the ships vanished, even those smashed or wrecked. In their place appeared a swirling vortex; much like a conventional Spacebridge, but this one was easily three times the size.

"Get us away from that thing!" Admiral Anderson yelled.

It was too late for three Liberty destroyers, and they were caught right in the path of the Rift. All of them were cut clean in half by the massive distortion. The rest of the fleet scattered in panic from the devastation wrought by the phenomenon. Sirens inside the ship blared loudly even though they had sustained no damage. Each of the ships powered away, scattering like prey from a predator. Admiral Anderson checked the data coming in, but it was the video stream of the Rift that attracted the most attention.

"I need T'Kron. Get him now!"

He watched as a large shape began pushing through the Rift. It looked nothing like a ship, yet it was larger than even the Rift control station. It moved slowly and then stopped, with a large section like the end of a bone that stuck out into Helion space. He grabbed the intercom and connected to the fleet.

"This is the Admiral. We have five and half hours before the Biomech reinforcements get here. Secure the perimeter, and move away from the Rift."

Most of the ships had already reached a safe distance and were now merging into four groups of twenty or more ships. The largest number moved in around ANS Warlord. At the same time, the Rift pulsed as though it was absorbing energy or trying to move. With each pulse came bursts of lighting that reached out like the limbs of some monster. Several lashed about the semi-derelict Rift control station and tore chunks off with each strike.

"Admiral," said a familiar voice.

Anderson looked to the right of the mainscreen where the image of the T'Kari commander appeared.

"Is this what you expected?"

"I expected nothing in particular, but this Rift is unlike anything we have seen before. The energy readings are incredible."

"Can your weapons close it?"

T'Kron looked back and said nothing for nearly four seconds.

"Admiral, my ships have been firing for the last thirty seconds. Our weapons are having no effect on the distortion."

He looked back at the mainscreen and the massive tear in space. The Biomech structure still sat right in the middle of the Rift while small shapes moved about it.

"Contact! We have signals coming through the Rift."

Admiral Anderson opened his mouth to speak, but no words came out. He coughed and tried again.

"All ships, watch the Rift. Here they come! Open fire!"

ANS Warlord began to pivot but only made it halfway around when the first dozen ships came through. Her starboard and dorsal turrets opened fire, as did the turrets on the other ships in the fleet. Four groups of Alliance vessels poured fire into the Rift and were rewarded by hundreds of explosions. Admiral Anderson even thought they were doing well for a moment, but through the debris field came scores more ships. Some even smashed their way through the wreckage to move out into Helion territory. Once they cleared the distortion, even more came in of all sizes.

"Keep firing!"

The ship's computer tagged and classified each of the threats as they came in. T'Kron watched on his own screen and appeared as dumfounded as Admiral Anderson.

"These ships, they match the stories of old. The Biomechs have returned."

Anderson looked once more at the screen and the scores of warships moving out in long lines. The end of the object in the Rift began to open in a dozen places, and from these gaps came a myriad of smaller fighters and robotic drones.

"Admiral, several of their ships are heading for the Rift back to Helios Prime," said the XO.

Anderson looked at the tactical display and rubbed his forehead. In all his concern about the Rift, he'd forgotten about the one they had created that went back to Helios Prime and their own collapsed Rift back home. For a fraction of a second, he considered issuing a withdrawal order. His small fleet of less than a hundred ships already faced a major threat, and there was no clear upper limit to the enemy strength.

What if they have three hundred ships, or a thousand?

He looked to his XO and nodded in agreement.

"Close the Rift. We will make our stand here, at the Black Rift."

He looked back at the mainscreen and issued his orders to each of the squadrons. One by one they presented their guns to the enemy while at the same time disgorged fighter squadrons into the fray. The Rift flickered and then vanished, leaving the fleet out on the periphery, weeks away from Helios Prime.

"Admiral, the structure inside the Rift appeared to be emitting a massive energy field into the Rift itself. A byproduct seems to be that it is stabilizing the Spacebridge, even with the T'Kari weapons firing into it," said the tactical officer.

"Byproduct?" asked the Admiral, "What else is it doing?"

The man looked back and rubbed his mouth with the back of his hand.

"Uh, our sensors show the structure of the Rift is changing. I could be wrong, but I think they are trying to create a permanent Spacebridge."

That was a possibility even he hadn't thought of.

"XO, ignore their fighters. I want everything we have firing at that structure. Tear it apart!"

* * *

ANS Dreadnought, Black Rift

Spartan, Khan, and Forty-Seven marched toward one of the waiting Maulers. Z'Kanthu was waiting for them, along with the Thegn file commanders, each of them with their distinctive colors and gray uniforms.

"Well, this is it," said Spartan.

Khan looked to his friend and was glad to see he was almost back to normal. The ship shuddered as gunfire from the few remaining Helion ships tried to force them back. None of this particularly concerned Spartan; his mind was focused on what he could control, the ground troops aboard the Black Ships.

"Are your soldiers ready?"

Each of the commanders nodded in agreement. Spartan looked to Z'Kanthu.

"What about you?"

The ancient machine stayed completely still as it spoke.

"My kin are ready, as are all eleven bandon. Just give us the target, and we will do the rest."

Another heavy blast shook the ship, and the XO's voice blasted out via the internal speakers.

"Brace, brace, brace. Enemy ships are coming through the Black Rift."

Spartan lifted an eyebrow and looked to Z'Kanthu.

"What is your assessment?"

The ancient machine considered the situation with all the data he had access to. Spartan and Khan had been granted full strategic and tactical access to the digital network, but the Biomech machines had a knack for tracking additional data, even when heavily encrypted.

"This vessel, it is unknown to us. Let me contact On'Sarax."

Again there was a pause, and the hull continued reverberating with the sound of gunfire clattering against the hull. Spartan and Khan watched and waited until finally Khan groaned.

"Come on, we know what's happening out there. Do we need these machines to explain it to us?"

Whether in confidence or not, Z'Kanthu chose that moment to speak.

"The signals from the structure indicate a Rift construction machine. These were in development in the war. They may be attempting a permanent wormhole directly to this system. If they succeed, it may never be collapsed."

An impact struck much louder this time, and the vessel made a groaning sound.

"I need to speak to the Admiral," said Spartan.

It took less than ten seconds for an image of the Admiral to appear inside his helmet.

"Admiral, what's happening out there?"

"Spartan, the Rift is open, and this base or ship is keeping it open."

"Can you destroy it?"

Anderson shook his head.

"Not a chance. We tried missiles, railguns, and particle beams. They have interceptor weapons to hit the ballistic rounds, and the particle beams are just not breaking it down fast enough. That thing is better protected than the bloody Arks."

"How long do we have?"

Admiral Anderson spoke a little quieter.

"My engineers estimate the Rift will reach maturity at the same time as the Biomech reinforcements arrive. It's a beautifully timed and executed plan. They are sending in an extra ship every two minutes now. I can hold what has come through, but every extra ship is making my job harder. I'm down three ships already. At this rate, the fleet will be gone well before the Rift is finished."

Spartan looked to Khan and the machine.

"Can it be stopped from the inside?"

Khan said nothing, but Z'Kanthu gave a slow nod.

"It is a machine, nothing more. If it can be slowed or shutdown, we could buy them more time."

Khan tilted his head and then nodded.

"Then we go in."

Spartan agreed.

"Admiral, I'll take the Black Ships right into the mouth. Keep them off my back."

"Spartan, what are you going to do?"

"Whatever I can."

* * *

The battle at the Black Rift had changed into a mass of ships and fighters with little organization on either side. The Alliance still maintained the greater numbers, but gunfire coming from newly arrived ships had pushed them further away. Fighters rushed about in squadrons of ten or more, and scores of wrecked ships littered the coldness of space around the Rift. Only one group made for the Rift, and at its head was ANS Dreadnought.

"All ahead full!" said Captain Vetlaya.

They went in at speed toward the ships coming out of the Rift. The forward guns flashed back and forth as both sides exchanged particle beam and gunfire. The Conqueror class Battlecruiser was a tough vessel and took the impact in her stride; even a thirty-round salvo against her port flank did little more than to create a minor gash and tear off the outer layer of armor.

"All ships create the opening."

The six Liberty destroyers added their own firepower to that of the Battlecruiser, opening up six holes in various parts of the structure deep inside the Rift. A few shots missed and struck yet more Biomechs coming through. If the Black Ships had been alone, they might easily have been destroyed at this range. Luckily, Anderson had brought in one of his divisions to offer support, and this group of eighteen ships, including his own flagship, was able to pound the Biomechs and provide a distraction, at least for a few minutes. Captain Vetlaya tapped the icon for Spartan.

"Legatus, you have your window. Now it's up to you."

"Thank you, Captain, good luck."

* * *

Spartan led the assault wave in the first of the Maulers. Dozens more followed, each carrying a deadly cargo of

Thegns and Decurions. Another eight Maulers moved with them and an additional two companies of Alliance Marines, each of them a volunteer to serve under Spartan's command. Behind this wave of armored vessels came a polyglot selection of ferries and passenger shuttles to carry the Jötnar contingents from the Hyperion flagged civilian ships. In total, more than a hundred small craft pushed away from the Black Ships and into the defensive fire of the Biomech warships.

"Spartan, I don't think this is your best plan," laughed Khan.

From their position inside the Mauler, the banging and crashing of debris and projectiles shook them about. There was no gravity or atmosphere, but the impact still would have killed them; had they not been strapped in their mag-harnesses.

Z'Kanthu waited at the rear of the craft where the clamps normally used for Vanguards had been modified to hold him. Even so, his massive metal frame shook and lurched about as the clamps strained to keep him in place.

"Six hundred meters," said the pilot over the comms channel.

Spartan looked at the other passengers, a fifty-fifty mixture of marines and Thegns. All of them were held in by the mag clamps and waiting patiently. He checked the figures on the visor overlay and shuddered at the sight of so many friendly and enemy vessels in such close proximity.

He could see the other units inside their craft as they made for the Rift. The Jötnar craft were catching up, and he tried to ignore the shock as three Biomantas caught one of the ferries out. They tore it apart with gunfire before themselves succumbing to fire from the Alliance warships. He tracked the Jötnar forces, identified the lead craft, and made contact.

"Olik, how are your people?"

The audio crackled a little and pulsed in and out, but most of it came through clearly.

"Spartan, good to hear from you. We're fine. Red Watch is right behind you, and we have another nine hundred Jötnar on the way. They are looking for a fight."

Spartan shook his head in amusement.

"You know this is probably a zero-g assault, don't you?"

"Most of them are from the mines on Hyperion or the engineer stations on Prometheus. Every single Jötnar has been equipped the same as us. Unlike your people Spartan, we're efficient. Just make sure you leave some for us."

It was bravado. He knew that. Even so, he couldn't help but feel concerned for them. They might have been equipped with fresh gear from the arsenals on Prometheus, but could they fight a conventional battle? He had to assume that Osk and Admiral Churchill had been behind their equipment.

If they gave them the equipment, then they probably trained them as well.

He recalled what he'd heard about the Red Watch and the militia. The Jötnar had been training for all kinds of situations, and only now had he realized there may have been other reasons for this.

That cunning dog, this must be Anderson's work. He was training up extra units of Jötnar, even though they weren't even technically in the military.

It made sense, of course. The Admiral had an excellent idea as to what was happening out in the Orion Nebula. The only other chance was that the Jötnar themselves had decided to do this, and that was something Spartan found hard to believe. They were great fighters, honorable, and reliable. The Jötnar were anything but great strategists.

"Fifty meters and closing," said the pilot.

"Right, get ready, people. This is gonna be rough."

Spartan looked down to his armor and checked everything was ready. His visor was already locked down and the protective screen raised. His carbine was loaded, the safety off, and the coils charged.

"Z'Kanthu, ready?"

Yes, was the only word that came back.

"Ten meters."

The craft shook violently as they smashed through the wrecked exterior of the structure. The Mauler's nose section was very heavily armored for just this purpose. It continued onwards until it almost became stuck.

"Out, now!"

The doors slid open and revealed the dark interior of some kind of massive facility. Spartan didn't hesitate and pulled himself out of the Mauler and into the wreckage. Khan came next and then Z'Kanthu. The other passengers were already clambering out through the other hatches and using their hands, feet, and additional reaction thrusters to move further inside. This particular area was very wide and nearly five meters tall. Spartan activated his exterior lamps, and the others did the same.

"Looks like a launch tube or hangar to me," said Khan.

The intercom crackled.

"Spartan, Major Terson. We've entered the dorsal breach and are moving inside. Be careful, this place is full of machines."

"Understood, Major, be careful."

He checked the rest of them were with him before pulling himself further forward. He could already see at least thirty marines and the same number of Thegns making their way through the ruined interior.

"I need this place mapped. Are the Decurions ready?"

"They await your command," replied Z'Kanthu.

"Good, send them in."

The machines were stored inside the landing craft wherever they had found space. As they received their orders, they extended their legs and then scuttled out of the craft and into the Biomech structure. Unlike the other units, they moved quickly, due to their multiple limbs and zero gravity agility; something they had been built to do. One by one they moved off into the distance. At the same time, the first indications of the enemy appeared at three other locations.

"Stand your ground; we need intelligence before we proceed," he said.

His body told him they needed to get inside fast, but his experience and training told him to be cautious. This was an unknown facility, and the enemy strength was even less known. In just a minute all of them had vanished from view, yet each sent back data that expanded the model Spartan and the other commanders had of the structure. Z'Kanthu quickly assessed the data as it arrived. He created a partially complete schematic and sent it to every officer in the boarding action.

"Yes, I see," said Z'Kanthu, "This is an outer transit coupling, an area for landing spacecraft. The shaft from here joins the primary shaft three meters in that direction."

He pointed away from where they had landed.

"The primary shaft runs along the entire length of this vessel and toward the field generators, here and here. Both sides of the structure are mirrored."

The flagged areas were in the center, one each side of the Rift. There were hundreds of spherical chambers running along the length, as well as a dozen larger sections above and below them.

"On'Sarax, Gorokk, and Bullyak are leading their

Thegns toward the nearest field generator. If they can bring it down, they will be able to slow down or halt their ability to reinforce the Spacebridge."

Spartan looked down his carbine's sights, but so far they were in the clear.

"We're nowhere near that part of the structure. The only way to join them is to get back in the Maulers and land at the same point at On'Sarax."

"No," said the machine in a robust, unflinching tone.

"You've got another plan to collapse this Rift?"

Two squads of marines moved on another twenty meters and then pulled themselves close to the floor, walls, and ceiling. Their lamps bathed the interior with a mixture of white, yellow, and orange hues. The first of the red armored Jötnar, six of them staggered, stumbled, and pulled their way through the zero gravity environment. Only two managed to get their magnetic boots functioning correctly. Z'Kanthu twisted to his left and moved one of his arms to point out extensions in the ceiling.

"You are thinking only of the objective, Spartan. There are many ways for us to complete this mission. Look, these are the heat exchangers, but this is the area that should concern us."

The area he had selected lay on the other side of the Rift, where a long cylindrical chamber connected to a vast series or tunnels and machines. It was the only section not mirrored in its entirety on the other side.

"The Primary Power Amplifier. This part of the Rift Engine is what is maintaining the stabilizer field, and it is at the end of the next passageway."

"That will stop this thing?"

The machine shook his head.

"No, the Rift will continue to exist."

Spartan sighed and took a step forward. Z'Kanthu traveled the same distance.

"If we overload the Amplifier, the stabilizer will fail, and the Rift we be like any other. It will make it vulnerable to weapons. If we overload it and cause it to fail, the T'Kari will be able to collapse the Rift and destroy this machine at the same time."

Spartan looked at Z'Kanthu and smiled.

"So we don't try and stop the machine itself, we just remove their ability to keep the Rift open. Are you sure the Amplifier is the place?"

"Yes. Each time the T'Kari fire their weapons into the Rift, this part of the station expends almost a third of its energy from the coils near the Amplifier. The Amplifier is charging them back up after each strike."

Spartan had almost been excited at their prospects, but now everything seemed to ride on this one objective, and that made him nervous.

"What about the station's main power unit? There's always a reactor of some kind."

Z'Kanthu snorted; it was a sound Spartan had never

heard before.

"I am detecting energy signatures, machine signatures all around it. Whoever is running this facility knows we are here. They are pulling back their forces to defend the weak points."

Spartan's helmet made a two-tone noise, and then a small icon popped up.

Anderson.

"Spartan, what's your status? We're getting hammered out here."

In the tense operation to get inside, Spartan had almost forgotten about the fight that was taking place outside. Every penetrating hit against a warship could kill scores of people, and he'd already expended substantial time getting this far. Spartan checked the details from his unit commanders that showed their current position and status.

"Admiral, I have four of our Kybernetes inside, plus upwards of four hundred Thegns and a company of marines. Olik has brought in Jötnar forces to assist. The other three Kybernetes are landing their forces along the port side of this vessel."

"And the enemy strength?"

Spartan's heart felt heavy at this question.

"Uncertain, Sir."

He could almost feel the nerves inside the Admiral.

"Don't worry, Sir. We have a plan. We will…"

"Spartan, don't waste time talking to me. A squadron of

Cephalons has come through and is pushing us back. Get inside, do what you must, and shut this wretched Rift."

Spartan glanced to Khan who had heard the same message. His comrade began to speak, but the sound of the Admiral's voice returned.

"Spare nothing, Spartan, end this today!"

That was finally the end of the message, but it filled Spartan with a sense of urgency. He selected the unit channel he'd used prior to starting the assault.

"All units, your commanders have their orders. Move quickly and get to your objectives. Set your thermite charges and then fall back to the boats. Each team will stay until their mission is complete."

Khan looked to him with a concerned look, but Spartan shook his head.

"Today is not a day for half measures. If we all do our job, we will have a chance. Let's do this thing."

One by one they inched further into the never-ending channel inside the facility. It looked like an underground railroad, with long beams on every side and indentations at regular intervals. Spartan threw another quick glance over his shoulder and spotted Z'Kanthu and lines of Thegns and marines walking along the metallic floor. Each of the marines was now making use of their anti-gravity boots, while the Thegns moved like animals on all fours. They made use of any grab rails, handles, or obtrusions to move at least as quickly as the marines.

"Z'Kanthu, what is this? A ship or space station?" Khan asked.

The machine kept on moving as it replied.

"This is neither. In our terms, we would call it a Rift Engine. It is a massive robotic installation with enough exterior weapons, power plants, and equipment to match an entire space station."

"Yeah, but where's the crew?" Spartan asked.

The hundreds of men and machines moved silently inside. Khan tapped his helmet and then pointed to the floor.

"Spartan, On'Sarax reports her forces are under fire at the secondary power convertors below us. Hundreds of machines are surrounding them."

Spartan looked to Z'Kanthu and shook his head.

"We stop for nothing, old friend. We keep forward. When the mission is complete, then we go for survivors."

"I agree," said the machine.

A light flashed on the inside of Spartan's visor, then another, and then the entire thing lit up red.

"Our Decurion scouts have made contact; multiple targets coming this way."

Spartan checked his carbine and looked to his visor.

"These are bigger than Decurions. What are they?"

The line of Thegns and marines advanced in the silent vacuum, all with their weapons raised and expecting trouble. The schematic created by Z'Kanthu showed that a wide chasm ahead would dip down and then join the massive passageway running the length of the Rift Engine. It would give them a quick way to progress, but it was also devoid of cover. They reached the edge of the downward gradient when Spartan could finally see their shapes on the enhanced optics of his visor.

"Biomech engineers," said Z'Kanthu.

He moved closer to Spartan and then stopped. With a single movement, his arms dropped down and his plasma weapons began to spool up.

"These are nothing like what you have seen before. Prepare yourselves."

"Get ready!" Spartan ordered.

His pulse began to increase, and he found his finger automatically moving to the trigger on his carbine. The shapes came closer, and he could see how big they were now. There were dozens of them, and each one at least the same size as Z'Kanthu. They had multiple legs, and from their torsos hung many more arms. An odd variety of tools and equipment was attached both to their torsos and to their limbs.

"Engineers. They are the oldest of the Biomechs, the most experienced, and the most intelligent. Their skills at the construction and operation of advanced machines are unknown even to me."

Blue flashes marked where the machines started firing their weapons. The pulse of energy moved at high-speed toward the advancing marines and their Thegn allies. Seven were vaporized in the first blast even though they kept their bodies low to the ground.

"Open fire!" Khan shouted.

He'd already taken aim with his new toy, one of the Jötnar L56 multi-barreled guns. The marines joined in with their own carbines, using only the high-power mode to smash the enemy machines. A sprinkling of L48 rifles sent explosive rounds hundreds of meters inside the Rift Engine.

CHAPTER SEVENTEEN

Spartan has always been a character of mixed fortunes. In the Uprising he was loved and hated in equal measure for his military successes, and for the bloody incursions that left so many dead and wounded. The Fall of Terra Nova, though a pivotal moment in Alliance history, is still subject to argument. The assault and battle on the surface left many dead, and much of the blame was placed on Spartan, a man renowned for frontal assault and body counts. Is it therefore surprising that the events of the Black Rift would leave him remembered as the man responsible for more death then any man since the great wars of Earth?

Heroes of the Great Uprising

Biomech Rift Engine, Black Rift

Two platoons of marines advanced, with Thegns moving along the walls and ceiling. They all fired repeatedly with great volleys of gunfire ripping through the tunnel. Every few seconds, another blast of energy would come back and tear apart whatever it struck. Even so, Spartan's assault had now penetrated into the primary passageway and was halfway along its length toward their objective. Additional passageways and rooms on both sides provided extra hiding places from which the defenders made quick attacks before melting away into the blackness.

"Spartan, we're getting close," said Khan.

Fifty meters ahead was a circular chamber with objects hanging down from the tall ceiling. It was a massive room, easily two hundred meters in diameter, and both the floor and ceiling disappeared into great pits. A pair of walkways wide enough for five or six people ran around the sides. There was an additional metal bridge over the great pit, but it was exposed with no protection of any kind.

"Yes, Z'Kanthu, is the plan still on?"

The machine headed for the central bridge and answered without even looking at the marines.

"Yes, the Amplifier system is on the other side of this structure."

He extended one arm and pointed ahead.

"Beyond the pit are four access points. Two of them lead to the Amplifier system. That is our objective."

Three heavy projectiles struck his chest, and the machine stumbled back, hurtling about before he could clamp onto the wall. Superheated blue material burned into his armor plating.

"And there is the enemy," Spartan said through gritted teeth.

The machines had so far avoided close range combat, but now they were coming out from the pit to block off access to the bridge and the two walkways. At this range, Spartan could see their shapes quite clearly. One took aim directly at him and fired. The blue energy narrowly missed him, burning through the wall instead.

"Put them down and keep moving!"

Line after line of Thegns threw themselves forward, only to be gunned down by the heat and power of the machines' weapons. Those that made it to within ten meters found they had keep their projectile weapons silent until now. The flash of white indicated dozens of barrels spitting out rounds that punched through marine and Thegn armor with ease. Spartan pulled himself back, watching in horror as more than thirty Thegns and marines were gunned down in a murderous salvo.

Bastards!

His visor showed there were seven of the machines, standing with a small gap to the next one. More were arriving from the other side of the pit and taking up position. Each was as different to the next with an odd array of arms, tools, and weapons. Many carried as many as five different limbs, and all were equally capable of tearing a man in half.

"Get in cover, now!" he yelled.

Khan had already taken cover behind a tall pillar flanked with pipes and thick cabling. Three Thegns clawed at the pillar and climbed up to reach the ceiling. It was a bizarre three-dimensional battlefield, a place where ceilings and walls became floors. Spartan lifted his carbine and took aim at the closest machine. Two high-power shots punched holes into its armor. His shots seemed to do no more than get the thing's attention. It rotated two of its six arms as though stretching and then moved away from the pit and toward the sheltering marines.

"Spartan, here they come," Khan said, excitement in his voice.

Spartan threw him a quick look and spotted a pair of serrated blades extending out from his friend's armor.

"You fool, Khan, you'll need more than blades against those things."

He looked back and all seven machines were marching in time. They stepped with one foot at a time, each crashing to the ground and connecting via magnetic links before the next. They had switched to their conventional guns now and blasted everything they could see. Spartan's helmet seemed to fill with sound.

"Come to us," said an odd voice.

"Did you hear that?" he asked Khan.

His friend was much too busy preparing himself for the approach of the metal monsters. Dozens of Thegns moved above the machines. They had somehow managed to avoid the guns and were moving along the walls to the pit. One lost its grip and spun out into the open, quickly drawing the attention of the machines. As soon as one saw the Thegn, they all did. Seven machines and sevens guns tore the unfortunate creature apart.

"Now!" Spartan called out.

Scores of marines and Thegns came out from cover and fired at the machines. It was almost impossible to miss at this range. Khan pushed away from the wall and landed on the side of the closest machine. He pushed the barrels of his L56 into its torso and fired. Sparks and flashes erupted all over the thing. Spartan tried to join in, but a red shape pushed past and threw itself at the machines. Another drifted past with blades held out in front of it before crashing headfirst into the next machine.

"Jötnar!" he said happily.

Dozens more of the Hyperion-marked warriors rushed into the fray, and only one stopped nearby and turned to look at him.

"Olik?" Spartan asked.

The Jötnar's armored visor lifted up so that only the transparent part remained.

"We're here. I'll keep the machines busy. You finish the mission."

More of the Jötnar moved in around the machines, and a deadly close range melee broke out. The machines were much better suited to the fight, and for each one destroyed, they killed or maimed three of the Jötnar. Even so, weight of numbers quickly turned against them. Spartan blasted the final machine, just as Khan embedded his blades into a power core on its back. The machine collapsed, and Khan pushed off and grabbed a nearby rail. Spartan placed his hand on Olik's shoulder, but Khan spoke.

"Always late to the fight!" he laughed.

They looked to the chasm and beyond where more machines were arriving.

"It's time," said Olik.

Spartan pushed in another magazine and climbed onto the wreckage of one of the fallen machines.

"You're right there."

He bent down into a low stoop and then pushed out. He moved effortlessly over the chasm in the zero gravity environment, easily avoiding the bridge and the vast gaps on either side. Other marines joined in, but the Thegns elected to stay in contact with solid surfaces.

* * *

ANS Warlord, Black Rift

"How many more?" Admiral Anderson asked.

His voice was bitter. Even after more than an hour's combat, the battle was still far from resolved. His crew was exhausted, yet they continued the fight even as gunfire raked her hull.

"Three more Cephalons have moved in. They have joined the other Biomech ships near the Rift Engine."

The ships were a major threat, but instead of attacking his ships, they had joined dozens more to create a strong defensive position. Any attempt to assist Spartan and his landing parties would require breaking through the Biomech blockade, something that had proven impossible. He looked to the tactical display that showed the remaining seventy-four Alliance ships. Every one was now damaged, but not one had even considered withdrawing. All but one of Spartan's Black Ships had also fallen back and to the rear of his own force.

"Sir, another assault wave is coming for us," said the XO.

The mainscreen showed sixteen Biomantas in an arrow formation, and a screen of at least fifty drone fighters of unknown configuration. They were already firing and heading for his ship. Admiral Anderson activated the communication protocols.

"All ships focus your fire on the approaching enemy vessels. Burn them!"

One by one they opened fired. Missiles, guns, and particle beams ripped the Biomantas apart, yet still they came. Four exploded simultaneously and then a Crusader joined them. The Biomech ships continued at an even faster pace even though they were taking heavy fire.

Admiral Anderson looked to the right where the bulk of the Biomechs sat patiently near the Black Rift.

They are just waiting for this to be over. They won't even help their comrades.

"Admiral. They are on a ramming course!" yelled the XO.

Admiral Anderson pulled himself to his feet and pointed at the Biomantas.

"Get our bow facing them. Concentrate all fire on the nearest ships."

The XO passed on his orders while a chorus of brace commands echoed through the massive warship. Admiral Anderson sat down and checked his mag belts were secured.

Come on, Spartan! End this! My ships can't take much more.

* * *

Biomech Rift Engine, Black Rift

Spartan looked back for a brief moment. The fighting around the pit had expanded to include machines, Thegns, and marines in a bloody battle. Hundreds of bodies, congealed blood, gore, and smashed chunks of machines drifted about the interior.

"We have to end this, Khan."

Khan was busily ripping off a gun mount from a fallen Biomech machine as Z'Kanthu held it down. The weapon came off with a flash of sparks, and Khan rested it under his arm. Just six other marines had made it this far plus a pair of Thegns; the rest were busy in the massive battle for the pit.

"The Amplifier, we need to end it now," said Spartan.

Z'Kanthu looked about, beckoning to the large arches ahead and to the right. A smashed Biomech war machine drifted out near an arch, and two more had taken cover behind the pillars.

"Two machines stand before us and the prize," he said through clenched teeth.

"Keep it simple," said Spartan, "High power and aim for the heads."

Z'Kanthu was already off though, his metal limbs propelling him along the wall with speed and precision. The two defenders fired at him and began to inflict substantial damage to his left side.

"Help him!" Spartan yelled.

The last few members of the assault force pulled themselves along and fired where possible. Spartan managed to blast three limbs off one of the machines, but Z'Kanthu ended them both when he reached them. It wasn't so much a fight, more a sequence of machine operations that saw chunks of metal, arms, legs, and pieces of armor ripped from each of them. The two were finally destroyed, and the battered Z'Kanthu grabbed the wall and pulled himself through the arch. Spartan moved in right beside him and face-to-face with one remaining machine. This one looked almost identical to Z'Kanthu. It was large and looked ancient, yet was colored bright red. It carried no obvious gun, but both of its arms were heavy and fitted out with powerful-looking clamps that might easily stand in for claws. It swung both its arms and sent the ancient Steersman flying through the air.

"Spartan, move back!" called out the machine.

He refused, of course, and pulled himself past and to the side of the machine. Khan and the others were right beside him, and rather than retreating were looking for cover. The chamber was large but with a much lower ceiling, and bank after bank of large cylinders. A huge three-dimensional model lay in the center of the room that showed a pulsing cylindrical object. The machine twisted about and pressed a panel. A holographic control unit appeared, and with a few subtle movements, the room flickered. Spartan found himself falling. The impact was hard, but luckily for him the drop was just two meters.

"Watch out!"

He rolled to the side without looking, and one of the machine's blades came down hard into the floor. More shapes appeared at the entrance, and Spartan waved them in. A pair of marine engineers carried one of the many portable thermite charges, equipment designed specifically for this operation. Behind them came one of the Biomech machines, but it dropped to its knees as dozens of Decurions clambered over its torso.

"Set the charges. Move it!"

The marines move with much greater speed now that artificial gravity had been activated. As more came inside, they split up and to the control and power cells for the Amplifier. The machine continued its deadly fight, and any coming too close, were quickly dispatched by its deadly arms. One marine tried to stab it with a bayoneted rifle, but one of the arms cut him clean in two.

"On'Sarax!" said Z'Kanthu from where he lay on the ground, battered and badly damaged.

Spartan looked at the machine, but he had no idea what he was talking about.

"She has succeeded. Her forces are falling back to the boats."

Just as he finished speaking, the Rift Engine shuddered. One of the overhead beams swung down and crashed into the ground. Khan and two marines lost their balance and slid along the floor toward the enemy machine. It clamped its feet to the ground and snapped at Khan. Unable to avoid it, the arm latched onto his leg and swung him closer. The crazed warrior opened fire with the looted Biomech weapon. Incredibly, the power of the weapon tore the limb apart and sent him flying through the air.

"Z'Kanthu!" hissed the machine.

They were the first and only words any of them had heard from the machine. Gas vented into the chamber, but Spartan had no time to work out how sound was now traveling inside the Rift Engine. Maybe it had activated its own internal air pressure, or it might have hacked into his communication system. All he needed to know was that the thing had moved in on Z'Kanthu.

"No!" Spartan shouted out.

Part of the wall ripped apart and mechanical arms appeared. Machines slightly larger than a Decurion fanned out to clear a path to the fallen Steersman. They moved on four legs, while another four utility arms fanned out along their flanks. One ran straight into the path of Khan. He dispatched it with a single shot from the Biomech weapon he carried in his two arms. It exploded and sent pieces of broken metal in all directions.

"I love this gun!" he yelled as he turned it on the rest of them.

Spartan twisted from left to right to assess the situation. More marines were coming in from their side, and there was ample cover to move about while avoiding gunfire. The machinery, computers, and equipment filled the open space, yet the machines almost entirely ignored them and concentrated on getting to Z'Kanthu. Incredibly, he lifted himself back to his feet and blast two more of the attackers just as they arrived. The machines were still outnumbered, but they were powerful and quickly halted the advance of the marines.

"Spartan, they've got him!" Khan shouted.

Off to the left, the struggling Steersman had been grabbed by one of the Biomech engineers, and half a dozen of the eight-limbed fighting machines had formed a wall of limbs to shield them both. Spartan broke from cover and ran at the machines, firing his carbine as he went. Holes appeared in their thick armor but not enough to halt their attacks on Z'Kanthu. He made it halfway when for no apparent reason the machine turned about and bolted away from him. Fire from the other marines struck at its armor, but it made off with great speed, dragging the smashed machine behind it.

"Khan, finish the mission."

He looked back and tried to look calm.

"As soon as the charges are set, blow them. Don't wait for me!"

He didn't wait for an answer and ran after the machine. Khan still ran along with Spartan and destroyed two of the eight-legged walkers. They both moved to the back of the room while ducking to avoid return fire from the machines.

"Spartan, there's something else coming through, something big. How much longer?" Anderson asked over the network.

A machine blocked Spartan's path but instead of stopping he dropped down, grabbed a section of a machine's shattered leg, and then swung it with all his might at the thing. The club cracked metal plating and one of the limbs with ease. It struck back, leaving gouge marks across his back.

"You bastard!" he cried out. The warning sensors in his suit flagged the breaches.

"Get down!" said another voice.

He ducked to the right just as a metal bar swung over his head. The impact tore the head from the machine, and then Olik and two more Jötnar smashed it to the ground. There were arched doorways on all of the walls, and Spartan tracked the engineer as it made for the largest, one that was covered in the sculptured forms of machines.

"Spartan?" Admiral Anderson called out again, "I need that Rift collapsed, now!"

Spartan stopped and looked back, just as part of the ceiling crashed down on top of two of the fallen enemy machines. Jötnar and marine alike scattered as more sections fell through. The facility shuddered, and the subtle vibrations from explosions shook the very floor.

"What's happening?" he asked.

Khan stabbed a piece of shattered metal through the chest of yet another fallen machine and glanced up to Spartan. They were separated by no more than twenty meters now.

"The other teams must have set their charges. Major Terson and the other commanders have given the all-clear signal. We're the only ones left."

The Jötnar were making good progress as they ripped

through the machines, buying valuable time for the marines to rig up equipment and charges through the space. A few of the machines tried to stop them, but the Jötnar were efficient. Every time they tried to interfere with the demolition equipment, they were intercepted. A few dozen Thegns had also made it inside and were busily throwing their bodies at the machines, even though many were gunned down. Then a light flashed inside his visor.

"The charges are set, Spartan. We have to go," said Khan.

Spartan shook his head.

"Get them out of here. I have to get Z'Kanthu."

A triple explosion rippled through the room, and two marines were vaporized by gunfire as a pair of engineers entered from the breached wall. Both were armed with powerful guns and mantlet-like shields on one side. Around them came dozens more of the medium-sized machines, and as quickly as that the fight began to turn against the attackers. Khan stepped closer, and Spartan lifted his hand.

"We don't have the time. Get them out of here. I'll be back. I promise."

Spartan didn't wait for an answer, and Khan watched him crash through the broken wall, narrowly avoiding the strikes of a third engineer. Khan wanted nothing more than to join his friend, but he could see marines, Thegns, and fellow Jötnar being hacked and shot at.

"Hell, no!" he snarled.

Ignoring his comrades, he chased after Spartan and into the path of another pair of engineers. Olik reached his side, and together they threw themselves at the two engineers.

"Activate the charges. Everybody else out, now!" Khan roared.

There was no disagreement, and the marines quickly gave ground while putting down an impressive level of covering fire. Many of the machines were forced to ground or to hide behind their already destroyed comrades. Khan was struck in the chest and again in the head with such power his armor was cracked in four places.

"Mutant, slave," said the machine.

Khan had no idea how the thing was communicating, or even how it knew his language. It didn't matter to him. He punched and kicked with all of his strength and somehow broke free of its embrace. That gave him the chance to duck under its attacks and then rip the mantlet shield from Olik's opponent. He held onto the piece of armor and smashed it against their foes.

"Destroy them!"

Both were far too busy to see that all but four Thegns now remained in the Amplifier chamber. Their personal battle with the two engineers had taken all of their focus and energy. Only Khan noticed the countdown in his visor and began to laugh as the thermite charges triggered one after the other. One detonated right behind his opponent, and he took the opportunity to sidestep and smash the cracked edge of the shield into a breach in the thing's armored torso.

* * *

On each side of the passageway were statues of more machines, many of which seemed no different to the one he was chasing. The machine was only a few meters ahead, and he used every last ounce of his strength and energy to keep going. They went through yet another arch and into a vast hallway filled with enormous pieces of equipment. Elevators moved up and down shafts, and dozens, perhaps hundreds more walking machines continued their work on the vast Rift Engine. Sparks flashed in a hundred places, but it was the massive window on the one side looking out into space that dumbfounded him. It was a huge dome-shaped object that must have been at least a hundred meters in height.

"What the hell is going on?"

The view on the other side showed a black world, a planet or moon. Behind it burned a bright red star that seemed to almost engulf the black world in its glow. It was the number of ships that stunned him. These were not the Biomantas and Ravagers that he was familiar with. They were easily two or three times their size. He counted hundreds of them, with dozens of them waiting in long columns. It reminded him of regiments of marines on parade, and the view from the window was the perfect spot to observe them. A noise from Z'Kanthu pulled his attention back to the enemy machines.

That's enough ships to defeat every world we've ever discovered.

He stopped and looked to his right and then to his left. A machine the size of a marine came into view, and he pulled the trigger of his carbine. The gun punched dozens of holes into the thing before sending it to the ground in a pile of broken parts and sparks. He spotted Z'Kanthu being held down by a pair of machines while a third, much larger machine in bright red armor spoke to him.

"Hey, you!" he shouted.

Spartan had little to no chance, yet he still blasted at the thing with his carbine. He managed to punch three holes into its chest armor before it moved to the side and made an odd noise. Spartan rushed from a jog to a run and began to scream. He lifted the carbine and emptied the clip into the three of them in a wild spray of magnetic rounds. He kept on running and then found he had no grip. Spartan flailed about, but he was spinning and completely out of control.

Artificial gravity has gone!

He grabbed at anything he could see, but the path he'd taken was devoid of anything but the smooth floor. Instead of an aggressive attack, he now drifted helplessly.

Movement caught his eye, and then something heavy swung at his face. He lifted his artificial arm to protect himself just as the Biomech arm crashed into his own limb. He spun about and crashed to the floor. As his vision blacked out, he heard just one word.

"Spartan."

* * *

Khan kicked against the wall and propelled himself toward the Mauler. He did his best to ignore the fusillade of shots smashing into the retreating boarding party and kept the shield between him and the enemy. Every meter they covered saw another chunk of the facility crash down around them. He still carried in his right arm the shield he'd torn from the Biomechs. With his left, he tugged at the wounded Olik. The lack of gravity had at least assisted in his removal of the badly hurt warrior.

"Khan, just go!" said Olik.

"Be quiet, you fool. We're getting off this thing. I didn't drag your worthless hide all this way to leave you next to a Mauler."

Another volley of shouts pattered around them, but the columns of marines and Thegns were not impotent. Each time a Biomech warrior showed its head it was hit by a dozen rounds from those retreating. There were five Maulers waiting in the wrecked area, and scores of warriors drifting about in zero gravity. The ball turrets on the flanks of the Maulers continued to blast away while the boarding parties dragged themselves inside. Khan reached the door of the nearest, and helping hands reached out to pull Olik inside. Khan laughed at realizing the helping hands were actually Thegn and human, with both dragging a synthetic Jötnar inside.

"Good times," he laughed as they pulled him inside.

He watched the door hiss shut behind him, leaving behind the scores of dead warriors from both sides.

Z'Kanthu, this had better work.

* * *

ANS Warlord, Black Rift

"Admiral, we've got breaches throughout the port hull. Multiple damage and a reactor leak on the secondary power plant," said the XO.

Admiral Anderson wiped the sweat from his face and focused his attention on the mainscreen. The newly arrived formation of Biomech ships had massively turned the odds against the Alliance forces by a ratio of two to one. Even worse, these new arrivals were fresh and relatively undamaged. His own fleet was the exact opposite.

We're stuck between a rock and a hard place now.

The Black Rift was a hive of activity, as dozens more Biomech ships congregated near the massive structure protruding from the Rift.

"Any change on that thing? We can't stay here indefinitely."

"Science station is picking up power fluctuations. Nothing major yet though, Sir."

There was now so must dust and debris around the entrance to the Black Rift that the energy beams were now visible. Both sides had sustained heavy casualties, yet still the Alliance vessels kept up the fight. ANS Warlord took the lead position and focused its fire on the nearest damaged Ravager. Other ships concentrated their gun turrets and covered the target in projectiles while the Liberty destroyers used their speed to race around the newly arrived Biomech ships. The entire battle was a single long delaying action that he knew they could ultimately never win.

"What the hell is that?"

Admiral Anderson pointed at the Rift. The others looked in the same direction, but not even the XO could see it.

"All ships; concentrate fire on their reinforcements," Admiral Anderson snapped.

His orders were acknowledged, and the gunfire stopped within a few seconds and quickly moved to those vessels that had come from inside the Helios System. Even just a few seconds respite allowed the area around the Black Rift to clear a little.

"Contacts! It's the Maulers!" said the tactical officer.

At the same time a video stream appeared on the mainscreen. It was Major Terson, and his face was bloodied from some violent encounter.

"Admiral…the station's stabilizers and amplification systems are offline. You need…"

The video flickered and then vanished. Admiral Anderson looked to his XO and frowned.

"The amplification systems are offline? What does that even mean?"

He walked past various screens and to the science station. The officers were busily scanning their own ship as well as the massive structure sat inside the Rift.

"Well, what is happening out there?"

The two junior officers looked back to him. The older, balding man spoke first.

"We are getting odd readings, but the station is still functional. The Rift is stable. Wait…"

Admiral Anderson leaned in and looked at the screens himself. The wormhole-shaped Spacebridge was shown on a three-dimensional lattice model. Right in the center was the Rift Engine with a bulbous section on each side of the Rift. The younger science officer almost fell off his seat in excitement.

"The amplifiers, of course."

He pointed to the Spacebridge.

"It's no longer being held open. Those crazy fools have

done it."

He looked back to the tactical display, and his heart nearly stopped.

"The T'Kari, where are they?"

A dozen pairs of eyes scoured the unit, but there was one, and only one of the alien ships left.

"T'Kron, he's still in the fight."

Admiral Anderson signaled to the communications officer.

"Get me T'Kron, right now."

He looked back to the Rift as he waited.

"I want full fighter cover for the Maulers. All other ships move in and help them. I want our people out of there!"

He looked back to the tactical display and the hordes of ships from both sides. For all the armor and guns of his own vessels, it looked as though the fate of the fleets, perhaps even the entire star system, would come down to the last of the T'Kari Exiles. With the planetary defense systems offline, he could think of no other way of doing what needed to be done.

This had better work. I need that Rift closed, and fast!

The image of the T'Kari commander appeared.

"Admiral. We're ready."

Anderson's lip quivered. He looked at the mainscreen and the mass of ships and fighters now swirling about the entrance of the Rift.

"Do it, do it now!"

The beam was invisible, yet the effect was instantaneous. The Rift changed in form from a doorway to another place and into a whirlpool. The Rift Engine ripped apart as it was cut clean in half, and explosions ripped though the section in Helion territory. A great pulse of energy pushed out and struck the nearest Biomech ships, and even a few Maulers that cast them out into space on a spinning course. Admiral Anderson watched the collapse with a mixture of terror and relief. Most of those ships near the Rift were now vulnerable, and he knew he had seconds to seize the initiative.

"All ships break and attack anything near the Rift. We end this, today!"

* * *

Biomech Command Ship, Uncharted Space

Spartan opened his eyes and looked directly into the face of his tormentor. As before, it was the large red machine, and at its flanks were dozens of similar machines of different colors and configurations. They were somewhere else, perhaps still on the station, but it could easily have been another ship. The lighting was poor, and he could see no further than just hundred meters, perhaps less. The open space was cavernous, and the walls were ribbed and curved in an odd fusion of flesh and machine.

"Where am I?" he demanded.

The red machine leaned in a little closer and then turned to indicate to the battered figure of Z'Kanthu. The machine looked at Spartan, but rather than speak or struggle, it simply lowered its head in a gentle nod. The enemy Biomech commander then looked back at him and reached out with a single limb. As it touched Spartan, he felt a jolt run though his body, something like an electric shock that instantly took him back to his time as a prisoner aboard the Biomech warship; when he and Khan had spoken with Z'Kanthu back before the mission.

"Spartan, remember..." said the machine directly into his mind.

Images flashed through his mind, many of them looking familiar. There was the Rift Machine, then Mars. He saw glimpses of Teresa and then back to the prison ship. More and more appeared, many of them going back to his fights on Prometheus as a pit fighter. Back and back the images went until one stayed in his mind. It was the interior of a ship, a derelict vessel with failing lights and blood-soaked bodies everywhere.

"The Bright Horizon," he muttered.

The images flickered, and then he was back at the Biomech ship. The machines were pushing long needles into his body and then his head. He began to scream, but then the pain stopped as quickly as it had started.

"It is your time, Spartan."

The images vanished and his eyes opened. He could see clearly now. The Biomech machines were waiting in long columns and watching him with interest. Behind them were a number of large domed windows, showing a similar view to that he had seen before. In the distance was the crackling energy of the collapsed Rift. The remains of the mighty engine that had labored away inside it still floated about. Hundreds of massive ships waited at the now closed doorway. Spartan heard sounds from the machine, odd, alien sounds, but somehow he could understand them. He looked down, and the shackles holding his half-naked form dropped down. He rubbed his hands and looked back at the main Biomech. He could feel suggestions and ideas swimming through his mind before something pushed them back to his subconscious.

"What do you want?"

The machine looked at Z'Kanthu lying helplessly on the ground. The Biomech moved closer to Spartan and handed him a cruel-looking weapon. It was nearly a meter long and shaped like a spearhead.

"Destroy the traitor."

Spartan saw images of Z'Kanthu in his mind; the talk they had had on ANS Dreadnought. He saw the old machine in his mind, and to his amazement it spoke to him.

Do whatever has to be done.

His hands were already tightening around the weapon.

"Show us your loyalty."

There was no hesitation. He jumped forward and stabbed down hard as though he was putting an animal out of its misery. The blade punched through the already ruined armor of the machine, and as it pushed inside his body, the tip flashed in a micro-charge that vaporized the innards of the machine. He discarded the handle of the weapon and turned to face the machine.

"Good," it said.

The machine then pivoted and pointed to the black space behind him. Strobe lights flickered and activated one line at a time. The open space seemed to increase a hundredfold to show thousands upon thousands of machines. Many were multi-limbed, but others carried vast weapons about their torsos. It was a truly massive army.

"Your mind betrays you. Your allies see you as their savior, a man reborn with a destiny as a warlord. They are not wrong. You will lead armies, and you will burn their worlds. Then you will take your place as one of our own. The great cull has begun."

They both watched as another three massive Rift Engines moved slowly toward the crackling energy of the Rift. Spartan's eyes looked on like glass, not a single emotion showed anywhere on his face.

"They are weak, broken. They will not stand," he said calmly.

The machine moved a little closer.

"If they do, what will you do?"

Spartan looked into the face of the machine and tensed his jaw. There was a slight flicker below his eye and a twitch. Something inside his mind whispered, and try as he might, he couldn't help smiling.

"I'll kill them all."